QUESTION IN THE NIGHT

He came that night. "Have you missed me, sweet?" he whispered as he put his hard cheek against her soft one, and gathered her into his arms.

His hands moved lower, curving in at her waist, and out again to explore every inch of her body. He captured her mouth, to savor her. Elinor had never experienced such intense feelings, such defenselessness, as if she were being drawn down into a maelstrom. As he slipped her nightrobe from her shoulders, and bent to kiss her breasts, she grasped his shoulders, holding them tightly.

He drew back when he heard her moan. "Elinor," he sighed. "Yes? Say yes!"

Elinor did not know who or what he was. But she knew what her answer would be. . . .

Midnight Magic

Barbara Hazard

AN ONYX BOOK

Special thanks to my "new" daughter,
Loree Hazard, M.S., C.C.C.,
for her expert help on speech disorders
—BH

ONYX
Published by the Penguin Group
Penguin Books USA Inc., 375 Hudson Street,
New York, New York 10014, U.S.A.
Penguin Books Ltd, 27 Wrights Lane,
London W8 5TZ, England
Penguin Books Australia Ltd, Ringwood,
Victoria, Australia
Penguin Books Canada Ltd, 2801 John Street,
Markham, Ontario, Canada L3R 1B4
Penguin Books (N.Z.) Ltd, 182-190 Wairau Road,
Auckland 10, New Zealand

Penguin Books Ltd, Registered Offices:
Harmondsworth, Middlesex, England

First published by Onyx, an imprint of New American Library,
a division of Penguin Books USA Inc.

First Printing, June, 1991
10 9 8 7 6 5 4 3 2 1

Printed in the United States of America

Dedicated to all lovers of fantasy, everywhere.

Prologue

"ALL RIGHT, ALL RIGHT! No need to bang the house down at this hour o' night! I'm coming! Just let me put the candle down so I can deal with the bolt.

"There! Oh, can it be . . . ? It *is* you, isn't it?"

"As you see."

"Now, who would have thought you'd turn up here, after all these years? Why, I never thought to see you again."

"Perhaps I'm a one-time-only bad penny?"

"Hmmph! Who's that driving away?"

"Only the trap I hired in Truro to bring me here."

"And the driver's going back now? He'll never find the road over the moor on a black night like this!"

"Yes, he will. He knows the turnings now, the dangers, and he couldn't wait to be on his way."

"Well, since you're here, you'd best come in, I suppose. There's a damp wind blowing."

"I agree it goes right through you. Still, I'd not dare ask for a warm drop of something. . . ."

"So, you remember I don't like spirits, do you? I've a jug of cider, if you're so minded, or I can make you a pot of tea."

"Neither, thank you. I came prepared with a flask of brandy."

"Brandy, is it? Next you'll be telling me it's only for medicinal purposes!"

"I wouldn't be so untruthful, not to you. However, it does have some excellent attributes. I don't suppose it's any use asking you to join me?"

"Hmmph! Sit down while I poke up the fire. It's been a wet winter."

"Now why do I remember that it always was? And just as drear and depressing as it is now?"

"Why are you here, then? Why *did* you come back after all this time?"

"Perhaps so I could congratulate myself on what I've escaped? No, no, don't look so indignant! I came, of course, because this is my birthplace, and I've not seen it for nigh on twenty years. At least that's the most acceptable of my reasons, so let's leave it at that."

"Aye. It has been a long time, hasn't it? And they have been twenty *peaceful* years. But I expect all that will change now *you're* back. There'll be trouble again. I can feel it in my bones. Trouble always did trail you like a tattered shadow. Better you had stayed away!"

"I am desolated to have disappointed you. I couldn't. I've a matter to settle here, once and for all—for my own sanity, if you like. But I'm sure you understand. You, at least, always did try to understand me."

"Hmmph! But why came you at night, in the windy dark, like a thief? Surely it would have been more sensible to put up at an inn on the moors till morning."

"I don't want anyone to know I've returned."

"I see you haven't changed a bit, more's the pity! *Now* what are you up to?"

"I advise you to wait and see."

"I'll have to, won't I, since you won't tell me? You always were a stubborn one! But perhaps it's just as well I don't know. Er, I gather you intend to stay with me, then?"

"Yes, for the present. I'll be no trouble to you. I'll be—hmm—out most of the time. Oh, by the way, I stabled my horse. My baggage is on the porch."

"Mighty sure of your welcome, weren't you?"

"I doubted you would turn me away. There is still our blood tie. And I rather thought you would approve my getting at the truth of the matter, even after all this time."

"Hmmph! I must say you're looking well—quite the fancy gentleman, in fact. You never had that coat from Kernow."

"Certainly not. I bought it in London."

"Hearken to ye. London, is it? Is that where you've been?"

"There, among other places."

"I notice you don't ask about the others."

"No need. I shall find out about them—*all* about them—soon enough."

"*More* brandy?"

"It is, as you yourself have remarked, a gloomy night. And I've had a long and tiresome journey."

"Hmmph! Well, I've no mind to sit here watching you swill spirits till all hours. I intend to teen an eye before daybreak, even if you don't. I'll red up the spare bedchamber. Prithee bank the fire and shoot that bolt when you come upstairs."

"I will. Good night. And thank you. I knew *you* wouldn't fail me."

"None of that now! But still, I'm glad to see you again, in spite of everything. I've—I've missed you."

"And I, you. You were always—my friend."

"Hmmph!"

1

As she stared out the streaked, dirty window of the carriage, Elinor Fielding decided the moors of Cornwall had to be the loneliest part of England—indeed, perhaps even of the world—for since they had left the last small hamlet behind, two hours previous, they had not seen a single person or animal, not another wayfarer, nor even the rudest habitation. Only an occasional formation of rough stones broke the monotony of the landscape, from one horizon to the other.

The road they were traveling was nothing but a rough track, cut through the coarse vegetation and stunted trees that covered the moor. She was glad it was light, although a gloomy day, for the gray sky with its scudding, low, heavy clouds foretold rain before much longer. She peered up at those clouds, and the flight of a hawk caught her eye. Even that little bit of life and motion was a relief to the eye.

As she watched, the bird soared upward, to circle at last far above them, his flight effortless now as he rode the air currents while his sharp eyes searched the ground beneath him for his next meal.

What must this carriage appear to him? she wondered. A huge, ungainly black beetle scurrying across the desolate landscape as fast as it could go, as if anxious to reach the safety of its hole? She smiled a little at her fancies then, and settled back on the cracked squabs of the hired carriage. Beside her, her maid kept her eyes firmly on the new dressing case she held clutched in her hands.

Elinor Fielding shook her head a little. She could sense the maid's uneasiness at the wide, empty moors in which nothing moved, and the only sounds were those of the wind and their own rattling passage. But Doll was London-born, and these moors were an alien place to her. As they are to me, Elinor reminded herself. I've never been far from town myself. But unlike Doll, somehow I'm not afraid here. Instead, I find myself looking forward to it all so eagerly, almost holding my breath in anticipation. I wonder why that should be so? 'Tis not likely such a desolate place will bring excitement of any kind. Indeed, I'll probably find it dull and boring after town, with all its noise and confusion.

But the London she had left behind was no longer a haven for her; instead, it had become the place she had fled in disgrace.

As she remembered this, the pure, clear green of her eyes darkened. Yes, she had been forced to leave. How fortunate it was that her father's boyhood friend had invited her to come to Cornwall after her mother's death, to make her home with his own family.

Not that I'll stay, if I find I don't care for it, Elinor told herself stoutly. When she had written to accept his invitation, she had mentioned only a visit, not liking to commit herself to an unknown future. And she had enough money to live anywhere she chose.

Her soft lips tightened for a moment as she considered that money. She had never imagined such wealth would be hers. And if it had not been, nonc of what had transpired in London would ever have happened. Frowning, she decided that being wealthy was a mixed blessing.

Inadvertently, her hand smoothed her clothing. Her gown was made of glossy alemade, a silk as thin and light as air, and her cloak was of the best velvet. She had never owned such finery. Of course she was dressed in black, for she was still in mourning, and would be for some months yet. But at her wrists and the neck of her gown, she had white cuffs and a collar of lawn trimmed with delicate lace. And the large, becoming bonnet she wore had come from London's premier modiste. Unseen, but even closer to her skin were her silk petticoats and a pale green chemise of lawn as fine as a cobweb.

No, she decided, no matter what happened, I am glad I am wealthy now. And I wouldn't have married Austin Denby even if I'd been a pauper. In fact, I'd rather have starved!

Her maid shifted on the hard seat then, and she made herself forget the past. "It does seem an endless way, does it not, Doll?" she asked. "But surely the place we seek cannot be much further. We have been traveling for hours!"

"I do so hope so, Miss Elinor," the maid told her with a toss of her black curls. "Much longer and the two of us will have to stop the carriage and find us a bush! But perhaps we'll come upon a cozy inn instead?"

Her mistress chuckled. "I very much doubt there's an inn, cozy or otherwise, for miles around," she said.

Her maid shifted her gaze to the landscape rushing by outside the window, and she didn't even bother to hide her shudder. "Eerie is what I calls it," she said. "So lonesome, like. It's as if we're the only two people left in the world."

"Surely not! You forget the coachman and groom."

"Thank heavens for even such small mercies as *them,*" Doll Bundy muttered, shifting to relieve the ache in her posterior. The seats of the old carriage were hard and uncomfortable, and the ancient springs beneath the body of it did little to ease their passage. But then, they'd hardly had a choice. This was the only carriage and coachman they had been able to hire to take them to this Mordyn Miss Elinor was so intent on reaching.

Following instructions, from London they had sailed to Falmouth. Doll hadn't cared for that part of the journey either. She had never been to sea, and although the sailing had been uneventful, due to the clement weather, she had been afraid the whole time. Their tiny vessel seemed a mere cockleshell on a vast expanse of deep water, and she had always been aware that only a few flimsy planks separated them from watery death.

At Falmouth, they had hired the carriage to carry them over the moors to Mordyn, situated as it was on the opposite coast. Shifting again from one well-rounded buttock to the other, Doll remembered how comfortable in retrospect the ship had been. Ah well, she thought philosophically, every journey, no matter how long, has to end sometime.

She stole a sideways glance at her mistress then. The girl was in profile to her, leaning forward a little to stare out the window. What she found to look at there, Doll couldn't say. Yet from Miss Elinor's eager expression, you would have thought she beheld wonders. Her lips were slightly parted, and her eyes wide with interest. Doll's own lips twisted in a grimace. Pray the mistress would be happy here; learn to love these strangers who had offered her a home, she thought. But as soon as Miss Elinor settles in like, Doll Bundy's heading back to London just as fast as she can go. Why, I'd rather die than live in such a lonely, out of the way place! Idly, she wondered what people here did for a bit of fun or excitement, and then decided she really didn't care enough to find out.

Doll was forced to grasp the strap beside her as the carriage rumbled into a deeper hole than usual. She could hear the coachman yelling encouragement to his team, and the homely rough sound of his voice reassured her.

Suddenly the desolate silence was shattered by the sound of a gun shot close by. Elinor and her maid exchanged glances of startled horror. They could hear the frightened neighing of the horses and the coachman's hoarse cries as he struggled to control the team. Elinor peered out the window, but she could see nothing. Then, as the carriage came to an abrupt halt, she was thrown in a heap on the floorboards. Doll had suffered a similar fate, and for a moment the two struggled to untangle themselves and regain their seats.

"What can it be, miss?" Doll asked, her dark eyes full of fright.

Elinor shook her head before both of them looked up as they heard the sound of someone scrambling over the roof of the carriage. Fearfully now, Elinor looked from the window again, to see a man on horseback a little distance away. He was dressed in dark shabby clothes, with a wide-brimmed felt hat pulled well down over his face. As he called a direction, two other men rose from the gorse where they had been hidden to run to the horses' heads. Everything was noise and confusion. The groom's frightened cries, the cursing of the coachman, the horses' neighing and the stamp of their hooves mingled with the rough voices of the men who had attacked the carriage.

As the door of that carriage was wrenched open, Elinor said a fervent prayer. She could not restrain a gasp as she stared up into the face of the man on horseback. His features seemed carved from stone, so harsh was his expression.

"Get down," he ordered in a quiet monotone.

Elinor did not move, nor did Doll, for they were rigid with fear.

The man pointed his pistol at them. "I said get down," he repeated in the same quiet tones that were all the more threatening for the lack of any animation in them.

Elinor forced her body to obey. "Come, Doll. We must do as he says," she whispered.

Doll's quick breathing showed her terror, but Elinor was relieved to see she followed her from the carriage.

"Stand over there," their captor ordered, waving them a little distance away.

Both women hurried to do his bidding. As he turned aside, Elinor drew a deep breath to steady herself, and put her arm around her maid. Doll was trembling so, she was afraid she might fall. Then she wondered if she had not done so for her own benefit, for the sound of her heartbeats seemed to thunder in her ears.

The scene the two stared at would have frightened anyone. There were six robbers, all of them busy, and all strangely silent. There was none of the loud gloating, the self-congratulation, that Elinor would have expected. Instead, three of the thieves were unloading the trunks and portmanteaus from the boot, while the rest guarded the coachman and groom and held the still restless team.

The baggage was thrown to the ground and opened. Elinor gasped as dirty hands pawed through it, tossing everything out on the coarse grass beside the track. Somehow this seemed the worst thing of all, to see such creatures handling her clothes, and it was all she could do not to cry out in protest.

The leader rode toward them again. "Where's the money, then?" he asked.

"Mon—money?" Elinor repeated, her voice cracking with the strain. Then she remembered her purse, and she held it out to him.

He inspected the contents, and pocketed the money inside, tossing the purse back to her when he was through.

"That's all ye got?" he asked, his pistol again in evidence.

Elinor swallowed. There was a large amount hidden in her needlework case. The men searching the baggage had given the case only a cursory inspection before throwing it aside, and they had not found it. Now, Elinor wondered whether if she told the leader about it, he would let them go unharmed.

"That's all," Doll said, speaking up for the first timc.

Elinor was startled at her suddenly firm voice. She thought it sounded almost defiant.

"Where ye be goin'?" the leader asked next.

When neither woman replied, he motioned to the man guarding the groom. Elinor thought she must faint when she saw the knife he produced and held close to the boy's throat.

"I asked yer a question," the leader said. "Answer me."

"To Mordyn Castle," Elinor said. "Oh, please, do not kill him!"

To her relief, the leader signaled his henchman, and the knife disappeared. Then he turned to the cowering women and said, "To Mordyn, is it?" He made a rough sound in his throat then, and turned his head to spit on the ground.

"Hold out yer hands," he said next.

As Elinor did so, she wished they were not shaking so badly.

The man dismounted and came to stand before them. He was not very tall, but he had a strong, compact body beneath his shabby clothes. Even in all her fright, Elinor wondered at the reddish color that seemed to cling to his hat, his coat—even his skin.

He grasped her right hand and began to remove the small gold ring set with pearls that she wore. It was her only jewelry.

At once, Elinor began to try to free her hand. "Oh, please, do not take my ring, sir!" she cried. "It was my mother's and it is all I have left to remember her!"

He paused for a moment, eyeing her black mourning attire, and then he shrugged and pocketed the ring.

"Ye have yer memories, missus, and they'll have to do fer ye," he told her in his quiet, lifeless voice. "There's many here starvin'."

He turned away to speak to his men. They had finished going through the baggage, and they were holding up some of her things in inspection. An argument commenced, and Elinor could see the leader wanted them to leave the clothes, although his men seemed determined to keep them. To sell? she wondered. They were very fine. She was surprised when the men threw down their booty and backed away, without even being menaced by that large pistol.

The leader turned back to her again. "Ye can be on yer way, missus. But don't come up here on the moors again. Next time ye might not be so lucky."

Elinor could only stare at him. She was holding her breath, willing him with all her might to leave and take his ugly band with him. As she watched, the men seemed to melt away, to be lost from sight in the dips and rough gorse of the moor. Their leader waited for a long endless time, his pistol covering the coachman and groom. Elinor wondered why. Neither of them looked at all a danger to anyone.

Then, with one last glance at the women standing beside the track, he wheeled his horse and rode away. No one moved until all sounds of his horse's pounding hooves died away.

To her surprise, Doll spoke up then. "Well, what are you starin' at?" she demanded of the frightened groom. "Come here and help me with Miss Elinor's things! The sooner we pack 'em up, the sooner we can be gone!"

The boy hurried to obey, while the coachman went to inspect the harness of his now-quiet team. Bemused, Elinor went to help her maid.

She wished they might leave immediately, and she was glad when Doll did not try to pack everything neatly again. Instead, the clothes were crammed any which way into the trunks and boxes, and the groom hurried to secure them in the boot again.

"There, that's the last of them, miss," Doll said, after searching through the bushes one more time. "Get in the carriage, do!"

Elinor was only too happy to obey. But before she did so, she spoke to the coachman, to ask him about his team.

His reply was terse, as all his remarks had been since first meeting. A man of few words, Elinor thought as she settled down on the hard seat again. In a moment, the groom had swung up behind, and they were on their way again. For the first time in ages, Elinor felt she could relax. She wondered how long they had been stopped. It had seemed an endless time, but she was aware it had probably been only a matter of minutes.

"Are you all right, Miss Elinor?" Doll asked from beside her.

When she did not answer at once, the maid took her hands in hers, to stroke them. "You're sorry about your mother's ring, aren't you?" she asked. "But we're alive, and surely that's the important thing."

"I know," Elinor said, squeezing her hands. "I wonder who those men were?"

"We'll probably never know," Doll replied, shrugging a little. "Thieves, is all. I guess they're everywhere, not just in London town."

Half an hour later, the road suddenly turned downhill, and the two women saw signs of human habitation. First a lonely farmhouse or two, then a large collection of rough buildings and rusty machinery that looked deserted in the cold gray light.

Elinor lowered the window slightly and took a deep breath. "We're almost there, Doll," she said in some relief. "I can smell the sea again."

"Well, that's somethin', anyway," her maid muttered.

They passed other cottages and entered a small hamlet, but the carriage did not stop there. At last it slowed, and started down toward the sea. Ahead of them, Elinor could see another village. It was only a cluster of buildings huddled together at the head of a deep-cut narrow bay surrounded by towering rock cliffs. In the flat light, the village appeared as gray as the day was. The buildings that comprised it all had similar slate roofs above their grimy stone walls. Even the cobbles in the street were colorless except where someone had tossed a bucket of water that turned them dull black. There were but few people abroad, all of whom stood quietly and stared at the carriage, their faces expressionless.

Elinor inched forward on her seat expectantly, but still the coachman did not stop. Instead, they left the village behind, and it was some minutes later before they slowed to take the turn into another, narrower road, and began to climb.

She glanced from side to side. But where had the sea gone? she wondered. Now, all that was visible were trees, an occasional patch of thin brown grass, and large rock formations.

And then she saw Mordyn for the first time. She opened the window beside her to lean out.

Ahead of them, up a steep rise, was a large castle,

the likes of which she had only read of in fairy tales before. Its towering walls of gray stone, punctuated by a few high-set narrow windows, rose from a rocky promontory. Before the castle, the land had been cleared to a rough approximation of lawn, but that amenity did little to civilize the place. It seemed to cling to the rock it was perched on, massive and brooding. Elinor felt very small. The wind that ruffled her hair and whistled past her cheeks was heavy with the briny smell she associated with the sea. As she stared upward in awe, some white gulls passed over the battlements to head out to that sea, and she could hear the distant rumble of its breakers as they crashed against the rocks and then retreated, in an endless rhythm as old as the world itself. Beside her, Doll stirred, to lean forward and look for herself.

"Brr!" she exclaimed. "Be that where we're goin' then, Miss Elinor?"

"It must be indeed," Elinor murmured. As she spoke, the sun found a ragged tear in the dark clouds, and for a brief, tantalizing second, it shone down full on the rugged castle, revealing all its features, limning it in hard brilliance. Elinor had to close her eyes for a moment against the glare.

"The sun! I believe it must be a good omen," she said. But even as she spoke, the clouds covered that one dazzling shaft of light, and the castle returned to its former melancholy. Beside her, Doll Bundy sat speechless.

The team struggled up the last steep rise to the castle, rumbled over a narrow drawbridge, and came to a halt before a massive door.

Motioning the groom away to sound the knocker, Elinor stepped down unaided to look around. The courtyard she stood in was bare of any vegetation, although two stone urns stood on either side of the door. She reminded herself it was only April—much too soon for flowers.

As she waited, the skies darkened even more, and rain began to fall. Fortunately, the door swung open then, and an elderly servant in dark livery held it wide.

He was short and stocky, and his grave face, etched with deep harsh lines, held no welcoming smile.

The rain was coming down harder now, and Elinor moved forward, anxious to gain shelter before her new cloak was ruined. "Good afternoon," she said pleasantly. "I am Elinor Fielding. I believe I am expected?"

"Come in then, do," the old servant said with a slight bow. "And you men, unload that baggage. And no haverin' about it, mind!"

Gratefully, Elinor stepped into an empty, low-ceilinged room made all of stone. It was windowless and had only another, much smaller door set near the end of the opposite wall. Doll was close behind her, so close she could feel her breath on her cheek. Sensing the maid's uneasiness, Elinor wouldn't have been surprised to feel her nervous fingers clutching her cloak.

"Come along," the servant said as he led the way to the other door. "Sir Robert is waiting on ye in the hall."

"Might my maid and I have a moment to tidy ourselves first?" Elinor asked with another smile. "I feel we are much the worse for the journey, for we were waylaid by thieves along the way. I would not meet Sir Robert in such a state."

The old servant ignored her. He had reached the door leading out of this cold, empty room, and he was tugging at it. Elinor waited, apprehensive now. It was almost as if she were a new prisoner being admitted to Newgate, and she couldn't help shivering at the thought. But I am only here on a visit, she reminded herself as she put up her chin.

The door swung open then, and she bit back a gasp. The hall before her, with its high, open-timbered roof, was as massive as any London church, yet it held little furniture. Some faded old tapestries hung on the stone walls, interspersed with arrangements of lances, shields, and battleaxes. The rough stone floor was bare, and there were no windows here either. Two huge fireplaces lit both ends of the room, however, and near the one set in the far wall, a man rose from a heavy leather chair and stood waiting. Elinor hesitated for a moment. He was dressed in dark clothing, and the firelight only served to silhouette his large form. She could not see his face.

As the servant stood aside, she moved forward to curtsy. She had the oddest thought that the man before her hesitated too, before he came toward her, hands outstretched.

"Welcome, child, welcome to Mordyn," he said in the strange Cornish burr she remembered from his one visit to London all those weeks ago. Relieved that it was Sir Robert Grenville indeed, she smiled.

"Come nearer the fire and warm yourself," he said. "I'm sure you are delighted to reach journey's end, are you not?"

Elinor grasped his warm hands gratefully. "Indeed I am, Sir Robert, especially since my carriage was held up on the moors not many miles away."

"Held up, you say?" he asked. "I shall want to hear all about that presently."

Turning to his old retainer, he said, "Fetch Mrs. Greene, Whitman, and then show Miss Fielding's maid to the rooms that have been prepared for her mistress. Oh, and see to her baggage and the hire of the carriage as well."

Elinor spoke up quickly. "Thank you, Sir Robert. I have more money the thieves did not find, but it is hidden in my trunks. I shall repay you later."

Sir Robert ignored her to wave the servant away, before he said, "Sit down, Miss Fielding. In a short time we'll have some tea, but I am sure you would like to retire for a while first, would you not? Especially after the fright you have had? As soon as my housekeeper comes, I'll have her take you up."

As Elinor took the seat he indicated, he went on, "Tell me, if you please, about this robbery you suffered. For if it occurred not far from Mordyn, it must be investigated."

Elinor told him as much as she could remember. Sir

Robert listened gravely, staring into the fire as she spoke.

"You say there were seven men? And only one of them was mounted?" he asked. At her nod, he continued, "What did the leader look like?"

Now Elinor frowned a little. In her fright at the time, she had not registered that, and now she struggled to recall some details.

"He was not a tall man, but he was powerfully built," she said at last. "Somehow I received the impression he had once weighed a great deal more. His face was very thin, and hard. His features were unremarkable. And he was covered in red dust," she concluded, still wondering about that.

"Aha! A tinner!" Sir Robert exclaimed. "I imagine they were all tinners." He shook his head in disgust, before he went on, "You were very fortunate, Miss Fielding. The tinners are desperate men, and dangerous now the mines are closing down. Even the old Ding Dong is gone, and my own Wheal Beatrice closed last year. The price of tin is such, it is not profitable to mine anymore.

"Tell me, do you think you could identify this man, if you were to see him again?" he asked.

As Elinor nodded, he said, "I shall have some men out searching. I have a fair idea of his identity. He's given me trouble before."

Elinor's smile was tremulous. She felt so much better now she was safe inside these thick stone walls, with a man like Sir Robert Grenville to protect her.

She thought him a fine looking man for his age. Tall and broad-shouldered, he wore his graying hair long, and he still had a thick wavy thatch of it. His dark eyes observed her keenly, and his broad forehead and strong nose, above a firm-lipped mouth, were attractive. How different he was from the shabby miners who had held up the carriage!

He had kept his figure, too, unlike many other older gentlemen. She knew he was a widower; she wondered he had never cared to marry again after the death of his wife so many years before.

He had told her something of the family situation when he had called on her in London, shortly after her mother's death. His wife had died giving birth to a daughter, and now there was only that daughter and his son left to him. She remembered he had stressed what a favor she would be bestowing if she would come and live with them. In fact, he said his invitation had little to do with his boyhood friendship with her father.

"No, it is because my daughter Fiona needs company," he had explained. "Someone her own age. True, her governess is still with her, but Miss Ward is too old to be a companion for a young woman. And we're isolated at Mordyn. Besides, Fiona is not like other girls, and I would not hide it from you. She had a childhood accident, and she cannot speak. No, no, she is not deranged, you must not fear that! She is only a little slow, a little simple. But you'll like my daughter. Everyone does."

Elinor was recalled to the present when a tall, stout woman wearing an immaculate apron over her dark dress came in and curtsied.

"Ah, there you are, Mrs. Greene," Sir Robert said. "This is our guest from London, Miss Elinor Fielding. Kindly take her to her rooms, and extend her every courtesy. And when she is ready, bring her to the gold salon."

"Certainly, sir," the woman said. Elinor was a little amused at the careful scrutiny she and her clothes were receiving. Nothing about her escaped the housekeeper's faded blue eyes.

"I shall see you presently, Miss Fielding," Sir Robert told her as they both rose. "You may look forward to a lavish tea. Mrs. Greene and Cook quite spoil us all."

The housekeeper curtsied, but she did not smile in reply to his compliment. Nor did she speak as she led the way to the door. Elinor followed in her wake.

On the other side of that door, she stepped into another part of the castle. This had walls of the same stone as the large hall they had just quitted, but it was much more habitable and modern. Colorful rugs were scattered on the stone floor, and highly polished furniture lined the walls, on which were hung several landscapes done in oils.

Looking neither left nor right, Mrs. Greene strode along to a wide staircase at the end of the hall. Elinor had to skip to keep up with her.

The staircase was covered in deep red carpeting, accented with gold. Halfway up the flight, there was a large window draped in the same color brocade. It was the first window Elinor had seen since she entered Mordyn Castle, and she could not resist taking a glance out of it. She saw it overlooked a large enclosed garden with a dormant fountain at its center.

"How lovely that must be in summer," she remarked to her guide.

"Aye, that's The Lady's Garden. It be full of flowers and birds by May. Miss Fiona spends every fine day there."

She moved quickly ahead then, as if she begrudged even that tiny bit of conversation. At the top of the flight, she marched down another passageway. This one had several doors along it, all now firmly closed. At its end, another flight led upward.

Elinor took a deep breath. The exercise felt wonderful after being cooped up in the carriage for so many hours, but she hoped they did not have much farther to go.

At the top of the flight, she saw they had entered a large square room, with tall windows all down one side. The three other walls were covered with portraits, no doubt of the Grenvilles, both past and present. It was all very grand to Elinor, but then, she reminded herself, she was only a London merchant's daughter with no such exalted heritage.

As the housekeeper moved forward again, Elinor's eye was caught by an almost life-size, full-length portrait of a gentleman dressed as a cavalier. It occupied a place of honor in the middle of the far wall. He wore pale blue velvet completed with a ruff of delicate lace, and he held his plumed velvet hat in his left hand while his right grasped the hilt of a sword. Elinor stole a glance at his face. Framed by dark brown hair arranged in curls many a girl would sigh for, it was almost too handsome with its sensuous lips. Even so, it was thoroughly masculine. As she stared at it, mesmerized, the dark eyes under their arched brows seemed to twinkle at her, those well-shaped lips twitch a little at her interest. She was annoyed to find herself flushing. It was only a painting, after all!

"These are your rooms, miss," Mrs. Greene said then, opening a door close by.

Elinor walked past her into a small sitting room. Through the open door beyond, she could see Doll unpacking one of her trunks. "Thank you, Mrs. Greene. This is delightful," she said.

"You have only to ask for anything you need," the housekeeper replied in her stiff burr. "Ring the bell when you're ready for tea. One o' the maids will come to show you the way."

Elinor nodded and closed the door gently behind her, before she picked up her skirts and ran into the bedchamber.

After she had used the close stool in the dressing room, and washed her hands and face in the hot water provided, Elinor came back and looked around her with more interest. "But what a beautiful room, Doll!" she exclaimed.

She saw there was a large tester bed set against one wall, plump with a feather bed and pillows, and a chaise near the windows. A fireplace with a white overmantel was set in one wall with comfortable chairs flanking it, and she was glad to see it had a cheerful fire burning in it. And then her eye was caught by the graceful dressing table with its delicate appointments and gold-framed mirror, and the walnut armoire where Doll was hanging up her clothes.

"I've never seen anything so fine!" she went on, her voice full of admiration.

"Maybe so," her maid said, giving one of her gowns a hard shake to remove the wrinkles and the bits of gorse that clung to it. "But for all it's pretty, it's still here in this scary old castle in this lonesome spot, with thieves wandering about outside. Brr!"

Elinor ignored her, still lost in admiration of the room. It was decorated in soft shades of rose and gold that were echoed by a large tapestry on the wall. Elinor touched the damask that covered one of the chairs, then caressed the embroidered satin counterpane that covered the bed.

She wandered over to the pair of long windows next. The rain had ceased to beat against the panes, and she could see they led to a small balcony. Opening them, she stepped outside.

"Here now, Miss Elinor!" she heard her maid cry behind her. "How do you know 'tis safe?"

Her warning fell on deaf ears, for to Elinor, Doll had ceased to exist. Stretched out before her as far as she could see was the ocean. It was dark and mysterious under the gloomy sky, and in constant motion as its waves swept in around the castle on both sides. Elinor could almost imagine she was standing at the prow of a very tall ship. She took a deep breath, admiring a small schooner that was beating to windward far offshore. She wondered to which part of the world she was headed?

She looked down then, and her eyes widened. The balcony hung over a sheer drop straight down the castle walls and the promontory itself. Far, far below, at the base of the cliff, the breakers she had heard earlier thundered to shore, to cast huge fountains of spray against the resisting rock. Relentlessly, one followed another in a solemn march, as if determined to undermine it. Strangely, Elinor was not afraid. The rock the castle was built on seemed impregnable, and no doubt those waves had been beating at it just this way for centuries.

Her hands tightened on the balcony's railing as she turned to stare up at the battlements above her, to scan as much of the front of the castle as she could see. There were other balconies, other windows as well as hers, dotted across its face. How different it was from the secretive, closed aspect the castle presented on the landside approach. Then a gust of wind whipped her thin gown against her body, and she shivered as she retreated to the warm room again.

As she smoothed her hair back, her eyes were shining. Doll shook her head at her, her mouth turned down in disgust.

"You might have blown away, miss, to say nothing of the possibility of that rickety old thing's falling into the sea," she scolded, coming to push Elinor toward the dressing table. "Sit down, do, and let me fix your hair. Can't go down to tea looking like a coster maid, not in this fancy place you can't!"

Elinor chuckled as Doll took out the hairpins and began to brush her long, windblown hair. "Just think how grand that balcony will be in summer, Doll! Perhaps we can move the chaise out there, for a more delightful spot to read I cannot imagine. And the view, why, it is outstanding!"

"I'd rather look at London town, fog 'n all, meself," Doll muttered around a mouthful of hairpins. "And all that fresh air ain't good for a body. You take care you don't catch your death!"

Elinor regarded her maid's reflection in the mirror. Doll was only a few years older than she was herself, certainly not yet thirty. She wondered if she would be happy here, and sensed somehow that she would not. And she knew she couldn't beg her to stay if she wanted to leave, not when she had already done so much for her! But still, she prayed she would remain for a while at least, until she herself felt more at home, or had decided to leave, too.

After Doll finished doing her hair, Elinor said, "Ring for the maid, will you, Doll? She's to take me down to tea. And a good thing, too! I'd never find the right salon by myself. This place is huge! And while I'm gone, you have some tea as well. The maid can show you where to get it, or you can order a tray brought up here."

Doll snorted as Elinor stood up so her skirts could be straightened. "Not bloody likely I can," she said tartly as she knelt to twitch at the silk. "That would be to start out on the wrong foot entirely, Miss Elinor. No, best I go and meet the others right away. They don't seem a friendly lot, do they? Mostly so far all I've had from 'em is a stare. Ah, well, they be a bunch o' peasants, so it can't be helped. Peasants is very wary o' strangers, or so I've heard tell.''

''You'll have them best friends in no time, Doll,'' Elinor assured her. ''There, that looks very well. I'm sure Sir Robert will forgive me for not changing my gown. I'm too hungry to wait for that!''

2

THE TEA was as lavish as Sir Robert had promised. Elinor was a little disappointed they enjoyed it alone, just the two of them, for she had been looking forward to making Fiona Grenville's acquaintaince, to say nothing of that of Sir Robert's son. Her host explained she would meet his daughter at dinner.

"Fiona's shy," he said gruffly, holding out a dish of clotted cream so she could help herself. "It will take her a while to get used to you, Miss Fielding, for we seldom have visitors here. Tell me, do you like to read, do needlework? Do you enjoy music? I want you to be happy here, but there's no denying 'tis not a social place, with a ball or a party every week of the year."

Elinor smiled to herself, even as she assured the gentleman she was quite used to solitude. And that was to understate the matter to an extreme, she thought. In London, she had stayed very much to home. Her mother had been timid, and had not liked her to go abroad, even with Doll to accompany her. Indeed, ever since her husband had been killed by a runaway horse on a busy London street when Elinor was ten years old, Anne Fielding had never left the house again in her lifetime. She would not even go to church. Elinor had tried to persuade her that her fears were irrational, but her mother, so gentle in other ways, remained stubborn. She would not go out; that was that. There was no need. The housekeeper, Mrs. Bundy, and her daughter, Doll, could do the shopping. She trusted Mrs. Bundy completely. Still, Mrs. Fielding had realized it was not right for Elinor to be kept so confined, and she tried very hard to allow her some freedom. But she was always in such a state of nerves when her daughter returned from one of her outings that Elinor soon found herself staying in most of the time. She went out only to church or to a nearby lending library. Not for her, pleasant afternoon strolls in one of the London parks or leisurely shopping trips.

Fortunately, Elinor loved to read, and the books she was able to borrow did a great deal to make her lonely lot more bearable. She especially loved reading romances, and adventure and poetry. It was so easy then, for a few hours at least, to leave Compton Street and travel anywhere in the world, and without disturbing her mother in the bargain. And fortunately, Mrs. Fielding had a number of neighborhood acquaintances who came to call on a regular basis, so the two were not completely isolated.

Elinor also enjoyed painting. Now, as Sir Robert quizzed her about other activities she engaged in, she remembered her box of watercolors, carefully packed at the bottom of her trunk. The thieves who had rummaged through it, had not disturbed them. She was glad, for she could hardly wait to try a painting of the ocean. Up to now, her efforts had all been of flowers, or the fruits and vegetables that Doll brought back from market. Mordyn opened a new world to her, and her fingers itched to explore it with her pencils and brush.

"Truly, it does not matter, sir," she said at last. "I am still in mourning, and could not attend parties even if they were available. I do assure you that I have led a quiet life."

Her host looked relieved as he spread another scone with honey. "I am sorry Jonathan is not here today," he said as Elinor refilled his cup. "He has gone to spend the day and evening with friends. There are a few of the gentry about: the Wilkensons at Trecarrag, the Brownells of Glyn."

"What fascinating names," Elinor remarked as she handed him his tea. "They are like nothing I have ever heard before."

"They are Cornish, of course," Sir Robert told her. "But none here speak the old dialect anymore. It died out as we became more and more anglicized. Trecarrag, for example, means homerock, and Glyn, deep valley.

"And what does Mordyn mean?" Elinor asked, leaning forward a little in her eagerness.

"Ah, Mordyn. *Mor* is Cornish for sea, and *dyn* means a hill fort. Ergo, a fort on a hill by the sea."

"It is well named. But I was surprised to see all the windows on the ocean side. There are so few anywhere else."

Sir Robert smiled at her, a little smile that curved his lips but did not expose his teeth. "Originally, many centuries ago, the castle was built as a fortification. The only approach to it is by land, for no boats can put in at the cliffs, nor can those cliffs be scaled. There were only slits for archers on the approach side. Of course, the castle has been modernized to a great extent. The balconies, the broader expanse of windows, are new amenities."

"But you left the approach and that huge hall the way they were built, did you not?" Elinor asked. "It is most impressive, although a little daunting to a visitor."

"Yes, it is true nothing has been changed there. I suppose because none of my ancestors wanted to forget Mordyn's original purpose, its proud history. Nor did I."

She looked a question, and he went on, "Mordyn was built to keep out Grenville enemies, to withstand seige. Do you remember that first room you stepped into, Miss Fielding?"

At her nod, he continued, "That had a purpose, too. If by any chance attackers managed to fight their way through the defenders outside the walls, survive the arrows from the battlements, to cross the moat and batter down the door, they found themselves in that bare, narrow room.

"It has an ingenious roof that opens so more destruction could be poured down on them in the form of boiling oil and torches. They were like animals in Mordyn's trap, you see. No place to advance, and no place to retreat. They could be killed almost at leisure."

He chuckled then, not noticing his guest's ill-disguised shudder, the way she put her cake down untasted. "Mordyn was only conquered once, and it took many long months to accomplish that. You see, there was no way to take it except by seige."

"But the Grenvilles recovered the castle, of course," Elinor prompted.

"Ah, yes. They never stayed long, those foreign invaders. No one could subdue Cornishmen, and eventually they gave up trying and went away."

He sipped his tea before he chuckled again. "I was just remembering Lady Mary Grenville, one of my more illustrious ancestors. She lived in Drake's time, when the Spanish Armada was a real threat to our shores. A ship from that Armada arrived at Mordyn. Her captain decided it would make a fine base, with its deep, narrow harbor. Accordingly, he called at the castle. Lady Mary's husband was from home at the time, and he had taken most of the men with him. Knowing she could not defend the castle herself, the Lady Mary decided on another way."

He paused for another sip of tea, and Elinor leaned forward, caught up in the story. "How did she do that?" she asked.

"She pretended to welcome the Spaniards, asked them to dine that evening. And it is on record she gave them a most lavish feast, all those officers. But they never returned to their ship. They were ambushed when they went back to their boats. Those few who escaped the marksmen, soon found themselves drowning. You see, while they had been at the banquet, Lady Mary had had men drilling holes in their boats. Not a one of them escaped."

He laughed heartily then, but Elinor was horrified.

"Cornishmen—and women—are good fighters. Now, of course, we are all Englishmen, although there are still some who mutter under their breath about it. An insular race, the Cornish."

"How did you meet my father? Was he from near here?" Elinor asked, not at all anxious to learn more of Mordyn's bloody history. Imagine sitting down to dine with men you were going to have killed a short time later. The Lady Mary sounded a ghoul!

"Yes, Gerald was born only a few miles away," Sir Robert told her. "I'll show you the place someday soon. His father, who came from somewhere in the north of England, managed the tin mines for my father. We were instantly compatible, perhaps because there were so few boys here of our age and station. I missed Gerald when he went away to London to make his fortune, but I understood. There was nothing for him here, and he hated the mines.

"And he did make his fortune, did he not, Miss Fielding?" he asked. "Good for him!"

Elinor nodded and tried to smile. Yes, her father had made a fortune, but he had not spent it. Outside of the house on Compton Street, there had been no amenities. Why, for servants they had only had Mrs. Bundy and Doll. The Fieldings had lived close, so frugally that she had always thought they were poor. She had worn turned dresses cut down from her mother's old gowns, darned her hose till it was hard in some places to see the original wool, and carefully preserved her shoes for years. And after her father's death, his widow had continued to live in the same manner. But perhaps she had not known there were all those thousands of pounds sterling, all safely invested, Elinor thought. Perhaps the solicitor was at fault there. Or it might just have been another instance of her mother's strangeness, like fearing the outside world so much. But what a shock it had been to her, to learn she was an heiress! She remembered how angry she had been at both her parents when she found out, for all she could think of was the many things she had missed over her childhood. Pretty clothes and toys, a real governess to teach her, instead of just her mother to see to her education, perhaps even painting lessons.

"Tomorrow you must ask Mrs. Greene to show you over the castle," Sir Robert was saying now, and she forced herself to concentrate. "I want you to be happy here, and comfortably at home. And may I call you Elinor, my dear? Miss Fielding is so formal for one I hope will become one of the family, another daughter to me."

"I should be delighted, Sir Robert," Elinor told him. The concern in his glance, the light in his dark gray eyes, warmed her. She had been alone for such a long time that his kindness touched her.

"Thank you. Now, I suggest you go and rest till dinner. We dine at eight—quite unfashionable, of course, but it is our custom here. You can find your way to your room? Oh, and there is no need to dress, my dear. That gown you are wearing is very rich, is it not? And we do not stand on ceremony here."

Elinor's hand went to her alemade skirts, to feel the thin soft silk under her fingers. Had she heard a little disapproval in Sir Robert's voice? Did he dislike her London gown, think it much too elaborate for the country?

Well, she had not known what to expect here. She would wait and see how Miss Grenville was dressed, and take her clue from her. But even so, she could not regret all her beautiful new clothes. After living with hand-me-downs for so many years, her orgy of shopping must surely be justified. And she knew how much she loved the rich fabrics, the sensual touch of them next to her skin.

Perhaps Sir Robert was such a man as her father had been, close with his money? But Mordyn Castle belied that supposition, for it was filled with beautiful things.

She went up the stairs to her room deep in thought. Doll was not there, although she saw the maid had finished unpacking before she went to tea.

Still, Elinor spent some time rearranging things to her own taste. The books she had brought with her were put in her sitting room, along with her painting equipment, and on the table next to the bed, she set the miniatures she had of her father and mother.

At last, she wandered over to the long windows again. She supposed she should pull the curtains across them, for the wind had risen; she could hear it buffeting the panes. But she could not bear to shut out the magnificent view a moment before she had to. As she watched, the sun slipped beneath the cloud cover to hover over the western horizon. The bottoms of those clouds were suddenly lit with soft gold and rose, and the ocean sparkled as well. Elinor caught her breath at the splendor of the scene, and she stood unmoving as that sun grew smaller and smaller, till finally it slipped beneath the waves.

In the faint afterglow, she lit a candle and closed the curtains at last. She saw how the flame flickered, how the curtains moved a little in the draft, and when she turned, she noticed the tapestry stirring as well. In an old castle like this, there was bound to be many a draft to contend with, and wasn't it a good thing she did not have Doll's fear of fresh air? she thought, smiling to herself.

As Elinor settled down on the chaise and closed her eyes, she found herself hoping it would all turn out all right; that her stay here would be a long and happy one. She admitted she was strangely attracted to Mordyn Castle, high on its Cornish cliff above the restless ocean, and she knew she would be loathe to leave it. And just before she dropped off to sleep, she remembered it was 1829. There would be no more attackers or boiling oil, no uncomfortable seige to face here. Not anymore.

Elinor woke early the following morning. For a moment, she was confused and did not know where she was. And then, as she inspected the sumptuous bedchamber, felt the satin counterpane under her hand, it all came back to her. Cornwall, and Mordyn Castle.

She did not ring for Doll immediately. Instead, she lay back on her pillows, staring up at the tester far above her while she reviewed the previous evening. She had gone down to dinner just before eight, to find

Sir Robert waiting for her, in company with his daughter.

Now she recalled how frightened Miss Fiona Grenville had seemed, and how much she had wished she might reassure her. Perhaps Sir Robert had been aware of her fright too. As he introduced the two, he had kept a firm grip on his daughter's arm, almost as if he were afraid she might try to run away. Elinor had smiled warmly as she curtsied, trying to convey to Miss Grenville her wish that they might be friends.

It had seemed awkward to Elinor at table, and afterward, for even if Fiona Grenville had been so inclined, she could make no contribution to the conversation. Elinor knew she could hear, however, for Sir Robert always couched his remarks to her in such a way that she could answer by nodding or shaking her head.

Tall and pretty, Miss Grenville had been wearing a white gown trimmed with blue ribbons. It had seemed rather childish to Elinor, and not in the height of current fashion, but it was of excellent quality. Her dark brown hair had been brushed smooth, and it was held back with a matching ribbon. All entirely suitable for a very young miss. But that in itself was a puzzle, for Fiona Grenville was not a girl. Indeed, Elinor was sure she was at least as old as she was herself, and she was twenty-four.

Sir Robert carried most of the burden of conversation. He told Elinor more stories of the neighborhood, and of her father, after explaining his boyhood friendship with Mr. Fielding to his daughter.

"And I shall hope you and Elinor become just as fast friends, my dear," he had said with his little smile. "But you'll see. I'm sure Elinor will be much more amusing company for you than Miss Ward."

Elinor had looked up quickly then to see Fiona looking rebellious, her color slightly heightened. When her father had stared at her, however, she had only nodded meekly, as if at his direct order.

Now, Elinor sighed a little as she stretched and sat up. She could see it would take quite a while to scale the walls the girl had retreated behind. Perhaps even as long as any seige Mordyn had ever known? She did so hope not! Sir Robert seemed a nice man, but he was older, not company for her. And she had yet to meet the son of the house. No doubt he would be too busy with his own pursuits to spare much time for her.

Before she rang for Doll, Elinor carefully pulled some of the bedcurtains tight around the bed, and retrieved her nightcap from under the pillow. It was something she did every morning, since she threw back all the curtains and tossed that confining cap aside the minute Doll left her at night. She did not like sleeping in a small, enclosed place, and the nightcap bothered her rest. Now, as she tied it under her chin again, she sighed. But it would not do to offend Doll's sensibilities about what was proper and healthful.

Elinor thought her maid was looking stern when she came in with a cup of chocolate on a tray. And as she sat up in bed to sip it, Elinor watched Doll open all the curtains so abruptly, it was almost as if she were angry. But when she questioned her, Doll merely remarked that she found the Cornish very hard to understand, and she did not think she was going to support living here for long.

Elinor's heart sank. "Oh, please try, for my sake, Doll!" she cried. "I don't think I would like it half as much without you beside me."

Her maid's lips only tightened, and she still looked mulish.

Elinor took a deep breath and decided to try another tack. "But perhaps I won't like living here either," she said more calmly. "And if I do decide to leave, we will be able to travel together."

"Would we go back to London, miss?" Doll asked as she picked up her mistress's slippers and wrapper.

"Why, yes, I suppose so," Elinor said, frowning now. "I would not know where else to go. Of course, I will *not* go back to Compton Street. On that point, I am adamant!"

She shrugged then, as she threw back the covers and held out her feet so Doll could put her slippers on.

"But it is too early to make any decisions. We must wait a bit and see. Sir Robert has very kindly invited me to live here. I cannot be so rude as to rush off without giving the place a fair trial. Do say you will stay for that, Doll!"

"We'll see," Doll mumbled, holding out the dark green satin robe. Elinor slipped off the bed so Doll could put it on her. As she pulled it close, the soft fabric caressed her body and she smiled. She had loved this robe from the moment she had seen it in the modiste's shop. Trimmed with pale green and gold embroidery, it was slippery and smooth, like a whisper against the skin.

When she came back from the dressing room, Doll was inspecting the gowns hung in the armoir.

"And what would you be wearing today, Miss Elinor?" she asked.

Elinor sat down at the dressing table to remove her nightcap and unbraid her hair. As she did so, she said, "What does it matter? They are all black! Oh, Doll, I did love my mother, but I will be so glad when this period of mourning is over! To think there are still six months of the year to go! And I am weary of looking like a rook all the time!"

Doll smiled a little at her outburst. Miss Elinor had no idea how flattering her black gowns were with her golden blond hair and fair skin. And the absence of rival color seemed to call attention to the pure green of her eyes, the peach tint of her cheeks, and especially her full, rosy mouth.

"How about the new taffeta, miss?" she asked, her fingers stroking it. "It makes such a nice sound when you move!"

Elinor laughed as she shook her head to loosen the braid. Her hair was her one vanity. It was almost long enough to sit on, for she had never had it cut, no matter the current style. Now she picked up her hairbrush to begin long, slow strokes through it.

"No, not the taffeta," she said. With her head bent, her voice was muffled by a curtain of hair. "I am sure that would be much too formal for morning wear.

What a terrible lot I have to learn, Doll, never having moved in genteel society before! And I could tell Sir Robert thought my alemade gown much too elaborate for traveling. The wool gown will do very nicely, and it is my plainest. I must remember that I am in the country now."

As Doll took the designated gown from the cupboard, she sniffed. "Not likely either o' us will be able to forget where we are, miss!" she said, her voice tart. "Not with that awful racket dinning in our ears night and day!"

"You mean the breakers?" Elinor asked as she brushed her hair to one side. "But I rather like that. It—it is soothing somehow, and steady, like a heartbeat."

"Soothing is it?" Doll asked. "Well, each to 'is own taste, as the 'ackney said when he kissed 'is 'orse! But I'll never get used to it, never! Give me a good old London street, full o' cackle and bustle, any day!"

"How do you find the other servants, Doll?" Elinor asked, in an effort to change the subject lest Doll begin to bemoan her exile yet again, "I hope they were not unfriendly to you."

"Very stiff and suspicious, although they did loosen up a bit after I told them about the robbers," Doll admitted as she laid out Elinor's hose and petticoats, her lace-trimmed chemise. "And at supper they was quite chatty."

She sniffed again, and Elinor spun around on the stool to stare at her. "That was nice," she said. "Did they tell you about the castle? The surrounding villages?"

Doll came over to take the brush from her hand before she answer. "No," she said dryly. "All they talked about were the ghosts."

"Ghosts?" Elinor echoed as she watched her maid's enigmatic face in the glass. Expertly, Doll swirled her heavy tresses into a soft chignon.

"Aye, the ghosts," she repeated, around the hairpins she held in her teeth. "Seems this old castle got a lot o' them, it do. First, there's The Lady. She's seen a lot, always wearin' white. She wanders about the halls, wringin' her hands and moanin', although about what, no one seems to know. Then there's the Sailor. He drowned right out there in sight of the castle, before anyone could reach 'im, or so they said."

Doll sniffed again. "No one knows why he can never rest, or why he haunts the castle, but they told me never to open the door to 'im when 'e knocks, or I'd be cursed."

"But how would you know it was him?" Elinor asked, getting into the spirit of things. "Perhaps it might only be another member of the household."

Doll could see how Miss Elinor's eyes were twinkling, the little smile that curved her lips, and she snorted. "Oh, I'll know, and so will you, Miss Elinor! They told me there's a strange odor then, like oreweed, whatever that might be. I didn't ask. And suddenly, near the door, it gets very cold and clammy-like. Brr."

She put in the last hairpin, and stepped back to survey her work. " 'Course they also mentioned somethin' they called piskies. I don't rightly believe in *them.*"

"What on earth is a piskie?" Elinor demanded.

"Some sort of fairy, from what I could make out. All households here have 'em. Sometimes they're full of mischief, like naughty children. Then they spoil food, and sour the milk. Huh! What silly notions these Cornish folk have!"

As Elinor rose to remove her wrapper and shrug off her nightrobe, she shook her head. "I do believe they were trying to frighten you, Doll. You're new here, and they were having sport with you."

"Oh, I ken that, Miss Elinor," the maid said as she lowered the flimsy chemise carefully over Elinor's head. "In spite o' the fact not a one o' 'em cracked a smile! So hard-faced they be! But when I went up to bed later, one o' the younger maids, Molly's her name, told me they really do have ghosts here. And the worst one o' all is the one they call the Cavalier."

"What does he do?" Elinor asked, sitting down so

she could pull on her hose and roll them over the garters.

"He touches you!" Doll said, sounding agitated for the first time. "You can't see him, not clear anyway, but you can feel his hand. Brr! Like to jump out o' my skin if he ever touched me, miss, that I would!"

As Doll put on her sandals, Elinor thought she would too, but she did not say so. "Does he appear often, or only on nights when there is a full moon?" she asked. "My, the castle appears to be very crowded. 'Tis a wonder this Cavalier and the Lady haven't taken up with each other long before this, and stopped bothering the mortals here. Surely they must, er, bump into each other now and then in their hauntings."

The hands on her ankle tightened. "You're makin' fun o' me, Miss Elinor, but for all we know, it might be true. And if it is, I'm off, I am, and so I'm warning you!"

As Doll lowered her petticoats over her head, Elinor said contritely, "I'm sorry, Doll. But give Mordyn a fair trial, for my sake, won't you? And don't be seeing ghosts around every door. If there were so many, why has everyone else stayed? But they're not afraid! It's my belief it was all a hoax, done for your benefit. After all, they know you're from London. They were probably trying to impress you."

Doll looked thoughtful as she put on the wool gown and fastened it. "No doubt you're right, miss," she said meekly. "It will take a lot, though, for a pack of peasants, who've never been over fifteen miles from here, to get the best o' me!

"Now, you be off to breakfast," she said, after giving Elinor's skirts a last smoothing. "I'll gather up the laundry. It's a nice day, and I've all the wash from the journey to do."

Impulsively, Elinor leaned forward to kiss her maid on the cheek. "Thank you, Doll," she said, hugging her close for a moment. "You are so good to me. You always were, even when those others were reviling me. But you stood up for me—stayed with me. I don't know what I would have done without you!"

"Pooh, enough o' that, now, Miss Elinor! Just you put it all behind you, is my advice. You'll never have to see those people again, you won't. It's over now, for good."

Elinor nodded before she left the room, closing the door behind her. As she turned, her eye was caught by the large painting of the gentleman in blue velvet. Could he be the Cavalier? she wondered. The one who touched people?

She paused for a moment to go closer and regard him, her head tilted to one side. As they had yesterday, his eyes smiled down into hers, and she found herself unable to look away. Those dark eyes were hypnotic, and there was a devil dancing in them. He *was* handsome, she thought. When he was alive, I imagine a great many women prayed he would notice them. And he looks as if he must have enjoyed making a lot of them very happy.

She turned away then and walked to the stairs, but as she started down, something compelled her to turn back and stare at him again. But how could it be? How could he be looking at her still? Yet it seemed his eyes had followed her across the room. That is impossible, she told herself. As she went down the stairs, she warned herself most sternly not to become fanciful and nervy here. She didn't believe in ghosts, no matter how handsome they were. There just weren't any. It was only people's ghoulish imaginations that conjured them up, and she would keep a tight rein on hers!

3

WHITMAN, the elderly butler, showed Elinor to the breakfast room. She found Fiona Grenville there, seated at the table with another lady who rose from her chair immediately to curtsy.

"But you are Miss Fielding, of course!" she said in a quick, almost breathless voice. "How charming to meet you! I am Rebecca Ward, Fiona's companion. Well, that is to say, now I am. I was her governess many years ago, but now we are very close companions. Isn't that so, Fiona?"

As she turned to her charge to accept her smile and fervent nod, Elinor studied the lady carefully. Only one word came to mind as apt to describe Miss Ward. That word was *ordinary.* She was of medium height, neither too tall nor too short, nor was she too fat or too thin. Her features were undistinguished, although she was not precisely plain. She was obviously the eldest in the room, but it was impossible to even guess just how old she might be. And she was dressed in quiet, unassuming clothes. Even her eyes were ordinary, some faded color between gray and blue. Elinor was sure if she had passed her in a London street, nothing about the woman would remain in her mind for more than a second, and she would be forgotten long before the next crossing. A most unmemorable person.

Now that same lady beamed as she came to take Elinor's arm. "Breakfast is always set out on the sideboard, Miss Fielding, so we can help ourselves," she said.

As she spoke, she handed Elinor a plate and began

lifting the various covers so Elinor might inspect the dishes. As she did so, she maintained a gentle flow of talk about the selections, recommending one or the other. After Elinor had made her choice, Miss Ward escorted her to the table.

"Now, Miss Fielding, do sit down opposite dear Fiona. I am sure you two will be great friends, although there is no denying Fiona is a trifle shy with strangers, aren't you, dear? Oh, do allow me to pass you the blackberry jam! Fiona and I picked the berries for it ourselves last summer, didn't we, dear?"

Elinor began to eat, somewhat startled by the waves of nonstop chatter that emanated from such a nondescript woman.

After ascertaining if she would prefer tea or coffee, and pouring her a cup, Miss Ward continued to talk. And it was not long before Elinor realized she was being most carefully quizzed. The questions came gently, never more than one at a time, but by the time she had finished her breakfast, Miss Ward and the silent Fiona knew where she had lived in London, when her father and mother had died, and how, and whether she had any living relatives.

"How sad that you do not!" Miss Ward mourned as she placed her napkin beside her plate. "But we do hope you will be happy with us, Miss Fielding. Of course, there are not many who enjoy the coast of Cornwall for more than a visit. Oh, not that it's not a lovely place on certain sunny summer days when the sky is so blue, the ocean so calm."

She tittered behind her hand then and added, "Those days are precious to us, for there are so few of them. Mostly it is stormy here. Indeed, there is an old Cornish saying that when the wind blows, a man wants two other men just to hold the hair on his head! And then there are the mists. We are famous for our mists. They can last for days. So depressing for the uninitiated. And, of course, it is so lonely here, especially for the young. There is little gaiety to be had. Quite a complete change from London, you know. Still, we do hope you will like it, don't we, Fiona?"

Elinor looked straight at the girl across the table from her. She was startled to see the fear still in her eyes, fear and something else. Could it be animosity? Miss Grenville lowered her eyes to her lap so quickly, Elinor could not be sure she had not just imagined that sudden flash of dislike.

"I am positive I shall enjoy it," she said in the sudden, blessed silence. "I am used to living secluded."

"In London?" Miss Ward asked, incredulous. "I find that hard to believe! Why, there are so many activities in town—the plays and shops and parties. I have heard some young ladies in society attend as many as three in an evening. But of course, you are in mourning. Do forgive me! I forgot! Perhaps that is what you meant?"

Elinor shook her head. "Not at all. My mother did not care to socialize. We lived very much to ourselves."

"Well, in that case, Mordyn might well appeal to you," Miss Ward commented, still looking doubtful. "Now, what are you planning to do this morning? Perhaps Fiona and I can be of assistance?"

"Sir Robert suggested I ask Mrs. Greene to show me around the castle. I confess, I am afraid I would get lost in it alone, so massive as it is."

"Oh, there is no need to bother Mrs. Greene," Miss Ward assured her. "She will be very busy with her household duties, and Fiona and I will be delighted to take you around. Indeed, although of course I should not be the one to say it, I am certainly a much better guide than an uneducated servant! Why, I know all of Mordyn's history! Do say you will allow me to serve you."

"I should be pleased," Elinor replied, although she was not being completely honest as she did so. Miss Ward talked entirely too much. But perhaps living so long with a mute girl had made her so? Poor lady, Elinor thought, trying to be kind. I must not judge her prematurely. And perhaps spending some time with Miss Grenville will relieve her mind about me. I wonder why she seems to dislike my presence here so very much?

When the three rose from the table, however, Miss Grenville declined to accompany them. Instead, she shook her head quite violently, when Miss Ward took her hand.

"You have something else you wish to do, dear?" the lady asked.

Elinor was intrigued when her charge raised both hands with the fingers curled over, and began to wiggle them rapidly. At the end of the display, she raised her right forefinger and drew it rapidly across her throat.

"Ah, but of course! You want to play the piano this morning, and you do not wish to be disturbed. I understand. I shall see you later, my dear Fiona," Miss Ward said with a smile.

Barely taking the time to curtsy, Miss Grenville fled.

As Elinor watched her hasty retreat, a little frown creased her brow. She sensed the older woman watching her, and she made herself say, "Miss Grenville is fortunate you are with her, Miss Ward. You understand her so well."

"I daresay," the lady agreed. "But it would be a strange thing if I did not. I was a distant relation of her mother's, brought here after my dear Papa died to keep Lady Grenville company. Of course, I was only a child then, or almost one," she added. "I was here when Fiona was born, and since she had her accident, we have been very close. I like to think, in some small way, I took her mother's place in her life."

"She could speak before the accident?" Elinor asked, curious. "How old was she when it happened?"

"She was only six. But come, enough of these reminiscences! Shall be begin here?"

She opened the door to a salon then, and began to explain the furnishings and paintings, and the room's use. For the next two hours, Elinor tagged after her, from one large room to another. She seldom had to make any comments at all, for Miss Ward appeared only too happy to conduct a monologue. They only neglected one room. Elinor could hear the sounds of a piano being played within, and Miss Ward explained that that room was Fiona Grenville's private sitting room.

Of all the many apartments, Elinor was drawn most to the smallest morning room. It was decorated in soft peach and cream, and it was so lovely, yet so comfortable looking, that she smiled.

"This was Lady Grenville's favorite room," Miss Ward explained. "She used to sit here and write her letters, read her books, and oversee the household accounts. She received the servants here every morning, to give them their orders. But it is not used much anymore."

"I notice it faces the garden," Elinor said. "How pleasant!"

"Yes, Beatrice did not care for the sea. She always said that she could pretend she was miles away from it here."

As they had been speaking, Miss Ward led the way across the wide hall to another room. As she opened the door, she said, "And here we have the library. Do observe the number of volumes, the—Oh, Sir Robert, your pardon, sir! And yours, Mr. Jonathan! I had no idea you were both here, or I would never have disturbed you. You must excuse me, and Miss Fielding, too!"

Sir Robert rose from the desk where he had been sitting as Miss Ward began to back from the room, looking flustered.

"No, do not leave, Elinor," he said. "Come in and meet my son."

Elinor wondered at the tension in the room. She could almost feel it, and she wondered if they had interrupted an argument between father and son. If that were the case, she would much prefer to leave with the garrulous Miss Ward. And after all, they had yet to visit the picture gallery. She very much wanted to ask the lady about the handsome cavalier.

Sir Robert turned to his daughter's companion then

and said, "We will excuse you, Rebecca. How very kind of you to show Elinor around. But we will not keep you. I am sure there is a great deal for you to do this morning, is there not?"

Miss Ward curtsied. "Indeed there is, Sir Robert. Why, I have been most derelict to my duties! But our honored guest, you see, quite took my mind from them. Now, however, I must speak to Cook—one of the sauces last evening was not of her usual excellence. And then I—"

"Yes, yes," Sir Robert interrupted. "Do run along at once."

No matter how hard she listened, his voice seemed expressionless to Elinor, and it did not hold a trace of the impatience or the dislike she had almost expected for the woman's dithering. Obediently, Miss Ward turned and whisked herself out the door without another word.

As it closed behind her, Sir Robert came to take Elinor's hand to lead her forward to where a much younger man was standing before the fireplace. As they neared him, Elinor's eyes widened, for he was the image of the cavalier in the painting outside her room! Tall and handsome, with strong features and dark brown hair, he regarded her impassively from a pair of fine gray eyes. Elinor noted he had his father's broad shoulders, an even narrower waist, and well-muscled legs clad in tight riding breeches. She felt very small standing before him, for the top of her head didn't even reach those broad shoulders he sported.

"May I present my son Jonathan, my dear? Jonathan, this is Miss Elinor Fielding, the young lady who has come to live with us."

Jonathan Grenville bowed. "Delighted, Miss Fielding," he said.

As she curtsied in return, Elinor considered his voice. A deep baritone, it had been almost toneless, without any inflection at all. Indeed, she had no idea if he were delighted to meet her or not. Somehow she rather imagined it to be not.

And as he took her hand and bent over it, Elinor

thought her first impression of his similarity to the man in the portrait much exaggerated. But when he rose and released her hand, he smiled at her, a little, knowing smile, and the similarity was striking again.

"I hope you will enjoy it here, Miss Fielding," he said. "Will you be seated?"

Elinor took the chair he indicated. She looked to her host then, to see him watching them intently. "But you must not be so formal, Jonathan," he said. "We are all to call the young lady Elinor. I have told her I hope she will become another daughter to me."

"Then I am sure she shall be," the younger man said, his voice toneless again as he took up his place by the fireplace. Turning to Elinor, he asked, "Do you ride, Miss Fi—er, Elinor?"

She shook her head. "No, I am afraid I never learned. Growing up in London made it unnecessary."

"Too bad. But it is never too late to start," Jonathan Grenville told her. "And it is the perfect way to explore the countryside, get away from Mordyn's grim walls every now and again. If you would care for it, I can make arrangements with our head groom for you to learn. His name is McCarthy, and he taught all of us to ride when we were children. In a month or so, why, you'll be able to share the family jaunts."

"It sounds delightful," Elinor replied, smiling at him a little. "I only pray I am an apt pupil!"

"As I said, it is never too late to learn. I am sure you will have a splendid seat."

"Be sure McCarthy starts her out on a gentle mare," his father interrupted.

His son waved an impatient hand. "Of course! I had in mind nothing more taxing than Jenny, sir."

Sir Robert chuckled. "Ah, Elinor, with Jenny you will have nothing to fear. She is a lamb."

He waved his arm to the floor-to-ceiling bookcases then. "You told me you liked to read. Do feel free to choose any book in my library you would care to peruse. As you see, there is a set of steps so you can reach the topmost volumes. And you will find the catalog on that table over there."

Elinor rose to inspect the volumes nearest her. "You have had your library catalogued, sir? How foresighted of you, and how much easier for me. Yes, I will most certainly take you up on your kind offer, and I thank you. I am fond of reading, but the lending library I patronized in London did not have that large a selection."

Sir Robert saw her eyes wandering eagerly over the shelves, and he beckoned to his son. "Come, Jonathan, let us leave Elinor to make her choice. I've a matter of business to speak to Bothwell about, and you might just as well alert McCarthy to the arrival of his new pupil."

Elinor tore her eyes away from the wealth before her, to turn and curtsy.

"We shall see you at luncheon, my dear," Sir Robert said over his shoulder as he walked to the door with his son. "Till then."

Jonathan Grenville waved a careless hand as the two disappeared. Elinor forgot them in a minute.

She was late to luncheon, and she apologized profusely.

"We are not such sticklers here, Elinor," Sir Robert said, as his son helped her to her chair. He and his father sat at opposite ends of the table, while Miss Ward and Fiona were seated together on one side. Elinor's seat faced them. She thought Miss Ward looked reproving, as if she regretted Elinor's lack of manners personally. Elinor tried not to flush as she spread her napkin in her lap. The library had been a revelation to her. She was sure she would have been there for hours yet if Whitman had not come to find her.

"I cannot understand why you did not hear the gong," Miss Ward remarked now. "Such a din it makes! And clearly audible in every room of the castle, for Sir Robert employs an old man whose only task is to sound the gong for luncheon and dinner as he walks through the halls. Why, many times I—"

"I understand Miss Fielding's preoccupation completely," Jonathan Grenville remarked, interrupting the older woman's discourse without apology. "She is a great reader. Perhaps she has that in common with you, Fiona?"

Elinor saw the girl was looking frightened again, and she wondered why. Was she afraid she was to be chastised for her reading? But it must be such a consolation for her, she thought. Unable to speak, to voice her thoughts, even to argue or cry out when she was angry or hurt, what a relief it must be to escape into a book, as she herself had always done.

When Fiona nodded almost reluctantly, Elinor said with a smile for her, "Perhaps Miss Grenville can point out some of her favorites to me. I was so lost in choice I did not even select one to carry away with me."

Sir Robert took a spoonful of the soup that had just been served him, and nodded to his butler before he said, "An excellent idea! Why don't the two of you go there after luncheon? And perhaps you might take Elinor for a stroll this afternoon, Fiona? You must not waste these mild, sunny days."

Elinor saw his daughter was looking mutinous again, and she wished everyone was not so eager to push them into friendship. It might be better to let it evolve at its own tempo, if it were going to, for forcing the girl to something she did not want to do could only make her more stubborn.

Miss Ward spoke up then. "What an excellent suggestion, Sir Robert! We can go as far as the Home Farm. It is quite one of Fiona's favorite walks, is it not, dear? And that way Miss Fielding can meet some of your people and—"

"Do stop by the stables, Fiona; see Elinor meets McCarthy. She is to begin riding lessons tomorrow," Jonathan said, interrupting Miss Ward yet again.

He was to do so many times throughout the course of the meal. Elinor thought it very singular, but Miss Ward did not appear at all discomposed by his discourtesy. Indeed, it was as if she were very used to stopping in midsentence. Sir Robert was as guilty as his son. Elinor wondered that it had not dawned on the woman that her conversation was rambling and involved, and not very interesting to gentlemen, and that she had not tried to correct the fault.

After luncheon, Elinor discovered that her return to the library with Fiona as guide seemed to have been forgotten. Instead, Miss Ward sent both girls to their rooms to collect their cloaks and bonnets. As they went up side by side, they could hear her voice still going on about the dangers of catching a cold, the uncertainty of the weather, and her hopes that it would not come on to rain. Elinor shut her door and closed her eyes. It appeared she was doomed to an afternoon of chatter, and she prayed for patience.

They left the castle by a side door that led into The Lady's Garden. Elinor would have stopped to explore it, but Fiona Grenville hurried along, looking neither left nor right. Elinor followed obediently, although she wondered if she were to spend the outing at a dead run. She lacked several of Fiona's inches. Eventually, she gave up trying to keep up with the much taller girl, and walked along at her own pace. Miss Ward kindly slowed down as well, to keep her company.

But when Elinor suggested there was no need for her to do so, since the path was well marked, Miss Ward only shook her head. "It is quite all right, Miss Fielding. Fiona likes to be independent on occasion, and it appears she does not want companionship this afternoon."

"I am afraid she does not like me," Elinor remarked with a sideways glance at the older woman. "Perhaps she did not entirely welcome my visit here? She seems to resent me somehow."

"I cannot say," Miss Ward admitted. "Of course, she could not tell me if she did, and since she has never learned to write, there is no way for me to ascertain her feelings. But you must not be hurt! No doubt she'll come about before long. Just be patient."

"You said she had never learned to write?" Elinor asked, curious. "But how is that, when she is such a great reader?"

"It is strange, is it not? But writing seemed beyond her as a child, and my attempts to teach her disturbed her so much that the effort was soon discarded. Sir Robert decided she would do very well without that skill. I do admit it would have made it easier to converse with her if she had learned to communicate that way. Now I must guess from her expression, her few hand signals, what she wants and how she feels."

She paused for breath as they came out of the woods they had been strolling through to the edge of a large field. Ahead of them they could see Fiona Grenville striding along, her hooded red cape streaming out behind her.

"This is the beginning of the Home Farm," Miss Ward explained. "Those buildings you see ahead are the stables. And those are some of the Grenville horses in the field. Such handsome animals, are they not? Sir Robert insists on the finest."

Elinor studied them with more interest than she had ever studied horses before. She wondered which one of them was the gentle Jenny, and she said a small prayer that Jenny at least would like her, and that she herself would be an apt pupil.

When they reached the stables, they found Fiona on her knees, playing with some new kittens. She was smiling so broadly as she did so that everyone smiled with her. Miss Ward introduced Elinor to McCarthy, the head groom. He was a smallish Irishman with a mop of white hair, and the bowed legs of a man who has spent most of his lifetime on horseback. As he tugged his forelock and bowed a little, he asked what time tomorrow Miss would care to begin her lessons. But before Elinor could reply, he questioned her about boots.

"I fear I don't have any," she confessed.

"Hmm. Can't ride without boots, miss," he said, looking stern.

"Oh, dear. I wonder where I can get a pair?" she asked.

"Well, Miss Fiona's won't fit such a little lady as

ye be,'' McCarthy said. ''But perhaps one of the lads? Joe? Bring me those extra boots o' Danny-Boy!''

Elinor tried to refuse such largesse, but McCarthy waved her protests aside, and as she tried on the heavy leather boots, Miss Ward assured her that this Danny would be honored. And she, herself, would see that the bootmaker in Portreath had Miss Fielding's measurements so he could make her a pair.

The old scuffed boots were a little large, but McCarthy promised to stuff the toes of them with rags, to make them fit.

A time was agreed on for ten the following morning, ''If it don't come on to rain,'' McCarthy said in his broad brogue as the three women prepared to leave his immaculate stables. Fiona Grenville was most reluctant to be separated from the furry little balls that were the new kittens, until Miss Ward pointed out she could return and visit them tomorrow.

As the girl ran off ahead of them once more, Elinor thought her a most graceful figure. What a shame it was she had such a disability!

Since their way back to the castle led uphill now, Miss Ward was often forced to pause and rest. And during one of those pauses, Elinor suddenly thought to ask her where the ocean was.

''It seems strange we have not even caught a glimpse of it,'' she said. ''Why, I have to listen very hard just to hear the breakers.''

Miss Ward waved a gloved hand toward the west. ''It lies over there. We never go that way, for Fiona does not care for the ocean or the cliffs. Indeed, she used to become so agitated when taken near them that I have taken care to avoid them ever since. I fear she has inherited her mother's aversion.''

''Is there a path to it? Any way to get down the cliffs?'' Elinor asked.

''Oh yes, there is a lovely cliff walk Sir Robert had built some years ago, and yes, there is a way down. But my dear Miss Fielding, you must not make the attempt! I do believe that it is very dangerous, crumbling away in spots. If you want to visit the beach, I pray you will follow the walk to the end, where the cliffs dwindle to nothing."

"I shall do so the next nice day," Elinor told her. "I have never been close to the ocean before. I find it fascinating, those waves, the sharp smell, and the flights of the gulls."

For once, Miss Ward had no answering comment. As they began to walk again, Elinor thought that the beach would be wonderful place to find solitude as well. Suddenly she remembered the tinners on the moor. "Does anyone else go there? Strangers or villagers?" she asked.

Miss Ward tittered. "Oh, no, my dear. The beach all the way to the cove is part of Mordyn, and private property. No one would dare! Sir Robert is very strict with trespassers and poachers, although in the summer he does allow the village huer to stand on the cliffs, to spot the shoals of pilchards. No doubt you will see the process for yourself, if you are still with us then. It is fascinating."

When they reached the enclosed garden again, Elinor voiced her desire to explore it. Miss Ward nodded, but she was looking anxiously toward the side door through which her charge had already disappeared.

"Of course, whatever you like," she murmured. "Please excuse me, however. I must see if Fiona is all right. She seemed agitated this afternoon."

"Please go ahead. There is no need to keep me company all the time," Elinor said. And then, feeling that had not been quite gracious, she added, "Thank you for accompanying me this afternoon. It was kind of you."

Miss Ward looked startled. "Oh, no, Miss Fielding, you must not thank me! It is my duty to try to make any visitor's stay at Mordyn more pleasant. If I can," she added, almost as an afterthought.

She hurried away then, and Elinor drew a deep breath of the salt air. As she strolled the paths, trying to guess what would grow in the beds later in the spring, she pondered the very ordinary Miss Rebecca Ward. So eager to please, so deep in her concern for her charge, and yet there was something about the woman—some little glance surprised, some inflection in that high, breathless voice—that sometimes did not quite agree with her honeyed words. Elinor found she did not completely trust her, although she did not know why. But she was sure there was more to the accommodating, ordinary Miss Ward than she showed the world. Perhaps she would discover what it was some day?

But as she went inside at last, Elinor was quick to put all speculation about Fiona Grenville's companion from her mind. There was still the library to be explored, and by herself, too. She would look for the perfect book to read until teatime.

Both Miss Ward and Fiona, as well as Jonathan Grenville joined Sir Robert and herself for that event. In an attempt to make conversation, Elinor expressed her admiration of the castle that she had inspected that morning, the lovely drawing rooms and salons, the beautiful furniture and fabrics.

"Do you have a favorite, Elinor?" Sir Robert asked as he picked up his teacup.

"Why, yes, I do," she said, smiling at him. "The small morning room that opens into The Lady's Garden. It is so very lovely!"

"That was my wife's favorite room too," Sir Robert said. He sipped his tea, and then he said, "You must make it your own private retreat, Elinor. I shall instruct Mrs. Greene to be sure there is always a fire lit there for your comfort."

"Oh, no, please do not do that!" Elinor said quickly, stunned by this largesse. "I do not need a private sitting room, indeed I do not, and I would not presume."

Even in her surprise, Elinor had noticed how Miss Ward had drawn in a startled breath at Sir Robert's suggestion, how her face had paled. But of course she would dislike a stranger's invasion of her close relative's former quarters, Elinor told herself.

"It would not be presumption, since it comes at my express invitation," Sir Robert told her. "The room has not been used in recent years, and it would please me to think someone as lovely as you are, my dear, would be happy there. Yes, bring down your needle-work, your books, and arrange them as you wish. And if there is anything special you would like to have added to the room, some unique piece of furniture, or a painting you have admired, don't hesitate to ask."

Elinor tried again to refuse, for she felt most uncomfortable. It was Jonathan Grenville who waved away her protests.

"I do advise you to accept, Miss—er, Elinor," he said as he took another of the scones Elinor had learned were called splitters. "When my father makes up his mind to something, it is as good as done. It is no use at all to protest. Fiona and I learned that years ago."

Elinor was forced to nod then, but when she would have voiced her thanks for Sir Robert's kindness, he changed the subject to ask when she was to have her first riding lesson.

When he learned she had no boots, he asked her to give him a tracing of her foot so he could send a groom to Portreath the next day. "And you must have a habit as well," he added. "See to that, Rebecca."

Miss Ward only nodded, for she was suddenly dumb.

Elinor was feeling vaguely uneasy. This open-handed treatment of a stranger seemed excessive. For that was what she was, of course, a stranger here. And although Sir Robert had told her she was to be another daughter, she had not taken his words seriously. Yet he seemed determined to treat her as one.

"She will need a waterproof cloak as well," Jonathan said. "Since there are so few good days, you will need it, Miss—er, Elinor. Otherwise, all your lessons will be in vain, for you will never be able to use them. Ah, there's no doubt about it, the sun makes herself a stranger in Kernow. But we have learned not to let a little drizzle or mist deter us. You must not, either."

When the family gathered for dinner that evening, Miss Ward was not among their number. Elinor remembered she had not been present last evening either, and she wondered why she did not take this particular meal with the family. It was very singular, but she did not feel she could ask the reason. She had to admit, however, that it was a more pleasant meal without her incessant chatter.

Tired from her exercise and the fresh air, Elinor excused herself soon after dinner to go to her room. As she climbed the stairs she told herself it was better to leave the others to their own devices once in a while. That way they would not be put to the strain of entertaining her, and could discuss family matters by themselves if they cared to. The rippling notes of a skilled pianist wafted up the stairs behind her. Fiona, no doubt. She was very talented.

Elinor had intended to read for a spell, but she was so sleepy, she rang for Doll almost at once, and was soon tucked up in bed, fast asleep.

The next morning, she walked down to the stables by herself. She was wearing her black wool gown again, and a matching cape, the most practical garments she had with her. She hoped they would do, but she was so nervous about actually climbing up on a horse, she soon forgot her clothes. Pray I don't fall off! she thought as she entered the stable.

McCarthy was waiting for her, with Danny-Boy's boots. When she was shod in them, he led her outside to where a chestnut mare was waiting patiently. Elinor saw the horse was very placid, even as huge as she seemed, and she was relieved.

The head groom explained the names of the various parts of the tack, before he helped her to mount sidesaddle and adjusted the stirrup. As he explained how she was to hold the reins, Elinor was relieved to see he had a long rope he called a longe with which he would control the horse. At least she did not have to be responsible for that as yet! she thought as he led her to a riding ring. Elinor began to relax. She did not seem in any danger, and Jenny's broad back was wide enough so she could stop feeling she was in imminent peril of falling off at any moment. She kept her eyes resolutely ahead, however, for she did seem very far from the ground.

McCarthy walked Jenny around and around the ring, calling instructions to Elinor as he did so. She tried very hard to obey them, and when at last he came to help her down, he was smiling.

"Ye'll do very well, miss," he said, his white hair blowing in the fresh breeze. "A good pupil ye are."

Elinor beamed at the compliment. "But surely we have stopped too soon," she said. "I do assure you I am not at all tired yet."

McCarthy chortled as he handed the mare over to a stable boy. "No, pr'haps not. But by tomorrow, ye'll know ye've had yer first lesson, miss. Don't be discouraged by the aches and pains. They'll soon go away as ye get more accustomed-like."

"Is she a good student, McCarthy?" she heard a voice ask, and she turned to see Jonathan Grenville astride a big gray hunter. He must have just returned from a ride. He dismounted and came over to them, leading the hunter. The horse tried to free his head and he pawed the ground, as if his ride had not tired him at all, but Mr. Grenville held him firmly with one big hand. Watching the hunter's antics, the way he rolled his eyes and snorted, Elinor was even more delighted with her Jenny.

"Aye, that she be," the head groom answered. "Soon have her trottin', I will. But I was jess tellin' her, better to start slow than overdo it. Otherwise, she'd be needin' some o' the liniment for her aches."

Jonathan smiled a little at the sally before he offered Elinor his arm. "Are you going back to Mordyn now, Miss—er, Elinor?" he asked. "Allow me to escort you."

Elinor nodded, and after she promised to return tomorrow at the same time, the two walked away. As they did so, she admired the day, the bright sunlight and salt-laden air.

When she remarked the weather, Jonathan Grenville said, "Cornwall has a mild climate. Flowers bloom early, sometimes even in February. And there is a long growing season; the harvest is always late. We rarely have snow or ice, but that does not mean we do not have storms. Most of them roar out of the southwest, accompanied by high seas and lashing rain. They are apt to end in a sullen calm, although sometimes they dwindle into fog or mist that can linger for days. Enjoy this weather while you can, Miss—er, Elinor. It will not last. Indeed, we have an old saying here that says Cornwall will take a shower every day, and two on Sundays."

He told her more about Cornwall and its coastline then, and Elinor asked many questions. Almost without realizing it, they arrived back at the enclosed garden. As they strolled to the castle, Elinor's skirt became caught on a dormant rose bush, and she stooped to disentangle it. As she stood up, she saw Jonathan Grenville looking at her intently, his face stern, and somewhat cold.

Startled, Elinor looked up at him, a question in her eyes.

"Your pardon!" he said at once, smiling easily now. "It is rude to stare, is it not? But I could not help admiring your hair. It is very beautiful—such a warm golden color. It reminds me of marigolds in the sunlight."

Elinor felt herself blushing, and she only smiled briefly to thank him before she hurried inside. In truth, she did not know how to reply to this unexpected compliment, delivered as it had been, in the warmest tone she had ever heard Jonathan Grenville employ.

As she turned to close the door behind her, she saw that he remained unmoving where she had left him. He was still staring at her, and he was not smiling now. Instead, the expression on his handsome face was enigmatic, his fine gray eyes half closed. For some reason, she felt a little shiver run up her spine.

4

TWO WEEKS LATER, Elinor was feeling much more at home in the grandeur that was Mordyn Castle. Her riding lessons had progressed well, and after she became accustomed to the aches in her bottom and the inside of her thighs and knees, "toughened up-like," as McCarthy put it, the lessons were easier. Thc head groom soon had her trotting around the ring, and one day, without her knowledge, had let her control Jenny by herself. When she refused to believe she had done such a thing, he removed the longe line so she could prove it to herself. Elinor was very proud, for it was, after all, a significant milestone. And she was beginning to look forward to riding freely, exploring Mordyn's lands and villages. The ring where she was training seemed boring now. But even when she saw Fiona ride off alone one day, she did not beg McCarthy to let her try it too. He would know when she was ready. She would not rush it.

The situation in the castle had eased as well. Sir Robert was just the same, smiling and gracious, but Miss Ward began to leave her to her own devices, at least some of the time, which suited Elinor very well. Fiona Grenville still held aloof, but Elinor had decided on patience where that young lady was concerned. After all, it was all she could do. As for the son of the house, he had progressed to the point where he no longer called her "Miss, er, Elinor." His smiles were no more frequent, nor his conversation any more intimate, but Elinor told herself that must just be his nature. Some people were like that. Cool and contained. She must not take it personally. And he often complimented her on her appearance. Like his father, he was quick to note a gown she had not worn before.

Sir Robert had located the man he believed to be the head of the gang of thieves who had robbed Elinor's carriage, and one day he called her down to see him. She remembered how frightened she had been to see the man again, standing in Mordyn's medieval hall and glaring at them both. Even though he was held close by two footmen, Elinor was still apprehensive.

"Is this the man, Elinor?" Sir Robert had asked. "Observe him carefully, and do not be afraid. He cannot hurt you now."

Elinor had made herself walk closer. Her heart was pounding almost as much as it had the day he had stopped the carriage. Yes, it was the same man. He wore the same shabby clothing, and his expression was just as bitter, although now he also looked hopeless.

Elinor had had enough tales from Doll by then to understand his plight. The tinners could find no work, and their families were in danger of starving. The situation had turned them into desperate men. She wondered if this Timothy Coryton had a family, small children perhaps, who cried with a hunger he could not assuage. She still remembered his words to her when he had stripped off her ring.

Suddenly, she made a decision. True, he had taken her money and her only remembrance of her mother, but he had not hurt her, nor Doll either, and that was in his favor for they had been helpless in his hands. He could have raped them, murdered them even, but he had not.

"No, he is not the one who held us up," she said from a dry throat.

"No?" Sir Robert asked, his voice incredulous. "Are you sure, Elinor? Look very carefully."

Elinor moved closer, her eyes intent on that proud, yet despairing face. "He is somewhat similar, but no, he is not the same man," she repeated. She looked straight into Coryton's face then. His expression had not changed, but she thought she saw a little relief deep in his eyes.

Sir Robert had dismissed the tinner then, with a brief admonition to watch his step if he knew what was good for him. Elinor watched Coryton shrug off the hold of his captors, give Sir Robert a searing glance of contempt, and turn on his heel without a word to anyone.

When Sir Robert had questioned her more carefully after he had gone, Elinor had invented a number of differences in appearance. The man who had held her up was taller, his nose was not quite so long, and his eyes more blue. It was decided that the search must continue, although privately, Elinor thought Sir Robert had lost heart in it. He seemed to have wanted the culprit to be Timothy Coryton very badly, and she wondered why that should be so.

But there were so many things to do at Mordyn, she soon forgot the incident. The books she read were wonderful, each more intriguing than the last, and she had come to adore her own pretty, private sitting room. There she could read, do her needlepoint, or draw just as she wished and without fear of interruption. And she could step out the long doors to walk the garden paths when she wanted a breath of air. This was especially important when one of the mists Jonathan Grenville had told her about shrouded the castle, and it was dangerous to wander far from its walls.

Elinor had made the acquaintance of many of the servants, too, and it was pleasant to be able to call them by name, and occasionally receive a little smile of acknowledgment as she did so.

She still found herself pausing once or twice a day to stare up at the portrait of the gentleman in blue velvet that hung outside her room. It was as if she had no control over her actions. Somehow, she was forced to that daily ritual now, forced to meet those handsome, knowing eyes. Rebecca Ward had told her the gentleman's name had been Sir Miles Jason De-Fountaine Grenville, and he was indeed the cavalier ghost the maids were so afraid of. Miss Ward had scoffed at the tales of his walking, his touching people, for, she said, she had lived there for many years, and he had never appeared to her, and most certainly he had never touched her.

As the two stared up at the painting, Elinor thought his eyes twinkled even more brightly, and she had to swallow a giggle. The Cavalier seemed to be telling her that touching that particular lady had never appealed to him.

Elinor herself had never seen a ghost, and she had all but forgotten them until one morning, Doll informed her that she had almost run right into The Lady, dressed all in white.

"It was right after I left you late last night, Miss Elinor," she said, her lips compressed. "There she was at the end of the hall, just standin' there and moanin'. I don't mind tellin' you, it shook me some. And if Molly hadn't come along, I'd pr'bly be standin' there still, if I hadn't died o' fright, like. I don't like it here, Miss Elinor, and that's a fact! It's that scary!"

Elinor's heart sank. She knew that even without this ghostly encounter, Doll was still not happy here. She had often spoken with scorn of the other servants and their unfriendliness, calling them provincial and standoffish. And when advised to give them more of a chance, she had only sniffed.

Now she said, "I'm leavin', Miss Elinor. I'm sorry to do it to you, but I can't stay here. Ghosts and cold people, gales and fog. Look out there, do!" she added, throwing the curtains before the long windows wide. Elinor did as she suggested, although she could see nothing but the thick white mist outside. She could not even see the railing of the balcony, and it had been that way for days.

She wanted desperately to beg Doll to remain, but she made herself say, "All right, if you must, Doll. I cannot ask you to stay, no matter how much I will miss you. But I, myself, am beginning to like it here. I cannot come with you, not just yet."

"I know," Doll said, coming to put her hand on Elinor's shoulder for a moment. She squeezed it and went on, "But if you ever do decide to live in London again, you know where to find me. I'll be with me

Ma, and if I'm not, she'll tell you where I am. I'll come to you gladly then. You're a kind mistress, an'—an' I'll miss you something awful, too, that I will!"

It had seemed only a short time later that Doll had left by cart for Portreath. From there she would travel by stage to Falmouth, to take ship for London. So anxious was she to be gone, that even the daunting trip over the moors failed to sway her from her purpose.

Elinor did miss her very much, and the new maid Sir Robert acquired for her, a Cornish girl named Betsy, could not take Doll's place. Betsy was a silent type, not given to chatter, although she did her chores impeccably, even to arranging Elinor's long golden hair in a becoming style.

Elinor told herself she must not cry over spilt milk. Doll was gone for good, and she must make the best of it.

One day, a few days after Doll's departure, Elinor decided to explore the beach. She had not been there as yet, for she had been so busy with her riding lessons and her reading, and the weather had been so uncertain. But that particular day was pleasant and sunny. There were only a few clouds far away on the horizon, and the mists had blown themselves away.

She left the castle right after luncheon. She knew Miss Ward and Fiona had planned a drive to Portreath that afternoon to shop, for she had refused an invitation to join them, one that had been offered only by the garrulous Miss Ward. And Sir Robert was going to be closeted with his agent, while his son planned a ride on the moors with the Wilkensons of Trecarrag. Elinor would be quite alone.

When she had made her way around to the back of the castle, Elinor caught her breath. The cliff walk wound very close to the edge of the precipice, and although there was a stout stone wall separating it from the drop, it was not a place for anyone afraid of heights. The wind had come up a little as well, swirling Elinor's skirts around her ankles. But she set off with a light heart, anxious to see what views lay around the next turn of the path.

It took her well over an hour to reach the end of the walk, so often did she stop to stare out to sea, and once to pause to watch the fishing boats from Mordyn Harbor as they beat their way home with their catch. Far below her, the breakers rolled up on the narrow beach, and then reluctantly retreated. Once, she admired a flight of gannets, as they swept around in great curves some two hundred feet above the ocean. She watched anxiously whenever one of them plummeted straight down to catch a fish. Sometimes they did not resurface for several seconds, but each time they did so safely, it was a small miracle, and she felt like applauding.

At the end of the walk, there was a short flight of steps leading to the beach proper. Elinor inspected that beach carefully, but there was no one in sight, just as Miss Ward had promised. For a while, she strolled back the way she had come, picking up shells and playing tag with the breakers. At last, tired out, she sat down on the sand well above the tide line, to prop her elbows on her knees so she could admire the ocean before her. So vast it was, so mysterious, even in the bright sunlight! Elinor could see why it fascinated men so, called some of them to venture on it again and again, no matter the danger. She wished she might do so as well, to see all those foreign lands she had only read of before.

She was watching a strange little brown bird, running on thin little legs as it inspected the piles of seaweed left by the last high tide, when suddenly she felt a cold chill on the back of her neck. Somehow, she was sure someone was watching her. She turned quickly, to scan the beach as far as she could see in both directions, and to look up to the top of the cliff. There was no one there, but still the feeling that she was no longer alone would not leave her. She rose then, brushing the sand from her skirts. She would go back now. Someone was there, even if she could not see who it was.

As she started to trudge through the sand, she sighed a little. It seemed a very long way back to the beginning of the cliff walk, for she had wandered along the beach almost half the distance to the castle.

As she scanned the cliff again, still searching the top of it for the intruder she was sure was there, she saw a set of stone steps leading up from the beach. There was a railing as well, and she wondered why she had not noticed it before. The steps zigzagged across the face of the cliff, and curious, she went closer. When she reached them, they seemed sturdy, and not at all in the bad repair Miss Ward had claimed. And she was young, and strong, too. Perhaps Rebecca Ward, being older, would not dare the ascent, but she saw no reason why she could not do so herself. And it would cut in half the time she had to spend to reach the safety of the castle again. Besides, she had on her sturdiest shoes, stout leather ones for walking.

Taking a deep breath, Elinor began to climb. What an adventure, she thought as she tested each step carefully before trusting her weight to it. She was almost to the top when she found herself suddenly in danger. The step she was on, that had seemed so reliable a moment ago, began to crumble under her feet. Quickly, Elinor moved to the next one. This one shifted a little, and horrified, she watched part of it break off and fall way, way down to the beach. The railing she was grasping so tightly was not a safeguard anymore either. It trembled in her hand, and appeared likely to pull away and follow the edge of the step at any moment. Gasping, she released her hold on it and pressed back against the cliff.

Well, my girl, now you're for it, she told herself. Miss Ward had spoken truth. The steps *were* dangerous. It appeared to Elinor that she had two choices. She could continue to go up, as quickly and carefully as she could, or she could retreat. But it was a long way down, and so few steps to the top. Taking a deep breath, she started to climb again. Sometimes the steps were firm and she was tempted to rest on them, but sometimes they moved a little, and more than once, pieces of them broke off and fell. She was shaking now, but she made herself remain calm. And then, just two steps from the top, when she was beginning to congratulate herself on escaping certain death, the step she was standing on gave way. The railing tore away with it, and gasping, Elinor reached out to grab a piece of protruding rock on the cliff face, to clutch it with both hands while her feet dangled over the abyss. Her breath was coming in little pants. She was all right for the moment, but she knew she could not hang on for long. Already, her muscles were beginning to ache with the strain. And despairing, she realized there was no one to hear her even if she cried out for help.

"Here, give me your hand," a deep voice said, and startled, she almost let go of the rock she was clinging to. Looking up, she saw a frowning Jonathan Grenville stretched out on his stomach on the top of the cliff wall. He was leaning over it, extending his hand. Gratefully, she loosened one hand to grab hold. Her feet scrabbled frantically for some purchase on the next step so she could help, but although she did not dare to look down, she could hear that step breaking up, too.

"Give me your other hand now. Don't worry. I have you," Jonathan told her, his voice calm.

Elinor closed her eyes and said a prayer. She could only hope his words were true, for in letting go of the rock, she was entrusting her life to him.

"Do as I say! Quickly!" he ordered.

Elinor obeyed him, clinging to his hand with both of hers and all her strength. She felt him lifting her then, pulling her up to what was left of the top step. When he was sure it was still fairly safe, he reached down with his other hand to wrap his arm around her waist. "Put your arms around my neck, and whatever you do, don't let go!" he commanded.

Again, Elinor did as she was bade. And then she closed her eyes as she felt herself lifted off the step. For a moment, she swung in the air, before he had her up and over the wall to lower her to the cliff walk.

As she felt solid ground beneath her feet again, Elinor opened her eyes. She was panting with the strain, and she saw Jonathan was gasping for breath as well.

Her knees were suddenly weak, and she collapsed against him, sobbing a little in her relief. He held her close to him, cradling her head against his chest, his fingers tightening in her hair. Neither spoke.

At last, Elinor had some control of herself, and she moved back a little. He let her go at once.

"Thank you, Jonathan!" she murmured. "I do not know why you are here, why you did not go riding as you had planned, but I am very grateful you did not. If you had not been here, I would have fallen to my death. Oh, thank you, thank you!"

Her green eyes were full of springing tears, but even though her vision was blurred, she could see the ferocious frown on his face.

"Little fool!" he said roughly. "Did no one warn you that the steps were dangerous?"

Stunned by a tone in his voice that she had never heard there before, Elinor could not answer at once. Then she said, "Why yes, Miss Ward did tell me, but they certainly seemed safe, at least at the bottom."

Jonathan continued to stare at her, his frown growing even blacker. "You should have heeded her," he said abruptly.

"But why didn't *you* stop me?" Elinor demanded, growing a little angry herself now. "After all, you *have* been watching me, have you not? I felt your eyes on me. All you had to do was call out. But you didn't."

She saw him draw a deep breath. "Yes, I was watching you," he admitted. "I was loathe to interrupt your privacy, for you seemed so happy to be alone on the beach. But when you looked around, got up, I could see you were distressed. I stepped back then, out of sight. When I chanced to glance back, you had disappeared from the shoreline. Indeed, you were already halfway to the top of the stairs."

"Still, you could have warned me even then," Elinor persisted.

He seemed to hesitate for a moment, and she wondered why. "You did not appear to be in any danger then," he said finally. "And I did not realize the steps were in such bad repair. I—I have not been this way in some time."

Elinor turned away then, to stare back down the cliff. Far below her, she could see the wreckage of the piece of railing that had torn away, and she shivered. That might have been her down there, lying broken and inanimate.

The wind that had been freshening all afternoon, blew a strand of her hair across her face, and she reached up to smooth it back. It was then she realized she had lost all her hairpins, and her hair was streaming loose down her back. Flushing a little, she searched the ground for them, but no doubt they had gone the way of that rotten railing.

"You had better get back to the castle," Jonathan told her, his voice toneless now, more like the man she remembered.

"Yes," she agreed. "But I would you do not blame yourself, Jonathan. It was all my own feckless fault. and perhaps the steps were damaged in that last storm. If you remember, it was a bad one. You could not have known."

She began to walk back toward the castle then, and he fell in step beside her. "I advise you not to mention this incident to anyone, most especially, not to my father," he said.

At her questioning, sideway glance, he added, "He would be most perturbed to think you had been in any danger. No doubt he would set Miss Ward to watching over you. You would not have a moment a day free of her conversation, if that is the correct word for the nattering she does."

Elinor turned toward him and smiled a little at his asperity, and it was then she noticed for the first time that he had changed his clothes since luncheon. Then he had been dressed for his riding party, but now he wore plain buff breeches, and he had slung a dark blue coat over his shoulders. She saw how the linen of his white shirt was stretched tight across those shoulders, and remembering his strength, she knew she had reason to be grateful he was so muscular.

"You are back early from your ride, are you not?" she asked, uneasy at the silence that had fallen between them. "I thought you said you would be away all afternoon, perhaps even remain at Trecarrag for tea."

The look in his dark gray eyes was intent, and his frown was back. Did he think she was keeping track of him and his movements? Did he dislike it?

"I did not go. I changed my mind," he said.

He was watching her through narrowed eyes now, and Elinor made herself smile a little. Jonathan seemed different to her this afternoon, although she could not have said why.

The wind blew her skirts against her legs then, whipped her long hair about her face, and she reached up with both hands to clear it from her eyes.

"You have such beautiful hair," he said quietly.

"But you told me that once before," Elinor reminded him. "Don't you remember?"

He nodded. "Seeing it loose made me forget. Can you get back to the castle by yourself from here? I have some business at the farm."

"Of course," she assured him. "Thank you again, Jonathan. I will never forget how you saved me. Never."

He waved a careless hand. "I suggest you put it from your mind. We will not speak of it again. And you must promise me you will say nothing of what happened, not even to your maid. From her, it would be only a small step to my father's ears. There was a similar accident there many years ago that resulted in a death, and I would not have him reminded of it."

He did not wait for her promise, but turned away rather abruptly to stride to a path that led down from the clifftop to the woods. Elinor watched him until he was lost from sight among the beeches and oaks.

As she walked on alone, Elinor was deep in thought. Jonathan *had* been different today. Something about his voice, his mannerisms. But of course he had been unnerved, she told herself, fearful lest she be fatally injured. Funny, that. He had never seemed to care very much before about her. Only a little more than Fiona did, which was, of course, not at all. Elinor frowned, wondering not for the first time, if he, as well as Fiona, resented her coming into their family group. A stranger. An intruder.

But his words to her this afternoon, the way he had watched her, his eyes so intent on her face, the tautness of his muscular body that seemed somehow so aware of her, belied that. If it had been anyone else, she would have been sure he was attracted to her. But she knew she did not have to worry about that, not from Jonathan Grenville, in any case. He had always treated her to an aloof courtesy, in an almost avuncular way.

By teatime, Elinor had rested, changed her gown, and had Betsy redo her hair. As she entered the gold salon to join Sir Robert, she was her immaculate self again. She noticed at once that Fiona and Rebecca Ward had not returned from Portreath as yet, although Jonathan Grenville was there, dressed once more in the riding clothes he had sported at luncheon.

"Ah, Elinor, there you are!" Sir Robert said with his little smile. "Jonathan and I were just trying to decide which one of us must play mother and pour out the tea."

Elinor smiled at them both as she took her place behind the teapot and began to prepare it.

"You had a pleasant afternoon, Elinor?" Jonathan asked, as he gave off lounging against the mantel and came to take his seat.

Startled, Elinor could only stare at him for a moment. What an enigma the man was, so cool and calm! You would never have thought to listen to him, that they had been together an hour ago, and in such a way, too!

"Yes, it was delightful," she said, holding his eye. "I went the length of the cliff walk, and then strolled the beach below. It is a wonderful spot."

"Do not ever attempt to use the cliff steps, my

dear,'' Sir Robert ordered, frowning now. ''They have been in bad repair for years, and the family has ceased to use them.''

As he accepted the cup she handed him, he added, ''Perhaps I should have them dismantled.''

''Surely there is no need to bother, sir, not when you have had the approach to them walled up. Only a fool would attempt the descent now, the state they're in,'' Jonathan said.

Elinor could feel the color rising in her cheeks, and she was glad when he changed the subject.

''I forgot to mention the other day that Mr. Wilkenson would like to have you call on him sometime in the near future, Father. At your convenience, of course. Some trouble with the tinners. Trecarrag is nearer the mines, Elinor, and there have been thefts, and some vandalism, too, I believe. Now his farmers are being harried by these men who steal their stock. Mr. Wilkenson says something must be done, and soon, to put a stop to their arrogance.''

''I agree,'' Sir Robert said, frowning again. ''That damned Coryton! Oh, I do beg your pardon, Elinor, but the man's a thorn in all our sides! An abomination!''

''I have heard that the miners are in distress, sir,'' Elinor said. ''Can nothing be done for them? Their families are so hungry, and they cannot find other work.''

''Then they must leave the neighborhood—go down the line, as we say here,'' Sir Robert told her. ''I cannot provide jobs where there are none. Of course, if the price of tin stops fluctuating so wildly, it might be profitable to open the mine again. But until it does so, there is no sense in tinning. And I am not a philanthropist.''

Elinor lowered her eyes to sip her tea, afraid he would see the dislike she suddenly felt. There were more important things in the world than profits, surely? A hungry child, for example? Even after her afternoon on the beach in the fresh air, and all her exercise, she suddenly lost her appetite for the delicacies spread out before them. The thin-cut sandwiches of meat and cheese and fish, the little cakes, the muffins and scones, all the silver dishes filled with jam and honey, clotted cream and fresh butter. And there was enough here for several people, not just three. What a hungry tinner's family could have done with such a feast!

"Do eat up, Elinor, lest my father think you are sickening with something, and send for the doctor," Jonathan said as he helped himself to another sandwich. "Now I, myself, have a sharp appetite this afternoon. The air on the moors, and the exercise, I suppose."

Elinor forced herself to take a small cake, but she could not help staring straight into Jonathan Grenville's eyes. He returned the stare, his face blank of any expression, and she was forced to look away first. He had certainly meant it when he said this afternoon must be forgotten, she thought.

But still, when she rose to curtsy and leave them, she gave him her warmest smile. He might forget, if he so chose. For herself, she would always feel an unending gratitude to him.

A week later, the daffodils began to bloom in the enclosed garden, to join the crocuses peeping up there. When Elinor looked out her sitting room window, she saw a little old man busy with hoe and rake and barrow. She had opened the long windows earlier to sniff the air, and in it there had been more than a hint of spring. And this afternoon, McCarthy had promised to take her for her first ride as well. She could hardly wait! She had progressed from a trot to a canter by now and, mounted on Jenny at least, she was confident she would not put the head groom to shame. And she had her bespoke shiny boots, and a new habit at last. It was made of broadcloth, in black, of course, and although she knew it would be unremarkable in London, perhaps even scorned as provincial, it fit her well, and it made her feel a real horsewoman. She had ordered another, lighter one for summer.

And by October, she would be able to leave off her

blacks for good. Even the pastels of half mourning seemed enticing to her, starved as she was for color. She had taken to wearing a rather daring scarlet wrapper in her room. She could tell Betsy did not approve of such a thing, although she never said a word. Elinor ignored her little sniffs, her pursed lips. What she wore when she was by herself was not disrespectful to her mother's memory, and it was no one's business but her own.

It turned out to be a memorable day, the kind one recalls years later and smiles about. Sir Robert had joined her for her initial venture beyond the riding ring, and he had been admiring in his congratulations for her new skill and her confidence.

And dinner that evening had been especially festive. Even Fiona had smiled at her once, and Jonathan, too, seemed affected by the softer, warmer air. He had entertained them all with tales of his last trip to London some months before, the plays he had seen, the gowns of the ladies, and the crowds in the park. His description of the fat King George IV had had them all laughing.

When she went up to bed, Elinor was still smiling. Fiona had given them a piano concert after dinner, after which they had played cards. It was late when Elinor reached the picture gallery. In the light of her candle, she could see the Cavalier smiling down at her, as if in approval of her delight in Mordyn and the day.

Intrigued as always by those handsome eyes, Elinor had gone closer, to hold up the candle so she could see his face more clearly.

"If only you could talk, what tales you would have to tell!" she told him. "Although in looking at you, I am sure all of them would be most unsuitable for unmarried ladies to hear. You do look the complete scoundrel, sir, and a confirmed rake as well!"

The candlelight wavered then in a slight draft, and it made it seem as if he were nodding at her in hearty agreement. Laughing at her fancies, and still feeling lighthearted, Elinor turned at her bedroom door and blew the once-dangerous Cavalier a kiss.

Much later, after Betsy had helped her undress, braided her hair, and left her for the night, Elinor yawned. She was so sleepy now that she set aside her book, after carefully marking her place. Climbing into bed without closing the curtains or donning her nightcap, she snuggled down under the warm covers, lying on her right side, as was her custom. She was almost asleep, in that world halfway between dreams and reality, and lulled by the sound of the breakers behind the windowpanes, when she felt a touch at her brow, and she stiffened.

She had heard no footsteps. She was sure there was no human presence in the room. Her heart began to beat wildly, as the hand moved slowly down her braid in a gentle caress. She did not dare to open her eyes, she was so frightened of what she might—or might not—see. The fingers of that hand entwined themselves in the curl at the end of her braid for some moments, and then were reluctantly withdrawn.

Still, she remained rigid, her eyes squeezed shut for a very long time. At last she sensed that whoever—*what*ever—it had been, had gone, and she opened her eyes. In the faint glow of the dying fire, she could see that she was completely alone. There was no one there, neither the quick nor the dead. No one at all.

Had she imagined that touch? she wondered. Dreamed it? But no, it had been so real! She remembered then how she had spoken lightly to the painted gentleman, even blown him a kiss before she closed her door. Dear God, had she, all unwittingly, conjured up his ghost?

5

THE MINUTE she opened her eyes the following morning, Elinor remembered what had happened to her the night before. She had tried to stay awake after the ghostly presence had left her, to think about the strange happening, but worn out from the long, exciting day she had spent, she had fallen asleep almost at once.

Now, she rose from bed and wrapped her scarlet robe around her as she padded barefoot to the windows. When she had opened the curtains, she saw a day like none other she had ever beheld at Mordyn Castle. The ocean lay quiet and serene beneath her balcony, the waves coming ashore in an almost lazy fashion. The sky was softly lucent, and the color of the first blucbclls. She opened the doors and stepped out on the balcony to breathe deeply of the warm, salty air. Why, it was almost like summer, even though it was still only April. She knew she would not stay indoors today, not a moment longer than she had to.

Ringing the bell for Betsy, she began to dress. This morning she did not mind that her new maid was so taciturn, for she wanted to be alone with her thoughts. And by the time she had been buttoned into her gown and had her hair arranged, she had decided that she had invented the whole episode late last night. No one had been in her room, neither ghost nor man. Perhaps it had been the stargazey pie at dinner? She had never had any before. But although Sir Robert had assured her it was a delicacy in Cornwall, she had not cared for it. Pilchards, she had discovered, were a very oily fish, although she had finished her portion lest she be thought rude. Yes, that must be it. For even if she had always loved reading romances, she had never tried to put herself in the heroine's place, imagined *she* was being kissed and caressed.

Still, when she left her room, she looked resolutely ahead, for the very first time ignoring the painting of the handsome Cavalier. She could almost feel his eyes piercing her back as she started down the stairs, but still, she refused to turn around. There was no such thing as ghosts. She had no intention of being beguiled into thinking there was.

Miss Ward and Fiona were already at breakfast. Elinor smiled impartially at them both before she selected her meal.

"Isn't this going to be a beautiful day?" she asked as she took her customary seat. "I can hardly wait to go outside."

"Yes, one of Cornwall's finest," Miss Ward agreed. "How sad it is that there are so few days like it. No doubt tomorrow it will come on to storm again, or the mist will come rolling back. I wonder you can support life here, Miss Fielding."

Elinor was buttering her scone, and did not answer.

"Do you know, I suddenly remember where Compton Street is in town," Miss Ward went on. "What a strange place to live! You did not tell us your home was among the merchants and the shops."

"You didn't ask me," Elinor said calmly as she stirred cream into her coffee.

"Can it be your father was *in trade?*" Miss Ward persisted, her voice horrified.

"Why, yes, he was," Elinor admitted, wondering what the woman was up to now.

Miss Ward tittered. "Then it is no wonder you are so attracted to Mordyn's grandeur, its *aristocratic* inhabitants. I quite understand now, although it is not at all what I am used to."

Perplexed and a little hurt, Elinor lowered her fork to stare at the garrulous woman. She saw Miss Ward was staring back at her, her expression haughty.

"Come, Fiona. Let us be off, my dear. Miss Fielding."

Elinor watched them both go to the door. It was obvious Miss Ward thought her unworthy to be a guest at the castle. She had not excused them, nor had she curtsied. Well, that is just too bad, Elinor told herself as the door closed behind the two. Sir Robert knew my background when he invited me.

She was not left alone for long. Jonathan came in only a short time later to join her. His nod for her was brusque, and he did not speak until he had filled his plate with beefsteak, eggs, and fish.

"Tea? Coffee?" Elinor asked, her heart beating a little faster that they were alone together. Would he speak of yesterday, remind her of their adventure at the cliffs?

But Jonathan only waved a hand toward the tea urn, and she filled a cup for him. Since he did not appear to want to talk, Elinor continued to eat her breakfast. But as she refilled her coffee cup, he pushed his plate away and said, "Your pardon, Elinor. I hate chatter at the breakfast table, don't you? But of course you must be used to it by now. I saw Miss Ward leaving a few minutes ago. In fact, I waited until she was safely out of the way since I cannot endure her gibble-gabble, most especially *not* in the morning."

"Jonathan, why does Miss Ward never eat dinner with us?" Elinor asked.

"My father convinced her it would not be—er, appropriate," Jonathan told her, grinning now. Elinor admired the way the corners of his dark gray eyes crinkled in his amusement.

"He told her he wanted to see Fiona alone, at least once a day, and that he considered the dinner hour should be reserved for the immediate family. Heaven be praised for that! Luncheon and tea with her are quite enough, thank you!"

Elinor lowered her cup to the saucer. "But I am not of the immediate family either, yet I dine with you all," she said, horrified. What a terrible slight to Miss Ward. No wonder she had become less than cordial!

"No, but you are our guest, and furthermore, my father has decreed you *are* one of the family. He rules supreme at Mordyn. Whatever old 'Becca thinks about it, there is nothing she can do."

Elinor remained silent. It seemed cruel to her, and callous, too. The woman had been a mother to Fiona, loving and caring for her, and educating her as far as she had been able to do, with Fiona's limited understanding. And she had been at Mordyn for years. Furthermore, she had been the late Lady Grenville's relative.

"No doubt you are wondering why my father did not send her packing years ago?" Jonathan asked as he reached for the toast rack and jam. "It was impossible for him to do so. She had no place to go, and she made herself invaluable to Fiona, so we have had to tolerate her. But when I am master here, she'll find herself taking coach, bag and baggage, in the twinkling of an eye!"

"But wasn't she also a mother to you? After all, you were only a small child when Fiona was born," Elinor asked. She admitted to herself that Jonathan Grenville's image was becoming a little tarnished in her eyes. He sounded so uncaring, so pitiless.

He laughed. "Her? Not likely! Even at four I disliked her. She was a wispy thing at eighteen, with no starch to her. And even then she could not keep her mouth shut. No, I went my own way." His face hardened as he added, "I always have."

He rose then and threw down his napkin. "You must excuse me, Elinor. A matter of business with my father. And you should not be dawdling here this beautiful day. Get out—enjoy it."

"I intend to," Elinor said, rising as well. She stared after him as he waved a careless hand and left her.

As she went to her sitting room to collect her painting equipment, she pondered the strange man who was Jonathan Grenville. He was certainly a man of many moods! And he appeared to have forgotten yesterday as completely as he had said she should forget it.

She made her way down the drive, and took a path through the woods that led to the cliff on the harborside. She had found this spot on one of her rambles, and had promised herself that on the first nice day that she was able, she would come here and attempt to paint the harbor. When she reached the clearing at the edge of the cliff, she studied the scene before her. There, at the head of the bay, was the village. "Downlong," Betsy had called it, to differentiate it from the village nearer the moors which was known locally as "Uplong."

Today it was not nearly as gray and colorless as it had appeared on the day of her arrival. The stone houses with their slate roofs, all sharing a common wall with their next door neighbors, were a softer color in the spring sunlight, and down on the narrow shore, some old fishermen sat on upended dories mending their nets. In the harbor proper, only a few boats remained at anchor.

Elinor soon arranged her equipment, opened the large jar of water, and set out her brushes and paintbox. Sitting down on the rug she had brought, she rested her pad on her knees and began. The water of the harbor was not just blue, she noted, nor was it green, and it was in constant motion even though it was a quiet day. How was she to capture that?

Two hours later, she was still at work when she heard someone coming through the woods, and she turned to see Fiona standing there. She made herself smile at the girl, although she wished she were still alone.

Then she looked back at the watercolor she had labored over so, and she frowned. "Oh, dear, it is all wrong!" she said, her voice exasperated. "There is something askew with the perspective, and the colors are muddy. How discouraging it is not to be able to put down what you see! I guess I will never make an artist. I have been fooling myself, thinking I could paint, for this is awful!"

She had forgotten Fiona as she studied her work. The girl had crept nearer to look over her shoulder, and now, perhaps because she had heard the despair in her voice, Fiona reached out to squeeze Elinor's shoulder in sympathy. Elinor was startled, but she pretended nothing was out of the ordinary in the unexpected gesture.

She turned then and smiled shyly. Fiona's hand dropped, and she backed away. Her gray eyes, so like her brother's, were wary now—indeed, she looked like she might take flight at any moment.

"I do admire your piano playing so much," Elinor told her as she began to collect her equipment. "You are so very talented and skillful. If only I could paint half as well as you play!"

She emptied the dirty water jar and replaced the cover. Then she picked up the still-damp painting. "I suppose I had better tear this up," she said, almost to herself.

Fiona clapped her hands then, and Elinor looked back to see her shaking her head violently.

"No? You do not want me to destroy it?" she asked in wonder. "But it is no good at all."

To her surprise, Fiona stretched out her hand for it. Elinor gave the painting to her, and the girl smiled.

"Well, you are certainly welcome to it, but please don't show it to anyone else," Elinor said. "I guess I will just have to work harder. And someday, Fiona, maybe I can give you a painting that I am proud of. I do so hope so!"

She began to walk back to the castle then, the silent Fiona by her side. As she went, she wondered if she should ask the girl to go riding with her, or perhaps walk the beach—but no! Miss Ward had said Fiona became upset when she was near the ocean or the cliffs. Perhaps after luncheon they could explore together a part of Mordyn she had never seen as yet? Thinking hard, Elinor decided against such a move. Slowly, slowly, she told herself. Fiona has come a little way toward friendship, but I must let her choose the pace.

"I like that yellow gown you are wearing," she said instead. "It is springlike, just like the daffodils in The Lady's Garden."

Fiona looked down at her gown as if surprised anyone would remark it. But Elinor was glad to see her little smile as she smoothed her skirts.

Everyone was at the luncheon table, including the very ordinary, very chatty Miss Ward. "I did not hear you practicing for long this morning, my dear," she said to Fiona as she took some game from the platter the footman was holding out. "Now I must wonder where you went, and what you were doing. It is naughty of you to run away and hide from me, Fiona. It worries me very much."

Elinor was about to speak and explain, but Fiona caught her eye and shook her head slightly. Elinor remained silent.

"Oh, do let her be, 'Becca," Jonathan Grenville said carelessly. "She cannot be in your company all the time, lest she go mad."

Miss Ward seemed to shrivel in her chair at the rebuff, and Elinor was horrified to see her eyes fill with tears.

"That's enough, Jonathan," Sir Robert said curtly. "Miss Ward does us a great service, none more so than Fiona. I am sure we should all have nothing but gratitude for her efforts. But Rebecca, Fiona is not a child anymore. She is twenty-six, and she is in no danger on Mordyn's grounds. You must allow her more freedom."

Before Miss Ward could reply, he turned to Elinor to inquire how she had spent her morning. Elinor told him about her painting, but when he said he would like to see it, she said it was much too bad, and she had destroyed it.

At these words, her eyes met Fiona's for a fleeting moment, and she was glad to see the twinkle in them.

"What a shame you were not able to have a good drawing master as a child," Miss Ward remarked. Her voice held just a hint of sarcasm, and Elinor could see she had quite recovered from her depression at Jonathan's earlier rebuff. "As the twig is bent, so it grows," she added with a sniff.

"But Elinor is not a bush," Jonathan said, eyeing Miss Ward with dislike.

Her laughter bubbling up and threatening to disgrace her, Elinor said, "Of course it might be that I have no talent, That is something any number of drawing masters could not correct. I shall keep trying, however. I do so enjoy painting."

As Sir Robert crooked his finger to his butler to refill his wine glass, he said, "It occurred to me last evening that it might be a very good thing for us to have a party soon, to introduce Elinor to the neighborhood. Oh, you must not worry, my dear! There won't be any dancing, nothing unsuitable for someone in mourning. But you should meet the Brownells and the Wilkensons, and a few others. A small dinner party, some conversation and cards, perhaps next week right after Furry Day. I shall speak to Mrs. Greene about it—send invitations."

"Oh, please, dear, *dear* Sir Robert, let me," Miss Ward said earnestly, looking at him adoringly. "I should be glad to take care of everything for you. Do say I may! Why, I know just what you have in mind, and certainly, being gentry myself, I am better equipped to plan such an occasion than Mrs. Greene! Although an excellent woman in her own way, she is, when all is said and done, merely a commoner, and not one of *us.*"

Sir Robert frowned a little, and then he nodded. "Very well. When you have made some plans, consult me, Rebecca."

Elinor caught the triumphant little smirk Miss Ward sent her way, but she did not wonder at it. It was becoming obvious to her that Miss Ward intended to tweak her about her less than noble background every chance she got. Elinor wondered why the woman seemed to have taken her in such antipathy all of a sudden? Surely she did not fear she would usurp her place here, did she? It was absurd! Determined to ignore the jibe, Elinor said, "What is Furry Day? Such a funny name!"

"It comes from the Celtic *feur,* meaning fair or holiday," Sir Robert explained. "The Cornish celebrate it every year on May 8th. The villagers get together and dance in and out of each other's houses, to help drive winter away, and welcome the coming of spring."

"I'm off to Glyn this afternoon," Jonathan remarked as he rose from his chair and bowed. "And I might take a ride up on the moors later. Have you any message for Mr. Brownell, Father?"

Sir Robert shook his head, frowning now. "Have a care up there, son. Those tinners! They have no love for Grenvilles at the moment. I'd not lose you to a stray bullet. You are my heir."

"I'll be careful," Jonathan said easily. "As you have insisted, sir, I never leave the grounds unarmed. But I cannot let these disreputable miners keep me penned up here. I must have *some* freedom."

"Take Harry Brownell, some grooms or gamekeepers with you, then," his father persisted. Elinor saw Jonathan looked annoyed, although he did nod.

After luncheon, Elinor put on her cloak and her stout walking shoes again. The beautiful day and The Lady's Garden beckoned, but somehow she was feeling restless today. She wanted to walk as fast and as far as she could. Perhaps the exercise would still these unsettled feelings she had had ever since that hand had touched her hair last night. Why, even while she had been painting this morning, she had remembered it. And she did not want to think about that strange happening again. With all her heart, she wanted to forget it, for it was only a dream. But somehow, it had disconcerted her, made her restive—for what, she did not know. Strange thoughts came unbidden to her mind—a remembered glimpse of a couple embracing in a London doorway, the girl's arm tight around her lover's neck, his hands caressing her back, cupping her bottom and pressing her closer still. And she wanted to forget how Jonathan's body had felt when he had held her and comforted her yesterday afternoon, the whole long, hard length of him. Her breasts crushed against his chest, the strength yet the warm tenderness of his hands . . . Yes, a good brisk walk would blow all these infantile fantasies from her mind. She was sure of that.

She walked past the Home Farm, not stopping to speak to McCarthy or the lads, or to give Jenny a sugar lump, as was her custom now. The path she was following was not well marked. It was overgrown, as if it were not used much anymore, but she was not afraid of getting lost.

Once the fields of the Home Farm were behind her, the path entered a little wood. She could see it would be cool and shady there in the summer. Now, of course, only a few small tender green leaves were in evidence. Using a set of stepping stones, she crossed a small stream that laughed over the stones of its bed as it went on its way. The banks of the stream were covered with primroses, and she stopped to admire them. Surely it was very early for them to bloom! But perhaps in this sheltered spot, well away from the sea, and in such a mild climate, anything was possible. She saw rhododendrons already well in bud, and above her a pair of swallows dipped and swooped over the stream. In their formal plummage, they looked dressed for an evening party. Perhaps she might be able to capture the scene with her paints, she thought.

Coming around a bend, Elinor saw the woods ended quite abruptly, and she stopped. Ahead of her, was a large, untidy garden, with a slate-roofed stone cottage beyond. A woman was bent over some plants in the middle of the garden, and suddenly, as if aware she was being watched, she straightened, one hand on the small of her back.

As she gazed at the intruder, Elinor gasped a little. The woman looked so very like Sir Robert Grenville—why, the resemblance was astounding.

"Well, you've come this far, you might as well take the last few steps," the woman called. "Come here, do."

Obediently, Elinor moved forward, taking care not to step on any of the plants just beginning to sprout. She studied the woman as she came. She was tall, and as sturdy as Sir Robert, but the resemblance did not end there. She had the same broad forehead and strong nose, the same thatch of graying brown hair. But her dress! Unlike her immaculate host, this woman looked like a peasant in her rusty skirt and the faded shawl that was knotted over her breast. The skirt was hiked up over a pair of high leather boots, and she held a hoe in one work-roughened hand.

"I'm Gwyneth Grenville," she said, transferring the hoe so she could extend her hand. Elinor began to curtsy, but the gesture was waved aside. "No need to do the pretty with me, Miss Fielding," she said with a wry twist of her mouth. Elinor noted her gray-blue eyes had a distinct twinkle in them, and she smiled in response.

"You know my name?" she asked.

Gwyneth Grenville laughed heartily. " 'Course I do! We've no strangers about but you. Everyone for miles knows your name. Heard you told m'brother that Timothy Coryton was not the man who held up your carriage. I've been wanting to meet you ever since."

Suddenly she leaned close. "Why'd you deny it, then?"

Elinor lowered her lashes. "I wasn't positive it was him," she invented, afraid of revealing anything to a stranger.

Miss Grenville laughed again, and turned back to her hoeing. "A likely story!" she scoffed. " 'Course it was Timmy, and some others. They're hungry. Their families are in a bad way. I'd speak to Robert if I thought it would do any good, but of course it wouldn't. He'll not be pressured by anyone, and he doesn't believe in charity. No more do the miners. They're stubborn men, proud and independent. But it can't go on. There's a day coming . . ."

She shook her head, her hoe biting into the clumps of earth around the plants.

"What an extensive garden you have," Elinor said politely.

"Like nothing you've ever seen before, I've no doubt, but you're too nice to remark it," Miss Grenville said cheerfully. "There are no flowers for milady's drawing room here."

"What are these plants, then?" Elinor asked, curious.

Miss Grenville paused to wipe her brow with the

back of her hand. "They're herbs," she said. "I grow them for medicine."

As Elinor looked a question, she went on, "The villagers and farmers can't afford the doctor from Portreath, not for every little thing. I've made a study of herbs, which ones help which illness, so they come to me for their medicine. Of course, I send for the doctor if it's something beyond my skill. But it's amazing how herbs do cure."

"What is this one?" Elinor asked, intrigued. "It looks familiar."

"Oh, that's rosemary. An infusion made of the tops stops spasms. It's also good as a tonic. It alleviates nervous headaches, and stimulates the circulation. Too much of it can be toxic, of course."

"But there are violets," Elinor said, a little surprised to see the humble flower among the other plants.

"Aye. The leaves are used for skin disorders, and the flowers for gout. It also makes a good cough medicine. There's woodruff over there. That's a diuretic. And there's lamb's quarter. It's a powerful styptic for hemorrhaging. And over on the side there, is burdock. It's a most useful weed. In a tisane it is used as a wash for wounds and bruises. It even gets rid of ringworm and rashes. O' course, some of the plants I use, I don't have to cultivate. I can gather all I need on a walk over the moor.

"Well, 'tis a fascinating study, but I forget everyone is not as interested as I am."

She laughed then, and shook her head. "But you'd be surprised at how many village girls find their way here after dark. At first they come for a lovendrant, all blushes and embarrassment."

"What's that?"

"A love potion. They slip it into their young man's cider or ale, to make him more eager." Miss Grenville gave her hearty laugh again, and added, "Not that they need much encouragement, those young men. My, no! And then, a few months later, some of the same girls are back, this time for my special potion to rid them of an unwanted birth. It's made of angelica, among other things. But it's my secret, that one. Of course, sometimes there's a hasty wedding, and later I help deliver the baby."

She shook her head. "The world goes 'round and 'round, Miss Fielding. Some things, like the seasons, never change. And sometimes, after I treat a young girl, the next knock on the door is an old man, seeking a special tea made of plantain to cure his impotence. I've seen it all, over and over again."

"It—it is fascinating," Elinor said. "However did you learn how to do it?"

"Trial and error, at first," Miss Grenville admitted. "But there's learned books about it, too. And some of the old country recipes do cure. It isn't witchcraft, no matter what my brother claims.

"But come, enough of that. Tell me of the castle. All are well there?"

"Yes, they are all well," Elinor told her, wondering why she never visited to find out for herself.

"I haven't been to the castle in years," Miss Grenville volunteered, reading her mind. "I don't dress fine enough for one thing. You see, I'm considered an eccentric. There's lots of us in Kernow, Miss Fielding. Must be something in the air here, to make us so different. Not for me, useless grandeur and worthless lives. I prefer my own cottage, my own way."

She looked back at the cottage then, and a smile of satisfaction creased her face. Elinor saw some chickens scratching in the yard, and a large orange cat sunning itself on the doorstep. Over on the edge of the garden were a few bee hives, and a cow placidly chewing her cud. Everything was there for a purpose. It was peaceful and serene, and not at all a bad way to live, she decided.

"My brother James is much the same," Miss Grenville went on. "He's next oldest to Robert, but he left the castle as soon as he reached his majority. He lives in a farmhouse beyond Uplong on the moors. A real hermit, James is."

Before Elinor could comment, she went on, "My niece, Fiona? She is well, you say?"

As Elinor nodded, she went on, "Still can't speak?"

"No, she can't. It is very sad."

Miss Grenville nodded, but there was a frown between her eyebrows now. "Well, Miss Fielding, you seem a sensible girl. Do come and visit me again," she said as she picked up a nearby basket. "Now I must make a call in the village. Mary Wigg's baby has the colic."

Waving a careless hand, she strode off toward the cottage. Elinor watched her for a moment, before she turned and made her way back to the path through the woods. What a strange person Gwyneth Grenville was! she thought. Yet obviously she did much good here, more surely than if she had been sitting in The Lady's Garden dressed in a fine gown, her needlepoint on her lap.

When she reached the Home Farm again, Elinor saw the head groom striding in the direction of the sea. He carried a large burlap sack that seemed alive with motion.

Elinor pointed to it as she came closer. "What on earth is in there?" she asked.

" 'Tis the kittens, miss," McCarthy told her, shifting the wriggling sack to his other hand so he could tip his hat. "I'm to put 'em to cliff."

Seeing she did not understand, McCarthy explained that all unwanted dogs and cats were tied in bags and thrown over the cliffs, "put to cliff" as it was called here.

Elinor could not suppress a shudder. It seemed so cruel, although she knew the barns and stables would have been overrun with cats if such steps were not taken.

Then she remembered Fiona. "Oh, how sad Miss Grenville will be!" she exclaimed. "You know how she loves to play with them!"

McCarthy's faded blue eyes grew sad. "Aye, the lass does at that," he admitted. "But orders is orders, miss. And she'll forget 'em, if she don't see 'em about-like. She always has before."

"But couldn't we keep just one?" Elinor begged.

"Can't keep even one in the stables, miss. Orders," McCarthy told her.

"No, I suppose not," Elinor said slowly. Then her expression brightened. "I know! I'll come back tomorrow with a covered basket, and I'll smuggle the kitten into the castle to Fiona. Between us, we can take care of it."

McCarthy chortled. "And which one do you fancy, miss? There's four to choose from."

"I seem to remember Fiona played the most with the all-black one," Elinor said. "Yes, do keep that one safe until I come."

McCarthy agreed, his eyes twinkling, and they parted. As she went on back to the castle, Elinor wondered, however, if she had done a wise thing. Sir Robert didn't even keep dogs. Perhaps he did not care for animals. But one little kitten isn't going to cause any trouble, she told herself. And if Fiona keeps it in her rooms, or mine, it won't be able to get into mischief. Why, perhaps no one will even have to know that it's there.

She did not mention the kitten to Fiona at tea, not even at dinner. At tea, Miss Ward hovered too close to her charge to allow a moment to whisper the news. Still, Elinor was not disappointed. It would make a wonderful surprise tomorrow, she decided as she went up the stairs to bed. I can go to the stables early and get it, bring it back here when Fiona is practicing the piano. She was always alone then, for Miss Ward spent that time harrying Mrs. Greene and the other servants.

At the top of the flight, Elinor's eyes met those of the Cavalier again, and she looked hastily away. No, she told herself as she marched to her door, stepped inside, and shut it firmly. No more of that!

Still, she found it very hard to get to sleep that night. She lay awake for what seemed like hours, waiting—waiting, in a strange mixture of dread and anticipation. But no one—nothing—came. No one—nothing—touched her.

As she drifted off at last, she did not know whether to be relieved or disappointed.

6

THE NEXT MORNING, the mist was back, as thick and impenetrable as ever. Elinor wondered if it were wise to try and walk to the stables alone. But as Betsy helped her dress, she remembered the path was well marked, and she had been that way so many times now, she was sure she would have no trouble.

After breakfast, she left the castle by the long windows in her sitting room. She was wearing her hooded, waterproof cloak, and she carried a small covered basket that Betsy had fetched for her from the kitchen.

The mist swirled around her, now in tendrils, now in a dense fog of cotton wool. In The Lady's Garden, familiar objects took on weird shapes, distances were hard to judge—it was as if she had stepped into another world. It seemed very still to Elinor as well, for not a single bird called. Once she was on the path through the woods, the world became an even more alien place, frightening and mysterious. Elinor kept her eyes firmly on the path, moving slowly and cautiously. She knew she could come to no harm even if she should miss her way, but she had no desire to spend hours wandering around in this white, eerie world. Droplets of mist occasionally struck the leaves above her, and every so often she could hear strange, rustling noises in the bushes. Resolute, she continued on. It is just the same as it would be in bright sunlight, she told herself stoutly. Don't be making up tales to frighten children, now! There are no ghosts in the woods, any more than there are in the castle, nor ogres nor wild animals either.

Thinking about it later, she still did not see how she

could have missed her way so completely. One moment she was on familiar ground, and the next she was thoroughly lost and confused, for the path simply seemed to disappear. Perhaps she had let her mind wander for a moment when she had taken that first, errant step. Now, suddenly, nothing around her was familiar. The mist lay thick on the ground, and she could feel bushes snagging at her cloak as she struggled forward, trying to see. But there was nothing there. Nothing.

She leaned against a tree then, her breath coming fast in her dismay. Listen! she told herself fiercely. The path is close, you know it is! Stand still until the mist lifts a little, else you'll lose yourself even more.

But the mist did not lift. To Elinor's horrified eyes, it appeared to be thickening, wrapping itself around her like a shroud, as if it were intent on keeping her captive here. She drew a ragged breath. What was she to do? What *could* she do?

"Don't be afraid," she heard a deep voice whisper, and she whirled toward the sound, straining to pierce the fog.

"Take four steps to the left, then turn to the right and take three more," the whisper told her.

She hesitated. It was as if this tree trunk she clung to had become the only safe place in an unknown world, and if she let go of it, she would be forever lost. "Who are you?" she called. "Come out, let me see you!"

There was a long silence, so long she was sure whoever it was had gone away. She almost sobbed in relief when the whisper came again.

"Do as I tell you, and you will be safe again," it said.

Slowly, Elinor pushed herself away from the tree. Four steps to the left, the voice had said. Turn right, take three more. She counted the steps as she obeyed that disembodied voice, although her knees were trembling so, she was afraid she might fall. When she had done as commanded, she looked around, and her heart sank. There was no path here, there was nothing but more woods and mist—she was as lost as ever.

The mist moved then, and as it thinned for a moment, Elinor could see the path, not three steps in front of her. Hurriedly, before those white tendrils could envelop her again, she pushed past the last bushes, panting in her eagerness. She said a little prayer as she recognized the spot. Then she turned back the way she had come. "Thank you. Whoever you are—thank you!" she said. No one answered. There was only a gentle sigh of the wind as it moved through the branches above her.

As she continued on her way, Elinor wondered about that voice. She had not been able to identify it, not from just a sibilant whisper. Had it been Jonathan? But if so, why hadn't he come forward and led her to safety himself? Why all this secrecy? Was he trying to frighten her?

As she reached the edge of the woods, and knew the fields and stables were just ahead of her, Elinor felt a little chill. For perhaps it had not been Jonathan at all. Perhaps it had not even been human, that phantom voice. Could it have been the Cavalier? Could it be possible that he not only haunted the castle, but the grounds of Mordyn as well?

She barely listened to McCarthy as he put the kitten in her basket and fastened the lid for her, and although a part of her wanted to remain there, enveloped in the warmth and the smell of the horses, safe with the head groom and his admiring "lads," she made herself go out into the strange white world again.

But somehow, the walk back did not seem so threatening to her now, perhaps because she had company. The black kitten did not like being confined in the basket, and he let her know about it. Elinor tried to soothe him, speaking in a soft, low voice. Before she knew it, she was safe inside the castle walls again.

Although Fiona was distressed to learn of the fate of the other kittens, she was delighted with Elinor's surprise, so delighted she gave her a warm hug. Pleased, Elinor offered to tell Sir Robert, and Miss

Ward as well, but Fiona frowned and shook her head. Obviously, she wanted to keep the kitten a secret between them as long as she could.

Elinor began to mention names for the kitten then—Midnight, Blackie, Ebony, Shadow. But it was not until the kitten pulled a cloth off a small table and some books tumbled to the carpet that she mentioned Mischief. Fiona smiled then and clapped her hands in agreement.

That afternoon, Elinor went to the library after luncheon was over. She had noticed that there was a history of the Grenville family in the catalog, and she was eager to read it. Perhaps she could learn more about the Cavalier, even more about his haunting, she thought.

Strangely, she could not locate it on the shelves, and she was still searching when Sir Robert came in and learned her plight.

"Oh, that book," he said. "I keep it in the vault, for there is only one, handwritten copy. I'll fetch it for you. I'm glad you are interested in our history."

"Do you think I should, if it is the only one?" Elinor asked. "What if something should happen to it?"

"Nonsense, my dear," Sir Robert said as he went to the safe that was hidden behind a large oil painting on the wall. "What could possibly happen to it? Although perhaps it would be better for you to read it only in this room.

"You remind me I should have another copy made as a safeguard. It was written by an uncle of mine some years ago, and it would be a shame if all his work was lost. I suppose I must have it updated at a future time as well, for now it only covers up to my generation's birth."

He frowned as he opened the safe and reached inside. Elinor began to wish she had never mentioned the book, for he looked almost distressed by whatever he was thinking.

"Here it is," he said at last, drawing it out to hand it to her. "Let me know when you are finished so I can put it away again."

Waving away her thanks, he went to his desk and was soon deep in some papers. Elinor took the heavy book to a windowseat some distance away where she would not disturb him, and curled up there with the book on her knees. The mist swirled outside the panes, but she did not notice, for here was the history of Mordyn from its very beginnings. And here were all the marriages, births, and deaths of so many, many Grenvilles, and their adventures as well. She was startled to discover that the ghoulish Lady Mary had had eighteen children, only five of whom she had raised to adulthood. Sad, that, but not unexpected at that time in history.

And then she came to the section devoted to the Cavalier, the one she had really wanted to read all along, and her eyes widened. Sir Miles Jason DeFountaine Grenville had been born June 19, 1613, in the rule of King James I. He had certainly had an exciting life, Elinor thought as she read the old, crabbed writing. First involved in the Civil War, then putting down uprisings in the West Country, before sailing ships from Mordyn Harbor to fight the Dutch, and, it was implied, involved later in a great deal of smuggling. He had not married until he was forty, although the chronicler had written, a little wryly, on the number of Grenville bastards strewn about the countryside. Sir Miles's wife, a much younger woman than her husband, had presented him with twelve children. And, Elinor saw, she, like herself, had not been noble.

Struck, she stared out at the mist for a long moment, her eyes far away. Sir Miles had indeed been a great rake, and not above illegality either, but for all that, he must have been a fascinating man. And then she wondered, even as she scoffed at herself, if the wife he had chosen at long last had been below average height, with long golden-blond hair.

She looked up, startled, as a voice said, "Here I am at last, sir. Whitman said you wished to see me?"

Peeking around a corner of the windowseat, Elinor watched Jonathan Grenville as he strolled up the room to his father's desk.

"Don't tell me, let me guess," he said, his voice sounding a little insolent to Elinor's ears.

"You have summoned me, yet again, to berate me for—"

"Elinor, my dear, would you excuse us?" Sir Robert asked, without even turning his head to where she sat.

She rose at once, bringing the book with her to place on his desk. She thought Jonathan looked at little discomposed, and she wondered at it as she said, "Of course, sir. I was quite lost in the pages, and did not notice how much time had passed. Jonathan?"

She curtsied and left the library. As she closed the door behind her, she realized that neither man had said a word. Surely whatever it was, was serious.

But everything seemed the same at dinner, and the next day as well. The mist continued to blanket the castle, and for the first time, Elinor found herself growing impatient with the weather. She was keyed up, unable to settle to anything for long. Books were discarded, half-read, drawings crumbled up in disgust, and she hardly touched her needlework.

It was at luncheon the following day that her secret and Fiona's was discovered. Miss Ward happened to notice Fiona putting a piece of fish in the pocket of her gown.

"My dear child, whatever are you doing that for?" she asked, her expression astounded. As every eye looked at her, Fiona hung her head and blushed crimson.

"Now, my dear, it is all right," Sir Robert said gently. "But I cannot understand why you wish to remove food from the table."

Elinor looked at Fiona. Her eyes were begging for help.

"Shall I explain, Fiona?" she asked quietly.

The girl nodded, and beside her, Miss Ward bristled. "You? Explain? Whatever do you mean, Miss Fielding? Why, what would you know of Fiona? She is my charge, and my responsibility, and if I do not know anything of this, then why should . . ."

"If you would just stop nattering, perhaps we might find out," Jonathan told her. "Do go ahead, Elinor."

"The fish is for Fiona's kitten," Elinor explained. "I brought one of the stable kittens to her the other day. She loved them so, I could not bear for all of them to be killed. I hope you will not disapprove of such a thing, Sir Robert, but I—"

"Well, of course he does!" Miss Ward interrupted, looking horrified. "A *cat?* In Mordyn Castle? The very idea!"

Elinor ignored her blustering. She knew now it was not for Miss Ward to say what would be allowed here. But as she glanced at Sir Robert, she saw he looked most stern, and her heart sank. Then Fiona rose in a whirl of skirts, to come and put her arms around her father and rest her cheek against his. After a moment, she backed away, and raised her hands as if in prayer. Her eyes were full of her pleading, and Sir Robert was not proof against her wiles.

"Very well, you may keep your cat," he said. "Just don't let it roam the castle unattended, do you hear?"

"But Sir Robert, I believe cats are very bad for one's health," Miss Ward sputtered. "And they are dirty, too. Fiona might catch something from it. Oh dear, I do think you should reconsider. She will soon forget it, and—"

"Does this creature have a name yet?" Jonathan asked, sounding more than a little bored.

"Er, I suggested Mischief, and Fiona agreed," Elinor told him.

Sir Robert chuckled. "Let us hope that is a misnomer. Come, Fiona, sit down and finish your luncheon. There will be plenty of fish left for Mischief. But remember, you are in charge. That will be quite enough, Rebecca," he added, seeing the lady's mouth opening and closing in her distress. "It is only a kitten."

"But it will be a cat soon, and have kittens of its own," Miss Ward continued, determined to win the battle still. "We will be overrun with them!"

"I hardly think so, ma'am," Elinor said before she thought. "Mischief is a male."

The two men laughed, but Elinor could see from the look in Miss Ward's eyes that she had made an enemy, and a fierce one at that.

By Furry Day on May 8th, the mist had still not disappeared, although it was less dense. That afternoon, Fiona came to fetch Elinor, urging her to put on her cloak and come along. Mystified, for she had forgotten the celebration, Elinor did as she was bade. She was closer to Fiona now, and she was glad of it. As soon as the weather turned pleasant again, they would be able to go for walks and rides together, and it would be nice sometimes to have company, even as silent as Fiona was.

Now Fiona hurried her down the drive, and then onto another path that cut the distance between the castle and the village in half. Elinor had not been there since her arrival, and when she saw the direction they were taking, she was a little afraid, and hung back. Fiona only grasped her hand tighter, and pulled her along the road, smiling and nodding.

The streets of Downlong were crowded today, for none of the farmers or their families had stayed home, nor had the fishermen left port. And there was singing and laughter, people selling food and drink. Elinor relaxed a bit after she saw that the villagers were not going to be a problem. For although some of them stared at her before they turned away, with nary a smile on their rock-hard faces, everyone's expression brightened when their eyes lit on Fiona in her red cape.

Elinor saw that they did indeed dance in and out of each other's houses, weaving back and forth in a seemingly wild, aimless dance. Fiona took her hand, and urged her to join in too, but Elinor refused. The villagers were used to Fiona. They loved her. But they might not care for a stranger from London parading through their homes. She wouldn't have liked it either.

She pressed back against a fish barrow then, to wait until Fiona was ready to go home. As she looked around, she saw a man staring at her, much more openly than any of the others had done, and as he came toward her, she saw that it was Timothy Coryton.

He paused by the barrow for a moment, supposedly to light his pipe. He wore the same shabby clothes, although they seemed to hang a bit more loosely than they had before. The red dust still clung to him. As he sucked in the fragrant pipe smoke, his gaunt cheeks were hollowed. "Thank ye for what ye done, miss," he said in an aside only Elinor could hear. "I'll repay the kindness someday, if I can."

Elinor would have spoken to him, but he moved away too quickly, calling out to his mates as he went.

The evening of the party Sir Robert had planned at Mordyn, Elinor dressed carefully in a gown she had not worn before. It was cut low, perhaps too low for Cornwall, she thought as Betsy fastened it up the back and she observed the expanse of bosom revealed. But it was a lovely gown, perfect for an evening party; she had no other as festive. Made of black brocade, and caught close under her breasts, it fell in easy folds to her ankles. The sleeves were puffed to the elbow, and then worn tight to the wrist. There was a tiny ruff of white lace to adorn the square neckline, and Elinor had a matching piece of lace, worked with a black velvet ribbon to put around her throat. She was sorry she did not have a pearl necklet, but the frippery was pretty enough.

She was feeling a little nervous when she was ready at last, and she paused for a moment before the painting of the Cavalier. As she stood there and those dark eyes smiled down into hers, she wondered why she felt she needed his approval. Annoyed at herself then, she turned in a rush of skirts, and hurried to the stairs.

Behind her, the Cavalier continued to smile at her.

Both Sir Robert and his son rose when she came in to the gold salon to join them. Fiona, dressed in soft rose this evening, smiled and nodded, but Miss Ward, who by special dispensation perhaps, was also present, did nothing more than nod distantly. Elinor saw her eyeing her gown with distaste, however, even as she smoothed her own sedate navy blue skirts.

"You are very smart indeed," Sir Robert told her with a twinkle in his eye. "You'll set all the ladies agog with this new fashion, Elinor. But no doubt their husbands will be annoyed, opportuned as they are sure to be all the way home for a shopping trip to London!"

"I do hope it is not too elaborate, although it is the latest fashion," Elinor said with a little frown.

"You look lovely," Jonathan told her, his gray eyes warm as they inspected the soft cream of her skin. "With your golden hair, black becomes you as it would few others."

Whitman introduced the first guests then, and before long, the salon was filled with more. Elinor tried hard to remember all the names. The Brownells of Glyn came first, a husband and wife with two sons and a daughter.

Miss Phoebe Brownell was a vivacious brunette in her early twenties, but although she greeted Fiona with friendly warmth, she was not so effusive when introduced to Elinor. Elinor concentrated very hard on standing up straight and keeping a little smile pinned to her lips. As the Brownells moved away, Miss Ward murmured behind her, "Dear Phoebe! Such a beautiful girl, is she not? There have been expectations there, you know. She and Jonathan—well, it is no wonder, is it not, with such a lovely, suitable girl? I am not the only one who has always considered them half promised."

Elinor forgot her words, for she was trying not to laugh at Harry Brownell's expression as he came toward her. He looked so eager, yet he was trying so hard for an air of sophistication. His younger brother, Dick, who surely at not much more than eighteen could only recently have begun to attend evening parties, blushed scarlet as he bowed over her hand.

But as the three stood chatting, Elinor considered Miss Ward's remarks. She could see Jonathan and Phoebe Brownell deep in conversation on the other side of the room, but she could detect nothing between them beyond common courtesy. She did agree they made a handsome, well-matched couple. Miss Brownell was tall and willowy, and very graceful, yet still she had to look up to meet Jonathan Grenville's eyes.

The contingent from Portreath was the next to arrive. A Doctor Hepplewait accompanied his sister and her husband, Mr. and Mrs. Booth, and their daughter, Willa, as well as an elderly lady dressed all in black.

"That is the new mourning in London?" Elinor heard this Mrs. Jenkins ask Miss Ward as she moved away. "My word! We must all scurry about, Rebecca, lest we be thought dowdy!"

Last to come were the Wilkenson party. Mrs. Wilkenson apologized profusely for being tardy. Something to do with a mistake as to when the carriage had been required, from what Elinor could gather. She liked the Wilkensons immediately. Jolly and outgoing, with no pretensions, they seemed a comfortable pair. Elinor was to learn later that they had quite a number of children, some of whom were still in the nursery. This evening they were accompanied only by their eldest son and daughter. The daughter, whose name was Maud, and who was only sixteen, made no secret of her adoration for Jonathan Grenville, for she scarcely took her eyes from him all evening. As for their son Nigel, he went at once to Fiona's side, and was soon talking to her quietly. Elinor was delighted to see Fiona's nods and smiles. What a nice young man, to bring Fiona into things! she thought as she went in to dinner on Harry Brownell's arm.

Miss Ward, or more likely Mrs. Greene and Cook, had planned a feast that was much appreciated by all. Talk was general. There was none of the formality that Elinor had been half expecting and thoroughly dreading. And since it was her first dinner party, she was relieved. She had admitted she had been feeling apprehensive, not knowing quite what to expect. But even here in the grandeur of Mordyn, there was only the laughter and easy goodwill of people who had known each other for years.

"I hear there's been rioting at Redruth as well at Truro, Robert," Horatio Brownell informed his host.

"I wonder when we will see the end of all this dissention? The tinners are getting hard to control."

"But the troops were called out, were they not?" Mrs. Wilkenson inquired, spooning up the last delicious bit of her prawn bisque.

"Yes, and I imagine the tinners will soon be put in their place. A few of their deaths, and the rest will scurry back to the moors where they belong," Sir Robert said. "Things any better at Trecarrag, Charles?"

Mr. Wilkenson frowned as he accepted a serving of haddock in parsley sauce. "No, I'm afraid I can't say they are. My outlying farmers are the most pressed, of course, but only two days ago, we, ourselves, lost several laying hens. I don't know what the dogs were about, not to sound the alarm."

"Keep your guns handy and loaded," Sir Robert advised.

"All very well for you to say, away down here at the shore," Mr. Wilkenson said cheerfully. "And tucked away in the castle, too."

"But surely there's no danger of any of us being attacked, is there?" Mrs. Brownell asked, a little fearfully. Elinor saw her eyes go to her pretty daughter, her two stalwart sons.

"There, there," Dr. Hepplewait said, putting down his fork to pat the lady's hand. "No need to borrow trouble, ma'am. And what would be the use of them attacking the gentry? Just bring His Majesty's troops here to root them out that much sooner. No, they might steal a few hens, a pig or two, but they'll not harm us."

"I'm sure you're right, sir," Nigel Wilkenson said. "After all, they are men we've known all our lives. I cannot believe they would suddenly turn savage."

"Hunger makes a man act strangely, saint or sinner," Sir Robert remarked dryly, signaling his butler to serve more wine.

"I do so hope you are not afraid, Miss Fielding," Harry Brownell said, turning already adoring eyes her way.

"Oh, Elinor has already had a meeting with the rascals,'' Jonathan said. ''Her carriage was stopped on the moors the very day she came here.''

''Never say so!'' Mrs. Wilkenson said, abandoning her pigeon pie for a moment. ''My dear girl, what a welcome to Cornwall for you! I hope it did not overset you too much!''

''It was frightening, but no, I was not hurt, nor my maid either, and for that I must thank the tinners, if that is who they were,'' Elinor said. ''They did not harm me. They only relieved me of the money that was in my purse, and a ring of my mother's I was wearing.''

''I hope that doesn't mean you will not venture to Glyn some day soon, Miss Fielding,'' Harry Brownell said. ''It is only a pleasant ride from Mordyn.''

''I should like to come,'' Elinor told him with a smile. ''But first I must gain our head groom's permission. McCarthy has been teaching me to ride, and until he tells me I am competent, I would not dare to leave the grounds. It has nothing to do with the tinners.''

''Perhaps we could have a riding party,'' Nigel Wilkenson said. ''If Jonathan and Fiona come, as well as Miss Fielding, and Phoebe and Harry and myself, there will be safety in numbers.''

''Yes, and we can show Miss Fielding the sights,'' Harry agreed. ''Perhaps we can even go up on the moors.''

Remembering Timothy Coryton's warning about the moors, Elinor decided she would veto any plan to do so, if such a plan was proposed.

Course followed course, to be climaxed by a grand trifle, thick with custard and cream and fruit, and smelling deliciously of brandy. Miss Ward was quick to mention she had ordered it especially, since it was her dear Sir Robert's favorite. As the ladies rose to leave the gentlemen to their port, Elinor was sure she was about to burst the seams of her new gown.

''A most delicious dinner, Miss Ward,'' Phoebe Brownell said as the ladies reentered the gold salon. ''And I knew it was all your doing even before you told us so. How well you supervise things at Mordyn!''

Miss Ward blushed a little and simpered as she thanked the girl before she bustled away to make sure the other, older ladies were comfortable.

"Do come and sit by me, Miss Fielding," Mrs. Wilkenson invited, patting the sofa beside her. "I do not feel we have had a chance to get acquainted as yet."

Elinor obeyed, although she was sorry to leave Fiona to Phoebe Brownell's company. It was obvious that Phoebe was only vivacious when there were gentlemen in attendance.

"And how do you like Cornwall, my dear?" Letty Wilkenson asked with a smile. "Not undone by our gales and mists as yet?"

"Not at all," Elinor told her. "Or, I should say, only when they last well over a week!"

"Be patient; wait for one of our perfect summer days," the older woman said. "I think that only one of them can make up for a month of mist! But it must be vastly different here, to one who is London-bred. I have heard that you recently lost your mother, too. Poor girl, I am so sorry, for I know what losing a mother can mean."

Looking into her sympathetic eyes, Elinor could see she was sincere, and she had to swallow a lump in her throat at her concern. "Yes, it was very sad," she said softly. "But Sir Robert has been so kind—indeed, everyone here. They have made me feel at home."

Mrs. Wilkenson patted her arm. "My good girl, it would be impossible for them not to welcome you, you are so very pretty, and so nice. Now if my Francis were older, or Nigel not so involved—but alas, Francis is only fourteen. I suppose there is no use in my asking you to wait for him to grow up?"

Elinor saw she was joking, and she laughed. "I doubt your young son would want a woman ten years older than himself," she said.

"You might be surprised, Miss Fielding," Mrs. Jenkins chimed in, in the loud voice of the hard of hearing. "Most men have no sense at all!"

When the maligned gentlemen rejoined them, Fiona went to the piano to entertain them, Nigel Wilkenson beside her to turn the pages of her music. And then there was cards and conversation, while the youngest among the guests played a game in an adjoining salon. For a group that ranged in age from sixteen to well over sixty, it was a pleasant and easy party.

Elinor never did have much chance to talk to Phoebe Brownell, even though she was the closest to her in age. The girl seemed to be avoiding her, and Elinor wondered if Phoebe had taken her in dislike. Once, in passing her chair, she thought she heard her say to Mrs. Booth, ". . . in trade, if you can believe it!", but she could not be positive. But where had Miss Brownell gotten that information? Not from Fiona, at any rate! No, it had to have been Rebecca Ward who had dropped that little tidbit in Phoebe Brownell's eager ear. Elinor tried to forget it. No one seemed to treat her any differently from then on except Phoebe and her mother. But it was hard to tell about Mrs. Brownell. She was a straitlaced-looking woman who had little to say for herself, one who preserved a stiff, unbending front even among these friends she had known all her life.

It was late when the guests finally took their leave, and Elinor went up to bed, arm in arm with Fiona. Miss Ward had hurried away to speak to the butler about the cleaning up, and Sir Robert and Jonathan had retired to the library for a last snifter of brandy.

After she left Fiona at her door, Elinor ascended the next flight, holding her candle up to light her way. She was tired now, tired from the excitement and the nervousness she had felt to be meeting so many people all at once. As she crossed the picture gallery, she frowned, completely forgetting the Cavalier who always seemed to watch her from his place on the wall.

Would Miss Ward's revealing her background make any difference to the people here? she wondered. She wanted so desperately for them to like her, to be accepted as one of them. But Phoebe Brownell didn't like her already. Perhaps because she was afraid that Jonathan Grenville might fall in love with her? But he was not about to do that, Elinor scoffed as she shut her door, moved to her bedchamber, and lit a branch of candles. True, I know he admired my gown tonight, and me, as well, but he is much too cool and contained to lose his heart to anyone—for any reason. And then she wondered how she was so sure of that. Jonathan had never been very open with her.

She summoned Betsy to help her undress and brush out her hair. But when the maid would have put it in its customary braid, Elinor dismissed her.

"I have a headache tonight, Betsy," she explained. "The braid will only make it worse, so long and heavy as it is. Thank you, and good night."

When the maid had left, Elinor wandered over to the long windows. It was black outside, but she could see a few stars. Perhaps tomorrow would be fair, bring an end to the mist? She opened the doors then, to breathe deeply of the salt air, hoping to clear her head. Yes, she had told her maid no lie. Her head did ache. The breeze blew her scarlet wrapper open, and she pulled it closer before she rested her head on the edge of the door. And then she prayed silently that she would be approved, popular here, for she was coming to love everything about Mordyn and Cornwall.

She wanted to walk the beaches, ride the moors, attend the local festivities, and take tea with friends. Yes, *friends.* With all her heart she wanted to be one of them. She had never been a part of any group in her life, had never had a single friend outside of her maid, Doll Bundy. She had always lived alone with her mother, locked away from the rest of the world in the house on Compton Street.

It was not that she yearned for endless gaiety, or parties. No, she only yearned for a smile, a hug, even a kind word—from *friends.* She wanted to be included not only in their joy, but in their grief and sadness, too.

Elinor sighed then, and closed the doors. Seated at the dressing table again, she pushed her hair back over her shoulders and tied a scarlet ribbon loosely around it.

As she climbed into bed and pulled the covers up, she realized that now she knew exactly how a poor child felt standing before a warm, lighted shop, with her nose pressed to the pane as she longed for just one of the confections displayed there, that were so close and yet so very far away. Sighing again, she drifted off to sleep.

It must have been very late when she suddenly woke, confused and apprehensive. In the dark, her heart began to pound.

"Don't be afraid," a deep voice whispered, close to her ear.

Elinor kept her eyes tightly closed. It was the same voice that had whispered to her when she had been lost in the mist that morning in the woods. But she did not dare to open her eyes. She did not feel she could move a single muscle. Instead, she held her breath and waited.

Gentle fingers entwined themselves in her hair, combing through it until they reached the ribbon. She could feel it being untied, and slipped away. The fingers were back then, smoothing, curling, losing themselves in all the long, luxuriant length of her hair. Playing with it.

The whisper came again. "How very beautiful you are, so lovely and yet so sweet. You were nervous down there tonight, weren't you? But there was no need."

Forced to take a shallow breath lest she faint, Elinor lay tensely. She could not speak.

"Nothing will hurt you," the voice whispered. "Be easy."

The hand abandoned her hair then, to caress her shoulder through the soft lawn of her nightrobe, and explore the contour of it to her neck. Little chills ran over Elinor's back and arms. She could feel herself shivering. The fingers of that hand traced her delicate jawline to her chin and, turning over, went back again to circle her ear. Slowly. So slowly and gently.

I must open my eyes, Elinor told herself. I must see who it is.

But she could not do it. She was afraid she would see the phantom of the Cavalier. She did not want her mysterious visitor to be a ghost. She wanted him to be a man.

The fingers caressing her were strong—full of life. Surely a ghost would not feel like that, she told herself. In spite of her terror, she began to relax, for she was sure whoever it was meant her no harm. Her body seemed full and languid, and yet every bit of it was alert, straining with keen awareness, waiting for what might come next.

As the fingers feathered down her cheek to the little hollow at the base of her throat, Elinor became one enormous throb of yearning. From the tip of her toes to the top of her head, she was aching for something, waiting—wanting something more than this, although she did not know what that might be.

With her eyes still closed, she turned her head slightly on the pillow to face this wonderful, unknown lover. The hand at her throat stilled for a moment, and she heard rustling as a pair of lips touched hers, tentatively at first, and then moving in easy exploration. She marveled that something so undemanding could yet, in some inexplicable way, demand so much more.

She seemed to catch a hint of some masculine scent, but in a moment it was gone, as were those lips, that gentle hand. She felt bereft, and she had to bite her lower lip to keep from crying out for more—much more.

She lay waiting for that "more" for what seemed a very long time. As before, when she dared to open her eyes at last, she was completely alone. But she had been listening hard this time, and she knew that no one had left the room by the only door. She had noticed before how it creaked slightly when it was opened or closed. There had been no such sound tonight. That seemed proof positive that it was a ghost after all, for men could not walk through walls.

But could ghosts kiss you? she asked herself. Did they have warm lips that seemed to speak a language of love that was all their own? Did they have hard cheeks and warm flesh; flesh that sported just the tiniest hint of leather and bay rum? And did ghosts have warm breath, breath laced with just the slightest tinge of old brandy?

7

Elinor woke late the following morning. She had tossed and turned in bed for a while, first too hot, and then, when she threw off the covers, too cold. Finally she had risen to put more wood on the fire and to light a candle so she could pace up and down, all the time wondering what was happening to her. Surely she had not made the whole thing up, nor had it been a dream! No, that was impossible. It had been real—much too real. And she knew she had to discover the identity of this person, or ghost, whoever he was, lest she go mad.

Now, she told her maid that she would not get up for breakfast. Indeed, she asked her not to disturb her until it was time to dress for luncheon.

"Be your headache worse then, miss?" Betsy asked. "That Miss Grenville do make a powerful powder for headache, an' I can fetch some o' it for ye, if ye like."

"No, thank you," Elinor said, touched by her concern. "My headache is gone. It is just that I did not sleep well, and I am still tired."

Curtsying, the maid went away. Elinor barely waited for the door to close behind her before she was out of bed, shrugging on her scarlet wrapper and pulling on her slippers. Just now, when Betsy left her, the door *had* creaked! she reminded herself.

All right. She had not heard that door either open or close last night. Whoever it had been had another way in and out of her room, and she would find it, right now. As she threw back the curtains, the bright sunlight streamed in through the windows, and she felt more in control. More normal, suddenly.

Ghosts! she scoffed. It has to have been Jonathan who was here. After all, I even heard him suggest a last snifter of brandy to Sir Robert as I went up the stairs with Fiona. And I know I smelled brandy when he kissed me. But why he is doing it, I do not know. Nor do I know why he treats me so coolly when we meet about the castle or at meals. But it has to be he. There is no one else it could have been.

The whispered voice had been that of an educated man, with none of the Cornish singsong or burr she associated with the servants, even with Sir Robert himself. She knew Jonathan had spent much time in London, attended Eton and Oxford. That, no doubt, was where he had lost his local accent.

Carefully, she inspected the walls of the bedchamber, feeling along them for cracks that might indicate a secret door. The stone walls were rough, and it took a very long time. She looked behind every picture hung on those walls, and felt behind the tapestry as well. She even went so far as to go out on the balcony to give the surrounding stonework a careful look. But that approach would be insane, she decided, looking down the long sheer drop to the ocean, measuring the great distance to the next window on this floor.

She moved the rugs back then to feel the floor. No telltale line appeared to indicate a trap door, and the mortar between the stones was undisturbed. She even investigated the little sitting room and the dressing room, to no avail. At last, putting everything back where it had been before, she sank down in a chair before the fire, defeated. There was no other way into this room. She would have wagered any amount on it.

But that led her back to the ghost again. Elinor frowned. She didn't believe in ghosts, but it seemed everyone in Cornwall, especially everyone here at Mordyn Castle, did. Perhaps there were such things as spirits after all.

Still frowning, Elinor got back into bed, propping her pillows against the headboard so she could stare into the fire. She must talk to someone, someone she could trust. Sir Robert? Fiona? Somehow she shied away from that. Sir Robert might think her a nervous woman, one who was unbalanced. She did not want to lose his good opinion of her. And poor Fiona couldn't communicate! As for Miss Ward, even if Elinor could have borne confessing such a thing to her, she had already scoffed at the very idea of ghosts.

Suddenly, a picture of Gywneth Grenville clad in her old clothes, with her hearty laugh, came to mind. Yes, of course! She had liked her at first meeting. And she was a practical woman, one well-versed in local lore and tradition. One, moreover, who had been raised in the castle. She was also educated—a healer. After luncheon, I will go there again and question her, she told herself as she yawned a little and slid down on her pillows. There was still some of the morning left. Perhaps she could doze for a while.

When she left her room later, the luncheon gong still echoing through the halls, Elinor paused before the portrait of Sir Miles Grenville again. She studied his knowing, masculine face carefully, but today, she did not linger on his eyes as she always had in the past. Instead, she stared hard at his sensuous lips. What would they feel like on hers? she wondered. Could they have been the pair that had kissed her so beautifully last night?

She knew little of such things. She had only been kissed once before in her life, and then she had hated it. Austin Denby's thin lips had been hot and dry, and they had hurt her, grinding her own lips against her teeth. And his hands had been all over her, clutching and squeezing before she had managed to push him away and scream to Doll for help.

But last night—ah, last night!—she had loved that kiss, the touch of that strong, yet gentle hand. Wanted more, she remembered, squirming a little under her smart black gown. And no doubt Sir Miles had been an accomplished lover in life. He had had more than enough practice, if everything that was written about him was true!

Still in a quandary, she went downstairs, and after a meal spent watching Jonathan Grenville as unobtrusively as she could, listening carefully to his cool conversation, his casual drawl, she felt sure that he could not have been her midnight visitor. Either that, or he was a consummate actor. After all, why would he do it? she asked herself as she buttered a roll. He had only to court her openly, and probably she would have fallen right into his arms. He was so tall and handsome—much more handsome than most men—and appealing when he put his mind to it. Now he was teasing Fiona about her kitten, and with the little smile he wore, and with his gray eyes alight, he was—well, breathtaking.

Elinor did not waste any more time. As soon as she excused herself from the table, she sent for her cloak. She thought Fiona looked at her a little longingly, but she could not take Fiona with her this afternoon. Instead, she gathered up her sketchbook and pencils as a ruse, lest the girl be hurt, and left the castle.

When she arrived at the cottage on the edge of Mordyn's grounds, she was disappointed, for there was no sign of Miss Grenville anywhere about. But then she saw the wisp of smoke coming from the chimney, and she walked through the garden and around the yard, to knock on the door that fronted the road.

"Come in, it's open!" Miss Grenville's voice called from deep inside. "I've something on the stove and I can't leave it."

Elinor lifted the latch and did as she was bade. She found herself in a narrow hall. Over to one side, a flight of stairs led upward, and to her left was a parlor that looked as if it did not get much use.

"Through here, in the kitchen," Miss Grenville called. Elinor walked down the hall and pushed open a door.

"Ah, so it's you, Miss Fielding," the older woman said, never stopping her vigorous stirring of a small pot. Steam and a rather unpleasant odor rose from it.

"Come in, do, and take off your cloak," Miss Grenville invited. "I'll make you a cup of tea presently, but I cannot stop this now, lest the infusion burn."

"I'm sorry to interrupt you," Elinor said as she put her cloak over the back of a wooden settle. "What is it? It smells awful!"

Gwyneth Grenville laughed, wiping her forehead with the back of her arm. "It does at that, doesn't it? But it makes good medicine. It's a mixture of garlic, sage, and pennyroyal—my own recipe. Does wonders for coughs and congestion. There's still a lot of that about the village, this damp spring. There, that should do it," she said as she removed the pot and set it to one side to cool.

Putting the kettle in its place, she went to get the teapot and cups from a large oak dresser. Elinor looked about the warm, friendly room. Next to an old rocking chair, the orange cat dozed before the fire, curled up in the one spot where a sunbeam from the window lit the floor. The deal table Elinor was seated at was spotlessly clean—in fact, the entire room, so homey and well-used, was spotless. Elinor found herself relaxing.

Miss Grenville did not chat as she went about her tasks, and Elinor was content to sit back, her hands clasped on the table before her, and watch.

As she set the tea tray between them and took the seat opposite, Gwyneth Grenville said, "And what brings you here, Miss Fielding? I sense there is a particular reason for your call."

Elinor looked right at her. "Yes, there is," she said. "You were the only one I could think of who might be able to help me."

"Of course I will, if I can. You are feeling poorly?" Miss Grenville demanded, her eyes sharp as she inspected the lovely, blooming face of her guest.

"No, it is nothing to do with my health," Elinor said. "It's—it's . . ."

As Miss Grenville waited patiently, she took a deep breath and said in a rush, "Do you believe in ghosts, ma'am?"

"Ghosts?" Miss Grenville repeated, the spoon stirring her tea stilling for a moment. "Well, I've seen a few, or thought I did, but I've never been able to decide if they were real. Tell me, Miss Fielding, are you impressionable? And have you been listening to the maids up at the castle? They've always been full of tales about The Lady. But it's my belief they tell the tales among themselves for the thrill of it. If they ever saw her close, they'd be off like a shot, good job or not."

"Yes, the maids have spoken of her, and my own maid, Doll, went back to London right after she saw her," Elinor said. "I've never seen her myself. But it's not that. I want to know if ghosts can touch you. And if they do, can you feel it?"

Miss Grenville put down her cup slowly and carefully. "Touch you?" she asked, her voice skeptical. "Oh, I see. You've heard about the Cavalier, too."

Elinor nodded. "Yes, but it's more than my reacting to a legend. Someone has been coming to my room late at night and—and touching me as I lie in bed. I—I have been too frightened both times to open my eyes, but I sense this is a real person. Yet there is no way out of my room except by the door, and that creaks when it is opened. The ghost, or the man, was there again last night, and when he left me, the door did not make a sound. I was listening for it. I know. This morning, I inspected all the walls, the floors, but I could find no other way in or out. I was forced to conclude it was a ghost after all."

She frowned down into her teacup then.

"Yes?" Miss Grenville prompted. "Yet somehow you still doubt it?"

"I have to," Elinor said. "He—it—kissed me. That was warm living flesh that touched mine; he had warm breath. And I'm sure ghosts don't drink brandy! But what else can I think? There is no one it could be except Jonathan, for when whoever it is whispers, it is with the words of an educated man, one, moreover, who does not have a Cornish accent. But why would Jonathan do such a thing? He doesn't even appear to like me very much sometimes."

She paused as a new idea occurred to her. "Could it be that he resents his father's asking me to make my home with them? Could he be trying to frighten me away?"

"I have no idea," Miss Grenville said a little absently. "It is an interesting solution. But I have not seen Jonathan for some time. I do not know if he would behave that way, now. Your arrival here has puzzled me, however. I cannot fathom why my brother would invite you. Yes, he knew your father, but they were not that close. They never kept in touch after Gerald went away."

Elinor saw her peering at her, and she said, "Sir Robert told me he wanted me to be a friend to Fiona. That she was too much alone in her affliction; that Miss Ward was not a suitable companion."

"Yes, he might do it for that reason," her hostess said. "He has great affection for Fiona, and I know he pities her."

"Perhaps the best thing I could do would be to confront Jonathan with what I suspect," Elinor said, bringing the subject back to her most immediate concern. "If only I was not so afraid of his scorn. And what if he denies it? Ridicules me?"

"Oh, no, no, you must not speak to Jonathan about this," Miss Grenville said hurriedly. "Nor must you tell this to anyone else, lest they think you mad."

"Do you think I am mad?" Elinor asked, leaning forward in her distress. "Do you think me young, hysterical perhaps? I assure you I am not!"

"My dear Miss Fielding, I have no idea. I don't know you very well. But you are calm, your arguments well reasoned and not at all hysterical. Now, if it had been Rebecca Ward who had come to me with your tale, I would have fixed her a draught. She's at that age, and she was always flighty. Poor woman, to waste her life on an impossible dream!"

"What dream is that?" Elinor asked, interested in spite of herself.

"She has fancied herself in love with my brother from the moment she arrived at the castle all those years ago. After Beatrice died, I know she had hopes that he would turn to her. Little fool! Robert's not for her. He can't stand her, if truth be told. Yet still she clings to the forlorn hope that someday, somehow—Fah! Some women are idiots!

"Miss Fielding, will you take my advice?" she asked next. When Elinor nodded, she went on, "Then I most strongly urge you to put this from your mind. It is true the castle has a history of hauntings, but Mordyn's ghosts are benign and cause no trouble. By the way, The Lady mourns her husband who never returned from the Crusades. When, as a girl, I learned about the chastity belt she was forced to wear during his long absence, I believed she still walked because she could never get free of the awkward, burdensome thing. Her husband had had the only key. Surely, that would be enough to make any woman weep and wring her hands through the ages! But as far as ghosts touching you, or kissing you—well! There must be another explanation. Ghosts have no earthly bodies. They are only spirits who can never rest."

She rose then to return to the stove. With her back turned, she asked, "Was it pleasurable? Did you like it?"

Elinor blushed. "I was frightened, but yes, I did like it," she admitted in a low voice. "It was not a bit threatening, and somehow—although it sounds silly to say so—so right."

"Hmmm," her hostess said as she poured the infusion through a strainer into a pitcher and then into some small bottles. "Well, I still suggest you try and forget it. It may never happen again. In fact, I'd be surprised if it did."

"But how can you know that?" Elinor asked, watching Miss Grenville cork the bottles tightly.

"Just a suspicion I have. Sometimes, speaking of such things to other people makes them stop happening. Wait and see."

"I suppose you could be right. But I must not keep you longer," Elinor said, going to pick up her cloak and drawing materials.

"There is no need to hurry off," Gwyneth Grenville told her as she came to her, wiping her hands on a rough towel. "Oh, you sketch! It is a talent I envy, for I have often thought of writing a book about herbs and their uses—putting down my hard-won recipes. But such a book cries out for illustrations, and at those I am a total failure."

"I am not so very talented," Elinor said shyly, "but if you would like me to help you, I would be delighted."

She put the sketchbook down, and opened it to show Miss Grenville a drawing of some crocus she had done a little while ago.

"That is very good," Gwyneth Grenville said, nodding her approval. "I would only need a simple line drawing of each weed and plant, showing the flowers, leaves, and roots. Do you think you could do that?"

"I am sure I can," Elinor said, her eyes shining. "And I would be glad to assist in such a worthy endeavor! I do so admire you for all the good you do."

"Very well, we shall be confederates then. Come down any time you have a free afternoon. If I should not be here, I'll leave you plants and some instructions on the table there. The door is never locked. And I do appreciate your help, Miss Fielding."

"Please call me Elinor," Elinor begged with a smile as she put on her cloak. "If we are to work together, you must not be so formal."

"Then you must call me Gwyneth," her hostess said with an answering smile. Seeing Elinor hesitate, she smiled even more broadly. "I dislike social conventions, Elinor, I always have," she said. "And any respect for my advanced age would send me into one of those declines so popular with certain ladies. Please spare me that!"

Elinor was pensive as she returned to the castle. As she walked, she thought hard, for Miss Grenville—no, Gwyneth!—had raised questions in her mind.

Why *had* Sir Robert asked her to live here? Was it at all possible that he had been so generous and welcoming just to gain a companion for his daughter? It was hard to believe, especially since Gwyneth had told her there had been no lingering camaraderie between him and Gerald Fielding over the years. There had to be something more beyond mere altruism and his care for a beloved daughter. But what it could be, she had no idea.

And why had Jonathan Grenville been so formal, so cool to her in the beginning? Perhaps he had resented her coming here, a complete stranger? And why was she herself so uncomfortable when she was with him? There was something about him, for all his good manners, that made her wary. Yet he was a handsome, appealing man, and lately he had been much more friendly. He smiled at her often now, even teased her, as he was wont to tease Fiona. Occasionally he looked at her the same way he had the afternoon he had saved her from the cliff steps. She also remembered his heartfelt approval of the gown she had worn to the party; how his warm glance and compliment had flustered her.

To offset such friendly gestures, there was his unconcern, even cruelty to others. Perhaps she could not like him for that reason?

Reminded of that cruelty, she remembered Rebecca Ward, a woman Jonathan obviously held in aversion. Why had Miss Ward changed so quickly from a welcoming person to one who snubbed their guest whenever she had the chance? Surely the fact that Elinor's father had been in trade was not enough to explain her sudden antipathy!

For Sir Robert himself had made no secret of how pleased he was when I came here, Elinor remembered, and she suspected that whatever Sir Robert Grenville approved had always won Miss Ward's smiling acquiescence before. She had made it plain to anyone of the meanest intelligence that she was in love with the man, and had been for years. Elinor had not needed Gwyneth's explanation to know that. Miss Ward's adoring smiles; her pressing Sir Robert to take a piece of his favorite cake at tea—one, she was always quick to point out she had insisted Cook make just for him; the breathless way she hung on his every word when he spoke, were all indications of her devotion. Elinor had seen no answering gleam in Sir Robert's eyes, however. Always formal with the lady, except when he interrupted one of her rambling discourses, he treated Rebecca Ward to nothing more than distant politeness and barely veiled indifference. Poor Miss Ward! Elinor thought.

Shaking her head, and putting the ordinary little woman from her mind, Elinor considered Fiona next. She had been unfriendly as well, in the beginning, but she had changed in a twinkling. Why would she do that?

As she reached The Lady's Garden, Elinor shrugged. The Grenvilles were a complicated family, more so than most, she suspected. Somehow she knew this even though her knowledge of families was very limited. But perhaps, if she were patient, she would discover their secrets someday.

She found Fiona in the garden, playing with her kitten. The morning's promise of a beautiful day had persisted, and the sun shone down warmly. Elinor smiled in response to Fiona's delighted smile of greeting, and she sank down beside her on the little bit of lawn that surrounded the fountain. Fiona was teasing the kitten with a little ball. Whenever Mischief pounced at it, his sharp claws extended, Fiona would snatch it away. At last, tiring of the game, Mischief curled up in a fold of Fiona's gown and went to sleep.

Elinor sat with her eyes closed and her face lifted to the sun, content to remain as silent as her companion. She was tired after her restless night, and she felt she could fall asleep now with no trouble at all. Above them, some birds trilled their little songs. They had been very quiet while the kitten was awake, but now they ventured to sing again. The sweet smell of the early flowers, as always overladen with the salty air, filled Elinor's nostrils.

Suddenly, she became aware that Fiona had started, and she opened her eyes to see the girl leaning forward and staring intently up at the castle. As she followed her gaze, Elinor gasped, for there, at the large window on the landing, was the figure of a woman dressed all in drifting white. She was holding the crimson drapery with one thin hand as she peered down into the garden, shaking her head sadly as she did so. The woman was very pale—bloodless—seemingly as ephemeral as mist.

As the two girls watched, the ghostly form let go of the drapery and began to wring her hands together, her face contorted now in a mask of misery. Elinor was sure she had never seen such agony.

To her surprise, Fiona carefully moved the kitten and rose with one fluid motion. Facing the window, she dropped a deep curtsy, holding it with her head bowed. As for herself, Elinor did not feel she could move.

When she dared to look up again, the woman at the window had stopped crying. She was nodding now, and she looked much calmer. And then, she simply disappeared. One moment she was there, and the next—she was gone.

Elinor became aware of the quiet. Even the birds had ceased to sing. Calmly, Fiona took her seat again, picking Mischief up to cuddle him next to her cheek.

"Was that The Lady?" Elinor asked when she could trust her voice. When Fiona nodded, she went on, "You do not appear to be afraid of her, Fiona, but I have never been so frightened in my life! I—I have never seen a ghost."

Fiona reached out to take her hand, to squeeze it in reassurance. Her smile was calm, soothing.

"There is no need for me to fear her?" Elinor asked. "But she is so unhappy, poor thing!"

Fiona nodded again, looking pensive and sad herself until Mischief began to squirm and demand to be let down.

Lost in the kitten's antics, Fiona seemed to forget The Lady very quickly. No doubt she was used to her, saw her all the time, Elinor thought as she stole a quick glance at the window again. To her relief, there was no one there now.

That evening, Sir Robert asked how she had spent her afternoon, and Elinor decided she had better not mention Mordyn's chief ghost. Instead, she told him about her visit to Gwyneth Grenville's cottage. "She has asked me to do some drawings for a book on herbs she is writing," she said, a little proudly. "I am thrilled to be part of such a noble effort. She does such good about the village.''

''How is Gwyneth?'' Sir Robert asked. Elinor noticed that he was not smiling now, and he did not appear to be best pleased at her new acquaintance. Elinor wondered why that should be so. She saw Fiona was staring at her, much astounded, although Jonathan appeared lost in revery.

''She is very well. She asked for everyone at the castle,'' Elinor told him.

''It was Gwyneth's decision to move to the cottage many years ago,'' Sir Robert told her. Elinor sensed that he felt some explanation for his sister's quitting Mordyn was required.

''She is strange. She always was, even as a girl,'' he went on. ''But to choose to live alone in a rustic cottage when she could be well taken care of in the comfort of the castle is ridiculous! Ah, well, there's no accounting for tastes, now is there?

''She should be grateful to you for your assistance. Do not let her overwork you, my dear. A book on those primitive ways of healing? I wonder who on earth would want to read it?

''Jonathan, did you have a chance to talk to McCarthy today about the new gelding?'' he asked then, turning to his son.

From then on, the conversation took other directions, and Elinor concentrated on her dinner. Obviously, Sir Robert did not care for his sister. Perhaps he would have preferred it if I had not met her, she thought. But he had not suggested it might be wiser not to visit her, or help with her book, and Elinor was glad of that.

She went up to bed fairly early. She admitted she was tired after last night, and the fright and strong emotions her unknown visitor had subjected her to. She even yawned widely as Betsy braided her hair, and not even her fears that that visitor—or The Lady—might come kept her from falling asleep as soon as her head touched the pillow.

But when Elinor awoke later, it was to the same,

heart-pounding fright. Instinctively, she knew she was not alone.

Taking a deep, ragged breath, she forced herself to open her eyes. The room was dark and chilly now, for the fire had almost gone out, and she could make out nothing but a large form bending over her. Before she could cry out in terror, the warm hand she remembered touched her brow and caressed her hair.

Immediately, Elinor felt strangely calm. From beneath half-closed lids, she watched whoever it was sit down on the bed beside her. But even though she peered at him intently, she could not distinguish a single feature of his face, for he had his back to the dim glow of the dying fire.

Both hands moved to her shoulders then, to press them gently. "Are you awake?" he whispered. "I have tried, but I find I cannot stay away from you. Without using any wiles at all, you are a lodestone, drawing me to you."

He bent closer then to draw her into his arms, and Elinor closed her eyes. His hands caressed her back, before one of them cradled her head. Once again, as his lips covered hers, she knew the ecstasy of his kiss. As before, it felt so right—so inevitable—that Elinor lost herself in it. Without even thinking of what she did, her lips parted under his, and she could feel her heart begin to race, keeping tempo with his own.

His mouth moved more urgently on hers then, pleading, demanding—seducing. Still held tight in one strong arm, his other hand pushed the covers down so he could explore her breasts through the flimsy fabric of her nightrobe. As his fingers traced their full outlines, Elinor gasped against his mouth. She knew she was almost lost, but she did not care. Indeed, she was aware how very much she wanted to lose herself in him.

When he lifted his head at last, she gasped, "Who are you? Why do you come to me like this?"

The hand at her breast stilled. "I cannot tell you who I am. Not yet," he whispered, laying his cheek against hers. "As to why I come, well, I cannot help myself. Sweet. You are so very sweet."

He turned his head only the few inches he had to to kiss her again, and Elinor lost all interest in questioning him. Whoever he was, it was enough that he was here. Tentatively, she put both hands on his lean face, his hair, touching him for the first time. She felt him stiffen, and he drew back a little as if to search her face in the dark.

Elinor's eyes flew open. She was afraid she had done something wrong. How she wished she were not so inexperienced, so new to all this! She wanted to let him know, by her kiss and her touch, how she longed to be closer to him, how she longed for something more than his kiss and caress. She was confused, even a little frightened at the strength of her emotions, the urgent desire she felt.

"It is late and you are tired," he whispered. "Go to sleep now, love."

Elinor had to bite her lip to keep from crying out to him and begging him not to leave her like this. As he lowered his head, she closed her eyes. She felt the soft touch of his lips on her brow, her cheek, even the tip of her nose, and she waited breathlessly for him to kiss her lips again.

To her surprise, he did so only fleetingly before he lowered her to her pillows and rose.

Elinor opened her eyes to search the dark shadows. She could not see him. She had no idea where he had gone. One minute he had been there beside her, and the next, he had simply—disappeared. She felt tears coming to her eyes, tears of disappointment. Lying there, staring up at the canopy she could not see above her, Elinor was aware of something more than just disappointment. Her whole body was aching, and she felt not only bereft but unfulfilled.

Tired as she was, it was a very long time before she slept.

8

ELINOR WOKE EARLY the following morning, and the first thing she thought of was her mysterious midnight visitor. My Cavalier, she murmured, and then she smiled at her fancies.

Snuggling under her covers, she remembered the wonderful clean scent of his skin, how his hands and mouth had felt, the deep whisper of his voice. When would she see him again? she wondered. It seemed such an endless time until midnight would come around again. All those long, dreary hours. But surely he would return to her then. She just had to be patient, no matter how she hungered for him.

But her mysterious Cavalier did not return, not that night, nor the next, nor even the next. Elinor began to worry—and to wonder. Surely she had not dreamed the whole thing—no, that could not be! Could it? It had all been so real, so intense, unlike any dream she had ever had.

She passed those days almost in a trance. She smiled and spoke, even laughed occasionally, and she knew she appeared just the same, for no one questioned her. Yet even as she rode Jenny, walked with Fiona, or started a new book, she felt as if only a small part of her was really there. The larger part held aloof from such everyday matters as eating and conversing. And it wondered, always wondered where he was. She found she had trouble sleeping, and as she paced her room late at night, she felt a wanton, she ached so for him. Where was he? Why didn't he come back?

He came that night. It was very late, well after midnight, and Elinor was almost asleep. She and Fiona had gone riding with Jonathan that afternoon, almost to Portreath, and she was tired, for it was her first lengthy expedition.

Still, she was awake as soon as his hand touched her brow in that familiar caress.

"You're here at last!" she cried, reaching up to touch his shoulders.

"Have you missed me, sweet?" he whispered as he put his hard cheek against her soft one and gathered her into his arms. Elinor cuddled closer and sighed, her eyes closing in pure delight.

When she did not answer, he chuckled a little. "No matter," he said, his voice easy. "You do not have to tell me, if you don't want to. But I shall confess how much I missed *you*. Believe me, I could not come till now, else I would have. Nothing could have kept me away. Nothing—no one."

His voice had grown deeper, more ragged as his hands caressed her, and suddenly he took her face in his hands and turned it to his to kiss. Elinor felt his lips on her brow and her cheeks before they captured her mouth.

When he raised his head, she gasped, "I did!"

"You did?" he asked, sounding confused.

"Yes, I did miss you," she told him. "I waited for you, wanted you every night."

His hands tightened on her back. "You darling," he whispered. "How wonderful to meet an honest woman!"

Elinor soon lost any interest in conversation as his kisses grew more passionate, and his hands cupped her breasts. She felt her nipples peak and swell under his suddenly urgent fingers, and that familiar ache returned, to pulse inside her and send waves of liquid fire along her veins. Slowly, his hand moved lower, curving in at her waist, and out again to explore her hips and belly, her thighs. Blindly, Elinor turned toward him, helpless with desire. She felt as if she could never get close enough to him.

His tongue parted her lips and captured her mouth, curling around her own as if to savor her. She had never experienced such intense feeling, and she felt as defenseless as if she were being drawn down into a maelstrom. But this particular maelstrom ended in another world, a world that was filled with the sensations only his hands and mouth and body could summon into being. Her hands abandoned his hair to rake the muscles of his arms, his back—to measure the breadth of his big shoulders under his linen shirt.

As he slipped her nightrobe from her shoulders, and bent to kiss her breasts, Elinor grasped his shoulders, holding them tightly as she arched her back and moaned a little.

He drew back finally and lifted his head, and she touched the column of his naked throat, her fingers trailing down it until they caught and held in the curly hair on his chest.

"Elinor?" he whispered, sounding tortured now. "Yes? Say yes!"

"Oh, yes," she breathed.

He moved away from her then. Elinor lay with her eyes closed, praying he would not be gone long. Even this little separation was hard to bear. She heard the sounds of his clothes as he dropped them to the floor, and then the coverlet was drawn back and he was beside her again, pulling her close in his arms, to throw a muscled leg over hers as if to claim her. His urgent kiss told her how much he wanted her.

Impatient fingers pulled her nightrobe down her arms and away from her body. And everywhere those fingers touched her bare skin lit a glowing ember of desire. As impatient as he was, Elinor kicked the robe free of her legs as he clasped her close again. And now there was nothing between them.

Neither spoke. His hands and lips adored her, waking her, tasting her—making her his. When he laid her back on the pillows and rolled over her, she felt something hard pressing against her thigh. But then he was exploring a part of her she had never imagined any man would ever touch.

Suddenly, in spite of her longing, she was frightened. Not of him and what he was doing—oh, no!—

but of herself. She had never known she could be so wanton, had never imagined she would surrender so quickly, and to an unknown lover at that! What was happening to her?

He hesitated, as if aware of her uncertainty, but she did not want him to stop. She reached up to put her arms around him to pull him closer still.

Yes, she thought as he caressed her again. Oh, yes! This was what she wanted, and she wanted it now. Right now.

There was a little pain at first, but it was gone in a moment, forgotten, while this wonderful man loved her so deeply, held her so close, surged with her, and brought her at last to unimagined emotion. Elinor cried out then in wonder, and he moved with more urgency. And still waves of feeling swept over her, threatening to engulf her. Was there no end to rapture? She was helpless in its grasp, yet she did not feel she could stand much more.

With a cry of his own, her lover shuddered before he collapsed in her arms. His breathing was ragged, and even in the coolness of the room, his skin felt fevered. Still one, they lay in each other's arms, struggling for breath, waiting for those enormous waves of passion to die away into little eddies. Elinor hardly dared move. She was sure if she did, the maelstrom would drown her again.

"My love," he whispered against her hair before he kissed it. One of his big hands softly brushed over her breasts.

"No, please!" she begged in a broken voice. "I cannot bear any more! Not now."

He left her then, to lie down beside her and cuddle her in the crook of his arm. His hand smoothed her hair, brushing back the tendrils that had come loose from her braid. So gently. So carefully.

Elinor lay with her eyes closed, a little smile playing over her lips. It had all been so wonderful, and now she had proof he was not a ghost as she had feared. He was *real!* No ghost could ever have made love as he had.

She did not know his name; she knew nothing about him. Strange how unimportant that was. But it didn't matter, for tonight she had found the one man in the world for her, and tonight they had claimed each other.

She knew she would never be the same, and that she would never forget what had happened. Not ever.

Drifting off to sleep, secure in his strong embrace, and with his warm breath stirring in her hair, Elinor put one hand on his chest and sighed in contentment.

When she woke in the first graying of the dawn, however, she was alone again. Sometime during the night, her lover had left her.

He came to her often from then on, and Elinor began to feel she was leading two lives. During the day she was cool and prim, the perfect lady guest as she whiled away the hours, but at night, ah! at night! she was a wanton, all hot abandonment as her Cavalier taught her the wonderful ways of love. They did not speak much, and then only of their desires, and how lucky they had been to find each other. Elinor sometimes thought words would break the spell she was under, and she did not want that spell to be broken by anything.

She did not even ask her lover his name again, or wonder if he were Jonathan indeed. It had suddenly become unimportant. It was enough that he was there, that they were together. For no matter how she pondered his identity occasionally during the day when she was alone and her face would not betray her, somehow when he was with her she ceased to care.

She felt like a princess in a fairy tale, hidden away from the world. Nothing would happen. No one would know. The nights became reality, more vivid than any daylight hours. Those moments in the dark were her secret world—hers and her Cavalier's.

The days were filled with all the usual activities. Sometimes, now, Jonathan joined her and Fiona on a walk, and sometimes he rode with them. Elinor had smiled to herself at how much friendlier Jonathan had become ever since Harry Brownell had begun to call on her with such regularity. And his impatience with the calls, his acerbic little comments about Harry, showed his jealousy clearly. Elinor found herself pitying that poor young man, with his so obvious attraction, and her smile in parting was always particularly sweet for him. Afterward, Mr. Brownell rode back to Glyn in a daze that would have surprised Elinor if she had but known of it, for she never intended to lead him on, she thought she was only being kind.

One afternoon the Wilkensons asked Elinor and Fiona to tea, and Sir Robert ordered the carriage for them while Jonathan rode his gray hunter alongside in escort. Elinor liked Trecarrag at once. It was a large, rambling house, built in the time of Queen Elizabeth, or so Letty Wilkenson told her amid the noise of her tea party. All the young Wilkensons were present, staring at the newcomer to the neighborhood even as they demanded another cake or a special muffin. Elinor was a little disturbed by the confusion and their loud voices, although her hostess seemed to accept it as normal practice, and made no effort to reprimand her children.

Nigel Wilkenson was there as well, sitting beside Fiona and talking to her softly. Elinor wondered if he were in love with the girl, and if Fiona felt anything for him. She invariably had a such a warm smile for him. But would any man want to marry a girl who was mute, a little backward? Perhaps he was only being kind. He did have a nice face, and in his company, Fiona remained calm. There was only one other person who affected her that way, and that was her brother Jonathan. When she was with him, she was always on her best behavior, and if he came into a room during one of her temper tantrums, it stopped at once.

By now, Elinor was used to Fiona's moods. Sometimes she lost her temper, even threw things or wept furiously, and sometimes she seemed like a very small child, stamping her foot and pouting until she got her way. It was hard to be kind to her then. Elinor often wished she could give her a good shaking. But then she would think, Poor Fiona! Why shouldn't she rage against the fate that had decreed she spend her life in silence? It was perfectly understandable, even though it was not pleasant to live with or endure. Reminded of her midnight Cavalier and his love, Elinor would vow to be more patient. She had so much richness, and Fiona, so little.

She had taken Fiona to Gwyneth Grenville's cottage a few times, although the visits could not have been said to be an unmitigated success. When Elinor became engrossed in her drawing, Fiona grew bored. She tried to play with the old orange cat, but it hissed at her and fled her petting.

It was not until her aunt took her in hand that the visits became more pleasant. Gwyneth Grenville gave her a book on herbs to read, talked to her about them, and let her work in the garden with her. She even let Fiona make one of the infusions and bottle it. Elinor reported none of this at the castle. She was not sure Sir Robert would approve his daughter visiting her aunt, becoming interested in herbs, or "witchcraft medicine," as he called it. And she knew Miss Ward would resent any other woman's influence over her precious charge.

One time at the cottage, when Fiona had gone out to pick some cowslip for her aunt, Elinor asked Miss Grenville about her accident.

"It seems so strange to me," she said, not noticing how the older woman's expression had grown wary. "Did she have a fall from her pony? Or perhaps some childhood disease? I have never heard of anything like her affliction, for I have been told she spoke perfectly normally until she was six years old."

To her surprise, Miss Grenville did not answer at once. Instead, she rose from the table and went to the window, to hold the curtain back so she could watch her niece in the garden.

"I cannot speak of it," she said at last, over her shoulder. "It is family business, and we have never discussed it with anyone else."

Elinor was embarrassed. "Do forgive me, dear ma'am," she stammered. "I—I did not mean to pry!"

"Of course you did, and very understandably, too," her hostess told her more cheerfully as she came and took her seat again. "But it was a very sad thing, and if Robert wants you to know, he'll tell you about it himself. I cannot take it upon myself to do so."

Fiona ran back into the kitchen then, and Elinor was glad to see her, for it allowed the subject to be changed. But as Gwyneth told Fiona how she planned to use the cowslip, she wondered about that "very sad thing." What could it be?

The drawings were going well, and Elinor was pleased with them. Not troubled now with the vast expanse of harbor and village to portray, or the mystery of perspective to solve, Elinor was able to make clean line drawings of each plant she was given. She liked the neatness of pennyroyal, each little leaf facing its fellow across the stem in perfect order. And the spiky leaves of agrimony, its drooping, flowering tops, were a challenge. Even the bulbous root of the angelica plant, its thick stem and large leaves, and the flowers that reminded her of Queen Anne's lace, was intriguing. And she found that when she was engrossed with her drawing she was able to forget her lover, however briefly. Through all the rest of her daily activities, he was her silent companion, hovering in the back of her mind, waiting to be remembered. As if she could ever forget him! Elinor scoffed to herself. His strong arms, caressing hands, and his intoxicating kisses were never far from memory. She could conjure them up in a moment, no matter what else she was doing.

All Cornwall was a garden that May. The roses and wild orchids were in bloom, and on her rides, Elinor saw that every field and hedgerow, every country lane, sported ferns, red poppies, blue flax, foxgloves, and ragged robin. Smiling, she felt they bloomed for her alone, to share her secret joy.

One day, when Miss Ward and Fiona had gone early to Portreath for a fitting on some new gowns, Jonathan surprised Elinor at luncheon by asking her if she would like to minch with him.

"Minch?" she asked. "I think I had better withhold my answer until I know what that word means."

"In Cornwall, minching means running away from your duties," he said with a knowing little smile. "It's a beautiful day. Let's go for a ride, just the two of us. I'll show you some of our Cornish secrets. A Crows an Wra—that's a witch's cross—and a logan—that's a rocking stone. Perhaps you'll even see a Men an Tol."

"You are speaking a foreign language!" Elinor protested. "What on earth is a Men an Tol?"

Sir Robert chuckled. Elinor saw he looked very pleased. She wondered why.

"A Men an Tol is a large granite stone with a two-foot hole in it, my dear," he told her. "It's also known here as a crickstone. For generations, people believed that if you crawled through the hole, backward and forward, you could cure backache, even get rid of rickets."

"And can you?" Elinor asked, a little skeptical.

"I don't have the faintest idea," Sir Robert admitted. "I've never tried it."

"Because it would be beneath your dignity, sir," his son said. "Still, with my own eyes, I've seen you touch one of the ancient memorial stones, and then spit for good luck. You are not quite without superstition, admit it!"

"Run along, both of you, before Elinor loses her good opinion of me," Sir Robert growled. "And have a good time minching!"

It turned out to be the pleasantest time Elinor had ever spent in Jonathan Grenville's company. He seemed intent only on her happiness and well-being, and his gray eyes gleamed into hers whenever she looked at him. He was more than willing to go out of his way to be entertaining, telling her things that would interest or amuse her. She was fascinated by his tale of King Arthur, born, or so it was claimed, at Tintagel and buried at Warbstow Barrows. Jonathan said some Cornishmen still whispered that he would come again, and set them free of English rule. And he told her the Connor River was called The Red, because the residue of the tin mining stained it that color; of the strange, shifting sands that sometimes buried whole villages and farms in certain areas of the coastline.

As they rode, side by side, Elinor's spirits were high. It was such a lovely day. There had been a shimmering of haze at dawn, but the sun had burned that away by noon, and there was no wind. But when Jonathan suggested they canter up on the moors, Elinor was firm in her refusal.

"Surely you're not afraid?" he taunted her.

"Yes, I am, and I admit it," she said, looking straight into his handsome, amused face. "I was warned to stay away from the moors, told I might not be so lucky if I ventured up there again. Even in a large company, I would be uneasy."

"Very well," Jonathan agreed, although she noted he did not look best pleased. "I shall bow to this irrational fear you have of a few grimy tinners, even though the moors are one of my favorite places. They are so lonesome, so treacherous. And now there is the added threat from the tinners, they are even more enticing to me. I like danger. I feel that only when you put yourself in danger, are you truly alive.

"And there are spots up there, Elinor—strange, swallowing bogs—where a man and his mount can disappear without a trace. The moors have a kind of weird, eerie beauty. But the only safe places are those on high ground that are barren and stony. The soft green bogs, those limpid pools and thick, springy grasses, are tempting, but they hide certain death for the unwary. We've lost more than sheep to the moors over the years."

Elinor shivered, and she was glad when he changed the subject by suggesting they ride to Glyn instead. When they arrived there, she saw the house was well named. Built at the head of a long, deep valley, the hills and moors reared up around and behind it. Yet it was pleasantly situated amid its farms and woods, and there was a wide stream meandering through the estate; even a small lake.

Neither Phoebe Brownell nor her mother seemed

pleased to see her in Jonathan's sole company, although they were both polite, inviting the riders to dismount for refreshments before they started the homeward trek.

Harry Brownell came in from the village while they were thus occupied, and he joined them with a special smile for Elinor. He took the seat beside her, and he would not allow them to leave later until he had Elinor's promise that she would go out sailing and fishing with him some fine day soon.

"Of course you plan a party, don't you, Harry?" Jonathan asked in his lazy drawl. "Not at all the thing, you and Elinor going out alone, you know."

Harry blushed, and then looked furious at himself for doing so. "Of course we shall have a party," he said. "I was just about to ask if you would care to join us, and my sister, too."

Phoebe hesitated until Jonathan gave a careless assent, then she was quick to agree to make one of the party too.

On the ride back to Mordyn, Jonathan teased Elinor about her beau. Elinor wished she might turn the tables on him, and twit him about Phoebe Brownwell, but she did not dare. Even as friendly as he had been lately, and as pleasant as he had been today, she felt there was something between them, some barrier, that effectively kept them from any real intimacy.

Still, when he lifted her down from Jenny's back after they reached the stables, he did not let her go at once. His big hands spanned her waist, squeezing it until his fingers touched.

"How enticing your waist is, Elinor," he said. "So very small."

Elinor found her breathing coming with difficulty, and she was glad when he set her on her feet and she could step back away from him. He was so big, so powerful. He quite overwhelmed her.

"And you are so tiny, too," he went on in a musing voice. "Not much bigger than a child. There is no doubt that in the London of our fathers' day, you would have been known as a Pocket Venus."

"Perhaps it is not that I am so short, but that you are so tall?" she asked. "You quite dwarf me!"

"Hardly well matched, are we?" he asked as he turned to give the mounts into the care of one of the lads. He reached for her hand then, and calmly stripped it of its glove. "Very pretty," he said, stroking it softly. Elinor pulled her hand away, her color heightened.

"But then all of you is pretty, indeed beautiful," he went on. "I must think Cornwall agrees with you. You have become so much lovelier here. There is almost a glow to you these days, a most intriguing warmth. Is it the mists, do you suppose? Or could it be a *human* element that has enhanced your beauty?"

Elinor shook her head in confusion, hoping she was not blushing. She knew very well who had put that glow on her face. Why, only last night her Cavalier had come to her in the dark and they had shared a tumultuous lovemaking.

She was recalled to present company when Jonathan laughed at her rosy confusion and held out his arm. "Come!" he said. "I shall say nothing more to embarrass you, Venus. Not at this time, anyway."

As they walked up to the castle, Elinor had little to say. She was pondering Jonathan's unexpected compliments. What did he mean by them? And how did he know *all* of her was "pretty"? Had he revealed himself by that little slip? Could he be her lover?

As he opened the side door and stood back for her to precede him, she forgot her musings in a moment, for the hall she entered seemed full of people. Whitman was there, and two of the footmen, as well as Mrs. Greene. Elinor's eyes widened when she saw Sir Robert holding a limp Rebecca Ward in his arms, and looking harried as he did so. Fiona stood nearby with the parcels. Elinor noted she did not appear upset in any way, and she was glad of it.

"What on earth?" Jonathan muttered as he hurried forward, Elinor right behind him. "What's to do, sir?" he asked his father.

"I have no idea," Sir Robert said, frowning. "Here,

Whitman, send for the coachman! Perhaps he knows. All I know now is that I could hear Rebecca wailing even behind closed doors, and I came out just in time for her to faint in my arms."

"How—how fortuitous your arrival was then, sir," his son said with a wry twist of his mouth. "And isn't it too bad Fiona can't make all clear?"

"Sir Robert, perhaps if you were to carry Miss Ward into my sitting room?" Elinor suggested, going to open the door. "It is closest, and you can put her down on the sofa there. Mrs. Greene, do you have a vinaigrette? Or I suppose we could burn some feathers? But at least we can make her more comfortable, fan her, until she revives."

The silent housekeeper nodded, her face noncommittal as she went away. Sir Robert deposited Miss Ward on the sofa, and Elinor arranged a pillow under her head. She noted her breathing was normal.

As she picked up Miss Ward's hands to chafe them, she saw that Fiona had disposed of the parcels she carried and wandered over to the window to stare into the garden. She certainly did not appear to be unduly concerned about her companion's indisposition.

"Aaaah," Miss Ward moaned, her hand tightening on Elinor's before she opened her eyes.

She seemed startled to see who it was bent over her, and she looked around wildly until she caught sight of Sir Robert.

"Oh, my dear sir," she said. "A thousand pardons for my weakness, but I am so distraught! Why, if anything had happened to Fiona while she was in my charge, I should never have been able to face you again! Oh, dear, it was dreadful—dreadful! We were both so frightened! But I made sure Fiona was safe in the carriage and away before any harm could come to her, and—"

"Perhaps, after the *great* shock you have had, it might be better to remain *quiet* for a time, 'Becca?" Jonathan suggested, sitting down on the arm of a char to swing one booted leg. His handsome face was devoid of any expression, although Elinor had no trouble detecting the note of boredom in his voice. Miss Ward seemed to hear it too, for she paled and fell silent.

"Yes, do rest quietly, Rebecca. And here is Whitman with some brandy. That will make you feel better," Sir Robert said.

"But you know I never touch spirits, sir," she protested, sinking weakly back on her pillow again.

"Nonsense!" he told her as he poured out a small tot. "Just what you need. Here now, sip it slowly, and then we can discuss what happened to overset you.'

He brought the brandy to her, and Elinor hurried to assist her to sit up. Miss Ward still looked as if she wanted to refuse the drink, but there was no denying Sir Robert. He held the glass to her lips until she was forced to take a tiny swallow. A coughing fit ensued, and it was several minutes before she was more at ease.

Elinor looked up to see Mrs. Greene in the doorway, holding a vinaigrette. She shook her head, and the housekeeper disappeared.

"There now, just a sip more," Sir Robert coaxed. "Come now, doctor's orders, Rebecca!"

The lady smiled weakly, and did as she was bade, infatuation written plain on her face. For some reason, Elinor hoped it would not be as obvious to Jonathan as it was to her.

Rebecca Ward was visibly disappointed when Sir Robert turned away to hand the glass to his butler and have a quiet word with him. Suddenly, she seemed aware of Elinor's arm around her shoulder, and she shrugged it off. "Thank you, Miss Fielding," she said stiffly. "I am quite able to sit alone now."

"But what happened?" Jonathan asked. "Was the carriage held up at our very gates?"

"No, it was in Portreath," Miss Ward said, taking a tiny handkerchief from her pocket to wipe her lips. "We had finished our shopping and were waiting for the carriage, when all at once we heard the sounds of a mob! I shall never forget it, never! They sounded like wild animals, not men!" She shuddered before she went on, "They were smashing windows, crying threats, breaking into houses, stealing food! Oh, my poor heart palpitates so, remembering!"

"Strange that you were not overcome until you reached the safety of the castle," Jonathan mused. "A rather delayed reaction, wouldn't you say, Father?"

Miss Ward paled, and she began to twist her handkerchief in her hands. Pitying her, Elinor took up her defense.

"Perhaps she might have been, if she hadn't been so concerned with getting Fiona safe away," she said.

"Spoilsport!" Jonathan said in a quiet aside. Aloud, he persisted, "But surely in the carriage later—it is several miles from Portreath to Mordyn after all."

"That will be enough, Jonathan," Sir Robert ordered. "Did you recognize anyone, Rebecca? Were they tinners, led by Timothy Coryton, perhaps?"

"I—I don't know," Miss Ward told him, turning her shoulder to shut out the amusement written plain on Jonathan Grenville's face. "I cannot be sure. They were—they were quite some distance away."

"Did you return to the shop for safety?" Elinor asked in the little silence that ensued.

"No, we did not. The carriage arrived then, and we hurried to climb in and drive away before the mob could reach us. To think we might have been attacked, robbed! To think dearest Fiona might have been harmed! Oh, the whole thing has shaken me so, I doubt I will ever be the same!"

As she spoke, her voice had been rising and quickening, and Elinor eyed her uneasily. There was more than a hint of hysteria in it—hysteria, and something else. A little horrified, she watched as Miss Ward went on, seemingly oblivious to the spittle that escaped her lips and ran down her chin. "Dirty commoners! Animals! Always making trouble, frightening gentlewomen! Every one of them should be hung, for prison's too good for them, and—"

"Rebecca! Compose yourself!" Sir Robert ordered in a loud voice. As she subsided, sobbing gustily, he went on, more calmly, "You must not dwell on it like this. Fiona is safe, and so are you."

Turning aside, he added, "Jonathan, remind me to thank Morrison for getting them away so quickly.

"And now, Rebecca, I think it would be best for you to go to your room. This has been a traumatic experience for you. Please do not attempt to join us for tea. You must rest; take a composing draught. I insist on it!"

He held out his hand to help her rise, and she placed her own, trembling hand in it. As she swayed toward him, Sir Robert looked almost desperately to Elinor, and she was quick to put her arm around the woman in support. Miss Ward collapsed against her, sobbing again.

"Whitman, a footman, and quickly!" Sir Robert ordered. "Have him take Miss Ward to her room. There, there, Rebecca, no more tears now! I am very grateful to you for your care of Fiona. You did just as you ought, but then, you have always been so dependable."

After the footman appeared and helped Miss Ward away, Sir Robert turned to his son. "I do think this incident will put paid to all your trips to Portreath, Jonathan. If the riots have really reached there, it can no longer be safe for any Grenville."

Elinor saw Jonathan's face grow cold, the hot anger in his handsome gray eyes, and she wondered at it. Yes, it was true that he had often been from home; sometimes he had even remained in Portreath overnight. She did not know who he went to see there, but it was obvious from his expression that the cessation of his visits would not please him.

"I'm sure old 'Becca was exaggerating, sir," was all he said, however. "We'll have the whole tale from Morrison and the groom and then we shall see. And I assure you, on my honor, that my visits there, are made only to—hmm—persons, who are delighted to see me."

Sir Robert stared at him for a moment before he nodded curtly. "Come, Fiona," he said, turning to his daughter. "You must be hungry for your tea!"

The girl nodded eagerly, smiling at him as she came

and took his hand. As the two left the room, Jonathan rose from the chair where he had been lounging, and said to Elinor, "It's my opinion 'Becca made the whole thing worse than it was as a way to engage my father's sympathy. What an idiot she is!"

He offered his arm. "Shall we have some tea, too? I'm looking forward to it, after our ride."

He smiled down at her as he tucked her hand in his arm, pressing it slightly with his other hand.

As they walked through the hall and up the stairs to the gold salon, Elinor thought of what he had said. Yes, she was sure he had been right, for Fiona had not seemed at all affected by her brush with danger. Had there been a mob, or only two or three men? And had Miss Ward and Fiona really been in any peril at their hands? If they had been too far away to even see them clearly, it did not seem likely.

Still, she wished Jonathan Grenville had been kinder to Miss Ward, or, if he could not have managed that, kept silent altogether. Sometimes, it seemed to her that he took an unholy delight in being caustic.

During tea, Sir Robert questioned Fiona about the riot, but she shook her head more often than she nodded, and all his leading questions about the identity of the rioters went unanswered. As Elinor sipped her tea and listened, she wondered once again why Sir Robert seemed to want Timothy Coryton to be among the culprits so very badly. Whatever had the man done to him to earn such enmity?

She went to the library right after tea, to select another book. She often read at night now, while she was waiting for her lover. He never came before the stroke of midnight, when the candles had been snuffed, the fire was dying, and Elinor was in bed. Reading helped pass the time.

She was on the library steps, taking out a volume, when Jonathan came in. She heard the door close behind him, and she turned. For some reason, the expression on his face startled her with its warm intensity, and as he came toward her, she hurried down the steps.

But still two from the bottom, he stopped her by reaching out and grasping her waist again.

"No, do not come all the way down, Elinor," he said. "I find this view of you entrancing, for now we are face to face."

It was true, Elinor was able to look right into his dark gray eyes. She felt entirely too close to those rugged features of his, his handsome sensuous mouth, now they were both the exact same height.

"Let me pass, sir," she managed to get out, even as she felt her heart begin to pound.

"Presently," he said in his lazy drawl.

His hands tightened for a moment on her waist as he leaned closer, and then he swept her into his arms. Before she could protest such treatment, his mouth came down on hers. Elinor closed her eyes.

To her surprise, his kiss stirred her senses. It did not threaten or demand. It was only a tender meeting of two pair of lips; a gentle exploration.

His hands held her close to him, caressing her back and hips. As he raised his head, one of those hands brushed her breast.

"How sweet you are," he murmured. "How very sweet!"

His lips captured hers again, lingering over them this time in deeper, more passionate fashion. Elinor realized that Jonathan was an expert lover, even as she tried to discover if his kiss was the same as that of the man who came to her at midnight. To her distress, she could not tell. It was different in a way, and yet in some ways, the same. Were there *two* Jonathans then? The heir of the house by day; the demanding, tempestuous cavalier by night?

He raised his head a few inches at last to whisper, "You are a very cool lady, aren't you, my darling? Whoever would have thought it? I see I have quite a challenge ahead of me, one I have seldom had to face. But I'll win in the end, just see if I don't."

He swung her to the floor then, Elinor holding the heavy volume she carried like a shield before her.

"Run along now, you enticing little jade," he said.

"I shall allow you to escape me this time, but 'ware our next meeting. Or, dare I hope, even look forward to it?"

As he chuckled, Elinor fled, running down the long library as if pursued by demons. And as she ran, a phrase he had used echoed in her head. He had called her "sweet" in the exact same words her Cavalier had used. What did it mean? Was he the one indeed?

9

ELINOR HAD EXPECTED to feel awkward at dinner that evening, but to her surprise, Jonathan reverted to his earlier, polite manner. He spoke to her only as he spoke to his sister and his father, and in the same, cool drawl. Indeed, in some way he seemed even more testy than usual, and where she had expected little intimate smiles and veiled innuendoes, she found only the same bored and superior gentleman. She wondered why that was so disappointing. How contrary she was!

Sir Robert had interviewed his coachman since teatime, and he regaled them all with the man's account of the incident at Portreath that afternoon. According to Morrison there had been some looting, even some broken windows, but it had all occurred in the poorer sections of town. The miller's and the bake shop had been the hardest hit by the hungry tinners. Certainly, neither Fiona nor Miss Ward had been in any danger. Sir Robert's mouth twisted wryly as he related how astounded Morrison had been to hear that anyone could even think such a thing.

"There, you see, sir? It was just as I said. 'Becca made the whole thing into a barely averted tragedy so she might star as the heroine of the piece. Idiot!"

"Perhaps you are right. It certainly appears that such was the case. But perhaps we are not being fair to poor Rebecca. She has always felt she had a heavy charge placed on her, for she is responsible for Fiona."

"Fiona is quite old enough to be in charge of herself, aren't you, my girl?" her fond brother demanded. "She is not, after all, a baby."

Elinor looked up from her plate to see the fright in

Fiona's eyes, the way she shrank back in her chair and paled.

"Of course she is able to take charge of herself," she said, to give Fiona time to compose herself. "Yet she is used to Miss Ward, fond of her, too. You must not frighten her so, Jonathan, by implying Miss Ward might be sent away."

"Sent away? Of course she'll not be sent away!" Sir Robert exclaimed. "She is my responsibility, and Mordyn's. However, I shall have a talk with her about loosening the leading strings. It is true Fiona cannot speak, but after all, she is not mentally deficient. A little more freedom might give her more self-confidence. And she has Elinor to go about with now."

He turned to their guest and added, "I have been so pleased to see the friendship that has grown between you and Fiona, my dear.

"And my thanks for your help this afternoon. I do assure you I felt quite helpless, and I do not think Jonathan's expertise with women would have shown to great advantage in the situation either."

Elinor stole a little look at Jonathan then. As he lowered his wine glass, he said, "Yes, I was delighted that Elinor was there to take care of all. A fainting, hysterical Miss Ward only made me feel an even more profound distaste for her than usual."

He beckoned to a footman to refill his glass before he added, "It is a shame you feel this responsibility for her, sir, especially since I begin to believe, after this afternoon's performance, the woman is more than a little dotty. Surely if she were given a yearly stipend, she could retire to another location? Someplace outside of Cornwall—nay, even England? How about China?"

Sir Robert was smiling, and Fiona began to look more cheerful when he shook his head at Jonathan's preposterous suggestion.

In the drawing room later, Elinor was content to sit quietly and listen to Fiona play the piano, for she was tired from her long ride that afternoon. She even excused herself early so she might seek her bed.

When she reached her room, she noticed it had begun to rain again. She could hear it lashing against the windowpanes, driven by the strong wind that moaned around the castle. And tonight the breakers seemed even more thunderous than usual as they attacked the base of the cliff. She shrugged as she resigned herself to spending the next day indoors.

Dismissing the silent Betsy at last, she climbed into bed and blew out her candle. She did not expect her Cavalier. He seldom came two nights in a row.

What a strange man Jonathan Grenville is! she thought sleepily as she snuggled into the soft goose-down of the mattress. Imagine kissing someone one minute, and acting as if she were only another sister of his the next. Why was he doing it? Would she ever understand him?

The remains of a log settling in the fireplace grate several minutes later caused her to open her eyes. Stifling a gasp, she quickly lowered her lashes to peer into the dim light that was all that was left. She was not alone anymore, for her Cavalier was coming toward the foot of the bed. Was it Jonathan? Was this the next meeting he had warned her about?

For some unknown reason, she was loathe to speak to him. She felt almost frightened, and she did not understand herself. But why, *why* was it taking him so much time to come and hold her in his arms again; make love to her? She ached, wanting him.

She noticed then that he was making no move to approach any nearer. Instead, he remained standing immobile at the foot of the bed, staring down at her. Elinor held her breath so she could listen carefully, but she could not hear his breathing. Was it really her Cavalier—the man—standing there, or was it only the ghost of that long-dead cavalier whose portrait hung in the gallery?

They remained that way for several moments, like participants in a tableau. Just when Elinor had decided she must finally speak, and find out who or what he was, the broad-shouldered figure moved away. So as not to startle him, Elinor turned her head slowly on the pillow, for she wanted to see where he went. It seemed to her that he paused before the tapestry across the room, but the fire was only embers now, and she could not be sure. And then he was gone. He simply disappeared from sight.

Tears sprang to her eyes as she struggled to support herself on her elbows while she tried to pierce the darkness. Angrily, she dashed those tears away. How could he do this to her? How could he come to her and then just leave, without even taking her in his arms? Was this some sort of new game he played? She wondered how many other times he might have stood there like that, late at night, and watched her while she slept? Why would he do such a thing?

Suddenly, Elinor became aware how chilly the room was, and she shivered as she lay back down on her pillows. She sighed, mindful yet again that no matter what he did, she loved him. She suspected she always would. But even if he were not a shade, he still seemed determined to remain an unknown shadow. It was very strange, and somehow, disquieting, too.

The next day was just as stormy as Elinor had predicted it would be. When she woke after a restless night, she felt as if she were at sea, there was such a constant ripple of the draperies and bed hangings in the draft. The rain still spat against the windowpanes, and the wind moaned, and she was glad she did not have to leave her warm bed until Betsy had lit a branch of candles and attended to the fire.

As she rang the bell, Elinor decided the weather suited her mood exactly; stormy, gray, depressing. She wished she might pull the covers over her head and sleep away all the days the gale might last. But even the thought of her maid's astonished face if she should propose such a course, could not cheer her.

Instead, rather listlessly, she chose a black taffeta gown she had not worn before. She thought it might lighten her mood with its smart lines and pretty ruching, and the sound it made when she moved that Doll had admired so much. But instead, she seemed to grow more and more downcast as the morning passed.

Fiona had had a tantrum at breakfast, something to do with the absence of her favorite muffins from what Elinor could gather, and when that had been resolved, Miss Ward's conversation seemed even more vapid than usual. Jonathan made no appearance at the table, although Elinor lingered there, hoping he might come in. When she went to her sitting room at last, Elinor found her current book dull, her needlework tiresome, and the drawing she turned her hand to, a disaster. And when she went in to luncheon, the gong still echoing in her head, she realized that somehow she had acquired a nagging headache. She wondered if she would feel better if she rested after the meal, or if she should change to her oldest clothes, her stout waterproof cloak, and go out? Perhaps if she dared the storm, walked long and hard, these megrims she suffered would be whipped away by the gusts, and washed away by the rain.

Luncheon was a subdued meal. Sir Robert apologized for his preoccupation, saying he had received a rather disquieting piece of news from his man in London in the morning post. For her part, Fiona still looked somewhat sulky and stormy, and for once Miss Ward held her tongue. Perhaps she was afraid her chatter might agitate her charge again, Elinor thought.

Jonathan made a few comments about the weather, teased Elinor about Harry Brownell yet again, and then lapsed into abstraction. Still, once or twice, Elinor looked up to catch him staring at her. His intent gray eyes held none of the warmth he had displayed yesterday, and she could read nothing in his regard. Rather, it confused her, for it was almost as if he were staring at an object he was considering purchasing, weighing the pros and cons of doing so, trying to decide if it were worth the price that had been asked. And then she wondered why such a bizarre thought should have occurred to her?

She was quick to excuse herself when the dessert plates were removed, and she did not mention her plan to escape the castle as she did so. Instead, she hurried to her room to change her clothes. She did not summon her maid to help her. Betsy would be sure to remonstrate with her on the foolishness of going abroad on such a nasty day.

As Elinor closed her door to go out, her eye was caught by the portrait of the Cavalier. It seemed to her that he was staring at her in amusement and disbelief, and she lifted her chin defiantly. "You've no right to look at me that way!" she told him. "I must escape these walls, if only for an hour or so, and you can't stop me. You're nothing but a ghost!"

Turning her back on him, she hurried down the stairs to let herself out into The Lady's Garden. There was no mist today and, fortunately, the rain had eased somewhat, although she could still feel it striking her hood and her cloak.

When she left the high, sheltered walls of the garden to make her way around to the cliff walk, the force of the wind staggered her and she had to lean into it to keep her balance. For some reason, she felt a fierce elation and she looked forward to pitting her strength against the storm's.

When she reached the wall that guarded the cliff, and looked down, she saw the breakers were magnificent. Dark and steep, they thundered ashore to cast huge sprays of white against the rocks. They were tossed higher than Elinor had ever seen before, and in only a few moments, her face was wet with the spume that was carried upward by the wind. Sir Robert had told her once that brine could be found on the crops even as far as ten miles inland. She had doubted the veracity of such a thing at the time, but she did not doubt it now. On such a day as this, it was only too plausible.

Putting the castle at her back, Elinor set off on her walk. It was a constant struggle, and sometimes the wind gusted so hard she was forced to the edge of the path so she could grasp a bush or a tree to remain upright. But she was soon feeling much better, and she took deep breaths of the cool, damp air. And as she fought her way forward, she wondered why she was beginning to feel uneasy at Mordyn. Somehow she felt as if she were sinking deeper and deeper into some dark morass. As if something awful lay just around the next corner, waiting for her—tomorrow, next week—and if she did not flee, she would not be able to escape it.

Shaking her head a little, she scoffed at her fancies. She was not a coward. Besides, Mordyn was a wonderful place most of the time, and she had come to love it. There was no danger here, she argued, and she would miss the kind Sir Robert, poor tortured Fiona alone in her silent world, even the handsome, cryptic man who was Jonathan Grenville. They were the only family she had ever really known, and they had taken her in as if she were one of them. Where could she find their replacement?

But all these excellent reasons only made her chuckle, for she knew in thinking them, she was being devious. It was not the luxury of Mordyn, or the Grenville family that held her here, and she knew it. Pushing back a lock of hair that had escaped her hood, she admitted it was because she could not bear to leave her Cavalier. For if she went away, she knew she would never see her lover again. And here she could be close to him. Smiling a little now, she forced herself to concentrate on conquering the cliff walk. Somehow, today, that was all-important.

It was almost time for tea when Elinor arrived back at the castle at last. She was tired, breathless, but she was triumphant, and she ran to change lest she be late. As she did so, she saw Jonathan just leaving the library across the hall, and she smiled at him. She was very conscious of her streaming cloak, her untidy hair, and the stout walking boots that were leaving damp spots all over the elegant carpet, for Jonathan himself was so dry and tidy.

She dropped a hasty curtsy, surprised that he only stared at her with a black frown on his face.

"Don't scold me, Jonathan," she said over her

shoulder as she hurried away. "I know I look a sight, but it was worth it!"

She could still feel his eyes on her back as she ran up the stairs, and she wondered that he had not said a single word to her, not even a sarcastic one about her bedraggled appearance or her foolhardiness.

In spite of her haste, Elinor was still tardy to tea, and she was surprised when she entered the gold salon to find that only Fiona and Miss Ward were before her.

As she took her seat and smiled at them both, she wondered at the strange currents in the room. Rebecca Ward was most perturbed, and she refused to meet her eye. When Elinor turned toward Fiona, she saw the girl was cringing back in her chair, her face as white as if she had just had a terrible shock. Even Whitman's generally immobile, hard-hewn face wore a frown.

"But where are Sir Robert and Jonathan?" she asked, hoping to lighten the atmosphere. "Perhaps we should wait for them to join us before we begin?"

"They will not be coming today," Miss Ward said as she fussed with the teapot. "I cannot say more. It is—it is *family* business."

Taking note of the snub, Elinor subsided, picking up Fiona's hand to squeeze it. She could feel it trembling in hers before it tightened convulsively. Whatever was going on here? she wondered.

"I hope you had a pleasant afternoon, Fiona," she said as she handed her the cup Miss Ward presented. "I, myself, did a foolish thing, although I must say I enjoyed it very much. You see, I went out to walk along the cliffs. The storm was magnificent, the waves so high and ferocious!"

Fiona's cup clattered in the saucer, and Elinor remembered, too late, that she was afraid of the cliffs. She bit her lip at her carelessness and fell silent in chagrin.

"Most unwise of you," Miss Ward told her absently as she stirred three heaping teaspoons of sugar into her tea. Elinor stared at her. She had never seen her do such a thing before. Indeed, Miss Ward had often made a point of how sparingly she used sugar.

"I suppose it was," Elinor made herself say. "No doubt I would have had an easier time of it if I had stayed in the woods. Would anyone care for a sandwich?"

Both of her companions refused, and Elinor took a chicken sandwich. She saw that neither of them was even making a pretense of eating, although Fiona's favorite white cake was prominently displayed on the top tier of the cake dish.

"I wonder how long this gale will last?" she asked next. It appeared that the burden of conversation was to fall firmly on her shoulders today, for the usually garrulous Miss Ward was strangely silent.

To her surprise, Miss Ward put down her cup and rose then, to draw Whitman aside for a quiet word. The old butler shook his head repeatedly, and Miss Ward was forced to resume her place, whatever question she had asked unanswered.

"Is there something wrong?" Elinor asked, looking straight at the older woman. "And is there anything I can do?"

Miss Ward sniffed. "Most certainly not!" she snapped. "As I told you before, this concerns only the Grenvilles. *You* have no place in it."

"I see," Elinor said slowly. "But Fiona seems so upset, and forgive me, Miss Ward, you do yourself. I only asked because I thought there might be something I could do to help you."

"There is nothing. Nothing," Rebecca Ward muttered. She took a sip of her tea, and Elinor noticed a look of utter astonishment cross her face as she peered into her cup, almost as if she wondered how the contents could have turned into such a sickening, distasteful brew.

The rest of teatime passed in complete silence, each lady deep in her own thoughts. When they rose at last, very few inroads had been made on the sumptuous spread. Elinor excused herself at once. She would not intrude, not after being warned twice about the sanctity of family affairs.

Instead, she returned to her sitting room to read.

Perhaps Fiona would come to her, as she had several times in the past when she was bothered about something. But Fiona did not come this afternoon, and Elinor spent the time alone until she heard the first dressing bell ring and she was forced to retire.

She wore her black taffeta gown to dinner, and as she went down the stairs, she wondered a little uneasily what mood she would find the household in this evening. She was looking forward to being with Sir Robert again, so she might reap the benefits of his calm maturity. Perhaps he might even explain to her what had happened to set everyone at sixes and sevens. Why, even prosaic Betsy had been flustered tonight, dropping things and fastening her gown all wrong as she helped her to dress.

As she entered the drawing room, Elinor found Sir Robert alone with Jonathan. They stood facing each other on either side of the fireplace, and as Elinor came forward to curtsy, she wondered if she had interrupted something portentous. They looked so serious, so preoccupied.

She heard the door open behind her then, and she turned with a smile on her face to greet Fiona. That welcoming smile was replaced with a shocked gasp, and she had to reach out to hold on to the back of a chair nearby, she was so startled. For surely that was Jonathan Grenville coming down the drawing room toward them!

Elinor whirled back so suddenly, her taffeta skirts whistled. It was not possible! How could *Jonathan* be entering the room, when *Jonathan* was standing there by the fire? She looked over her shoulder for a moment to make sure her eyes were not deceiving her. But no. The gentleman making a deep bow to Sir Robert now was Jonathan's exact counterpart. As tall and broad-shouldered, as narrow-waisted and with the same muscular legs, he also had the same features and fine gray eyes. Even his dark brown hair sprang from his brow in identical waves. Only his jawline seemed different, harder set than the one she was used to seeing at Mordyn. But perhaps that was only because he sported such a black sneer? she mused.

"I do beg yer pardon fer my tardiness, sir," the stranger said in a deep, careless drawl. "I confess ter a certain clumsiness when I am forced ter do without the services o' my man."

As he spoke, the hair rose on the back of Elinor's neck, and she could feel her face paling. Why, even though his words were coarser, the timbre of his voice was almost the same! Indeed, now he stood closer to Jonathan, she could see their resemblance was uncanny. The only difference was that Jonathan wore blue this evening, looking impeccable with not a hair out of place, while the stranger was dressed carelessly in gray.

Sir Robert noticed her distress, and he came to her, bending toward her in concern to put a hand under her elbow. "You must sit down, my dear Elinor," he said. "I can see this has been a shock to you. This is, er, my other son, Jason Grenville. He is, as I am sure you have fathomed, Jonathan's twin brother."

Elinor sank into the chair he helped her to, not even bothering to try and curtsy.

"Miss Elinor Fielding, Jason. Our guest from London," Sir Robert said, his face suddenly as dark as his newly returned son's.

Jason Grenville gave her a careless bow. "But is it possible no one told the girl o' me at all?" he asked, looking grimmer still, if that were possible.

"It wasn't thought at all necessary," Jonathan said, speaking for the first time. Elinor stole a peek at him and saw how very cold and displeased he looked, how tense, as if he held himself in readiness for some unpleasantness about to happen. "Since we never expected to see you again, why mention it?" he asked.

The stranger shrugged as he went to the drinks tray to pour himself a glass of sherry. "Unfortunate," he murmured. "How soon we are forgotten! But as I explained ter ye both this afternoon, I could not resist looking in on my old ancestral home. An' after twenty long years o' exile from it, I didn't expect ter find myself unwelcome. Surely I have paid my penance, wouldn't ye say?''

"You are not unwelcome," Sir Robert said stiffly. "I only wish—but never mind that."

He turned to Elinor then and said, "My dear, you must do the honors tonight. Fiona has declined to join us. I fear the sudden arrival of her long-gone brother has overset her, and she has retired early."

"I am sure she will soon be more easy in my company," the stranger said, his mouth twisting a little. "We used ter be great friends, little Fiona an' I, when I was ten an' she but six."

"You might find those twenty years more a chasm than you imagine," his twin remarked. "Fiona has changed. And it is more than just because she cannot speak."

"Yes, I am very interested in the persistence o' that failing," Jason Grenville remarked before he sipped his sherry. "Excellent, sir, excellent," he added, with a bow to Sir Robert. "But surely Fiona should have regained her power o' speech by now, wouldn't yer think? Ye have had her examined by physicians o' course, sir?"

As Sir Robert nodded, Elinor looked from one man to the others, trying to calm her racing pulse, the thudding of her heart, and her constricted breathing. That voice—that deep, coarse voice! Why did it perturb her so much? And why was he ignoring her, speaking to the others as if she were not even in the room? It was very rude of him, surely! But then she realized he was nowhere near as polished a gentleman as his twin. Instead, he was a rougher, much cruder version.

Whitman announced dinner in quavering tones, and Elinor was delighted when Sir Robert offered his arm to lead her in. Somehow her flesh crawled at the thought of either Jonathan or this Jason touching her. The massive table was set for four this evening, and she was dismayed to find herself seated across from the newly arrived member of the family. Sir Robert took his usual place at the head of the table; Jonathan faced him at the other end.

"You have only recently arrived in Cornwall, sir?" she asked Jason Grenville, determined to take the initiative; force him to acknowledge her.

He nodded carelessly, his glance wandering around a dining room that had no doubt been very familiar to him at one time. "As ye say. I had business 'ere. I must say, sir, I find the old place doesn't change. Still the same bad weather, the same mists and gales."

"I wonder you lingered then," Jonathan murmured as he arranged his napkin in his lap.

"Ah, as I wonder ye chose t' remain 'ere during the London Season, old boy," his twin riposted. "Somehow I was sure ye took part in those festivities every year. Indeed, I have often read o' ye in the journals. Mr. Jonathan Grenville, seen here, there, an' everywhere—now gracing a ball, now attending a race meet, now escorting Lady X ter the theater. Strange, ain't it, that this one particular spring ye decided to grace Mordyn with yer presence? Now why was that, I wonder?"

Elinor saw Jonathan's lips tighten, the angry gleam in his gray eyes, and she was glad when Sir Robert intervened.

"Where are you living at present, Jason?" he asked.

"But can it be yer not even aware I came into my Uncle Curtin's fortune a few years ago, sir? An' his estate?" the stranger asked, nodding as Whitman filled his wine glass.

"Say you so?" Sir Robert exclaimed, looking startled. "Why, I knew Lawrence Curtin to be an extremely wealthy man! How, er, how fortunate for you!"

Jason Grenville's face grew even colder, and he seemed to hesitate for a moment, as if he were choosing his words with care. "Yeah, wasn't it?" was all he said, however. "Mother's brother was a good man. And besides being an old bachelor, he were fond o' me."

He laughed harshly then. It seemed to Elinor that he was laughing at himself, or perhaps at this Mr. Curtin's folly in holding such an unworthy specimen in esteem. Or was he laughing because he had tricked his uncle into thinking him reputable enough to inherit a fortune?

"Where is your estate, sir?" Elinor asked, since the others did not appear willing to comment.

"In Northumberland. Ye know that county?"

"Not at all. I am London born and bred," she replied, sitting back so the footman could serve her soup.

"Do yer like Cornwall? It must seem lonely to ye."

"It was a little strange at first, but I soon became accustomed," Elinor told him as she picked up her spoon. She managed a polite smile as she went on, "I never expected to like it so well. Indeed, I have surprised myself."

Good girl, Elinor! she told herself as she ladled a spoonful of soup. No crude copy of Jonathan Grenville was going to be allowed to disturb her, not if she had anything to say about it!

"I've been in the neighborhood but a short time, but that's been long enough fer me ter see the troubles that have come ter the tinners," Jason Grenville said, turning his attention to his father, his brother.

"Yes, most unfortunate," Sir Robert said absently, as if his mind was far away, on another, more important matter.

"I understand all the mines is closing?" his son persisted.

"As you say. The price of tin is such—and then, too, tin has recently been discovered in Malaysia, or so I have been informed. There's nothing left for the miners here."

"Pr'haps the new discovery might give them employment," Jason Grenville suggested. "Several finds of kaolin, the porcelain clay, have been discovered in Cornwall. Makes me wonder if there be any on Mordyn land."

Sir Robert looked a little more interested. "I have no idea. But it would take a great deal of money to find it. A very great deal. I am not sure the game is worth the candle, and I'm tired of mining."

"And there are so many other ways to make money, isn't that so, Father?" Jonathan drawled, draining his glass of wine.

"Elinor, you must pardon us for discussing such boring matters while you are with us," Sir Robert said, ignoring his heir's last remark to turn and smile at her. "Pray tell me, how did you spend this stormy day?"

Elinor spoke briefly of her reading, her drawings. She did not mention her walk along the cliffs, nor the uneasy tea party she had shared with Fiona and Rebecca Ward.

"I see yer wearing mourning, miss. My condolences," Jason Grenville remarked as the footman served him some creamed cod. "A close member o' yer family? A fiancé, pr'haps?"

"My mother, sir," Elinor said, holding his dark gaze for a moment. "I—I have never been promised."

His dark brows arched in astonishment. "Now, whoever would o' imagined England's young men could be such laggards?" he drawled. Elinor flushed at the sarcasm in his voice.

"Jonathan, tell me more o' Mordyn, if ye please," he went on. "How is Aunt Gwyneth, by the way? She ever marry?"

Jonathan shook his head. Elinor noticed he was eating very little, although he had had his wine glass refilled several times.

"No, Gwyneth never married. She is still living in the old Macklin cottage. Do you remember it?" Sir Robert volunteered. At Jason Grenville's nod, he went on, "Gwyneth has become some sort of healer to the villagers. She mucks about with herbs and potions, mutters incantations over them, for all I know. I wonder she has not been taken up for a witch! We never see her anymore."

"Pity, that," Jason Grenville remarked. "I'll make it a point to call on 'er. Always liked Aunt Gwyneth, I did."

"Yes, you were quite a pet of hers, were you not, bro?" Jonathan sneered.

Before his twin could reply, Sir Robert changed the subject. Elinor could only be glad.

When dinner had concluded and she rose to leave the men to their port, she excused herself from waiting for them in the drawing room, saying she was feeling tired.

"I'm not surprised, ma'am," Jason Grenville remarked. "Ye looked quite done up when ye returned ter the castle this afternoon after yer walk. Ye called me Jonathan, but yes, that was me wot was in the hall. Yer bound ter make that mistake many more times. We have always been as like as two peas in a pod."

Elinor looked from one young man to the other. The stranger had risen well after the other two men when she had excused herself, almost as an afterthought, and he had loosened his cravat, run his hand so carelessly through his hair that several dark locks fell in disarray on his broad forehead. Jonathan Grenville, in spite of the wine he had consumed, was as neat and elegant as ever.

"Oh, I doubt that, sir," she said pleasantly. "There is still a certain difference between you, not so subtle as telling."

Jonathan began to laugh, and he himself came to escort Elinor to the door, pressing her hand as he bade her good night. Elinor could see how pleased he was at her response, for the black humor he had sported all through dinner had disappeared.

Once in her room, Elinor did not ring for Betsy at once. Instead, she built up the fire and sat down in the chair beside it to think. Who was this twin that no one had ever thought to mention to her? And why was he here? Why now? He had been gone and forgotten for twenty long years. Why would he suddenly make an appearance? He had never tried to communicate with his family, or see them before.

And why did Sir Robert look so disturbed? Why, in fact, had Fiona been so distraught that she had excused herself from eating dinner with them? And, most importantly, why had Jonathan been so taut, like an overtightened violin string about to snap?

It was obvious to the meanest observer that there was no love lost between these two twins. But wasn't that highly unusual in itself? She had imagined twins always compatible, closer to each other than any other siblings. When she had been a lonely little girl on Compton Street, she had even pretended she had a twin named Margaret. She had talked to Margaret by the hour, played with her, confided everything to her. But these two twins were enemies. As coldly courteous as they were, they were enemies for all that. The hardly veiled sarcasm, the little digs exchanged, all pointed to something stronger than mere rivalry or dislike.

Elinor rose then to walk over to the long windows to pull back the draperies. The storm continued to rage and the rain to beat against the panes. She could see nothing out there but blackness, the reflection of fire and candlelight behind her, her own troubled face in the glass.

Why had Jason Grenville been sent away from his family and his home when only a young boy of ten? she wondered. What could he have done to merit such cruel exile from everything dear and familiar? It had to have been something dire, for no father would decree such banishment without very good reason. Sir Robert was a kind man. His concern for Jonathan, his love for Fiona shone on his face. But twenty years ago, he had sent his only other son away to be raised by his wife's relatives in Northumberland. And he had never inquired for him, never communicated with him from that day to this. *Why?*

Elinor dropped the drapery then, to go back to the fire. It burned brightly, looking a lot more cheerful than her thoughts.

Was Jason Grenville as dangerous as he looked? she wondered as she took her seat again. But no, that could not be! Sir Robert would not have allowed him to remain at Mordyn for even a visit if that had been the case. Would he?

But Jason Grenville's sudden appearance here was shrouded in mystery. Somehow she sensed it was a dark, ugly mystery. And he looked dangerous—so cold and black! She knew she would have no trouble at all distinguishing between the twins, even if they didn't speak.

She wondered if Gwyneth had left the castle after this Jason had been sent away. In that case, she would know the reason why, for Jonathan had taunted his twin about being his aunt's favorite. Elinor decided she would go and ask her about it tomorrow.

She stretched and yawned then. The afternoon's exercise

and the heat of the fire were making her sleepy. As she went to ring for Betsy so she could have an early bedtime, she suddenly remembered the painting of the Cavalier.

Sir Miles *Jason* DeFountaine Grenville. Had this newly-come twin been named for him? And had he become as great an adventurer, as uncaring a rake, and as enthusiastic a lover as that ancestor of an earlier day? Could he be, in fact, a reincarnation of that most dangerous Grenville?

Elinor shook her head and smiled a little. She was air-dreaming, writing fairy tales. For surely, if Jason Grenville's cool indifference to her this evening had been any indication, at least the title lover could never have been applied to him. Far from it!

She woke hours later to feel her Cavalier's hands drawing her up into his arms, and she smiled a little, still half asleep. His kiss was gentle, so gentle she wondered if she were dreaming it.

"How cruel of me to wake you!" he whispered in her ear. Elinor sighed as her arms went around him to hold him close, and she buried her face in his shirt.

"Mmmm," she murmured, and he chuckled softly.

"I will not stay tonight, love," he told her, smoothing back her hair with careful fingers. "I only came to tell you I will not be able to see you for a while. There are some things I must do—important things, believe me, or they would never have been able to coax me from your side. Take care. Remember how important you are to me. Will you do that until I return?"

"Mmmm," she said, inhaling the dear scent of his skin and cuddling closer.

She heard his chuckle, rumbling deep in his chest as he lowered her to her pillows and arranged the covers around her.

"Sleep, love," he whispered. "But I do not have to tell you that, do I? You are asleep already."

There was no sound in the room but Elinor's deep breathing, and he rose and turned away.

10

THE RAIN CONTINUED the next day, although the sky did appear to be lightening somewhat in the southwest. The winds continued to shriek with as much fury as ever, though, and Elinor decided that her visit to Gwyneth Grenville must be put off for another day.

She was feeling lost and unsettled again, and she knew her mood resulted from her Cavalier's visit late last night. He had said she would not see him again for many days, and she was missing him already. The morning she spent alone, reading, seemed endless to her.

When the family assembled for luncheon, she noticed Jason Grenville was not among their number. Sir Robert told them all that he had gone out riding; how he had laughed at any suggestion that it would be better to remain by the fireside in such inclement weather.

That afternoon, as Elinor watched the flowers in The Lady's Garden drooping under the assault of the wind and rain, she was sure Sir Robert was right. Fiona crept into her sitting room a little while later to take a seat as close to Elinor as she could get. She held a book in her hands, but Elinor noticed she turned very few pages. Instead, she stared out at the garden, her eyes far away. It was one of the times Elinor wished desperately that Fiona could speak, for if she had been able to, she could have explained so very much that was hidden now.

Everyone was there in the gold salon for tea. Even Jason Grenville was there, his dark hair still damp from its soaking, although Elinor saw he had changed to dry clothes. Today he wore a rather elderly jacket, frayed at the cuffs, and his cravat was a mere travesty of a gentleman's neckwear. But he greeted Fiona with a warm smile, a smile Elinor saw quite changed his face. Why, he was an appealing man when he bothered to be, she thought as she took her seat. Across the tea tray, his elegantly dressed twin watched him, his identically handsome face emotionless.

By the time tea was almost over, Fiona had relaxed somewhat in Jason's presence. She even smiled shyly at him when he relayed a message to her from one of the villagers, and she was completely absorbed when he described his home in the north of England.

Elinor was amused to see Rebecca Ward remained stiff and silent, only darting little glances to Sir Robert every now and then, as if seeking some clue as to how she was to treat this new crude visitor to Mordyn. Elinor thought Sir Robert appeared strained today. His face had new lines on it, and his eyes looked tired, as if he had not had enough sleep. But he was as calm and contained as ever, although Elinor noted he treated his recently returned son with only the cool politeness he would have given any casual visitor. She wondered if Jason Grenville minded such treatment—what he thought of it? He did not appear to even notice it, further proof that he was not a sensitive man, alive to subtle nuances.

Once again he barely seemed aware that Elinor was in the room, for he never addressed a single remark to her. Somehow, Elinor found herself resenting this, until she took herself firmly in hand. Why, she told herself, she was sure any special recognition from Mr. Jason Grenville would be most unwelcome to her!

Suddenly, in a lull in the conversation, everyone heard a tiny "meow?" coming from the direction of the door. Whitman had left that door ajar, and now Mischief bounded in to run down the room straight into Fiona's arms.

"So this is your kitten, is it, my dear?" Sir Robert asked, smiling a little at the picture his daughter made with the kitten held close to her cheek. "He is Satanish, is he not? And I thought black cats were supposed to be bad luck.''

''Oh, Fiona,'' Miss Ward remonstrated. ''That animal should not be here! You know you promised your father that you would not let it roam the castle unattended. Let me have the footman take it away!''

Fiona tilted her chin defiantly, storm signals flying in her cheeks, and peace was not restored until Sir Robert assured Miss Ward it did not matter this once.

Mischief began to squirm then, demanding to be put down, and when Fiona placed him on the carpet near her feet, he did not hesitate. No doubt, Elinor thought later, he had been making his plans from the beginning. Freed, he jumped quickly up on the low table, heading straight for the platter there. In his eagerness to acquire one of the fish sandwiches, he took a swipe at the platter with one clumsy paw, and scattered its contents on both the table and the carpet. One particularly sticky sandwich landed in Jonathan's lap.

''My dear heavens, just see what that naughty thing has done!'' Miss Ward exclaimed. ''I knew there would be trouble with a cat in the castle, I just knew it! And the carpet and Mr. Jonathan's unmentionables will be quite ruined! Such disarray! Fiona, you must remove that horrid animal this minute!''

But Fiona was not to have the chance. Instead, Jonathan, having disposed of the sandwich on his lap, picked the kitten up from the table by the scruff of its neck and shook it before he put his other hand under it to keep it captive. Elinor saw he was coldly furious.

Mischief was not about to take such treatment calmly. Balked of his fishy prize, he hissed in fury. And as Jonathan began to hand him to the hovering footman, he unsheathed his tiny, sharp claws and scratched his captor on the back of the hand.

Cursing, Jonathan threw the kitten to the floor, and Fiona scrambled after him to save him.

''That damned wildcat!'' Jonathon swore, his gray eyes icy. ''Why, look—he's drawn blood!''

Jason Grenville strolled over from the mantel where

he had been leaning. " 'Tis nothing but a scratch, twin. Where's yer manliness?"

Jason went then to where Fiona still crouched on the carpet, clutching her kitten and looking stricken. "Give him ter me, Fiona, luv," he said calmly. "I'll see he comes ter no harm, me word on it."

But Fiona would not give up her kitten. Elinor saw her face pale, saw the panic in her eyes as she shook her head vehemently and cringed away from Jason's outstretched hand.

Brows raised, he shrugged before he retreated to the fireplace again.

"Fiona, get that animal from my sight!" Jonathan snarled, busy wrapping a snowy napkin around his injured hand. "For if you don't, I will, and nowhere near as gently. He is not fit for a gentleman's house!"

"But what can you expect from a stable kitten?" Sir Robert murmured. "I imagine it will be quite a while before Mischief learns his manners. There, Fiona, do stop crying," he said, coming to pat her on the shoulder. "But take Mischief to your room now, and make sure he does not escape it again. Jonathan's right, you know. A kitten is not fit company at teatime."

Fiona allowed her father to help her up, and she hurried away without looking at anyone in the room. Miss Ward sniffed as the footman picked up the scattered sandwiches and removed the tray, but when she opened her mouth to complain again, Jason Grenville forestalled her.

"Where did Fiona get the kitten?" he asked idly.

"I brought it to her," Elinor told him, her eyes lowered as she stirred her tea. "She loved all the stable ones so, that when the rest had to be put to cliff, I thought it might ease her loss to keep Mischief. This is the first time he has misbehaved in company."

"I've no doubt it will not be the last," Jason drawled. "Unless something happens to 'im to prevent it, and I've never believed that old tale that cats have nine lives, have ye?"

Elinor glanced up to see he was not looking at her.

Instead, he was studying Jonathan's still angry face, as if coolly assessing his fury.

"I saw Timothy Coryton on the moors today, sir," he said next, changing the subject to everyone's relief.

"I wonder you lived to tell the tale," Sir Robert said stiffly. "What were you doing up there? And why was Coryton there?"

"I went ter visit some o' my old haunts," Jason said easily. "As fer Timmy, I didn't ask. We only traded a few words."

"Beware the man, Jason," Sir Robert warned. "He's no love for the Grenvilles, you know. He took my closing Wheal Beatrice as a personal offense. There have been threats. . . ."

"But we was great friends as boys, an' he did not appear ter bear me any dislike," Jason said. "But pr'haps—an' rightly so, too—he does not consider me a Cornish Grenville anymore?"

There was an uneasy silence for a few moments then, until Elinor thought to ask Miss Ward about some redecorating she was supervising.

Fiona was very subdued at dinner later. She barely touched her food, and all her father's blandishments could not cheer her. Not even his suggestion that she might order some new gowns styled more like Elinor's could make her smile. Elinor could tell she was still worrying about her kitten. But though Jonathan did not even wear a bandage on his scratch, and made light of his injury, Fiona did not appear to be reassured.

The next day a watery sun made an appearance. Elinor had set out after luncheon to visit Gwyneth Grenville, but the damp wind and still threatening clouds forced her to settle for the Home Farm as her destination that day. After stroking Jenny and giving her a lump of sugar, she started back to the castle again. McCarthy had told her tomorrow was sure to be fine. She would visit Gwyneth then.

She met Jonathan coming down the path just as she reached the woods, and he asked if he might speak to her privately on a matter of some importance. He looked so serious that Elinor was quick to agree. He led her along a path through the woods that she had never followed before. The sound of the breakers grew louder and louder as they climbed.

Jonathan did not speak as they walked along. Stealing a sideways glance at him, Elinor could see he looked very stern and uncomfortable. Every so often a little muscle moved in his lean cheek, and his gray eyes were bleak. Elinor wondered at it. This was a Jonathan she had never seen before.

They came out of the woods near the crumbling steps to the beach on the cliff walk. Elinor wondered if Jonathan would remember the day he had saved her life here—speak of it, perhaps—but he made no move to do so.

Instead, he indicated the wall that guarded the walk, and Elinor took a seat there. Mystified, she watched him walk away from her, pause, and then turn back, squaring his shoulders as if he had made some silent resolution.

"I wish I did not have to tell you what I am about to, Elinor. I have never told anyone before," he said, pacing up and down before her. He stopped then, and came to put one booted foot on the wall beside her, leaning his arms on his knee so he could look down into her face. "Will you keep what I tell you in confidence?" he asked, in a strained, tortured voice. "Indeed, I must have your promise that you will never reveal to anyone that it was I who told you the tale."

"Of course I promise," Elinor vowed, still mystified.

"Believe that I only tell you now because I know how confused you must be at Jason's sudden appearance here, his absence from the family scene for twenty years. It must seem . . . odd to you."

He waited until she nodded before he went on, "And I tell you for your own protection as well. I would have you on your guard now."

"On my guard?" Elinor echoed faintly. "Whatever do you mean?"

Jonathan removed his hat then, to run his hand

through his dark hair. The weak sun lit highlights in its waves.

"Twenty years ago, when Jason and I were ten and Fiona only six, there was an accident here at the cliff steps," he began, staring past her out to sea. Elinor saw the little muscle in his cheek move convulsively, noted the pain in his eyes, and she pitied him.

"We had an older brother then, one you have never heard of before. We never speak of him anymore. He was named Robert, after my father. Rob was twelve at the time, but he was not as strong as Jason and myself, for he had always been a sickly child, thin and weak. He was my father's heir, of course, and his favorite. Oh, you must not think the rest of us resented it—at least Fiona and I did not. It seemed perfectly natural to us that Father would prefer him, take the greatest care of him. Rob needed it the most."

He paused again, and Elinor saw how the hand on his knee had closed in a tight fist.

"I will never forget the day of the accident to the end of my life," Jonathan said more softly. "It was the first day in over a week that the sun had shone, one of those perfect Cornish summer days that everyone extols here. We children had gone out to play on the beach, 'Becca Ward in charge, but she had forgotten her parasol, or some such thing, and she ran back to the castle to get it, after begging us to be careful going down the steps. Fiona was ordered to wait for her to return, not to attempt those steps on her own. We all thought 'Becca much too fussy and cautious, although Fiona, being a good little girl, settled down on the grass nearby to wait for her.

"Rob started down first. Immediately, Jason began to argue with me about who would go next, and we began to wrestle here at clifftop. Suddenly, we stumbled against Rob, who cried out in alarm. I drew back immediately, but Jason . . ."

Jonathan turned his face away then and swallowed. Elinor could see the perspiration beading his forehead, the lost look in his gray eyes, and she held her breath.

"I fear there is no easy way to say this," he said at

last in a strangled voice. "Rob had been leaning against the railing, watching our struggle, and so he could not save himself. He was bent over that railing, and he lost his balance and fell to the sand far below. The sound of his scream as he did so never leaves my memory, night or day."

"Oh, Jonathan, how perfectly terrible!" Elinor whispered. "Now I know why you were so upset the day you saved me from the exact same fate—why you didn't want me to tell anyone of it, remind them."

He turned back to her then, his eyes narrowed. His mouth had thinned, and Elinor suddenly had a glimpse of what he would look like when he was very old.

"Remember?" she prompted gently. "The day I went out to walk the beach, and climbed those steps not knowing how dangerous they were?"

To Elinor it seemed a long time before he said, "Of course. I had forgotten that day for a moment. Yes, you frightened me then, reminding me of the earlier tragedy."

Jonathan stared out to sea again, and for some minutes, neither spoke. Elinor saw the grim set of his mouth, his stiff jaw, and she wished there was some way she could comfort him.

"Excuse me, Elinor," he said after he had composed himself. "I know I must finish my story, even though I do not want to. The day Rob fell to his death I looked around, but Fiona had fled back to the castle. I was sick then, but Jason—well, Jason just stared at me, as if daring me to tell anyone what he had done.

"You see, I had seen him push Rob, and I know he did it deliberately, hoping to get him out of the way. Jason always had to be first in everything. He resented not being the heir, my father's favorite.

"I was too frightened to say anything then, but later, after the funeral was over and Rob buried—after my father ceased to mourn so deeply—I went and told him. He believed me. Jason had always had a cruel streak, and he was a wild, unmanageable boy. Sometimes, at night, he would dress up as the ghost of a sailor, carrying oreweed, to scare the youngest maids, and once he tied a piece of twine across the top of the stairs when he knew 'Becca would be coming down them shortly. She had a bad fall; broke her leg and some ribs and was laid up for weeks. And Jason refused to confess to it, and only laughed, although my father gave him a hard caning.

"I admit I was afraid of my twin then, for after disposing of Rob, he might well have decided to get rid of me, too. Oh, it was not that I couldn't best him in a fair fight, but I knew he wouldn't give me the chance of that. He was far too devious. He would arrange another 'accident.'

"And you see, having been born a few minutes before him, I was next in line to inherit Mordyn, and the title. If there is one thing in the world Jason loves and covets, it is Mordyn."

Jonathan sighed and took out a handkerchief to wipe his brow. "But even so, I've always been sorry for Jason," he said more quietly. "I don't think he can help this vicious streak he has, poor fellow. I protected him for a long time, hiding the small animals he tortured, burying them when they died. But that time I didn't protect him. I couldn't anymore. I—I had loved Rob, you see, and what Jason had done was—was evil."

Elinor swallowed and nodded, for she could not speak.

"My father felt he had no choice but to send Jason away. He did not tell my Uncle Lawrence everything. Instead, he claimed Jason's banishment was because he and I could not live in harmony together. He told him Rob's death had been a tragic accident. I knew it had not been, but I have held my tongue to this day, lest shame come to our house.

"Jason didn't even bother to deny the charge when my father taxed him with it. He just stood there, so white and strained looking. My father thought that indicated his guilt, but I knew it was because he was furious that his first step in gaining the baronetcy had been discovered.

"And now, after twenty long years, he has come

back to Mordyn. My father says we must hope he has outgrown this urge he had to hurt others. I am not so sanguine. I admit I am worried, and not just for myself. After all, we don't know what he has been up to all these years; what other deaths he might have caused. Why, even perhaps my uncle's, to gain his fortune."

He turned to her then and put his hands on her shoulders. "Elinor, you must be careful! Never be alone with Jason if you can avoid it. There must be no more 'accidents.'

"But why would he hurt me?" Elinor whispered, stunned by what he had told her. "I'm a stranger—only a guest here."

"Maybe he won't," he agreed, although he did not look like he believed what he said. "I have no idea how his mind works anymore. When we were boys together, I could sometimes sense when he was up to no good, but that closeness is gone. But even though you are only a guest at Mordyn, he might resent your being here where he longs to be and can never be again. You may be sure I shall be on my guard as well. For if anything happens to me, well, Mordyn would come to Jason. I hate to think that such a warped, evil man would be lord here."

Elinor shivered, and she reached up to clasp his hands where they rested on her shoulders. "Be *very* careful," she whispered.

Jonathan smiled down at her and took hold of her hands so he might draw her to her feet before he slipped his arms around her and bent down to kiss the tip of her nose. "There is another reason you must be careful as well, my dear," he told her. "Jason may well sense my interest in you, and if he does, he will do everything in his power to take you away from me. Not because he wants you—oh, no! But as a way to repay me for telling my father that he pushed Rob, and to thwart me—to be first with you, as he must be first in everything. I'm sure he could be a charming, persuasive man if he put his mind to it. Avoid him as much as you can."

As Elinor nodded, her eyes troubled, Jonathan kissed her and held her close for a moment. His gentle embrace was so different from his teasing, provocative lovemaking in the library that she was stunned, and did not even think of protesting.

Over her head, he said in a musing voice, "If only things were different . . ."

Confused, she drew back, but when she would have questioned him, he let her go to turn and face the ocean again. "It is such a shame that I am a gentleman. If I were not, this problem might be resolved now. Yes, it is—a shame."

He left her abruptly then, and only moments later was lost among the trees.

Elinor lingered by the cliff wall, thinking over everything he had told her. She put his last, incomprehensible remark from her mind. for she was remembering the story he had just told her. What a ghastly thing for him to have had to bear! she thought. No wonder he had not appeared glad to see his twin again; no wonder Sir Robert had looked so strained since Jason Grenville's arrival. Elinor stared down at the beach far below her. In her mind's eye she could see the thin, broken body of Rob Grenville, who had lost his life being "put to cliff" by his youngest brother. Shuddering, she hurried away.

When she let herself into The Lady's Garden a short time later, Elinor saw Fiona on her knees by the fountain. She was digging a deep hole there, and as Elinor hurried toward her, she saw why. Laying on the grass next to her was a small wooden box lined in soft flannel, and in that box was Fiona's kitten, dead.

"Oh, my dear Fiona!" she exclaimed, dropping to her knees to put an arm around her. She saw the tears streaming down Fiona's face, the way her face was twisted with grief.

"I am so very sorry," Elinor whispered, hugging her a little. "But what could have happened? How did Mischief come to die?"

Fiona dropped the trowel she was using, to wipe her

eyes on the back of her arm. She refused to look at Elinor and only shook her head sadly.

Elinor watched her pick up the box to run gentle fingers over the soft black fur of her kitten for the last time. Mischief looked so very tiny now. Then Fiona put the lid on tightly, and lowered the box into the hole she had dug. Elinor could feel her shaking as she did so, and her arm tightened in support.

The little grave was soon covered with dirt, the sod replaced, and unless one looked very hard, it was difficult even to see where the grave was.

Fiona put both hands over her face for a moment, her head bent. Then she shook off Elinor's comforting arm and rose to her feet. Ignoring her friend's outstretched hand, the loving concern in her eyes, she hurried inside.

Elinor rose more slowly to her feet. How had the kitten died? she wondered. It had been frisky enough yesterday! She decided she would have to speak to Sir Robert about it. Something was wrong here, and she was not entirely sure Mischief had died a natural death. And there was that horrible story Jonathan had just told her. She remembered he had mentioned how much delight Jason had taken as a boy, torturing small animals.

And there were Mr. Jason's Grenville's words yesterday as well. He had said in his careless drawl that he didn't believe cats had nine lives. And there had been Fiona's frightened reaction when he had tried to take Mischief from her. Elinor remembered now how pale she had been, how she had cringed away from his outstretched hand. Was it possible that he had killed Mischief? Even found it amusing to do so?

11

WHEN ELINOR ASKED the butler for Sir Robert, Whitman told her he had gone to visit Mr. Brownell that afternoon and he had no idea when he would return. Frustrated, Elinor sought out Miss Ward instead. She found her in one of the smaller salons, harrying Mrs. Greene about a pair of brass candlesticks she claimed the maids had neglected to polish. Elinor noted Mrs. Greene neither denied the charge nor defended the maids. Instead, she only stood stoically, looking into some distance over Miss Ward's head.

More cheerful now she had delivered her lecture, Rebecca Ward turned to see Elinor waiting for her. The smile she was wearing faded at once.

"If I might speak to you a moment, ma'am?" Elinor inquired. "Privately?"

Mrs. Greene was quick to curtsy and leave the room. She even gave Elinor a wintry little smile, as if to thank her for her deliverance.

"Yes? There was something you had to say to me, Miss Fielding?" Rebecca Ward asked. "I cannot imagine what that might be."

Elinor ignored the stiffness in her high, breathless voice. "I am worried about Fiona," she said. Miss Ward made no move to take a seat, nor did she indicate Elinor do so. Instead, the two faced each other standing, a green and gold brocade loveseat dividing them.

"Fiona?" Miss Ward echoed, sounding outraged. "Fiona is *my* charge, as I have told you many and many a time before, Miss Fielding. If she is upset, *I* shall take care of her. *You* have no place there."

"You don't understand," Elinor said as evenly as she could. She wanted to rage at the woman, shake her for this stupid defense of her authority, her senseless jealousy. "I have just returned to the castle. I found Fiona in The Lady's Garden, burying her kitten. She was—she still is!—distraught."

Watching her carefully, Elinor saw Miss Ward's face brighten just the tiniest amount.

"It is dead, you say?" she asked, leaning forward a little. "Well, and although I should not say so, good riddance! That animal had no place in a noble house. And if Fiona is upset he died, *you* must take the blame for it, my girl! Oh, yes! For it was *you* who brought it here in the first place. *You* who encouraged Fiona to give it house room, in spite of my protests. It is all *your* fault!"

Elinor counted slowly to ten. "Yes, it is true I brought her the kitten. But right now I am only concerned for Fiona. She loved Mischief so. And I do have to wonder how it died. Of course she cannot tell me. I thought to ask you if you had any ideas about that, but I see you have only just learned of his demise now."

"It probably ate something it shouldn't have, greedy little guts!" Miss Ward said carelessly. "Kittens often get into things.

"Excuse me, Miss Fielding. I must go to Fiona, try to comfort her. None of this would have been at all necessary if you had not taken it on yourself to—pushing in where you were not—well! I shall say no more!"

Miss Ward turned and rustled away, her head held high.

Elinor stared after her. She was sorry now she had told the woman about Mischief. Quite the opposite of comforting her, she would probably make Fiona only more miserable.

As she followed slowly in her wake, Elinor wished again that Sir Robert was home. Then she remembered Gwyneth Grenville, and she decided she had to see her today after all. Never mind that it was threatening to rain again and it was already late afternoon.

She donned her cloak and told Whitman she would not be joining the family for tea, then she left the castle.

Elinor wondered if she would meet Jonathan coming back from the stables, but she did not see him as she hurried by the Home Farm and entered the little woods.

She had crossed the stream near the end of them when she saw a man coming toward her. For a moment, she thought it was Jonathan, until she remembered that he never visited his aunt. Her heart began to pound.

Face to face with Jason Grenville, she bowed slightly and tried to hurry by.

"Yer in a tearing rush this afternoon, are ye not, Miss Fielding?" he asked. "Now what's ter do?"

"There is something I must speak to Miss Grenville about," Elinor managed to get out over the thudding of her heart. "I must not tarry!"

"Well, ye'll find her home, fer I jest left her," he said. "But if I'm not mistaken, it's about ter rain again. Pr'haps ye would allow me ter escort ye back ter the castle instead? Ye can always call on the lady tomorrow."

He held out his arm then, although the black look on his face contradicted his polite concern. Elinor backed away from him, her eyes wide. It was dark in the woods, and they were completely alone. Echoing in her mind were Jonathan's warnings about his twin. And here, all unwittingly, she had managed to put herself in a position where she was at his mercy. Why, even if she screamed for help, no one would hear her!

He bent closer to her then, his face grim. "What is it? Why do ye look at me that way?" he asked in an urgent voice. "An' why are ye frightened?"

Elinor shook her head and tried to smile. It was a very poor effort. "I cannot linger. Oh, please let me go, please!"

He stepped back. His bow was sardonic. "Well, o' course. I would not keep ye against yer will, Miss Fielding. I only thought ter help ye, if I could."

"Thank you. There is nothing you can do," Elinor said over her shoulder as she hurried away. She did not dare look back, although she was sure he remained standing there, staring after her, with that dark frown still on his face. She began to run a little, and she did not feel safe until she was standing on Gwyneth Grenville's doorstep, panting, and with a stitch in her side.

"Gracious, Elinor!" Miss Grenville exclaimed as she opened the door. "You look as if all the hounds of hell have been after you. What's the matter?"

"I—it is nothing. I hurried too fast . . ." Elinor managed to say as she stepped inside.

Miss Grenville refused to let her talk until her breathing slowed. Instead, she made tea for them both, and set out a plate of scones and some honey. As was her custom, she worked silently, and Elinor took a seat at the table and tried to arrange her thoughts.

Staring at Miss Grenville's broad back as she worked at the dresser, Elinor was reminded that she had promised Jonathan not to tell anyone she knew about his elder brother's death. Instead, she must question Gwyneth obliquely about Jason Grenville, and tell her about the death of Fiona's kitten in the hopes she would reveal something that might be helpful.

As her hostess took her seat at last, and poured out the tea, Elinor said, "I just saw Mr. Jason Grenville coming through the woods. He had been to call on you, ma'am?"

"As you say. It was such a delightful surprise seeing Jason after all these years. We were close when he was a child."

"Things have not been going well at Mordyn since his return," Elinor told her. "Sir Robert seems concerned by it, and Jonathan is upset as well. And Fiona—well, Fiona has changed too, become almost fearful."

"Indeed?" Miss Grenville asked. She was looking straight at Elinor as she spoke. Elinor could discern no shadows in her eyes, no subtle changes of expression.

"And today,—just a little while ago, in fact,—I

discovered Fiona burying her kitten in The Lady's Garden," she said. "The kitten was fine yesterday, although it made a shambles of our teatime. It had escaped Fiona's room, you see, and come in search of her. But Mischief was certainly lively then, jumping up on the table and upsetting a platter of sandwiches. You can imagine Miss Ward's chagrin! And then it scratched Jonathan when he picked it up."

"Did it really?" Gwyneth remarked. "How very unfortunate."

"But why should Mischief be dead today?" Elinor persisted. "He was not ailing."

"It is impossible to say," her hostess said, taking a scone. "And of course, Fiona cannot tell us. But kittens often succumb to mysterious diseases, you know. I am sure it was a natural death, Elinor, if that is what you are worried about."

She spread honey on her scone before she added, "You are not inventing things in your mind, are you, my dear? Imagining dire happenings, all associated with my nephew Jason's return?"

Elinor flushed a little. "It is only that it does seem strange to me," she said in defense. "He is such a dark, disagreeable man! And Mischief was so lively until he arrived on the scene."

"A mere coincidence. And you did say it had been Jonathan who had been scratched, not Jason, did you not? But come! You're not eating a thing! Do have a scone. Mrs. Andrews brought them to me this afternoon, and she is an excellent cook."

Elinor took a scone, and Gwyneth continued to chat of the villagers, the weather, the book they were both working on.

But Elinor did not forget the kitten's death, nor the things Jonathan had told her. She wished with all her heart that he had not extracted her promise, for she badly wanted to be open with Gwyneth, talk the whole thing over with her. She was so comfortable, so sensible. As she ate the excellent scone, Elinor wondered, however, that Gwyneth could be fond of Jason, monster that he was. But perhaps she did not know he had killed his brother? After all, she had not been living in the castle then. Or had she?

"May I ask you something of a personal nature, ma'am?" Elinor asked a little diffidently.

"Of course you may ask, but whether I will choose to answer is another matter," her hostess informed her, smiling as she did so, to take the sting from her words.

"Well, I was just wondering why you left the castle all those years ago. And was it before or after Jason Grenville was sent away to his mother's relatives?"

Miss Grenville refilled their cups before she answered. "It was before," she said at last. "Robert and I did not get on together; we hadn't in years. Robert has always tended to hem his womenfolk in, under the guise of protecting them. I found that frustrating. And I was interested in herbs, and above all, I wanted to be my own woman. It has been so wonderful living here alone, answering to no one but myself! You have no idea how delicious freedom can be! And, of course, Robert has never approved of my profession. 'Witchery,' he calls it. My removing from the castle was for those reasons. Not that I approved of Jason's being sent away. I thought my brother's handling of the situation a disaster. But all my protests didn't do any good. Robert doesn't listen to women's opinions. He considers our entire sex deficient in understanding."

She sighed then and stirred her tea. "It is a shame, really. He is such an intelligent man otherwise."

"Do you think this Mr. Grenville will stay here long?" Elinor asked, trying to bring the conversation back to her primary concern.

"I don't believe so. He is a man now, and involved with his own estate and the life he has forged for himself in the north. I sense, from what he told me this afternoon, that this visit was in the nature of a pilgrimage—a way of finally saying good-bye to his boyhood and his home, putting it all behind him at last.

"By the way, Elinor, I've been meaning to ask you if you have ever seen any of Mordyn's ghosts again?"

Elinor nodded, trying not to look self-conscious as

she remembered her missing, beloved "ghost." "Why yes, I have seen one of them," she said. "The Lady appeared to Fiona and me one day when we were in her garden. She was standing on the landing, looking out the window at us. I was very frightned, but Fiona took it as a matter of course. She even rose and curtsied to her! Then the ghost simply faded away. Brr! I still get shivers just remembering the occasion."

Gwyneth rose to remove the plates without commenting. When Elinor would have helped her, she waved a dismissive hand. "No, no, my dear. I know where everything goes, and I have my own way of doing things. Just you rest yourself a bit before you must start back."

Elinor nodded, and stared into the cheerful fire. It was getting late. The woods would be very dark when she reached them. She must leave soon.

Some little sound made her turn her head, to see Gwyneth standing in front of the cupboard where she kept her herbal concoctions. She was holding a thin, dark bottle up to the light and she was frowning.

"There is something wrong?" Elinor asked, startled by the grim expression on Gwyneth's generally genial face.

"What? Oh, no! It was just that I was sure I had more of this potion than is left in the bottle. Well, no matter. Can it be that I am getting old and forgetful?" she asked as she put the bottle back in its place and closed the cupboard door.

"You? Never!" Elinor told her as she rose to don her cloak. "You are wiser than any woman I have ever known, and you are certainly not old! You could never be, even at eighty!"

Gwyneth laughed then, and came to give her a kiss on the cheek. "Run along, flatterer," she said. "If you can manage to come tomorrow, I've a mind to start you on some new drawings. It's supposed to be a good day, and I intend to walk the moors. There are plants up there I must include in my book."

"I'll try to be here," Elinor said. "Thank you for

the tea and the scones. And thank Mrs. Andrews when you see her. They were delicious!"

The gentlemen did not linger over their after-dinner port that evening. Perhaps that was because there were only two of them, Sir Robert having sent word he would be dining at Glyn. Neither twin had had much to say during the meal. Jonathan had brooded into his wine glass; Jason had only looked black. Elinor herself had chatted on a number of innocuous subjects, trying to cheer up a sorrowing Fiona, but eventually, she had fallen silent too, and devoted herself to her excellent dinner.

So she was not best pleased when Jonathan and Jason rejoined them so quickly. Fiona had been playing the piano softly, but when they entered the drawing room, her hands faltered on the keys and she sat back, her head bowed.

"Do go on," Jason Grenville said as he came to take a seat nearby. "Ye play so well! And when I remember those endless scales, those simple one-finger airs that were all ye could manage at six, well! The artist ye've become is a miracle, like."

Elinor stared at him. He wore a little smile for his sister, a smile she saw was not mirrored on Fiona's still, white face.

Jonathan sat down on the sofa beside Elinor. Once again, he had drunk heavily with dinner. His face was flushed now, but he was in perfect control of himself. "Whatever is the matter with Fiona?" he asked Elinor. "Is she sulking about something?"

"No, she is not sulking. Her kitten died today," Elinor told him softly.

Jason Grenville appeared to have no trouble overhearing. "What's that ye say, Miss Fielding? Fiona's kitten, dead?"

Elinor looked to Fiona, to see she had turned her head away and was twisting her hands in her lap. When she looked at Jason Grenville next, she was startled to see his black frown was back.

"That is exceeding strange, wouldn't you say?"

Jonathan asked. "The animal was certainly in fighting form yesterday."

"Yes, he was," Jason agreed. "It is too bad Fiona can't tell us about it. Although I, fer one, can hardly be surprised. Small, helpless animals have so often come ter a bad end at Mordyn."

"I am astounded that you would say so, sir," Jonathan said.

Jason Grenville leaned forward, his gray eyes as icy as his twin's. "Yer know very well what I mean, sir. There were several similar incidences during m' boyhood years here. Birds, rabbits, even moles, all having strange an' painful deaths."

Fiona's hands crashed down on the piano keys then, and everyone jumped, for the loud, cacaphonous chord was startling. The next moment, Fiona had risen to her feet, to whirl away from the piano and run down the room. She moved so swiftly that no one had time to speak, much less detain her. Only seconds later, the drawing room doors slammed behind her.

Suddenly, Elinor was furious and she jumped up as well. As the two men rose to their feet, she glared at them, completely forgetting the ghastly tale Jonathan had told her that afternoon, the fact that she might be putting herself in danger.

"Now just see what you have done!" she exclaimed. "You have put an additional burden on that poor grieving girl! Never in my entire life have I seen such prime examples of selfishness and egotism! Had you no thought for your sister in her sorrow? Have you no feelings for anyone but your almighty selves? You ought to be ashamed of yourselves, you great, hulking stupids!"

Both Jason and Jonathan—all six foot one inches of handsome muscular masculinity multiplied by two—stood stunned, facing this golden-haired five-foot-two inch virago whose breast heaved, and whose fists were clenched, and whose green eyes flashed fire as she lambasted them.

Elinor marched to the door. Once there, she turned back to where the twins still stood frozen in place, like two identical Greek statues. "Bah! *Men!*" she spat. "I shall leave you to your idiotic quarrels. Since I have seldom spent an evening I have enjoyed less, I see no reason why I should prolong my suffering a moment longer. Good night!"

She closed the drawing room doors behind her on complete silence. Breathing hard, but feeling a great deal better, Elinor strode to the stairs. She did not even notice the deep bow Whitman gave her as he presented her candle, nor the awed respect of the two footmen standing at attention along the wall. But then, she had no idea how her impassioned speech had carried beyond the drawing room doors.

Elinor stopped at Fiona's door and knocked, but Fiona would not open it to her soft plea, and she was forced to leave without being able to commiserate with her as she had hoped to do.

Before she entered her room another flight up, Elinor's attention was caught by the painting of the Cavalier, and her mouth tightened again. "And don't you stand up there, you arrogant rake, being so all-knowing and superior, either!" she told him, moving closer and shaking her fist at him. "In your day, you were no better than they are, which is to say, not at all! Insensitive clods! Clumsy imbeciles who think of no one but themselves! Oooh, how I dislike you all, you damned Grenville *males!*"

The Cavalier continued to smile down at her, looking amused, and Elinor was tempted to throw something at him. Then the ridiculousness of her scolding an oil painting made her glare fade, and a weak chuckle escaped her as she went into her room.

She came late to breakfast the following morning, and she was delighted to discover she was to be completely alone. After her anger had cooled last evening, she had felt more than a little trepidation at what she had done. After all, Jonathan had told her how ruthless his twin was. Perhaps her chastising Jason would anger him? Put her in peril?

But still, she told herself as she selected a hearty meal, it had been worth it. Oh, my, yes. And that screeching chord that was all Fiona could manage, to express her agony and her fury at her brothers, had unleashed a tigress in Elinor that she had never suspected she could be. She was even secretly a little proud of herself.

At her place, she found a sealed note, addressed to her in a strong, slanted black handwriting. She ignored it until she had finished her breakfast and poured herself another cup of coffee. Only then did she slit the seal with her fruit knife, to read a most humble apology from Jonathan for his unforgiveable behavior. However, he did beg her pardon. As she folded the note, Elinor wondered if he had bothered to beg his sister's as well. From Mr. Jason Grenville, there was not a word, but then, she had hardly expected such a thing from a man she was beginning to consider a crude boor. But perhaps he had never learned to write?

Elinor decided that her first order of business this morning would be to see Sir Robert, after which she would go to Fiona, to try to get her to ride with her this beautiful May morning. A good canter might take Fiona's mind from Mischief's untimely death.

She rang for the butler then, to ask for Sir Robert. In the most respectful tones, Whitman told her that gentleman had been called to Portreath very early. As for Mr. Jonathan and Mr. Jason, they had gone out as well. Separately, he added, looking carefully over Elinor's head. He had no idea where they might be found.

Elinor nodded and excused him, frowning a little now. But before she could rise and go to Fiona's rooms, Miss Ward rushed in. Elinor's brows rose, the woman looked so distraught. Her normally neat hair was escaping its pins, and she was wringing her hands.

"Miss Fielding! Thank heavens you at least are here!" she exclaimed, skidding to a stop by Elinor's chair.

"What is it? What's the matter?" Elinor asked.

"It's Fiona! She's gone, disappeared!" Miss Ward moaned, her eyes wild. "She didn't come down to breakfast, and when I went to her room, questioned her maid, she said Fiona had not rung for her this morning. I looked through her clothes. Her habit and red cape are missing, and other things too. And Cook tells me considerable food is gone from the larder. Where can she be? Why did she leave the castle? Oh, dear, I cannot bear that my dear Sir Robert, with all the burdens he has right now, should have to suffer this as well! And what will he think of me? I was in charge of Fiona, I should have watched her more carefully, especially after her kitten died yesterday. I saw how upset she was! Why, she would not even let me remain with her, comfort her as I longed to do! And she was so harsh when she sent me away! And last night, when I tried to go to her to wish her good night, I found her door locked against me. She has never done that before—no, never!''

''Yes, it does sound unusual,'' Elinor managed to interject as Rebecca Ward was forced to stop and take a deep breath. ''But come! Is there no place you know of she might have gone to? Some friend of hers in the neighborhood, or a haunt she prefers when she wants to be alone?'

Miss Ward stood very still, an arrested, almost crafty expression on her face. ''There is one,'' she said slowly. '' 'Tis up on the moors. An empty, run-down tinner's shack. She took me there years ago in the jingle, for you know I do not ride.''

Suddenly she moved closer to grasp Elinor hands. ''Miss Fielding, you must go after her at once! At once, do you hear? I have no idea when Sir Robert or Mr. Jonathan will return! And I have the most awful premonition of disaster. You must make haste! Haste!''

''You want me to go up on the moors? But I have been warned against such a thing ever since I arrived here!''

''There is nothing for *you* to fear! *You* are not of the nobility, or a Grenville either! But Fiona, being both, may well be in danger. Oh, please, Miss Fielding, do say you will save her! Look, I will even go down on my knees to you and beg!''

Horrified, Elinor watched the older woman begin to

do just that, and as quickly as she could, she raised her to her feet.

Miss Ward clutched her hands so tightly, Elinor winced. Leaning forward to peer into Elinor's face, she said, "I can describe the place. It will not be hard for you to find, and it is no great distance. You take the first turning after the tin mine. It is a rugged, narrow track that winds back into the moors for a few miles. The shack is in a little dell by a small pond. But you must hurry, *hurry!* I am so concerned for Fiona, for she *is* a Grenville. Pray you can reach her before those horrid tinners do!"

"Very well," Elinor said slowly. "I shall change to my habit at once. Please send a message to the stables that I shall require Jenny saddled."

She hurried from the room, cutting short all Miss Ward's garbled and profusive thanks. It seemed only minutes later that she was running down the path to the Home Farm. She carried her hooded cloak with her, for sunny day or not, she knew Cornwall now, and the weather might well change before she found Fiona.

She had intended to ask McCarthy for the escort of one of the grooms, but she found everything in confusion at the stables.

True, Jenny had been saddled and was waiting for her, but Elinor could see the head groom and his lads were much too busy to help her. Two of the mares were foaling at the same time, something McCarthy said he had never had happen before. After helping her mount, and telling her to be careful in an absent-minded way, he hurried back to his mares.

As Elinor trotted to Downlong, she told herself she must not borrow trouble. It was still early. Perhaps she would find Fiona and they would be able to return in time for luncheon, long before the tinners got word that either one of them was up on the moors.

But as she went through the harbor village, she noticed how many curious eyes watched her, noting her direction. Realizing that everyone for miles around would know where she was going, she stopped at one of the outlying cottages to ask the whereabouts of Timothy Coryton, hoping to enlist his aid. She had seen how the villagers loved Fiona. She could not believe they would hurt her. The skinny woman she questioned was standing on her doorstep, a wailing baby in her arms and two toddlers peeking around her skirts. She only shook her head to Elinor's question, her sullen face blank. Elinor was forced to ride on.

She stopped again in Uplong, but she had no better luck there. No one had any knowledge of Coryton, or if they did, they were keeping that information to themselves.

"If you should by any chance see him, would you kindly tell him that I have gone up on the moors to search for Miss Grenville?" Elinor asked a very old man with a white beard who was leaning over his wall, pipe in hand.

"Aye, missus, that I will," the oldster said, turning his head to spit on the ground.

Elinor tried to smile at him, even though she had seldom felt less like doing so. Perhaps it would have been better to have avoided the villages all together, she told herself as Uplong fell behind Jenny's cantering hooves. But she had not known any other way to the mine, or that turning Miss Ward had told her about.

She supposed the mine was the Wheal Beatrice, and it looked sad and neglected even in the bright sunlight. Grass had grown up on the track to it, even poked up in the rusty machinery. The wind was stronger up here, and it moved the grass before it, making it ripple like a catspaw on the sea itself. And outside of that wind, the occasional creek of some loose boards, it was very quiet.

Elinor was glad to put the mine behind her. Strange that a place that had once been abustle with activity and noise could seem twice as desolate as the empty moor ahead, she mused.

If she had not been looking hard for it, surely she would have missed the turn into the rough track, for it was overgrown now, as if no one had come this way in years. Elinor reined Jenny in for a moment, patting her neck absently. Was this the right place? She had no idea. She would just have to try it, and if it did not lead her to the empty shack, she would have to come back here and search for another way.

In spite of her concern for Fiona, even the little tremor she felt to be here in a place where she had no right to be, Elinor began to enjoy her ride. The moor lay peaceful and empty under the May sky, as empty as she remembered it had been on her first journey over it some weeks before.

She saw it was a place of granite and gorse, bilberries and bracken, but there were also wildflowers now, their colors seeming even more brilliant in the monochromatic landscape. And there were plover and woodcock, and once she heard a titlark call. Several times, hares scurried out of sight. Elinor even saw an adder twisting away, a thin ribbon of death, and she realized the moor pulsed with a hidden life of its own. It did not need man.

Slowing Jenny to a walk to rest her, Elinor looked around with renewed interest, breathing deeply of the freshening air. She saw no sign of the empty shack Miss Ward had told her about. The track wound on, now disappearing for a while, then opening up ahead of her again. Several other tracks crossed it. She wondered who had made them, and for what reason?

Some minutes later, she saw a small pool only a short distance away, and she turned Jenny's head toward it, thinking to water her. The pool was surrounded by thick green grass, and it looked inviting in the sunlight. But to Elinor's surprise, Jenny refused to obey the pressure of her knee or the reins. But why was that? Elinor wondered, bewildered. It was well over an hour since they had left the stables. Surely Jenny must be thirsty!

It was then she remembered Jonathan's words about the moors. How the only safe place was on high, stony ground; how the tempting grass and tranquil pools, so innocent looking and calm, were traps for the unwary, hiding bogs that could suck a man and his mount down until they disappeared forever. Shuddering, Elinor turned back to the rocky track, patting Jenny to thank her for her good instincts.

She rode on for another mile or so, and she was just about to give up and retrace her route when she saw another small pool ahead. There was a grove of trees beside it. Perhaps the shack she sought was in that grove? Urging Jenny to a canter, Elinor hurried on, calling out Fiona's name as she did so.

But the grove was without sign of human habitation, either past or present. Elinor let Jenny water at a small brook, and as she loosened the top buttons of her habit, she wished she could dismount and get a drink herself. It was getting warm on the moors, so little shade was to be found. But she did not dare. She was afraid she would not be able to mount again without the help she had always had before.

Elinor took a long hard look ahead. The moor stretched out in an endless ripple of dips and small hills, but she could see no other grove in sight. Discouraged to have wasted so much time, she turned Jenny back toward Wheal Beatrice.

An hour later, she stopped again, finally admitting to herself that she was hopelessly lost. Somehow she had wandered off the main track at a tangent, and she had no idea how to find it again. The sun was high in the sky, and she could not tell, due to her ignorance of such things, whether she was heading west toward the ocean and Mordyn, or east toward the even more barren moors. Cursing her London girlhood, she realized she had found no trace of Fiona either.

Elinor called out Fiona's name then, as loudly as she could. Perhaps she would hear her, or perhaps someone would. Elinor did not much care at this point. Indeed, she would have welcomed any number of tinners, if they could just have pointed out the way to get home.

Only the echoes of her own voice answered her, and she slumped a little in the saddle. Coming up here had been a foolish move. She should have known better; insisted on waiting for Sir Robert or Jonathan to come back to lead the search, no matter what Fiona's companion had said.

For Rebecca Ward was given to hysteria, even mental instability, as Elinor was by now well aware. Yet she had allowed the woman to manipulate her, fallen under her influence, and raced away like any knight in a fairy tale to save the fair damsel—bah! In an effort to repay Sir Robert for all his kindness, she had been stupid.

Elinor shook her head and took a deep, steadying breath. She reminded herself that Fiona had known these moors since childhood. No, Fiona was not in any danger, no matter where she was, but she, herself, now thoroughly lost and confused, was the one in desperate need of rescuing.

Slowly, she rode on, for she did not know what else to do. She could tell Jenny was tiring, for she stumbled every now and then. Elinor was tired too, and thirsty and hungry and sore, and she could see clouds massing on the horizon, thin forerunners of them already casting filmy veils over the sun's brightness. It looked like a big storm was coming. Elinor shivered. Pray God she would not be lost up here, alone, when the mists curled in! she thought. She refused to consider what she would do if night fell and she was still wandering around, lost in the wind and the rain and the mist.

12

ELINOR CONTINUED to call out Fiona's name at regular intervals. Jenny could no longer manage anything but a walk, and Elinor tried not to urge her to any faster pace, even as she kept an anxious eye on the thickening clouds, felt the sudden chill of the rising wind.

Suddenly, she heard hoof beats behind her, and she halted Jenny to turn eagerly in their direction. "Over here!" she called. "I'm over here!"

To her relief, Timothy Coryton rode over a small rise then, to come directly to her side.

"What do ye think yer doing up here, missus?" he asked, his voice rough and his rock-hard face cold.

"Oh, please, I know you told me not to come, but I had to try and find Fiona—er, Miss Grenville," Elinor told him, blinking back her tears of relief. "She ran away from the castle this morning, and there was no one else to search for her. But—but I got lost. I am so glad to see you!"

Coryton did not respond to her brilliant smile. "Think ye ter call in that favor I owes yer then?" he asked, looking her up and down.

Elinor was suddenly aware that they were alone. Indeed, there was probably nobody about for miles. As his glance seared her, she remembered the undone buttons of her habit, and her face paled.

"I would be very grateful to you if you would tell me how to get back to the road to Uplong," she made herself say. "I have no idea where Fiona is, but I can see it would be wiser if someone who knows the moor tried to locate her."

A thought occurred to her then, and she stretched

out her hand to him. "Mr. Coryton, perhaps you could do so? I am sure you know these moors better than anyone, and if you were to search for her, why, she would be found in no time!"

She stopped as he began to laugh. It was a harsh laugh with little music in it, as if he had not had occasion to employ it lately.

"Ye want *me* ter help look fer a *Grenville?*" he asked, after that laughter died away. "Not bloody likely!"

"But—but you know Fiona! And surely you bear *her* no animosity," Elinor persisted. "And then there is Gwyneth Grenville, and all the good she does about the villages. Would you take your hatred out on them? Innocent women?"

For a moment, Timothy Coryton's face stiffened so, Elinor wondered if she had gone too far. Into her head came the irrelevant thought that under his shabby clothes, he held himself as proud as any king.

"Do ye have a cape?" he asked, ignoring her question. "Best ye put it on then. It's about ter rain, and we've a way ter go."

Elinor reached behind her for the cloak she had tied on the back of the saddle. As she donned it, Jenny stood quietly, her head down.

Coryton pointed to the mare, jeering at her. "Should o' been mounted on somethin' with a bit more life in 'er, missus," he said. "That one's no good fer the long haul no more."

He wheeled his own horse then. "Come along, do! I've no mind to get caught out in a downpour. These be the only clothes I got."

He set out then, never looking behind him to see if she were following. Elinor urged Jenny into a trot, peering ahead to keep Coryton in sight. "Wait!" she called. "Wait for me! Jenny cannot keep up!"

He did not turn his head, but Elinor noted with relief that he slowed the pace. He led her along a dozen paths, seemingly picked at random. Elinor was sure she would never be able to find her way back over them, and she prayed he was leading her to safety.

At last they came to a house, if you could call the rough shack ahead of them a house. It had no windows, and only one door, but Elinor could see smoke coming from the chimney at the end of it.

She waited, but Coryton's preoccupation with his own horse showed her he had no intention of helping her dismount. Stiff and tired, she slid carefully to the ground, hanging on to the stirrup until she could stand alone. Still, she found herself tottering when she tried to walk a few steps.

"Bring the mare this way," Coryton ordered without turning his head. "There's a shed."

Elinor obeyed him, trailing a tired Jenny. The shed was nothing more than a three-sided leanto, but it would be shelter for the horses in the coming storm. Watching Coryton carefully, Elinor loosened Jenny's girth and tied her to a post in the corner, although she did not think there was any danger of her wandering away. She did not unsaddle her. She didn't know how.

"Is there water? Feed?" she asked, watching Coryton rub down his horse with a handful of straw.

"Water, aye. Feed, no. Not fer *her*. I'll feed no Grenville nags!" Coryton muttered.

Elinor lost her temper. "Shame on you!" she said hotly. "Jenny is only a horse! She doesn't know she belongs to the Grenvilles, and she is tired and hungry!"

"Do 'er good to go without a bit," Coryton said callously. "Bit too much weight on 'er as it is. Too much lolling about in the green pastures of Mordyn, I've no doubt."

He walked out then, returning minutes later with a bucket of water. Elinor had been trying to rub Jenny down in the meantime. After Coryton had finished watering his own horse, he tossed the bucket to Elinor. "Well's around the corner," he said. "Come up ter the house when yer done."

By the time Elinor had managed the heavy bucket and started for the house, the skies had darkened and it had begun to rain, a hard, steady rain that seemed likely to go on for hours. She had relieved herself out behind the shed, then had a long drink of water and buttoned her habit to the throat, and now, as she tried to run, she wondered how long she would be cooped up here alone with Coryton. She hoped it would not be for long. She had not liked the considering look he had given her earlier.

But as she stepped inside the door of the rude house, Elinor stopped short, trying to hide a gasp. The place seemed full of men, all of whom had turned to stare at her.

"An' wot we got here?" one of the younger ones asked, getting to his feet and strolling toward her. "My, my, my."

Desperately, Elinor looked around for Coryton. She saw him standing by the fireplace, deep in whispered conversation with another man.

"Mr. Coryton," she called out, walking toward him and trying to ignore the leers she was receiving from some of the men. Others, she noted, didn't even bother to raise their eyes now as she passed.

She stopped near the fireplace, staying back a little so as not to interrupt Coryton's conversation.

At length, the other man nodded and hurried to the door, slamming it shut behind him.

"Sit down," Coryton told her, not looking at her.

Elinor glanced around. There was no furniture in the place. It was only a long windowless room with straw on the floor, but there was one rough shelf near the fireplace holding a few plates and mugs, a rusty frying pan and a battered kettle.

"What is this place?" she asked, sinking down to her knees in the straw.

"It's a miners' house," Coryton told her. "When the mines wuz open, lots o' the men stayed up here in houses like this, rather than trudge back ter the village at night. It saved time, and they wuz tired from all those hours underground, tinning."

"Who might the *leddy* be, Timmy?" the young man who had first accosted Elinor demanded, coming closer as he spoke.

"This be Miss Fielding. She got lost on the moors," Coryton told him. "Any more questions, Thomas?"

The man called Thomas settled down near Elinor, stretching out full length and picking up a straw to chew as he did so. His eyes raked her face, her body. "Wot's she up here fer, then?" he persisted. "And how do we know she won't tell Sir Robert where ter find us?"

"She didn't tell on me before, when she got the chance," Coryton said. "Leave be, Thomas—all o' ye! When the rain stops, I'll be sendin' her on her way. She's no Roger Tom!"

The men settled back, muttering among themselves. Thomas continued to watch Elinor, his eyes intent—sly, somehow.

Trying to ignore him, Elinor asked, "What's a Roger Tom?"

"Aw, it's just an old saying, like," Coryton said as he put the battered teakettle on the fire. "Years ago, Roger Tom informed on his mates ter the excise men, and they wuz caught smuggling. In Cornwall, anyone who rats is called by his name."

Elinor could hear the rain pounding on the roof, and she moved a little closer to the furze and turf fire. It smoked terribly, but it was warming.

"Did the miners really stay here, even in the wintertime?" she asked, curious. "But—but there are no beds!"

"There's straw. That's enow," Coryton said. "An' yes, they stayed up here, especially in the winter. We worked on tribute, an' we could put in longer days if we didn't have that long tramp home and back each day."

"What is working on tribute?" Elinor asked, holding out her hands to the sullen blaze.

"Some o' us—most o' us!—don't like workin' for men like Sir Robert Grenville," Coryton said, frowning as he put a pinch of tea in both the mugs and filled them with boiling water before he handed her one. "We'd rather have a share o' the yield than a fixed wage."

"Why is Sir Robert so angry at you especially?" Elinor asked, holding her watery tea and trying to forget the lavish spread being served at Mordyn even now.

"Ye ask a lot o' questions, don't ye, missus?" Coryton observed. The man called Thomas who was lolling nearby listening, laughed.

"He don't like Timmy, 'cause Timmy was the one wot got us ter quit working fer wage in the first place," he said. "Grenville's had it in fer him ever since. See, he could make more o' a profit paying pence fer wage, but afterward, when we hit a rich yield, he had ter split it with us, see?"

"An' he don't like losing a groat," another man remarked. "Nary a single one, the ol' pinchgut!"

"What's it like, tinning?" Elinor asked, trying to get the men to stop discussing Sir Robert. "Do you really go down into the ground? I cannot imagine such a thing!"

Coryton turned his head, his eyes narrowed. "Aye. It's hard work. So hard, most tinners don't last long. Me own Da died, worn out, when he wuzn't yet forty. Most o' 'em do, but 'tis all they know, see?

"An' yes, we go underground. Sometimes, the mines near the sea have shafts that go way out under the ocean."

"How do you see down there?" Elinor asked. "It must be dark!"

She shivered a little at the very thought of being deep in the earth. She could not even contemplate being underground and under the sea at the same time. It was too frightening.

"We wear stubs o' candles stuck on hard hats," Thomas told her. "Like ter see a mine, missus? I'd be glad ter show ye 'round, jess ye an' me, like."

There was some rough laughter at the back of the room, and Elinor moved closer to Coryton.

"Do you have a wife, sir? A family?" she asked.

He stared at her, unspeaking, and Elinor wondered if she had been wise to ask him that. Perhaps he considered such a question an invasion of his privacy.

"No, no wife. An' no family," he said brusquely

before he swallowed the last of his brew. "I got cured o' the thought o' marryin' a long time ago."

He grimaced before he said roughly, "That's enough talk. Don't ask no more, missus. Keep ter yerself."

Elinor nodded, and a few minutes later, she curled up in the straw and went to sleep. She had tried to fight her growing weariness, for she wanted to be alert for what the miners might do to her, but she had not been able to stay awake. And besides, she told herself drowsily, Timothy Coryton was there. And somehow I trust him, no matter how he looked at me on the moor.

Loud voices from the other end of the room awakened her later.

"An' I sez we hold 'er ter ransom, like," a deep voice growled. "Sir Robert would pay mighty good ter get the likes o' *'er* back!"

"Aye," two or three other voices agreed.

"She be a prime piece, ain't she?" a voice she recognized as Thomas's asked. "I'd be glad ter watch 'er, *all* the time!"

His offer was greeted with hoots of laughter.

"I say no. We'll not hold her ter ransom," Coryton's decisive voice said. Elinor felt a little safer, knowing he was still there.

"Grenville's lookin' fer us ter do somethin' like that, somethin' stupid! He'd have the troops here afore ye could blink an eye, an' they'd kill all o' us. Them they didn't save ter hang."

Elinor heard the men muttering among themselves, arguing for and against the plan, and she prayed Coryton would prevail.

"But they wouldn't kill us, not if we had *'er,*" the first voice persisted.

"How long wuz ye plannin' ter keep 'er then, our Bill?" Coryton asked. "Can't even feed ourselves an' our families. How we goin' ter feed the likes o' *'er?*

"An' if we had ter watch 'er all the time, we wouldn't be able ter go on raids. Ye know that's all wot's keepin' us alive."

"Still I say we ought ter try it," the deep voice

insisted. "We could make somethin' big out o' it. More 'n we can git on a raid."

"An' o' course we'd send 'er back jess like she come?" Coryton asked, his voice harsher now, colder. "Not a chance o' it! Jess look at Thomas there, an' Roger, an' our Walter. Can't hardly keep their breeches buttoned even now! Ye want rape on yer consciences? Think o' yer sisters, yer wives!

"No, 'twas a daft idea. We'll send 'er back jess like I planned, an' that's final."

Elinor drew a shaky breath as all argument ceased. But she had to wonder at the authority Coryton had over these rough men, even as she was exceeding grateful for it. She was reminded of the time he had held up her carriage on the moor. He had prevailed then, and without threatening the men with his pistol either. It appeared Timothy Coryton was a born leader. Even with his rough accent and his obvious lack of education, he was a man other men looked up to, and obeyed without question.

A loud knock on the door startled everyone. Elinor struggled to sit up, her eyes widening when she saw Coryton pull his pistol from his pocket.

Motioning the other men back, he went to the door to stand carefully to one side of it. "Who's there?" he demanded.

"Ye know who it is, Timmy. Lemme in."

Elinor did not know whether to be relieved or even more distressed to hear Jason Grenville's deep, coarse accents. Oh, why couldn't it have been Jonathan who found her? Or Sir Robert? she wondered as she brushed wisps of straw from her habit and her hair with hands that shook a little.

Coryton put his pistol away before he opened the door to a frowning, very wet Mr. Grenville. As he stepped inside to shake hands, he said, "Thank ye fer yer message, Timmy. I came as fast as I could, knowing how eager ye must be ter get rid o' such a weighty burden. I suppose I must thank ye fer saving the girl as well, although at the moment, I'm not at all sure I want ter. Women! Nothing but trouble from the moment they're born! *Bah!*"

He had not bothered to lower his voice, well aware that Elinor could hear him. It was obvious to her that he spoke to repay her for her set-down last night.

The tinners were all laughing at his sally, two of them clapping him on the shoulder, and Elinor seethed. Well! she thought indignantly. Well!

"She got a horse? Where is it?" Jason Grenville asked next.

"In the shed. But the mare's done up. Even riderless, I doubt ye could get her as far as Uplong, Jason."

Mr. Grenville shrugged his large shoulders. Under the rush light on the wall, his dark wet hair gleamed like satin. "I suppose it can't be helped. I'll put 'er up before me. And I'm not going ter Uplong, but ter a nearer place. I've no mind ter get pleurisy from this absurd affair."

He turned then to where Elinor still crouched in the straw, glaring at him.

"Whatever are ye waiting fer?" he asked carelessly. "Come along! It's late."

Elinor rose to her feet, wishing she might strike him. But though she looked daggers at him, he only turned away for a private word with Coryton. As she picked her way around the grinning tinners, holding the train of her habit high, Elinor saw Coryton nod before he grasped Jason Grenville on the arms again and smiled. It was the first time Elinor had ever seen Coryton smile, and it transformed his face. Why, she thought as she came to stand beside them, he is nowhere near as old a man as I had supposed! And he is pleasant-looking as well. Almost handsome.

"Fasten yer cape and yer hood securely," Jason Grenville told her. "It's still raining, and the wind's come up."

As she did so, Elinor thanked Timothy Coryton again for all his aid.

"We're even now, missus. A favor fer a favor, remember?" he said, his voice arrogant.

How proud he is! Elinor thought. What a terrible

thing it was that such a man had been brought down to this—this degradation.

Even before Elinor nodded, trying to hide her pity, Coryton had gone back to his men. Once outside, her breath was snatched by the wind, and she turned her head away from it, and the cold raindrops that were striking her face.

"Over 'ere! Hurry!" Jason Grenville said brusquely. She stumbled a little, obeying him.

He put his hands on her waist and lifted her to the front of the saddle. Elinor grasped the gelding's mane to steady herself, for the horse's back was so wet, she was afraid she would slide right back off. Every single one of her muscles protested another ride so, she had to bite her lip to restrain a sob of pain. Jason Grenville mounted behind her and took up the reins.

As they started off into the teeth of the gale at a walk, Elinor's face streamed with rain, and she could feel it making its way inside her hood to run in icy little rivulets down between her breasts. She shivered, wondering how far they had to go. Not that I will show this insulting boor any weakness! she vowed.

As he set the horse to a trot, Grenville said, "If ye don't lean back against me, ye'll be in grave danger o' fallin' under the horse's hooves, Miss Fielding. Come, this is no time fer silly modesty!"

Elinor would have refused, but she could see that at this faster pace, the danger of her doing so was all too real. And what if Grenville decided to canter? Reluctantly, she relaxed against his broad chest. His arms tightened and she gasped, but in a moment she could see he had only done so to keep her secure.

"Where—where are we going?" she asked over her shoulder.

"Ter the nearest sanctuary. Although whether ye'll consider it such is questionable," he said, his deep voice rumbling in his chest. They were so close, it made the moment a great deal more intimate than Elinor cared for. She was reminded she was alone with this dangerous man. A murderer at ten, a boy who had tortured small animals for his own perverted pleasure.

Where was he taking her? For what reason? She wished with all her heart that she was back at the tinners' house. She would have been safer there, even with a threat of rape to contend with.

"Why can't we go back to Mordyn?" she asked, trying to keep the panic she was feeling from showing in her voice.

"Come now, think!" Grenville said roughly. "If yer capable o' thinking, that is. Mordyn is miles away. We would both risk serious illness if we tried ter reach it. And the moors are treacherous at night, especially such a black night as this one."

He paused then, and his voice was softer, gentler, as he added, "Trust me, Miss Fielding. I'll see all well."

Elinor made herself nod, not even wondering why his unexpected kindness caused her such a tremor of unease. So might any evil man reassure his victim, until he had that victim safe in his trap.

They rode through the storm for what seemed a very long time. At last, Elinor saw a dim light ahead, and she leaned forward.

Jason Grenville turned the horse into a rutted drive that led toward the dark, looming shape of a farmhouse. He headed toward a small barn that was across the yard from the house, dismounting to open the doors and lead the horse inside.

Elinor slid to the ground before he could help her, for her skin was crawling from his touch. She waited beside the gelding until Grenville had lit a lantern. In the circle of light it cast, she could see the barn was crowded with all manner of rusty tools, frayed rope, an old plow, even feed sacks stuffed with heaven knows what—a miscellany of goods of all kinds. There was little open space. Even the stalls were full.

Jason Grenville tied his horse to a post before he stripped the saddle from him. After rubbing him down briskly, he put a ragged blanket over his back and then picked up the lantern.

"Come on!" he said, holding out his arm. "What ye waiting fer?"

Ignoring that arm, Elinor went before him to the door. She did not see the black look return to his face as he brushed by her to lead the way. The two of them struggled against the wind, Elinor bent almost double and wishing she dared grab hold of his cloak, until they reached the porch. To her surprise, Grenville knocked loudly, paused, and knocked again. As they waited, she could hear someone scurrying around inside, but when her companion opened the door at last, there was no one there.

As she stepped in, Elinor looked around in wonder. They stood in a very small square of open space, from which two narrow alleys led in opposite directions. Grenville nudged her toward the one at the left. Turning sideways, she went forward between towering piles of paper and boxes until she reached a fireplace. There was a small open space here as well, just large enough for a table and an old upholstered chair that was oozing its stuffing.

"What on earth?" she whispered, looking around. Beside the stacks of paper and boxes, there were also balls of string and twine, empty bottles, books without number, old broken furniture all in a heap, baskets of rags, even large jars of rusty keys and nails—why, she could not begin to count the items.

"Where are we?" she asked Jason Grenville. He was busy removing his cloak and hat, shaking them before he laid them over some kegs.

"We're at my Uncle James's farmhouse, 'bove Uplong. He, er, he saves things," he said, his gray eyes studying her face. "Ye'd better take off yer cloak, while I make up the fire."

Wonderingly, Elinor did as he suggested. There did not appear to be any place where she could sit down except that old ragged chair, and she was loathe to use that. Its cushions still held the dents of its previous occupant, and it smelled. Indeed, the entire room had a peculiar odor, of dusty, dry, decaying things.

Elinor moved closer to the fire then, holding out her hands to its warmth, and trying not to shiver with the cold. She felt wet through, and she wondered if there were any place in this crazy storehouse of the old and tossed away where she might be private; any other clothes she might put on.

But when she asked Grenville as he rose from the now blazing fire and wiped his hands on his breeches, he only laughed. Elinor thought it a very disagreeable sound.

"This be the only room yer allowed in, an' as fer women's clothes, they're probably the only thing my Uncle James wouldn't give house room. Ter tell truth, I had the greatest trouble getting his permission fer ye even ter seek shelter here. Uncle James hates women. Always has. Ye be the first one who's ever crossed his threshold. I trust yer properly honored, miss?"

When she stared at him, appalled, he said, "I s'ppose I must see about findin' a blanket fer ye. Oh, there's a close stool in there, an' a basin an' some water if ye need 'em," he added, pointing through an even narrower alley she had not noticed before.

He went away then, his big shoulders threatening to bring the piles of rubbish he passed between, down on him. Elinor almost begged him not to leave her here alone, until she took herself in hand. Instead, she shook out her wet skirts, and tried to ignore her damp petticoats and chemise, the clammy feeling of her stockings and her soggy boots.

It was some time before Jason Grenville returned. He held out an old ragged blanket that might once have been blue, but was now faded to an ugly gray. "It's clean," he said. "Well, at least cleaner than anything else here."

He paused then, scowling, before he added, "I'll leave ye ter get out o' yer wet things. Put them before the fire. It's hot, and they should dry quickly. I'll be in the barn seeing ter the horse."

He turned aside to get his cloak, and Elinor held out her hand to him. "Mr. Grenville, is there anything to eat?" she asked, hating herself for having to do so. "I—I have had nothing since breakfast, and I am very hungry."

His scowl deepened. "I'll see what I can do," he

said. "Ye do seem ter require a goodly amount fer yer comfort, don't ye? And a great deal o' waiting on as well."

Elinor stared at him. She was tired and wet and miserable—frightened, too—and she felt tears coming to her eyes at his sarcasm. Abruptly, she turned away from him, praying he would mistake the tears now running down her face for rain. She remained that way until she heard the outside door closing behind him.

Even then she hesitated. Taking off her clothes seemed a foolish thing to do in the company of such a man. But then she reminded herself, he could easily take them off her himself if he had a mind to do so. He was so much bigger and stronger. And she did not think, from what he had told her of his uncle, that that man would come to her assistance, no matter how she screamed. She would just have to trust to luck. Jason Grenville had not seemed dangerous this evening. Indeed, outside of his boorish manners, he had treated her with consideration. So far.

Quickly, then, she hung the old blanket before the fire to warm it while she stripped off her clothes. Ah, it felt so good! she thought, snuggling into the blanket's scratchy depths. Trailing it on the floor behind her, she arranged the kegs in a row before the fire, and draped her habit and her underclothes over them, setting her boots to one side so they would not get scorched.

Once she had washed and was more comfortable, she curled up in the old chair, making sure she was completely covered by the blanket, right down to her littlest toes.

When Jason Grenville returned, he ignored her as he rummaged through the cupboards till he found half a loaf of bread, the remains of a wheel of cheese, and one apple. There was a jug of cider as well, but only one plate, one knife, and one mug.

"I'm feared we must share, Miss Fielding," he said as he set the provisions on the table. His brows rose slightly as he eyed her clothes steaming before the fire, before he fetched another keg to sit on. Firmly, Elinor kept her eyes from those dainty silk petticoats, the pale peach chemise lavished with lace, and her delicate clocked stockings. A faint scent of her lilac perfume was in the air. It was unfortunate, she thought, but she had no intention of moving anything until it was bone-dry.

As Jason Grenville handed her a slice of bread and some cheese, Elinor asked, "Is your uncle here, sir?"

He nodded, concentrating on dividing the apple equally. "Yes, o' course. He's yer chaperone. But ye'll not sec him. I haven't seen him myself, since he would only talk ter me from another room." He shrugged. "A strange man, my Uncle James, a true hermit. He lives accordin' ter his own codes, and who's ter say he's wrong? An' he does no harm ter any other livin' thing, which is more than most o' us can say."

Munching a large mouthful of bread and cheese, Elinor could not answer. Then she noticed his black frown was back, and she decided she would rather not anyway. But what had he meant by his last statement? The food suddenly tasted like sawdust in her mouth.

"Some cider?" he asked, poising the jug above the mug. Elinor nodded. She would love to have asked for another piece of bread and cheese, but she did not want to deplete Mr. James Grenville's meager store.

"How does your uncle get his food if he is a hermit?" she asked.

"The farmer's wife a mile or so away brings it ter him, although she has ter come at a special time and leave it on the doorstep. He's wealthy, in spite o' this rat's nest he has here."

"I wonder why he feels he has to save such useless things?" Elinor asked wonderingly, looking up the high stacks to the dingy ceiling.

"He claims he never knows when he'll have need o' them," Grenville told her, biting into his half of the apple. Elinor was indignant to see him follow that with the rest of the cider he had poured in the mug for her, the way he wiped his mouth with the back of his hand. What crude manners he has! she thought.

Their small repast was soon finished right down to

the last crumb. As Grenville threw the apple core into the fire, he yawned. Elinor clutched her blanket tighter, watching him with apprehension.

He rose and stretched. "I shall leave ye ter the dubious comfort o' that chair, Miss Fielding," he said. His gray eyes narrowed as he saw how tightly she held the blanket, the way she stared at him so fearfully with wide green eyes. "There must be some other place fer me t' go. By the way, we must be off at dawn. I promised me uncle we wouldn't linger—not, I'm sure, that either one o' us has the least desire ter do so. Good night ter ye."

He did not wait for her reply, turning away at once to shoulder his way through the stacks of debris. Briefly, Elinor wondered where he would sleep, but she really didn't care as long as it was far away from her. She yawned. If all went well, she would be home at Mordyn tomorrow—safe within its thick stone walls again, under Sir Robert's protection.

She left the chair then to add a few more sticks to the fire, and she turned her clothes so they would dry equally before she settled down in the old chair again. It was very uncomfortable. She was sure between its lumps and her fear of Jason Grenville, she would not get a wink of sleep.

Elinor did not wake till dawn. The fire had died down and, stiff and uncomfortable, she struggled to her feet to tend to it before she repaired to the wash basin and close stool in the other room. Once dressed in her own clothes again, she felt better—safer somehow, as if a few yards of silk and wool made formidable armor. How ridiculous she was!

Yet all the time she performed her morning toilet, she wore a frown on her face, for she had had a most peculiar dream last night. Most peculiar indeed, and for some reason, she could not banish it from her mind.

She had dreamed she had been in her own bed at Mordyn. As had happened before, she had wakened there, sensing a man's presence in the room. And just like the first time, she had felt someone caressing her hair, smoothing it away from her face, tracing the line of her jaw from chin to earlobe. Those same gentle hands had adjusted her blanket as well, drawing it up over her arms and shoulders, tucking it close around her. She had not opened her eyes in the dream, for she was afraid of whom she might see. And surely that was singular, wasn't it, when she yearned for her lover so? Now she wished she *had* opened her eyes! She did not understand that dream at all, nor her reaction to it.

Elinor shrugged, longing for a cup of hot coffee to help her wake up and dispel this strange, empty feeling. But no doubt she was just hungry.

She forgot her musings as Jason Grenville came in, after calling out to make sure she was dressed.

"Come along," he ordered brusquely. Elinor wondered if he had slept at all, he looked so tired. The beard he had not been able to shave gave his face an ever darker, more saturnine cast, which the frown he sported did nothing to dispel.

Quickly, she finished braiding her hair. With neither comb nor brush, a braid was all she could manage.

Her rescuer turned abruptly to precede her down the narrow alley, and Elinor looked around to make sure she was leaving nothing behind. She wished she might see James Grenville, thank him for giving her sanctuary, but there was not a single sound in the old farmhouse.

The morning Elinor stepped out into was gray and misty, but at least it was not raining. And after the stuffy farmhouse, the air was cool and fresh. Then, as she saw her mare waiting for her near the barn, she picked up her train to run to her.

"How did Jenny get here?" she asked Jason Grenville as she patted the mare's neck.

"Timmy brought her only minutes ago. He's off ter find Fiona. He says he thinks he knows where she is; that he'll see she gets safe home."

He came to help Elinor before he mounted his own

gelding. "We must be on our way afore Sir Robert has the troops out after us," he told her curtly.

Obediently, Elinor urged Jenny into a trot, following the larger horse down the rutted track to Uplong. As she did so, she stared hard at Jason Grenville's broad-shouldered back, that arrogant dark head of his.

What was different about him this morning? she wondered. Why was he so abrupt? And why did he frown so darkly?

Half an hour later, they passed through Uplong. Her guide turned off to a smaller track then, one which Elinor was to discover was a shortcut to Mordyn. She was glad they could avoid the larger, seaside village. She had not liked the stares they had received in Uplong, the smiles carefully hidden, the little nudge one man gave to another as they passed. It was obvious the villagers had drawn their own conclusions as to what she and Mr. Grenville had been up to all this time.

How ludicrous! Elinor thought. As if she would ever willingly have anything to do with such an uneducated brute, or spend a moment more with him than she had to.

As they turned into the drive that led up to the castle, she stole a glance at him. He was riding beside her now, and she noted his strong profile, those glowering brows and narrowed eyes, the set jaw that was shadowed with the growth of new beard. How dark it made him look! she thought. Like a pirate, or a felon.

Yet as she watched his strong, competent hands on the reins, her breath caught in her throat and her heart began to pound, for she was struck suddenly with the possibility that that might not have been a dream she had had last night after all.

Instead, it was entirely possible that sometime, while she slept in that lumpy chair, Jason Grenville had come back to the fireside. Perhaps it had been Jason Grenville who had smoothed her hair, caressed her face so gently, just as her lover had done. Perhaps it had been Jason Grenville who had tucked the blanket around her so carefully, lest she feel the chill.

Jason Grenville—*murderer.*

13

ELINOR ONLY ARRIVED safely at the castle door by clinging to the front of the saddle and letting Jenny take her there unguided. Jenny, sensing her comfortable stall, as well as a hearty feed, was only too happy to do so.

Dressed for riding, Sir Robert and Jonathan were standing in the courtyard waiting for their horses to be brought up from the stables. As if through a mist, Elinor noted Sir Robert's frowning concern, the relief that spread over his face when he saw her, and she tried to smile at him, touched by his obvious caring.

Jonathan came to her side immediately, to hold up his arms to her. His handsome face was cold and set, those gray eyes narrowed as he stared into her face to search deep in her eyes.

Elinor slid down into his waiting arms and promptly fainted there.

When she woke, she was lying on her own bed, Betsy and Mrs. Greene watching over her.

"There now, miss, you're all right now," the housekeeper told her in her gruff way. "Mr. Jason told us you hadn't eaten all day yesterday. 'Tis no wonder you fainted. I'll see to a tray of food at once."

As she strode away, Elinor just stared straight ahead, her clear green eyes huge in her pale face. Was it true? Had Jason Grenville come to her last night? Touched her? Was it possible that he might even be her lover? Dear merciful God!

Betsy coughed a little. "Would ye care to undress, miss?" she asked. "I've warmed yer nightrobe, for Mrs. Greene says ye should stay in bed today to rest."

In a fog, Elinor allowed Betsy to help her up, stood like a wax doll as the maid removed her clothes, dropped the nightrobe over her head, and finally helped her to climb back into bed before she drew the covers over her.

When the tray came, Elinor made herself eat something, drink the hot tea. But the food and drink could not warm her. She did not think she would ever be warm again. Deep inside, there was a frozen core of ice that she was sure would never melt. What was she to do? What *could* she do to dispel the horrors in her mind?

After Betsy removed the tray, she reached out shyly to pat her mistress's hand, and her generally stolid face showed her concern.

"Why, miss, how cold ye are!" she exclaimed. "There now, slide down under the covers, do! I'll get a hot brick for yer feet."

She bustled away before Elinor could tell her a hot brick would do no good at all. Her pain was too deep inside, in a place neither warmth nor comfort—not even compassion could reach.

Wearily, she closed her eyes. Her hand rested on the satin counterpane. She was safe in bed, surrounded by soft pillows, clean silky sheets, all delicately scented with her own lilac sachets. She should have been at ease now.

But she was not easy. She felt lost—more lost even than she had been on the moors the afternoon before. And she was much more frightened.

The wind rattled the panes of the long windows, and she could hear the breakers pounding against the base of the cliff, just as they always had. Oh, why had she ever come to Mordyn? And why, when she had had that earlier premonition of some darkness ahead, hadn't she left, gone back to London while she had the chance? Oh Doll, she thought, where are you? I need you! You saved me before, but now I'm alone. And I do not think, alone, I can save myself this time either.

She cried aloud then, before she put her fist against

her mouth. It was too late to run to Doll now. And futile to cry out for her.

But perhaps it had always been too late to change what might well be inevitable. Perhaps she had been journeying all her life toward this dark future that was to be hers. She wondered what she had ever done to deserve such punishment? But to finally fall in love, to want someone, yearn to be with him always so she could cherish and adore him, only to discover he might well be . . .

But no. She could not even think of that. It was too horrible to contemplate. Not him! she prayed silently. Anyone but Jason Grenville!

It was a long time before Elinor finally fell asleep, worn out with her agonized thoughts. Thoughts that went around and around in her mind, like a dog on a treadmill to cook the roast.

Betsy tiptoed in at regular intervals, but her mistress continued to sleep. Only her tossing and turning in bed, the occasional low sigh she gave, showed her distress.

The maid saw nothing amiss in Miss Elinor's behavior. She had had a harrowing time of it, from what Betsy had been able to glean from the other servants. Mr. Jason had told his father and brother that when he had found her, she had been lost on the moor with night coming on. That the two of them had had to seek shelter from the storm at James Grenville's farmhouse. No wonder Miss was distraught! Betsy thought. She herself had been frightened since childhood of that crazy hermit. Even to think of spending a night in his house made shivers run up and down her spine. Besides, Miss hadn't found Miss Fiona, as she had set out to do. She must be worried about the girl still.

When Elinor finally awoke, it was late afternoon. For a moment, she lay quietly, savoring the luxury of her own room—her own bed—until memory came flooding back.

But now she did not despair as she had done earlier. Instead, she threw back the covers and padded to the dressing room to wash her hands and face in cold water.

Ringing for Betsy, she went to the long windows. The afternoon had brought clearing weather. It was sunny now, and the southwest wind had died. Before her was the ocean, a serene blue-green. She opened the doors to step out on the balcony and breathe deeply of the briny air, air that was making its first landfall after all those long miles from the Americas.

Elinor felt her spirits lift, and she was suddenly calmer. Very well, she told herself. She must make plans, and quickly, too. She could not cower up here alone forever. And perhaps the trauma of her adventure had caused her to imagine things that were not so. *Could* not be so. For after all, Jason Grenville spoke with a coarse, uneducated accent that was nothing at all like her Cavalier's whisper. Then, too, she had been visited at night long before Mr. Grenville had come back to Mordyn. Her expression brightened. But of course! It could not have been him after all. She wondered how she could have been so very foolish as to even have contemplated such a possibility! And she had only been dreaming last night. *Really* dreaming this time.

Suddenly she knew her magic midnights could be no more. The dream world she had reveled in, felt safe and loved and adored in, must be discarded. Reluctantly, to be sure, but put behind her now. She must discover her lover's name, no matter what she had to do to get him to confess it. When he returned to her, she would insist, and she would not let him kiss her, or touch her, until he confessed.

She wondered then where he was? It seemed such a a long time since she had seen him, held him in her arms, loved him. But no matter how she longed for him, she promised herself she would be firm. She had to be, now.

Feeling much better with her new resolutions, Elinor ordered tea, making herself speak normally to her maid as she told her to inform Sir Robert she would be joining the family for dinner. As Betsy curtsied and went to do her bidding, Elinor went to the armoir to look through her gowns. She intended to look as fashionable and stunning as she could this evening. The black silk with the velvet ribbon trim? The brocade she had worn to the party? She planned to wear her hair piled high on her head as well, to make her seem taller, more sophisticated.

As Betsy came in and set the tray on the table and Elinor took her seat beside it, the maid told her the latest news. Miss Fiona had arrived at the castle right before luncheon, she said as she went to straighten the bed. She did not know what Mr. Jason had said to his father and his brother, but both of them had canceled their search that morning and waited for Miss Fiona in the castle. Come alone, Miss Fiona had. It was very strange. And o' course, Betsy confided, unusually garrulous as she fluffed the pillows, Miss Fiona hadn't been able to tell anyone where she had been. But she had promised her father somehow that she would never run away again, or so Betsy had understood.

Just before the maid left to order a bath for Elinor, she said that that Miss Ward had been closeted with Sir Robert for ever the longest time this morning. When she had left him, she had been in hysterics, gibbering and carrying on like a crazy woman. She had even had to be carried to her room. Such a to-do! Don't know what *she* had to be upset about! Betsy scoffed as she closed the door softly behind her.

Later, bathed and dressed in the silk with velvet ribbon trim, and with her hair tied up with a matching ribbon, Elinor went downstairs. Her heart was beating rapidly, for in spite of all her logic, she was still not entirely sure that Jason Grenville had not touched her last night. There was something about the man that bothered her—something she could not quite understand. She had the feeling that she held the key to him somehow, even knew his secrets, but she could not put her finger on that key. It was some little thing about him that eluded her; something she had heard or seen, and since forgotten.

As she entered the drawing room, she saw that everyone was before her; Sir Robert, both tall twins, and a very subdued Fiona. Sir Robert came to take her hands, clasp her to him for such a warm hug that it brought tears to Elinor's eyes. He led her up to the others who were assembled before the fire. Elinor made herself smile impartially before she went to Fiona to kiss and hug her, tell her how very glad she was to see her safe home again.

"You are quite yourself again, Elinor?" Jonathan asked, his voice anxious. Elinor noted that his face was as cold and contained as it had been that morning. It appeared that besides his concern for her, he was burning with some deep resentment. She wondered what that could be?

"But of course she is!" Sir Robert said gruffly. "Just look at her! She's as pretty and blooming as a rose!"

"Indeed, I am myself, sir," Elinor told Jonathan with a warm smile. "And I do thank you for catching me up this morning. I can't imagine whatever came over me. I have never fainted in my entire life!"

"Perhaps the privation o' one day was too much fer ye," Jason Grenville suggested, in a sneering tone that implied she had merely been dramatizing the situation.

Elinor forced herself to turn and look at him. He was slouched against the mantel, glowering at her, and looking as if he thought much too much was being made of a very boring incident.

"I would be remiss not to thank you as well, Mr. Grenville," she made herself say. "You did find me yesterday, and I appreciate it."

She paused, but he did not even bother to shrug in deprecation before he sipped his wine. Nor did he smile.

"Well, the adventure is safely over, and I, for one, am extremely grateful it is," Elinor made herself say lightly as she nodded her thanks to Sir Robert for the glass of sherry he brought her. What a boor Jason Grenville was! she thought.

"But my dear, why did you tear off in that precipitous way?'' Sir Robert asked in a puzzled voice. Elinor made herself concentrate. ''You should have waited for one of us men to return. I simply cannot understand why you did not, not after your previous misadventure on the moor. And when I think of both you girls wandering around up there, separately and alone, my blood runs cold!''

Elinor flushed a little. ''Miss Ward was so concerned,'' she murmured. ''And truly, I did not think I would be gone for long, or that I would get lost up there. I see it was—it was stupid of me.''

''Aye, it was,'' Jason Grenville agreed coldly. ''Very stupid.''

''Rebecca has been severely chastised,'' Sir Robert said, ignoring his newly returned son. His face was set hard as he continued, ''Why, you might have stumbled into a bog and drowned, or been set upon by tinners!''

Elinor sipped her sherry. She could feel Jason Grenville's eyes on hers, could even imagine the dark light in them as he remembered that that was exactly what had happened, but she would not look at him again. Still, she wondered why she did not tell Sir Robert that it had been Timothy Coryton who had found her first, and taken her to the miner's house. Nor, it was obvious, had Jason Grenville mentioned that fact. Why was that? Was he protecting Coryton for some reason? Or did he want all the glory of rescuing her to fall on his head, perhaps as a way of ingratiating himself with his father again? From what his twin had told her of him, she would not put it past him.

She glanced at the unusually silent Jonathan Grenville then, and she had to stifle a gasp. He looked coldly furious. It was almost as if, under his impeccable evening dress, some wild thing lurked, seemingly tamed but not truly domesticated.

Dinner was announced, and Elinor rose to find him extending his arm. They followed Sir Robert and Fiona to the dining room, the brooding figure of Jason Grenville slouching behind. Elinor could feel that man's eyes on her back, and she had to wonder which twin was the more feral this evening.

"We must talk privately as soon as possible," her escort whispered, bending low so only Elinor could hear him. "There is much about all this I do not understand. Much I would have explained, Elinor."

She made herself nod as he seated her. She rather hoped she would not have to see him alone until he had had a chance to calm down. He looked as dangerous tonight as ever his twin had.

Dinner had never seemed longer to her. Course after endless course was served, eaten, and removed. Although Elinor tried to contribute to the conversation, she had seldom felt less like doing so. Fortunately, everyone appeared to put her reticence down to the trying experience she had just undergone, and thought nothing unusual about it. But across the table from her, Jason Grenville seemed to be watching her. And every time she felt his eyes on her, Elinor felt that core of ice inside her grow larger.

When Fiona rose at last to leave the gentlemen to their port, Elinor was only too happy to join her. And then, after curtsying to Sir Robert and smiling at Jonathan, she steeled herself to look straight into Jason Grenville's eyes. Did you come to me last night? she asked silently. What do you want? What manner of man are you?

She turned quickly to follow Fiona from the room, her head held high. At the door, she excused herself for the evening, claiming a lingering fatigue.

Sir Robert bade her have a good night, and told her to sleep as late as she wished the following morning, to regain her strength. Elinor smiled at him. So dear he was! So kind! How very unfortunate it was he was saddled with such an unworthy son!

Once in her room, Elinor tried to read for a while. It was not a successful diversion, for the printed page could not come between her and her thoughts. At last, she summoned Betsy to help her undress, even yawned a little as the maid did so. Perhaps she did need a good night's sleep. Perhaps tomorrow everything would seem brighter.

But after Betsy left her tucked up in bed, Elinor could not seem to fall asleep. Instead, she watched the fire die down to glowing embers, heard the gallery clock outside her room strike midnight, and then one. She wondered if she should light a candle, build up the fire, try to read for a while again. She felt edgy, unsettled, and her comfortable bed had become a scented, silken prison.

Sighing, she rolled over on her back to consider what she should do. She was just about to throw back the covers and rise when she heard a small sound. Cautiously, she opened her eyes to see a dark figure standing near her dressing table.

Her breathing grew shallow and her pulse raced, as whoever it was approached the bed to look down at her. Under lowered lashes, Elinor searched for a face in the dim light, before she realized, in frustration, that once again it was too dark for her to make out any features.

Pretending she was asleep, she sighed a little before she turned over on her side, facing him. She felt the bed sink as he sat down on it, although he did not make a sound now, and she was waiting when his hand touched her hair and her brow. It was just like the hand in her dream had touched her last night.

Suddenly, for some reason, she was frightened. Frightened, and yet still eager, her whole body awake and tingling with anticipation. His arms enfolded her, and she felt his lips on her hair, smelled the familiar scent of his warm skin. Her fear disappeared immediately, leaving in its wake a feeling of deep relief. Her Cavalier had come back to her! He was here at last!

"Elinor," her lover whispered, his hands caressing her before he lifted her and drew her closer to him. Already under the spell he wove with such ease, Elinor could not bring herself to protest, never mind question him.

Instead, as his lips came down on hers, she felt the

madness he had invoked so many times before return in such a burning flood of desire for him that she was shocked. Quite unthinking, her lips parted under his as she flung her arms around his neck and buried her hands in his thick hair. Oh, what a wretched thing a body is, that it can betray you so! she thought. It was to be the last sensible thought she was to have for some time.

When he could bear to stop kissing her mouth, his lips explored the soft skin of her face, her ears, her throat, while his hands unbraided her hair so he could comb his fingers through all the long length of it.

"Ah, love, how very sweet you are! How desirable and dear to me!" he whispered. "Every hour we have been apart has been painful. Can I hope you suffered just a little, too? Wanted me half as much as I wanted you? Missed me?"

Elinor was not allowed to answer, for his mouth was on hers again, this time both passionate and demanding. His tongue parted her lips, explored the tender insides of them before it captured her mouth, and Elinor felt herself aching with her need for him. Suffered? Wanted him? Dear heaven, surely he knew how wanton she was where he was concerned!

As his hands caressed her breasts, she sighed and surrendered. It was all wrong; it was not at all what she had planned to do when he came to her again, but she could not help herself. Damn him, oh, damn him! she thought, even as her tongue answered his, and her nipples peaked and hardened under his urgent hands. He had subdued her—seduced her—brought her to this melting acquiescence, with only a few soft words, the touch of his hands, and his wonderful mouth.

He was more impatient than he had ever been before. Tonight, there was none of the slow delicious stroking and exploring of those other times. Elinor was glad of it, for she was as avid to be part of him as he appeared avid to have her so.

Gasping a little now, she helped him pull her nightrobe over her head, and he took it and threw it aside before he drew her close to him again. The buttons on his shirt cut into her soft breasts, and she undid those buttons to pull the shirt away from his chest with hands that trembled a little. She was glad when he discarded his breeches so they could lie naked, hip to hip, thigh to thigh, her breasts crushed against his hard bare chest, while his hands pressed her closer still. She could feel his heart thudding, as her own was doing.

Wildly, Elinor even wished there were some way she could pass through his skin, mingle her heart and blood with his, so they would truly become one person.

As his hands caressed the soft inner skin of her thighs, Elinor became aware that another part of her was beginning to throb with a separate beat of its own. Wanting—no, demanding—release, begging him to touch her there, then make them one.

As he came to her, Elinor was surprised to find herself uttering a low, gutteral cry that issued from some dark part of her she had not known she possessed until this very moment. It was a primitive cry, perhaps handed down from the first woman on earth, to all the sisters who had come after her. And her body welcomed him, enclosed him, as women have embraced their lovers through the centuries.

His hands were urgent on her hips, and Elinor arched her back, already feeling the tiny ripples curling along her veins. He moved more quickly then, in the pulsing, sensuous rhythm she remembered, and was quick to answer. And all the time, he promised her, teased her with fulfillment, those enthralling, magic moments she wanted so badly. When it came, engulfing her in sensation, it was so quick she was almost disappointed. So soon! she mourned, the tears running down her face. Too soon!

Her lover uttered his own primitive cry then, his arms tightening on her back even as his hands twisted in the hair that tumbled over her shoulders and lay around them in a spill of gold.

Elinor lay quietly with her eyes closed, taking the shallow breaths that were all the confinement of his embrace allowed her, while she waited for her heart to slow its racing beat. Waited as well, for her mind and body to be hers to command again. She knew she should speak, ask him who he was, but she could not bring herself to do so. Later, perhaps. Not now. Oh no, not now.

He rolled over, taking her with him, still bound to him by love. One of his big hands smoothed her hair back.

"I love you," he whispered. "Dear God, how much I love you!"

Joy welled up in her, joy as incandescent and encompassing as the joy his lovemaking had brought to her. That joy pulsed with every one of her heartbeats, sang deep in her soul.

"I love you, too," she replied over the ache in her throat.

His hands tightened almost cruelly, and Elinor stifled a gasp. As if he sensed her discomfort, he relaxed his hold on her, and she sighed as one of his hands caressed her, tracing a slow path from her shoulder to her hip. Content, Elinor closed her eyes so she might relish that feathery touch more fully. She felt closer to her unknown Cavalier than she ever had to anyone in her life.

Reminded that he was unknown, and of her promise to herself, she whispered, "Who are you? You must tell me! It is not fair of you to keep me quite so literally in the dark all this time."

There was a long pause before he whispered, "I cannot. It would not be safe for you. But you will know soon, I promise you."

Elinor put her hands on his chest and pushed him away a little. The magic of their lovemaking had disappeared, leaving her suddenly petulant, and more than a bit disappointed. "When?" she demanded. "Can't you understand what this is doing to me? To be in love with someone you don't know—to wonder who you are, yet never find out? I have been patient long enough, and it has been agony! You say you love me. Well, if you do, you will tell me your name."

She sensed his withdrawal, not in any physical sense, but as if he were trying to distance his thoughts from her. Perversely, she longed to recall her words, be one with him again. She felt as if something precious had slipped away, some golden moment that would never come again.

"I cannot tell you for your own safety. There is danger at Mordyn. Great danger," he whispered, more coldly now. "I must ask you to trust me to see that all will be well. No harm will come to you if I can prevent it. My promise on that."

Elinor felt tears coming to her eyes, and she reached out for him, to put her arms around him and hold him close again. Suddenly there seemed to be nothing she could say.

At once, he bent his head to kiss the top of her head. As her hands ran down his back, circled his narrow waist, and crept up his broad chest, he gasped. At least I still have this much power over him, she thought sadly.

"I know this is hard for you, love, and not at all fair," his whisper came as he tucked her head under his chin and cuddled her. "Shall I tell you instead when I fell in love with you?"

He waited for her nod before he continued, "It was during those first days after your arrival at Mordyn. I thought you like a brilliant burst of sunlight in these gray old walls. So small and yet so perfect, with your beautiful figure, that lovely face and golden hair. You made me yearn to protect you—shelter you from all life's pains and disappointments.

"And when you moved, you were so graceful I ached. I wondered then whom you were mourning, hoping so fiercely it was not a husband, or a former lover. I wanted you to be mine—mine alone—as I wanted to be the only one for you. And when you spoke to your maid, laughed with her, talked about Mordyn and London—I was lost."

"You watched me here in my room?" Elinor whispered. "But how?"

"That must also be my secret. For now," he told her. His hands were moving over her body again, and wherever they touched her, they left lambent flame.

Losing interest in words, Elinor held up her lips for his kiss. It was a long, leisurely one, as if now they had all the time in the world.

Slowly, so slowly, he made love to her again, drawing out each moment of sensation until she thought she must die from it. And he whispered to her as he did so, precious words of love. It was exquisite, like nothing they had shared before—might ever share again. Elinor tried to make him feel as she did, and from his shortened breath, his thudding heartbeat, she sensed she was succeeding. After what seemed an age later, they lay close together, entwined in each other's arms, unable to speak or caress, or even to kiss. Oh, don't move, don't leave me! Elinor begged silently. Let me have this precious interlude longer!

Even later, she had to stifle a protest when he left her for a moment to reach down and pull the covers over them. The fire had died down completely, and the room had grown chill. But in his arms again, feeling all the delicious warmth of him against her, Elinor was content.

She was almost asleep when he stirred, and she whimpered a little as he drew away to rise and don his clothes.

"How I wish I did not have to go," he whispered minutes later as he leaned over to kiss her soft, swollen mouth. "But I must, even though I don't want to. Sleep now, and dream of the day when all this will be behind us, and we will be able to meet each other in bright sunlight, face to face at last, to love openly. You cannot know how much I want to see your eyes, your every expression, when I make love to you. Want you to see mine. How I long to sleep beside you every night, wake to take you in my arms, through all the years ahead. Call you—wife."

Elinor swallowed, to stifle her plea that he stay with her. Struggling, she clung to the little bit of pride she still had, as if to a lifeline.

"Must you go, truly?" she asked instead, her voice unsteady as she smoothed his tousled hair back from his brow and touched his lean cheeks with lingering fingertips. He turned his head to leave a kiss in the palm of her hand.

"Truly, I must. But we will be together soon again, my love," he promised her.

Elinor did not watch him as he moved away from the bed. She was staring up into the darkness instead, a puzzled little frown creasing her brow. Something he had said sometime—something that revealed his identity, even if he wouldn't do it openly—but she could not recall what it was. It remained elusive, hiding just beyond the far reaches of her mind.

When she turned her head again, he was gone, and there was nothing left of him but her memories, and this warm, boneless contentment she always felt all through her body after they had made love.

Who was he? she wondered once again. She did not know. She only knew she loved, and was loved in return—and for this little space of time at least, that would have to be enough. Right now, it was more than enough.

Sighing and smiling a little, she turned over and drifted off to sleep.

14

ELINOR WAS ALONE at breakfast. She was glad to have it so, glad that Fiona, Sir Robert, and both twins had come and gone before her. Only Miss Ward's place was still pristine, and somehow Elinor was sure she would not see that lady this morning.

As she ate strawberries and cream, shirred eggs and scones, and drank her coffee, Elinor was free to remember last night. She had been thinking of it almost continually since awakening. Indeed, she had had to take herself firmly in hand when Betsy stared at her oddly after she had asked a question twice and still gotten no response.

But now she was alone, Elinor was able to recall exactly how her lover's body had felt close to hers, how those long muscles of his had moved so smoothly under her hands, how his own hands—and his mouth—had touched her, and where . . .

She made herself stare out the window at the bright May morning then as she sipped her coffee, knowing it was not that hot brew that brought the flush to her face. Concentrating, she noted the sun was shining and it was a beautiful day. She wondered if Fiona would care to walk with her to Gwyneth Grenville's cottage later, for she herself must go there to explain why she had failed the other day. Or would Fiona be embarrassed by the errand?

She was about to go in search of her and inquire, when the butler entered to tell her Sir Robert wanted to see her as soon as she was through. He was waiting for her in the library, Whitman informed her as he bowed and held the door. Elinor smiled at the old butler, and she was delighted to see the little answering one that creased his face. First Mrs. Greene, now Whitman! She was becoming an accepted member of Mordyn at last.

Sir Robert was seated at his desk when Elinor entered the library and curtsied.

"You wished to see me, sir?" she asked, even as she wondered if he were feeling well. His face was so white and strained, and there were circles under his eyes. This morning, he looked every year of his age.

"Yes, I do, my dear. But sit down," he said, waving to a chair nearby and making an effort to smile.

As she did so, he continued, "I am most sorry to embroil you in this, Elinor. You have done so much already for the Grenvilles, and especially for my—my daughter. But I do not know where else to turn. Rebecca is of no use at all, and there is no one else."

"I should be delighted to help in any way I can, sir, if that is at all possible," Elinor assured him. "But forgive me, are you quite yourself? You look ill."

He rose then and came to take the chair across from her. "How like you to notice! But no, I am not ill. I am, however, upset. You see, it is Fiona . . ."

He looked away from her, to stare into the empty grate. His brows were contracted in a dark frown as he did so, and for some reason, Elinor was reminded of Jason Grenville.

"I have spoken to Fiona at great length this morning," Sir Robert went on, still not looking at her. "As you can imagine, it took me a long time to get at the truth, but finally she admitted. . ."

"Admitted?" Elinor prompted as he fell silent again.

Sir Robert turned back to her and reached out to take both her hands in his. He looked deep in her eyes as he said, sounding anguished, "Fiona confessed that she killed her kitten."

Elinor's eyes widened. "Fiona killed *Mischief?* I—I do not believe it!" she whispered. "Why, she loved her kitten, you know she did! Surely there must be some mistake!"

Sir Robert shook his head. "No, there is no mistake," he said sadly. "You see, I had a message from Gwyneth yesterday. In it, she told me she was missing a large amount of some herbal concoction she makes, one that can prove fatal if taken in excessive doses. I don't imagine Fiona would have needed much of it for a tiny kitten, would you?"

"But why does Miss Grenville accuse Fiona of taking it? Surely she must know how impossible it would be for her niece to do such a terrible thing! Perhaps someone else took the poison . . ."

"No, it was my daughter," Sir Robert said sternly, dropping her hands to rise and pace the floor. Elinor stared at him, appalled.

"Gwyneth told me Fiona was the only one who had the opportunity to do so. She said she noticed the loss of the drug the morning before Fiona disappeared. And the day before that, very early, as she was returning from an errand in the village, she saw Fiona running through the garden away from the cottage, in an almost furtive way. She called to her, but Fiona did not stop. It was as if she were in a hurry to reach the shelter of the woods before she could be detained. Gwyneth knows that scurrying figure was Fiona. She was wearing her red cape. No one else at Mordyn, indeed in the neighborhood, has one like it."

"But still, it might not have been Fiona even so. Someone might have borrowed the cape! And there was no proof she was inside Gwyneth's cottage, was there? She might have run down for an early visit, and finding her from home, gone away. And perhaps she might not have heard Gwyneth calling to her . . ."

Sir Robert had been shaking his head all through her defensive speech, and as she fell silent, he said, "No, none of that could be so. My sister assures me, on her honor, that Fiona was there. There were little signs of her presence, and Gwyneth's cat had hidden under her bed. That is something he does every time Fiona comes to visit, although he does not avoid other visitors, or so Gwyneth tells me.

"Besides, Fiona admitted the deed when I taxed her

with it, and on further questioning, she also admitted that that was why she had run away from home. She was afraid, you see, that she would be punished for it. I could not ask more. She was distraught, and she was weeping so, I feared hysteria. I excused her then, told her to go to her room and remain there."

Elinor stared at him. Fiona had *killed* Mischief? But *why?* There was no need for her to do such an awful thing, even if she had tired of caring for the kitten, which Elinor found hard to believe. McCarthy or one of the lads would have taken care of it for her gladly, spared her her grief and pain. It was most unnatural for her to feel she had to do it herself.

Sir Robert came and sat down again, interrupting her tangled thoughts. "Elinor, you have spent much time with Fiona. I would ask you if you have noticed anything strange about her lately. Any sudden changes in her behavior or routine."

"Why, no, I haven't," Elinor said slowly. "She has seemed content. The only new thing are her visits to her aunt. But she has enjoyed those, enjoyed helping her in her work with the herbs."

"It reassures me to hear you say so. I have been sitting here wondering if she were mentally ill. Deranged, even."

Elinor raised a startled hand. "Oh, my dear sir, surely not that!" she said quickly, concerned for the stark despair on his face. Then she frowned.

"Yes? Yes? What is it? What did you just think of?"

"It—it is only that ever since her brother Jason returned, Fiona has not been as happy," Elinor admitted. "She seems frightened of him—well, you have seen her with him yourself. Perhaps his appearance at Mordyn has distressed her, caused this peculiar behavior?"

Sir Robert thought hard. "He might have upset her by the suddenness of his arrival, with no warning. Jason is a stranger to Fiona now, and you, yourself, know how leery she is of strangers. Just remember how long it took for her to accept you.

"But surely there can be no connection between Jason's reappearance, and the killing of her kitten,'' he said firmly.

Elinor subsided.

''I intend to write to London. There is a physician there who has treated Fiona before, one who is aware of her condition. I shall ask him to travel to Mordyn, to examine her yet again. In the meantime, I would ask you, as a favor, to watch her carefully, and come and tell me if you see anything unusual about her.''

Elinor promised, but when she would have risen and left him, he held up his hand.

''There is something else. Jonathan tells me he informed you of the reason for Jason's exile from Mordyn,'' he said, two spots of color burning high on his cheeks.

''Yes, he did. I am very sorry. It was a very sad thing. But perhaps you would rather he had not told me?'' Elinor asked. ''I do assure you, the secret is safe with me.''

''No, no, not at all. I see that I was at fault not to have mentioned it before,'' Sir Robert said, trying to smile. ''After all, now you are one of the family, it is your right to know all our dark secrets.''

Somehow, Elinor was glad he went on before she was forced to comment on that statement. ''I would ask what you, as a comparative stranger here, think of Jason. I have not seen him for twenty years, and of course the man grown is vastly different from the boy I knew. And from the man Jonathan has become. How would you assess Jason?''

''I really don't know,'' Elinor replied, wishing with all her heart Sir Robert had not asked her that particular question. ''He—he is an enigma to me, so cold and black, so—so crude compared to his twin. I have wondered sometimes why he returned here at all, since he does not appear to be happy for having done so.''

''Perhaps he is overcome with guilt,'' Sir Robert suggested. ''Oh, not for what he did to his brother, after all this time, but for his part in Fiona's condition. After all, it is his fault alone that his sister can't speak. And he never knew, when he went away, that that would become a permanent condition."

"His fault? But how could that be his fault?" Elinor asked, perplexed.

"Why, didn't you know? Strange, I was so sure someone—Rebecca, perhaps—would have told you.

"Fiona never spoke another word after my son Rob died so tragically. At first we thought, the physicians and I, that it was just the trauma of the experience that made her mute. That surely in time she would regain her power of speech. But she has never done so. And Jason did not know that when he came back."

"He has a great deal to answer for," Elinor said carefully.

"Do you wonder why I permit him to remain here? Sometimes, I wonder myself. But Mordyn is Jason's home, and there have been occasions when I have felt that I was wrong to . . ."

Sir Robert rose again, and turned his back. His voice sounded tortured as he continued, "Occasions when I felt I had been too harsh with him. I have missed Jason—my son—very much over the years. Thought of him, wondered how he was making out, agonized over him, more than was good for my peace of mind. But the deed had been done then, the exile imposed. I could not bring him back, not ever."

Elinor was horrified to see Sir Robert wipe his eyes before he turned back to her.

"Strange, isn't it?" he said quietly. "Now, so long after, I find it hard to feel anything but deep regret for what I did to the boy in my grief all those years ago. No matter what he had done, he was as much my son as Rob was, or Jonathan either, for that matter. If I had only been able to find it in my heart to forgive him, he might have become a different man than he is today."

He came back to her and took her hands again. "Tell me, Elinor, did he talk much to you when you were alone together on the moor? Did he speak at all of Mordyn? Perhaps even voice his regrets that he had had to leave it?"

Elinor shook her head, although she wished she could have replied favorably. Sir Robert looked so eager. "No, he did not. He barely spoke to me at all. But he would not be likely to do so to a stranger, sir," she said.

Sir Robert dropped her hands and sighed. "No, I suppose not. I only asked because he will not speak to me, not openly. I guess I have forfeited that father's privilege by my own deed. But I hoped—well, no matter.

"Thank you, my dear. You have been very patient with my rambling confessions. I appreciate your kindness."

Elinor rose and curtsied. "My dear Sir Robert," she said, her voice not quite steady, "I am honored that you felt able to confide in me. Know I will watch Fiona carefully and come to you at once if I notice anything unusual."

Sir Robert had gone back to his desk to fuss over some papers there, and he only nodded. Understanding he could not speak just then, Elinor left the room quietly.

As she went across the hall to her sitting room, her mind tumbled with chaotic thoughts. Firmly, she put Mr. Jason Grenville away from them. Fiona must be her main, her only, concern now.

Staring with unseeing eyes into The Lady's Garden glowing with the color and scent of the blooming flowers in the sunshine, Elinor considered what Sir Robert had told her. Even now, with all that evidence to hand, she found it hard to believe that Fiona had poisoned Mischief. Why, she herself had seen Fiona's grief when she was burying him. It was incomprehensible that any normal human being would have done such a thing, not and wrapped him so carefully in a flannel-lined box, touched his fur so gently, and wept so copiously afterward.

Elinor's hand tightened on the brocade drapery as a new, more horrible thought entered her mind. Was it possible that Fiona was not normal? She could not be, to do what she had done. And even her father had suggested she might be deranged.

Elinor remembered how Jonathan had told her of his twin's sadistic habit of torturing small animals. Could such a trait run in the family? Be more marked in Fiona, perhaps? For even putting aside her dumbness, her inability to write, there had been times Fiona had not behaved normally. Those terrible temper tantrums of hers, the way she stamped her foot and could not be quieted. And sometimes those storms were only the result of the absence of her favorite muffins for breakfast! Surely that was not rational behavior!

Nor had it been rational for Fiona to run away to the moors. However had she imagined she was to survive up there? She had little food with her, and no chance of getting more. And where had she expected to find shelter? Any sane person, capable of even rudimentary logic, would have discarded the plan immediately.

Elinor decided she must talk to Gwyneth Grenville right away. And this time, Gwyneth must be open with her, since Sir Robert had told her of his heir's death. And she could ask her advice about Fiona, for even loving the girl as she did now, Elinor knew she could not be easy in her company anymore. Instead, she would always be on her guard, watching her with trepidation, waiting for her to do something odd.

Heavens, Fiona might even become dangerous! And hadn't her lover warned her that there was danger at Mordyn? Did he mean danger from Fiona Grenville?

Yes, she must see Gwyneth as soon as she could about this impossible situation. She needed Gwyneth's calm reason, her reassurance, if she were to succeed. And Gwyneth had been with her niece many times now. Perhaps she had noticed something about her that the rest of them had missed.

She was about to ring for Betsy to bring her a light stole when Whitman knocked and presented her with a note on his tray. "Come from Glyn, it did, miss," he said. "From Mr. Harry, no doubt."

Elinor missed his little smile as she broke the seal.

As she scanned the note quickly, her heart sank. The boating expedition was planned for this very afternoon. Harry had written he was sorry for the short notice, but the day was so perfect, he did not care to postpone it. Surely Miss Fielding could arrange to come! He said he had sent a note to Jonathan as well, and if he did not hear from them in an hour, he would continue his preparations. He, himself, would come and fetch them in his carriage at noon.

Why did it have to be today? Elinor wondered as she crumpled the note. She wished she might refuse, but she knew it would look strange if she did so, and it would be most impolite. Harry had planned the sail to give her pleasure. She must accept.

"Has Mr. Jonathan received his note, Whitman?" she asked.

"Aye, long before you did, miss, but you were with Sir Robert. Mr. Jonathan told me to tell you he'd be in the old hall at noon."

"Very well. Thank you," Elinor said, looking at the Cartel mantel clock and noting it was already past eleven. Her visit to Gwyneth Grenville must be postponed. As she hurried upstairs, she hoped Jonathan would be feeling more cheerful today; that the coldness she had noted last night had had time to dissipate.

Even as pressed for time as she was, she paused at Fiona's door, but she received no reply to her knock, and when she tried the door, she discovered it was locked. Shaking her head, she went along the corridor to Rebecca Ward's room, but the maid who answered her summons told her Miss Ward could not be disturbed, for she was still feeling quite done in.

Elinor ignored the girl's smirk as she turned away. She must inform Sir Robert she would not be in for luncheon and alert him to Fiona's lonely state, before she left. In her room, she wrote him a short note and summoned Betsy to deliver it, before she chose a simpler gown to wear. She had no idea what was suitable for fishing and sailing, but she hoped her plainest black muslin would do. At least it would be easy to clean if it became soiled or wet.

When she ran down to the medieval hall, carrying a light, hooded cloak, she discovered Harry Brownell had already arrived. He had been talking to Jonathan, but he sprang to his feet and came toward her with a beaming smile.

"Am I late? I am so sorry," Elinor said, as he bowed over her hands.

"No, our eager Harry was early," Jonathan drawled, looking almost amused.

Elinor glanced at him and she was relieved to see he had himself well in hand. At least his face no longer sported thunderheads, and for that she was grateful.

"Phoebe is waiting in the carriage with my mother," Harry said as the three left the hall via the little entrance room. Elinor could hardly wait to step outside the castle door, for ever since Sir Robert had told her the room's original purpose, she never lingered there a moment longer than she had to.

"Your mother is going with us?" Jonathan asked, his brows raised. "But surely she will be redundant, Harry. Believe me, I shall watch you most carefully, and you are welcome to watch me."

Harry blushed, looking as if he hated himself for doing so. "No, no, Jon, she is taking the carriage on to Trecarrag for the afternoon. She merely rides with us to the harbor, and she will be there at four to take us up again."

"You have thought of everything for our comfort, sir," Elinor complimented him, trying to be kind. Really, it was too bad of Jonathan to twit him so, she thought.

She greeted Mrs. Brownell and Phoebe as she took her seat beside them in the spacious family coach. The gentlemen rode facing back, sharing the seat with a large lunch basket, some rugs, and fishing poles.

On this occasion, Mrs. Brownell was more than gracious, asking Elinor about her stay at Mordyn, and saying she hoped she would find herself a good sailor.

"Of course Phoebe has been sailing since childhood," she said proudly. "As good as her brother she is, aren't you, my dear?"

"Mama! You will put me to the blush!" the girl said with a little smile for Jonathan Grenville. "Besides, Harry is outstanding. No one can best him at yacht racing."

"I wish Miss Fielding might see him at it, but alas, there is not enough wind today," Mrs. Brownell said. "But I am sure what breeze there is, will be more suitable for ladies."

Turning to Elinor then, she went on, "As his mother I should not be the one to say so, but Harry is a nonpareil on the water. You will be quite safe, Miss Fielding."

Elinor did not dare look at her host, for she was positive he must be crimson by now. "I am looking forward to the outing a great deal, ma'am," she said. "It was so kind of Mr. Brownell to include me."

"I do believe we have reached Downlong, Harry, old son," Jonathan drawled. "In a moment you may jump from the coach, thus escaping these fulsome encomiums on your prowess. Much to your relief, I'm sure."

As the coach pulled up at the front, Elinor saw a sailor with a small boat waiting to take them out to the yacht. Mr. Brownell confided she was a converted fishing yawl he had named *Siren.*

He hurried ahead carrying the lunch basket, with Jonathan following him at a more leisurely pace with the rugs and poles. Phoebe kissed her mother before she went after them. As Elinor stepped down and prepared to join the others, Mrs. Brownell said, "Enjoy yourself now, Miss Fielding! There is nothing like an afternoon under sail!"

Elinor smiled, touched by the kindness of this formerly straitlaced lady. "Thank you, ma'am, I am sure I shall," she said.

Just then Phoebe squealed in mock terror, and they both turned to see her backing away from Jonathan, who was threatening her in jest with a basket of bait.

"Jonathan is such a handsome beau, is he not?" Mrs. Brownell asked as she peered past Elinor's shoulder through the window of the coach.

Staring at that tall, well-built figure in the tight breeches and the open-necked shirt he wore today, with the sunlight glinting on his dark hair and his face alight with laughter, Elinor could only nod in agreement. She felt her heart quicken, and warmth course deep inside her. Jonathan was more than handsome, he was superb, almost godlike.

"And my Phoebe is so lovely as well, is she not? I do not fear a mother's prejudice makes me say so, for I have been complimented on her appearance many times. What a stunning couple they will make! The children are sure to be outstanding," Mrs. Brownell confided, smiling in delight. "I am sure Jonathan will be calling on my husband soon. We have all been expecting him to do so this age!"

Before she could say more, her son came back to help Elinor down the beach. "Have a pleasant afternoon, Mama," he said, giving that lady a quick kiss. "But don't forget we shall be back here waiting at four."

Mrs. Brownell promised she would not fail, and Elinor waved to her as the coach went on its way.

Elinor discovered that the sailor who rowed them all out to the *Siren* was to come along and help with the lines. As she took the seat that Harry Brownell indicated in the large, roomy yawl, she watched the two men raise the sails and anchor. As the yawl ghosted through the almost empty harbor, Elinor looked around with interest. How different the cliffs were from down here, she thought. So towering and powerful. It was an entirely different perspective from the clifftop where she had been painting earlier.

As they cleared the cliff walls, the breeze that had been in abeyance in the narrow, protected harbor freshened. As Elinor felt *Siren* heel over, she grasped the varnished coaming for support.

"You must not worry, Miss Fielding," Harry Brownell called from his position behind the wheel. "I assure you it is quite safe. Jerry, man, tighten that jib sheet and bring in the main a bit. She's luffing. I'll set the jigger."

The boatman grinned as he obeyed. Elinor took a deep breath, firmly holding on to her bonnet. Suddenly, she felt as free as any gull must feel wheeling over these sparkling waters, and her eager posture, her delighted smile, drew an answering one from her host.

Glancing at Jonathan Grenville then, Elinor saw he was watching her closely, his handsome eyes narrowed against the glare. Beside him, Phoebe Brownell edged closer, smiling for him alone. Yes, they were an outstanding couple, Elinor thought. She wondered they were not pledged as yet.

She was struck then by the thought that their coming alliance might well be the reason Jonathan had never asked *her* to marry him, why he had said it was a shame he was a gentleman, at the cliff the day he had told her about his brother Rob's death. For if he had even a casual understanding with Miss Brownell, he could hardly do so in good conscience. Perhaps he was trying to extricate himself from the entanglement before he came openly to her? For, Elinor reminded herself, he *had* kissed her, had warned her there were to be future meetings between them, had even told her of his interest in her.

And if he were indeed her late-night Cavalier, that might well be the reason he could not tell her his name as yet. But of course! Elinor told herself, wondering she had been so stupid. He had to treat her coolly and pretend he didn't care, in public. But he could not always stop himself from coming to her at night. Remembering the hours they had spent together last night, Elinor blushed. How very glad she was he had that weakness.

The boatman took over the helm then, and Harry joined her on the windward bench. Elinor was forced to put Jonathan from her mind as Harry pointed back to various landmarks, all now fast disappearing astern. Even Mordyn looked tiny, like a child's sand castle.

It was a pleasant afternoon. The picnic lunch was delicious, and Elinor caught a fish herself, a large pollock which Jonathan promised they would all enjoy for dinner. By the time they headed back to the harbor again, Elinor had discarded her bonnet, and rolled up the sleeves of her muslin gown, although she noted Phoebe Brownell had done neither, nor had she removed her gloves.

"I fear you will be sunburned tonight, Miss Fielding," the girl said in her well-bred, cool contralto.

Elinor laughed. "No doubt I will. But what care I? The sun feels so good on my face!"

"Come and take a turn at the wheel, Miss Fielding," Harry Brownell suggested with a happy grin. "Don't worry, I'll help you."

Elinor was quick to obey, but she was disgusted to find she could not steer anywhere near as straight a course as her host. Harry positioned himself behind her, to guide her hands. He stood very close to her as he did so, his arms enclosing her.

"Go and sit down, Elinor," Jonathan said moments later as he made his way aft toward them. "I'll take the helm now."

Happily involved with her first sailing lesson, Elinor was about to refuse when she noticed the cold expression on Jonathan's face, his angry gray eyes. Chilled, she stepped aside at once and went to sit beside Miss Brownell and chat with her.

Jonathan handed the helm back to Harry Brownell as they entered the harbor. He seemed in a better humor now, and Elinor was relieved. Had he been jealous? she wondered. But for what other reason would he have interrupted her fun? It was very strange, especially since Harry Brownell was like an eager puppy, with just about as much finesse as one, too. She had no interest in him except as a friend. Surely Jonathan did not fear she might be falling in love with Brownell!

Jonathan helped her into the rowing boat himself, and it was he who carried her ashore to the beach a few minutes later, leaving Harry to assist his pouting sister. Glyn's coach was nowhere in sight.

"Oh dear," Phoebe said petulantly. "Mama must have been delayed, and I have no desire to linger here. The beach smells so!"

Elinor had to agree that at low tide there was a rather fishy odor, now further enhanced by Harry's boatman, who was cleaning their catch. Gulls squawked and quarreled over the entrails he flung to them.

"She probably got talking to Mrs. Wilkenson and

forgot the time,'' Harry said easily. ''If only Downlong sported an inn, we might repair there to wait, even have some tea.''

''I rather think Elinor and I will walk back to Mordyn, Harry,'' Jonathan said. ''It is no great distance if we take the shortcut through the woods. For although it has been a pleasant time, Elinor is fast turning red. Best I get her under cover quickly.''

''You make me feel like a cooked lobster!'' Elinor protested. ''I am no such thing! Besides, it would be rude to leave the Brownells here alone.''

''Oh no, you must not consider us, my dear Miss Fielding,'' Harry assured her. ''I am only sorry Mama has been delayed.''

He blushed and held out his hand. ''Jonathan is right. You should go home and apply some lotion, not stand about here in this hot, sunny place.''

Elinor could feel Jonathan's firm, strong hand cupping her elbow, almost urging her away, and she knew he was anxious to be gone. ''Well, if you are sure,'' she said.

Thanks were given and received, and good-byes exchanged, before Jonathan escorted Elinor from the beach and along the road to the shortcut at a quick pace. Elinor insisted on carrying her pollock herself, carefully wrapped up in paper.

As they entered the shade of the woods, she breathed a sigh of relief. It was cooler here; she knew how flushed she must be.

''That was not very polite of you, Jonathan,'' she scolded as he held back a branch for her. ''But I must admit it is pleasanter here in the woods, for Phoebe was right. The beach did smell.''

In the little silence that followed, she realized he had not spoken a word since they had left the others, and she stole a glance at him. He looked angry again, and suddenly she was exasperated.

''*Now* what is it?'' she demanded, coming to a sudden stop in the path. ''I declare, you are the most prickly man! It takes nothing at all to set you off like a cannon, and looking as black as thunder, too! But what on earth could have offended you *this* time?''

He turned and stared at her, his dark brows contracted over narrowed gray eyes. "You're surprised?" he asked, between clenched teeth. 'You do not consider your outrageous behavior this afternoon with Harry Brownell offensive? Even common?"

"What outrageous behavior?" Elinor asked, much confused. "Whatever are you talking about?"

"When you took the helm, and he stood behind you, cuddling you so close!" Jonathan snapped. "I am sure Phoebe did not know where to look, she was so embarrassed!"

"Pooh!" Elinor said, tossing her head. "She only longed to be in my place, with you in her brother's. How sad it is she is such a good sailor, she could not ask for the guidance of your arms.

"Besides, you are ridiculous! He was only instructing me."

"Harry did not think of it that way," Jonathan said, coming closer. "I do assure you he enjoyed every moment of it. There was such an expression of bliss on his silly face, it was almost laughable!"

"A pity you could not laugh, then! Mr. Brownell is a very nice young man, but I have no interest in him except as a friend," Elinor said, suddenly aware that they were alone, far from the castle, and almost equally far from the village.

"And even if I did, it is none of your business," she rushed on, somewhat recklessly in the light of Jonathan's dangerous glare. "You do not own me!"

Suddenly, rage distorted his features, and Elinor was terrified. But then, to her surprise, his expression changed, and he began to laugh, long and loud and helplessly. She watched in amazement as he shook his head and said at last, "How ridiculous I must seem to you! I do beg your pardon, Elinor. You have discovered my most grievous fault—my jealousy.

"You see, my dear, I do not want anyone else touching you, nor do I want you to smile at other men. But to think I flared up over such a paltry specimen of manhood as insignificant, naive Harry Brownell with his girlish blushes and obvious infatuation, is ludicrous. You must have enchanted me, to make me behave in such an idiotic way."

He moved closer to her then, and bent slightly to ask, "Do you forgive me? Please say you do!"

"Well, of course I do," Elinor made herself reply, mesmerized by his warm intent gaze and rueful little smile—the feel of his hands as they caressed her arms.

He stepped closer still. "I admit I am a possessive man. What is mine, or in your case, what *will* be mine, I keep safe. Most women would adore to be treated that way. Surely, like them, you would prefer passion to, er, polite indifference?"

Elinor could only stare at him, speechless. Once again Jonathan had changed, this time from the stern accuser, to the merry joker, to the tender lover in only moments. What a complicated man he was! she thought. Would she ever understand him?

He took her in his arms and bent his head to kiss her slowly. His lips were warm on hers, warm and sure, and yes, they were possessive, yet still enticing. Confused, Elinor closed her eyes and surrendered to the sensations his kiss evoked.

When he lifted his head at last, he whispered, "Do you think you could possibly dispose of that fish you are clutching to your breast, my lovely one? I find it very much in the way, to say nothing of the fact that the aroma that clings to it is hardly conducive to seduction. Surely you must agree!"

Still retaining her catch, Elinor backed away from him, and he grinned at her, the corners of his eyes crinkling shut in that appealing way she remembered. In spite of herself, she grinned back.

"My, I do not seem to have much luck, do I?" he mused. "First that heavy tome in the library, and now a fish. I wonder what you will find to defend yourself with next time?"

"You'll have to wait and see, now won't you?" she asked, feeling breathless with her daring.

As he started toward her, the dangerous light back in his eyes, she added, "But you remind me I must get this fish to Cook as soon as possible, lest it become unfit to eat. I would be so disappointed if that should happen!"

She picked up her skirt and started to climb toward the castle again. For some reason, she felt a great relief when Jonathan came to her, to cup her elbow and help her, without trying to keep her there any longer, continue his lovemaking.

As they walked, he said, "Tell me, my dear, if you would be so good, what really happened to you and my twin on the moor. I did not find the story he told us rang true, for some reason."

"I can't imagine why, for it was the truth," Elinor said. "Just as he said, I was lost on the moor. I originally lost my way trying to find the old tinner's shack Miss Ward had told me about. I was frightened and tired, and there was that awful storm approaching. Mr. Grenville merely guided me to your uncle's house."

"Yes, and that is strange, too," Jonathon mused. "Uncle James never sees a soul, or lets anyone in his house. I have never seen him myself, for he left the castle before I was born. I find it hard to believe he would make an exception to his iron-clad rule, even for you."

"I didn't see your uncle either, so I have no idea what Mr. Grenville said to persuade him to do so," Elinor told him. "But thank heavens he managed it! I was wet through by then, and it was late, and much too dark to risk trying to get back to Mordyn."

"You were wet through?" Jonathan asked quickly. "Did you disrobe?"

"Why, yes, I had to," Elinor admitted, regretting she had let that part of the adventure slip out. "I wrapped up in an old blanket until my clothes dried out before the fire."

There was an ominous silence, and she added hotly, "Mr. Grenville was a perfect gentleman! He left me quite alone. I do not know where he slept, or even if he did. The whole farmhouse was packed from floor to ceiling with old papers, boxes, broken furniture, kegs—a million things. There were only narrow alleys to get from one place to another. It—it was awful."

Still the ominous silence continued, and she swallowed and said, "We left at dawn, and came straight home. And that was all there was to it."

A quick glance at Jonathan's face showed he was frowning again. "I see," he said slowly as they left the woods and began to cross the grass outside the castle walls. "Yes, I am sure it must have been as you say. Jason has grown to be quite the boor, but even he would not take advantage of you under the circumstances."

"I would never have allowed him to do so!" Elinor gasped.

"My dear, sweet Elinor, you would have had no say in the matter at all," he told her coldly. "If he had wanted to, he could have raped you any number of times. I can only be glad that his original breeding kept him from indulging in something I am sure has become one of his favorite pastimes."

"You are most unfair to your twin, Jonathan," Elinor said. "You do not know he is that kind of man. How could you?"

"No, that is true," he admitted, holding the door open for her. "I suppose sadist and murderer are quite bad enough, without adding rapist to his list. I must not be so severe."

As they went into the medieval hall, he added, "And perhaps he knew enough to be afraid of me, for I would have killed him if he had even touched you."

His voice was cold and flat, without inflection, and Elinor shivered. Yes, he would do just that, she was sure of it.

She gave her fish to a footman and sent him off with it to the kitchen. Bowing, Jonathan kissed her hand. His nose wrinkled as he did so, and she had to chuckle.

"After you wash off this lingering reminder of your catch, apply some cooling lotion to your face and arms, Elinor," he told her. She nodded as she turned toward the stairs.

Looking down the hall, she saw Jason Grenville lounging against the door of the gold salon, watching them. For a moment, the three of them stared at each other, before they went their separate ways without speaking.

At the top of the second flight, Elinor paused to look

up at the portrait of the Cavalier, her head tipped to one side as she considered him.

"I wonder if you were as difficult to understand as your descendants are, sir?" she asked him. "For I admit I cannot fathom Jonathan Grenville especially, decide what manner of man he is. He shows me so many sides to him—love, anger, jealousy—even indifference and cruelty sometimes. Are all Grenville males like that? And then there is Fiona, and I do not understand her, either. Oh why, I wonder, did I ever come here, become embroiled with the lot of you?"

The Cavalier smiled down at her, his painted eyes full of hidden amusement. It appeared to Elinor that he was laughing at her, but she did not put up her chin in defiance this time. Instead, she just stood there, looking lost and bewildered.

The clock in the gallery ticked quietly in its corner, and there was not another sound to be heard anywhere in the castle. Elinor sighed.

It was at that moment she felt a gentle touch on her shoulder. Instinctively, she knew no human hand was there, that she was still quite alone. And yet she also knew something was touching her. She tried not to panic. There was a real, not unpleasant chill surrounding her now, and as she stared upward, the painting of the Cavalier seemed to dim, as if a misty veil had been thrown over it.

The pressure on her shoulder lingered, almost, she thought wildly, as if it were trying to comfort her somehow.

She did not know the exact moment the touch was gone, she only knew the world returned to normal.

The chill around her dissipated, a maid appeared at the end of the hall and dropped her a curtsy, and below her, someone slammed a door and she heard voices. Relieved, Elinor retreated to her room without giving the Cavalier's portrait another glance.

Somehow she was positive he meant her no harm, nor ever had, but she also knew she would never look at him or talk to him again, for in doing so, she might summon up his ghost, however inadvertently.

The whole experience had been entirely too eerie to take that chance.

15

FIONA DID COME down to dinner, although from her closed face and timid demeanor, Elinor was sure it had been at her father's direct order. She also refused to play the piano after dinner, only shaking her head to all Elinor's entreaties. Sir Robert was no more successful, and at last he suggested a rubber or two of whist. Armed with a book, Fiona retreated to a distant armchair, while the twins, Sir Robert, and Elinor took their places at the card table.

As he dealt the first hand, Sir Robert said, with a twinkle in his eye, "The fish was delicious, Elinor, but I have to wonder if the game was worth the candle. You have such a glow about you this evening."

"Gently put, sir. I admire your adroitness," Jonathan remarked as he picked up his hand. "But it would be closer to the truth to say she is as red as a beet."

Elinor could only nod in agreement, chuckling as she did so, for as the sun had gone down, her color had risen. The lotion she had applied had done little to help. "It is not very kind of you to remark my sunburn," she said in mock reproof. "But yes, it was worth it, sir. Sailing is so exhilarating!"

She caught Jonathan's eye across the table then, and she was forced to lower her own, feeling a most unnecessary flush adding its bit to her already rosy complexion. Was he remembering her turn at the helm? Harry Brownell's arms around her? Elinor wondered as she sorted her cards according to suit. Perhaps his sudden frown was only because he had been dealt a poor hand. She did so hope so!

Even so, she and Jonathan won the hand easily, and

by the end of an hour, they had also won a great number of imaginary guineas, for Sir Robert had never allowed them to play for real money. As Elinor picked up the deck to shuffle them, she had to stifle a wide yawn.

"I do beg your pardon, sir," she said, more than a little mortified.

"Fresh ocean air will do it every time," Sir Robert told her. "But come, we have had enough of cards this evening. You run along to bed before you fall asleep right in front of our eyes. Jason and I are more than willing to concede such an unequal match, are we not, son?"

"Ter be sure," Mr. Grenville said, tilting back in his chair and raising both his arms over his head to stretch. "Bit tired, m'self."

"Where were you today?" Sir Robert said as he put the cards away. "You were gone from early morning to just before tea."

"I was up on the moors and in Portreath as well," Grenville told him. "Some business o' mine ter take care o', is all."

In the little silence that followed his remark, Elinor made her curtsies and excused herself. Stopping by Fiona's chair, she smiled and gently squeezed her shoulder. "Good night, dear," she said. "Shall I see you in the morning?"

Never taking her eyes from the printed page, Fiona shrugged her hand away. Peeking over her shoulder, Elinor saw she held a book of sermons. It would have seemed odd that Fiona could be engrossed in such a tome, except Elinor was well aware she was not engrossed in it at all. She merely held the book for protection, to help distance herself from the others, and any possible conversation.

And that was not abnormal, Elinor reminded herself as she climbed the stairs. Of course she is upset—embarassed even—to have been found out. She'll get over it in time, I know she will.

But tomorrow I shall call on Gwyneth, ask for her help, she promised herself as she passed the Cavalier's portrait without even raising her eyes to it. I will go early, too, before she can leave the cottage, and under no condition will I take Fiona with me. Not this time. This time I intend to have a very serious talk with Gwyneth about Fiona, and the problem she has become, and to do that, we have to be alone.

After Betsy put more lotion on her reddened skin, Elinor was glad to climb into bed and close her eyes. As she settled down to sleep, she rather hoped her Cavalier would not come tonight. She was sure even his gentle touch would hurt.

By morning, her skin felt much more comfortable, and the redness of the previous evening had become the healthy glow Sir Robert had mentioned. Dressing quickly, Elinor was early to breakfast. One of the twins was before her, and when he did not bother to rise and hold her chair for her, she had no trouble identifying him as Jason Grenville.

"Feelin' better?" he asked gruffly as she brought her plate to the table.

"Why, yes, thank you, Mr. Grenville," she said as she took her seat and spread her napkin in her lap. "May I have the jam, please?"

He passed it to her before he returned to the revery she had interrupted. Elinor ate her breakfast calmly, forgetting her unsatisfactory companion. She thought instead of her coming meeting with Gywneth, and she wondered where Fiona was this morning. Noticing no place had been set for her, she wondered when Rebecca Ward would quit her room. She could not stay secluded forever, after all. Elinor realized if it had been she who had been in such a position, she would have braved company long before this, for delaying unpleasantness could only make it more difficult in the end.

She left Jason Grenville still at the table a few minutes later. The Lady's Garden looked lovely in the bright May sunshine, alive with bees and birdsong, but she did not linger there. Instead, she made her way quickly through the woods and past the Home Farm with only a wave to McCarthy and the lads, who were clustered near the paddock, admiring the two new foals and their dams. Perhaps she would have a chance to admire them herself when she returned, Elinor thought as she took the path through the little wood that led to Gwyneth's farmhouse.

She found that lady busy with a large washing, and in spite of all her protests, she rolled up her sleeves to help. As she scrubbed and rinsed, she explained why she had failed to come as she had promised, the day she had gone up on the moor.

"Och, I know all about that! Knew it almost as soon as you left Mordyn. That's the thing about a small country place. Everyone knows everything about everybody, whether they want them to or not," Gwyneth told her as she wrung out a tablecloth and set it in a reed basket. "It was a silly thing for you to do, Elinor, but I expect you've heard that before, haven't you?"

"Several times!" Elinor said tartly.

"Time to forget it, then, move on to other things. It does no good at all to fret over 'what might have been, if only . . .' Besides, it was good of you to try and help Fiona, even though she was never in any danger, no matter what Rebecca Ward said. I expect my niece took refuge in the fourgou."

"What's that?"

"An underground chamber. We've several fourgous in Kernow. No one knows when they were built, or exactly for what purpose, but they are all very old. I don't care for them myself, although they give good shelter with their dry stone walls and huge rock slab ceilings. There's a disquieting feeling to them somehow. I suspect in ancient times they were used for storerooms, and perhaps they were also the setting for some heathen rituals. Fiona has been fascinated by the one above Wheal Beatrice ever since she was very small."

"I don't think I'd care for such a place myself," Elinor said thoughtfully as she handed over the last petticoat.

"Thank you. I'll just spread these on the bushes in the sun."

Following her out to the yard, Elinor helped with the chore.

"There, that's the last of them!" Gwyneth said, looking around at her snowy laundry with satisfaction. "And since I gave the house a good red-up this morning, I can minch awhile. Let's sit over there in the shade. You'd do better to avoid any more sun for a few days."

As she led the way to two rustic seats under a beech tree, she said, "Remind me to give you some of my special balm. You don't need it now, but since you're turning into such a countrywoman, you may get sunburned again. You'll like my lotion, and it smells nice, too. The base is lavender."

As they took their seats, she went on, "My, how my practice is growing! Even Rebecca Ward came by late yesterday, to ask me for a nerve tonic."

"She did? How strange! I thought her secluded in her room, where she had been ever since Sir Robert chastised her for sending me up on the moors."

Gwyneth shrugged. "Well, she managed to come here. Asked a great many questions about the herbs, too. She was especially interested in the potion Fiona stole to kill her kitten. I didn't tell her much. I dislike ghouls."

Reminded of her reason for visiting, Elinor forgot Miss Ward in a second.

"I want to speak to you about Fiona, if I may, and to ask your help," she said slowly. "Jonathan told me what happened to his older brother, and Sir Robert has spoken of the incident as well, so you need not feel you are talking out of turn."

She paused, but when Gwyneth had no comment, she took a deep breath and said, "I am so concerned for Fiona! I still find it incomprehensible that she could kill Mischief when she loved him so. Surely she cannot be normal."

"No, Fiona is not normal," Gwyneth agreed in a steady voice.

"Sir Robert told me he is afraid she is losing her mind, becoming deranged."

Gwyneth snorted. "Of course she's not deranged!" she said in exasperation. "If that isn't just like my brother, jumping to conclusions with not a shred of proof!"

"But to deliberately poison her kitten and then to weep so over his grave is not normal behavior," Elinor persisted.

"No, you are right there. However, there are many reasons my niece might have felt she had no other recourse."

"What possible reasons could she have?"

"Fear, perhaps," Gwyneth mused, her expression thoughtful. "Fear can make anyone act strangely. I do not know what Fiona is afraid of, but I do know she has had this fear for a very long time. I had thought she might outgrow it as she grew older, come to see it as irrational, but she has not done so. Nor has she begun to speak again."

"You mean you think she still can? But can that be?"

"It is strange, but sometimes when she is with me, working on the herb medicine, I sense she is about to do so, so she can ask me a question. But then she clamps her lips together and gives her head a tiny shake, and the moment passes. I have watched her many times, when she does not realize she is being observed."

"How—how extraordinary! But if what you say is true, her silence is not normal either." Elinor leaned forward in her seat so she could take her older friend's hands. "Gwyneth, Sir Robert has asked me to watch Fiona—tell him if I see anything strange about her. He is sending for a London physician to examine her again."

She paused and bit her lip before she went on, "I am ashamed to admit I don't really want to be near Fiona anymore, much as I have come to love her. I am more than a little afraid of her now. For after all, if she could coldly kill a kitten she loved, who knows what she might decide to do next? She might even be dangerous!"

Gwyneth held tight to her hands. ''Listen to me, Elinor, and trust me. I would never let harm come to you. Oh, no, not to you!

''You have nothing to fear from my niece. You are the first real friend she has ever had, and she loves you. She would never hurt you. Indeed, I do not think her capable of hurting a fly, under normal circumstances. What she did, she did for some very good reason, or at least it seemed so to her. For now, there is nothing anyone can do—no, not even Robert's fancy London physician. We must wait for Fiona herself to decide the time has come to stop hiding, to finally face up to whatever frightening bane she has been concealing, bring it out into the open, and deal with it.''

''Pray you are right, and thank you,'' Elinor said, releasing her hands and sitting back in her chair again. ''But tell me, if you would, how Fiona really lost her power of speech. I understand it was right after she saw her eldest brother fall to his death?''

''Yes, that is so. I ran up to the castle that afternoon as soon as word came of the accident, and I found Fiona in hysterics. She could not be calmed or comforted, not by anyone. Indeed, I had to give her a strong sedative, to make her sleep.''

''Was she crying normally then?''

Gwyneth nodded. ''Oh, yes, in loud wails and piercing shrieks. But when she woke the next day, she could not make any sound at all. Nor has she done so to this day.''

''And then Jason Grenville was sent away because he was the cause of his brother's death,'' Elinor mused.

''Yes, that is what Jonathan told his father, and he was very positive of his facts, although he was shaking with fear. But I must say I have often wondered about that. Jason, however, would not defend himself. His silence was taken for guilt. Bah! Even at ten he had such pride, and look where it has left him—left all of us.''

She sighed and shook her head. ''I am sure Jason's banishment reinforced Fiona's determination to remain mute. Oh, I have no proof of that. It is only a theory I have."

"I find it so hard to believe that she could really talk if she wanted to," Elinor marveled. "To think she has lived in a silent world for twenty long years, all by her own choice. Are you sure?"

"Of course not. It is only another theory of mine. She may very well have lost the power to speak after all this time. But she had a reason for it then, just as she had a reason for never wanting to learn to write. Fiona is intelligent. She was reading even before she turned six. Writing would have been a mere formality for her, for no one who can play the piano as well as she can, has any trouble with dexterity.

"But come, enough of Fiona today! Of course we shall talk of her again, any time you like, but right now I must know exactly what happened to you on the moor before Jason found you."

Elinor told her all about that long, frightening day—how she had become lost and how she had felt, how Timothy Coryton had found her and guided her to the tinner's house, even how Jason Grenville had come for her and taken her up before him on his horse to his uncle's farmhouse. Gwyneth laughed until the tears ran down her cheeks at Elinor's description of that pack rat's nest.

"But it doesn't surprise me," she said finally, wiping her eyes on the hem of her skirt. "Jamie always was a great one for saving things, even as a child. His room in the nurseries was a terrible mess, and oh! the tantrums he had when the housemaids periodically carted all his treasures away.

"Well, he can be happy now, save whatever he likes, for there is no one to take a single inch of string or one rusty nail away from him ever again.

"What memories your story brings back, Elinor! Why, I remember a time when he actually tried to save a large piece of whalebone and blubber. My, how it stank! And when my father ordered him to—"

"Miz Grenville, where are ye?" a frantic voice called. As a man ran into the yard, Gwyneth jumped to her feet. The man was panting from his exertion, and Elinor recognized him as one of the fishermen from Downlong. He must have run all the way.

"What is it, Barney? Who's hurt?" Gwyneth demanded.

" 'Tis—'tis Sary Farlow's youngest. He wuz playin' around the harbor beach, an' he fell hard on a rusty anchor an' cut himself up terrible. An' we—we can't stop the bleedin'!"

"Hitch the horse to the gig while I fetch my things," Gwyneth ordered crisply. "I'll be right with you."

As she hurried to the cottage, she called over her shoulder, "Forgive me, Elinor! I must make haste!"

Elinor wondered if she should offer to go along and help, but she realized that with no knowledge or skill, she would only be very much in the way. She waited to wave as Gwyneth ran from the cottage before she started back to Mordyn. As she walked, she prayed the little boy would be all right. She was sure if anyone could help him, it would be Gwyneth Grenville.

As she was crossing the stepping stones in the stream, she looked up, startled, to see Jason Grenville standing on the opposite bank, waiting for her to pass. He was staring at her, looking grim, and Elinor had to make herself move forward, not retreat.

"Mr. Grenville," she said as she stepped up onto the bank beside him. She noted he had not extended his hand to help her, and she was reminded of Jonathan's constant courtesy.

"If you intended to visit your aunt, I must tell you she has just left the cottage," Elinor said a little unsteadily. "A small boy in the village has cut himself badly, and she has gone to help."

Jason Grenville shrugged, and turned to walk beside her. As he did so, Elinor felt her breath grow short and her heartbeat quicken, and she forced herself to relax. Surely nothing was going to happen to her! She was ridiculous! But somehow, the tall, very masculine, and very threatening Mr. Grenville always brought this feeling of unease, and she hated to be alone with him.

"M'aunt is a great comfort ter the villagers," he remarked, sounding as if he grudged the few words he had to speak to her.

"Yes, she is a wonderful woman," Elinor replied, glad there was something they could agree on. "I do admire her so very much."

Silence fell between them until they left the woods and reached the fields of the Home Farm.

"Seen the foals yet?" he asked.

"No, I didn't stop on my way to the cottage, although I intended to on my return," Elinor admitted.

McCarthy hurried out of the stables and came toward them minutes later as they paused by the paddock fence. He was beaming so, it was almost as if he were the proud father, Elinor thought.

Her attention was caught by the two little foals, still so small and unsteady on their thin, long legs, and her expression softened. One of them, a chestnut with a white blaze, tried frisking, but his legs got tangled and he went down in a heap on the soft grass.

"Oh dear," she said, concerned. "Has he hurt himself?"

"No, no, miss," McCarthy said, removing his cap as he joined them at the fence. "Jest ye watch close, now."

The colt's large dam looked around, and when she saw her foal lying there, looking so frustrated and confused, she bent her head and nudged him gently. The colt made a valiant attempt, but it took several nudges before he got his legs straightened out, and was able to rise unsteadily to his feet again.

The other newborn, a pale gray filly, stood quietly beside her own dam, calmly watching his struggles.

"How superior the other looks!" Elinor said, smiling.

"Aye, a proper little lady she be," McCarthy agreed, smoothing back his white hair. "She'll make a good mount fer ye, one o' these days, miss. Now that rapscallion! Don't know about him! Too early ter tell whether that's heart o' his, er jest flash."

"But perhaps it is only that females are always better behaved than males? Learn their manners earlier?" Elinor suggested, teasing the old groom.

He chuckled. "Well, that might be truth, miss, but I've known some mares a sight nastier than any stallion ever was. I guess it all depends on the sire and dam, an' the luck o' the draw."

The two mares moved away, heads down as they took mouthfuls of grass. Their offspring followed closely, as if anxious not to get too far from their own food supply.

"They do put humans ter shame, don't they?" Grenville remarked.

"How d' ye mean, Mr. Jason?" McCarthy asked.

"Well, we certainly can't stand up an' move about when we're only a few days old," he pointed out.

"Very true. We're real laggards when it comes to animals," Elinor agreed, more than a little amazed. She had been thinking the same thing herself. "Have they been named yet?" she asked, turning to McCarthy.

"No, not yet. Sir Robert's been too busy, like. Wot would *ye* call 'em, if ye had the namin' o' 'em, miss?"

Elinor considered, her head tilted to one side. "Why, I think I would call the well-behaved little lady Misty," she said slowly. "As for that handsome, daring fellow, he can be nothing but Blaze."

"I'll tell Sir Robert," McCarthy promised. "Might be he'll let ye choose, Miss Fieldin'. That fond o' ye, he is!"

"Has Miss Grenville seen the foals yet?" Elinor asked, suddenly reminded of Fiona, who could not—or would not—speak to name a foal. As the groom shook his head, she said, "I'll bring her soon. How she'll love them!"

Then she remembered Mischief, and her face clouded over. Perhaps any new baby animal would only remind Fiona of the kitten's death, and her part in it. It might not be such a good idea to bring her here after all.

"It's gettin' on. Best we be goin'," Jason Grenville said, his harsh voice interrupting her thoughts.

Elinor nodded, but she lingered a moment more to ask the head groom about Jenny, and her well-being after her ordeal on the moor.

"Och, Jenny is fine!" he told her. "Needs exercising again, though, miss. I hope we'll see ye down here fer that."

Smiling at her mentor, Elinor agreed to come on the morrow.

"Shall we be gettin' on, now?" Grenville interrupted, sounding impatient at the delay.

As Elinor fell into step with him, her forehead was creased in a little frown.

"Now what's botherin' ye?" he asked, frowning in turn.

"I was just wondering if bringing Fiona down here might be a good idea," Elinor admitted. "She is still so upset—the kitten and all."

"Might take her mind off it. 'Sides, she's got ter get over it sometime."

He paused for a moment before he added, "Strange do, that were. Wonder why she did it? Ye got any guess?"

"No, and no one seems to know. Of course, she can't say. It seemed strange to me, too," Elinor said.

And how strange this conversation seems as well, she mused. Why do I feel so comfortable with Jason Grenville now, in spite of his loutish behavior and coarse accent? It is almost as if we share some kind of rapport!

They had reached the home woods by then, and Elinor felt her spirits sink as she spotted Jonathan striding down the path toward them. As soon as he saw them together, he frowned, looking as black as ever his twin had. She wished he had not come upon them, for it might mean trouble.

As they came to face to face, she gave him her warmest smile.

"Wherever have you been all this time, Elinor?" he asked harshly. "Whitman tells me you went out right after breakfast."

Elinor resented his tone, but she swallowed her first,

quick retort. "Why, just down to Miss Grenville's cottage for a visit. I met Mr Grenville here as I was returning, and we have just been admiring the new foals. Have you seen them yet? They are so dear!"

"Where did you meet him, and when?" Jonathan demanded, ignoring the foals' baby charm.

"What are ye then, her jailer?" Jason Grenville asked, his voice a cold sneer. "But since ye *demands* ter know, I'll tell ye. We met at the stream back there. I was goin' ter call on Aunt Gwynnie myself, when Miss Fielding here told me she'd been called ter the village."

Somehow, he sounded grimly amused, and Elinor shivered as she prayed he wouldn't exacerbate the situation any further. Jonathan had such a quick temper, and she knew how jealous he could be.

"Were you on your way to the stables, Jonathan?" she asked, keeping her voice mild as she tried to change the subject.

"No. I was looking for you, and now I've found you, I'll take you back to the castle," he told her, holding out his arm.

Elinor hesitated. She was standing beside Jason Grenville, facing Jonathan. Surely it would be rude to step away from him to take his twin's arm.

"There is no need for you to do so," she said. "I hardly need an escort for a few, short steps."

Jonathan did not move, and still he held out his arm to her.

"Like a dog with a real meaty bone, ain't he?" Jason Grenville remarked to no one in particular.

Jonathan's head swung toward his twin, and his eyes narrowed. "I do advise you to stay away from Miss Fielding if you know what's good for you, bro," he said coldly. "*Far* away. She is not for the likes of you."

"Aw, she's all right. Seen better, I have. Lots better. And she's way too short fer us. 'Sides, she's got a bad temper on her, if ye remember," his twin drawled.

"Stop it at once!" Elinor exclaimed, her patience

snapping. "This is the most ridiculous conversation I have ever heard. Let me pass, sir! I don't want your escort, or your insulting twin's either. In fact, it would give me a great deal of satisfaction if I never had to have anything to do with either one of you again!"

When Jonathan just stood there, still looking black, Elinor picked up her skirts and pushed past him. As she climbed the slope, she said over her shoulder, "Now you may enjoy your idiotic quarrel all by yourselves! I pray you get into fisticuffs and manage to not only knock each other down, but bloody your noses and loosen some teeth as well. Such childish behavior would suit both of you perfectly!"

Elinor had intended to sit on a bench in The Lady's Garden to enjoy the flowers for a while, but she did not dare to linger there now. Somehow, she was sure Jonathan would be coming after her shortly, and she did not care to see him. As for his brutish twin, she wished he had never come back to Mordyn. Seen better, had he? Too short and with a temper, was she? The consumate gall of the man to say such things to her face, even if they were true!

She marched inside her sitting room doors and shut them firmly behind her. Then she drew the underdraperies across the windows so neither one of them could look inside and spot her there.

As she removed her bonnet and laid it on a chair, she rubbed her forehead. She had a headache coming on, all the result of those *damned* Grenville males. Like two cocks on a dung heap! she thought, borrowing one of McCarthy's more pungent similes. Well, I'll not play hen to their crowing, and the sooner they learn it, the better!

She sank down on the sofa, wondering if a visit to London would be wise. It would be such a relief to get away from here! And while she was away, she could think long and hard about ever returning. Only a moment's reflection made her smile ruefully. She could not go away. Not now. First, because she could not leave Fiona, and second, because she could not leave her lover. So no matter how miserable those two, identical, handsome, masculine, *impossible* specimens made her, she must remain.

But how could it be that Jonathan was that lover? she wondered anew. So jealous by day, yet never showing any signs of such a failing when he was with her at night. Of course, there was no one around for him to be jealous of then, and he had other things on his mind. Elinor blushed at her thoughts, but still she had to wonder what marriage to such a man would be like.

Mentally changing the subject, she made herself remember what Gwyneth had told her that morning. Her theory that Fiona could speak but refused to do so, was startling still. And she had had no good explanation for Fiona's killing of Mischief. She had said that Fiona must have had a good reason, but for the life of her, Elinor could not imagine what such a reason might be! Nor could she understand Gwyneth's statement that Fiona might well be afraid of something, and had been for years. What did she have to fear? She was dearly loved, coddled, and protected here at Mordyn. It made no sense!

Elinor remembered then that she had forgotten to ask Gwyneth about Jason Grenville's friendship with Timothy Coryton. The two of them had been so easy in each other's company at the tinner's house, easy even after twenty years apart. It was almost as if they were equals, a liaison she knew Jonathan would disdain. Tinners were—nothing. Little better than animals to him.

She did not like that about Jonathan, but she supposed with his noble birth and upbringing, it was understandable, especially since Sir Robert considered them of no account too. Like father, like son. And she supposed that, as the commoner Rebecca Ward kept reminding her she was, it was beyond her ken to understand the nobility.

She sat up straight, her hand going to her face in horror. Was it possible that Jonathan had no intention of marrying her? Was he merely using her, a commoner, for his amusement during her stay here? Would he toss her aside eventually, to marry someone more worthy? Phoebe Brownell, perhaps? Why, he might not even be trying to extricate himself from his entanglement with that lady!

Elinor rose to pace the room. Was that why it was taking him such a long time to tell her who he was? Because when he did so, and she learned the true purpose of his midnight visits, she would either leave Mordyn or go to his father? And what would Sir Robert do if she confronted him with his son's iniquity? Look down his nose at her as a foolish woman who had let a man make love to her without her even knowing his name? It sounded so wanton, put like that! So lewd! Even, although she hated to admit it, so common.

Elinor put both hands to her blazing cheeks, and shook her head. No, no! None of it could be true!

She saw her latest book on a table then, and she made herself go and pick it up. There was still time left before luncheon for her to return it to the library and select another one. In doing so, she might be able to put these horrid, disquieting thoughts from her mind. But still, she told herself as she crossed the hall, I will make him tell me who he is when next he comes; find out what his intentions are. And I shall do so before he can overwhelm me with his lovemaking.

As Elinor stepped into the library and shut the door softly behind her, she stopped and gasped a little, for Rebecca Ward was there before her.

"Good morning, Miss Ward," she made herself say. "I trust your being below stairs means you are feeling more the thing?"

Miss Ward had spun around at the sound of her voice. She was clutching a book to her breast, and her face had paled so, Elinor was afraid she was about to faint, until she saw two spots of red begin to burn high on her cheeks.

"Yes, thank you," the woman managed to get out before she turned quickly away to replace the book she was holding. She remained standing that way with her head bent for such a long time that Elinor shrugged and went to put her own book in its proper place.

"If you are looking for something to read, I can recommend this novel by Sir Walter Scott," she said. "It is excellent!"

"I—I don't have much time for reading," Miss Ward muttered, her head still averted. "My duties are too onerous, Mordyn being such a large, *noble* house. Not that you would understand that, of course."

Elinor opened her mouth to reply and quickly closed it. There it was again, that little dig about her background, but she would not stoop to argue with this petty, ordinary woman. She had had more than enough arguments today.

She took down a slim volume of poetry instead, and opened it to scan a few lines, hoping Miss Ward would take the hint and go away to attend to all her onerous, *noble* chores.

"Miss Fielding, I have something I have to say to you," Rebecca Ward said instead, and in quite a different tone.

Startled, Elinor looked up. Her voice had sounded so strangled, it was as if every word had been dragged from her throat with great effort.

"I—I have to apologize to you for sending you up on the moors to find Fiona. I have been told it—it was not well done of me."

Elinor stared at her contorted face, and she felt a great pity for Miss Ward. That pity made her voice warmer as she said, "It is quite all right. I understand. You were upset, concerned for Fiona's safety. And although it is very good of you to ask my pardon, it is not at all necessary. I was as much at fault for going as you were for suggesting it, and so Sir Robert has told me."

Rebecca Ward nodded slightly before she hurried away. As she reached the library door, she turned and said, "There! Now I have begged your pardon as Sir Robert insisted I do, although to think he would demand such a thing of me, who is *noble* born, and who has never apologized to a commoner in her life, is almost too much to bear! But now it is done, and so I shall tell him!

"I hope you're satisfied, Miss Elinor Fielding! Coming here and disturbing everyone's peace, bringing dissention and family rifts, ingratiating yourself with Sir Robert and pulling the wool over his eyes till he cannot see the kind of woman you are—well! And you, nothing but a merchant's daughter, the granddaughter of a lowly tin mine manager, and heaven knows what scum on your mother's side! But know that I at least am on to all your tricks, my girl!"

She ran from the room, leaving a stunned Elinor still clutching her book of verse. As the door slammed behind her, Elinor sank into the nearest chair. Was the woman insane? Was *everyone* here insane?

It was several minutes before she could bring herself to put the distasteful episode behind her. In an absentminded way, she replaced the book of poetry on the shelves. Somehow, she was sure she would not be able to concentrate on reading for the remainder of the morning. Perhaps she would just go up to her room instead, sit on her balcony and let the view of the ocean and the fresh breeze calm and cleanse her, help her forget the terrible things Rebecca Ward has said about her family, and her so obvious hatred. Elinor swallowed a sob. She was discovering how very unpleasant it was to be hated.

She was about to leave the library when she started to wonder what book Miss Ward had been looking at. She had never seen her with a book; she knew she did not enjoy the pastime. Once, at tea, she had even twitted Elinor about her reading, darting a little glance at Sir Robert as she said Elinor was in danger of becoming a bluestocking, or one of those horrid women who thought she was as good as a man. Yet this morning, she herself had been studying a very weighty tome. And it had been one she had replaced on the shelves hurriedly—almost furtively, in fact.

Idly, Elinor went over to where Miss Ward had been standing. The fifth shelf from the top, she recalled, one finger tracing the spines there.

But how very strange! she thought. There were only scientific books here, and yes, there was the one Rebecca Ward had been looking at. She recognized the dark red binding. Taking it from the shelf, Elinor opened it to the title page.

Good heavens! she thought. Whatever in the world would Miss Ward want with this particular volume, a copy of a book written by a fourth-century B.C. herbalist named Diocles? The book, fortunately translated from the Greek, was entitled *Rhizotomika*, and as Elinor riffled through it, she saw it was a listing of medicinal plants and herbs, with notes on the specific effects of those plants on the various parts of the body.

Elinor could easily picture Gwyneth Grenville studying this book carefully, but Rebecca Ward?

Well, Gwyneth had certainly been right, she thought as she replaced the volume on the shelf. Miss Ward was taking up the study of herbs with a vengeance. But still, she had to wonder why. It was so very unlike her.

16

Elinor never did have a chance to go to her room and compose herself, for Whitman came to the library to tell her Mrs. Brownell, Miss Phoebe, and Mr. Dick had just arrived.

"I have taken them to the red salon, Miss Fielding," he said. Elinor felt a little apprehension. Outwardly, the butler was as contained as ever, but she could tell there was something amiss, just from his tone of voice.

"Since Sir Robert is not here, nor Miss Fiona either, I thought it best you be notified," Whitman went on. He coughed a little before he added, "I do not know if Miss Ward is receiving visitors for Mordyn as yet again, you see."

"Very well, I'll go and entertain them. But this is a rather unusual call, is it not, coming right before luncheon as it does?"

He bowed. "As you say, miss. But I do not believe it is a social call."

As Elinor preceded him to the door, she said, "In that case, perhaps it would be well to notify Jonathan of our guests? And Mr. Jason Grenville, too? But you will know what is best."

"It shall be taken care of immediately, miss. Fortunately, they are both within doors," Whitman told her holding the door for her to pass him, and following her down the hall so he could announce her.

Elinor was stunned when she entered the red salon to see Mrs. Brownwell seated on a damask sofa and sobbing loudly, her face buried in a tiny handkerchief. Her daughter Phoebe was trying to calm her, while her youngest son, Dick, stood behind the sofa and looked as if he would rather be anywhere else on earth.

"Dear ma'am!" Elinor exclaimed, hurrying to kneel beside the lady. "What is it? And what can I do to help you?"

The older woman waved a weak hand, and her daughter began to explain. "We have just escaped our home, Miss Fielding," she said in hurried tones, even as she continued to pat her mother's shoulder. "Glyn has been attacked by a band of tinners."

"Oh, no!" Elinor exclaimed, horrified.

"Oh, yes!" Dick Brownell said grimly. "My father felt Mama and Phoebe would be safer inside Mordyn's walls, and I was sent to guard them. But there was no need of that. We never saw a single tinner on our way here, and besides, Mama had the coachman and a groom. I still don't know why I couldn't have stayed with Father and Harry to fight them. I'm an excellent shot, and it is most unfair!"

"Oh, do stop your whining, Dick!" his fond sister said tartly. "You know how upset Mama was when you first proposed doing so. And it is all your insisting that you be allowed to return now that has given her this spell. You ought to be ashamed of yourself! And you are much too young to fight, anyway!"

Dick looked as if he would very much like to refute that remark, and hotly too, but a glance at Elinor's face recalled him to his surroundings. He was a guest at Mordyn, whether he wanted to be or not. He could hardly conduct a family quarrel here, although there were a number of cutting things he intended to say to Phoebe just as soon as they were alone.

The door of the salon opened then, and the twins entered. Jonathan was first, followed in more leisurely fashion by Jason. Jonathan's brows rose when he saw their visitors' state, and his bow was hurried as he asked what the trouble was. As he did so, Jason moved apart from them all to lounge against the mantel.

"Oh, Jonathan, how wonderful that you are here," Phoebe Brownell said in dulcet tones, quite unlike those she had just used to address her brother. "I feel so much better now. So much safer!"

Elinor noted her tremulous smile, the blush that stained her cheeks.

Mrs. Brownell managed to gather herself together long enough to tell Jonathan exactly what had happened.

"Was it a large band that attacked, Mrs. Brownell?" he asked, his gray eyes narrowed.

"Oh yes, there were several men, I believe. At least a dozen, probably more! At first, we thought they were only going to raid the Home Farm, but when Horatio rode out with Harry and some grooms to scare them away, they fired on them! Oh, how my heart palpitates just remembering that awful moment! I was so frightened until my dear ones returned to the safety of Glyn! And then Horatio ordered the carriage for us, and sent us here. I—I hated to leave him, but the thought of my lovely Phoebe in those tinners' hands . . ."

"It does not bear thinking of," Jonathan said absently. "Elinor, get Mrs. Brownell a glass of sherry, if you would. And perhaps a glass for Phoebe might not be amiss, either."

He rose then to pace the room, rubbing his jaw with one big hand. Busy at the drinks tray, Elinor managed a glance at his twin. Jason Grenville was studying his brother carefully, with gray eyes that were just as narrowed. She realized he had not spoken a word, nor had any of the company acknowledged him as he stood apart, listening carefully. She wondered what he was thinking.

"Here now, what's all this I've been hearing?" Sir Robert's stern voice asked from the doorway. "Whitman tells me a very disturbing story of tinners attacking Glyn. It is true, Agnes?"

"Oh, Robert, how glad I am you are here!" Mrs. Brownell exclaimed, extending shaking hands to him. "Alas, it is true."

"I think it might be best for me to take some grooms and ride to their assistance, sir," Jonathan said before his father could speak. "Together, we'll put those ragged tinners to flight in no time at all."

"No, you must not do that," Sir Robert said firmly. "We don't know the extent of this problem, and we can only hope and pray that Horatio and Harry and their men can hold them off. You must ride to Trecarrag and warn them. We can't be sure they are not to be attacked as well. Indeed, another group of tinners might already be there.

"If they are, do not get involved. Instead, ride as fast as you can for Portreath and summon the troops. Indeed, summon them anyway. This has all gone on quite long enough, and this unruly uprising—this *arrogance*, attacking the gentry!—must be put down with a firm hand by the authorities."

As she handed the ladies a glass of sherry, Elinor saw that Jonathan did not look best pleased with such a tame role, but she noticed he did not argue the point with his father.

"Very well, sir, I shall leave at once. And Dick, you'd better come with me."

The young man's face brightened, but his mother gave a little shriek. "Oh, no, not my *baby!* It is too dangerous!" she cried, much to her baby's disgust. He flushed crimson.

"Nonsense, Agnes!" Sir Robert said briskly. "Dick is eighteen, and grown. And Jonathan will see he comes to no harm.

"If you should run into any tinners, son, take care you avoid them. We are but a few men, and we must not be foolhardy. The troops will take care of them, it is their job. Take our fastest horses, and tell McCarthy and the lads to be ready for trouble, alert them all at the Home Farm."

Jonathan nodded and hurried from the room. Dick Brownell followed closely on his heels, as if he were afraid his mother might call him back and disgrace him further by refusing to let him go. Mrs. Brownell had collapsed in sobs again, however, and he managed to make good his escape.

As the two left, Elinor looked around, wondering

what Jason Grenville was to do. To her surprise, she discovered he had left the salon sometime during the last few minutes. She wondered where he had gone, and for what reason. Surely he had no intention of fetching troopers to attack his friends!

Sir Robert rang for his butler, and when he entered, told him to send Miss Ward to him at once. "And then make sure the castle is secured after Jonathan leaves. Lock and bar all outside doors. Open the gun room as well. I'll be with you presently."

"Guns, Sir Robert? Do you think they will dare to come here?" Phoebe asked, her dark eyes troubled.

"It will not matter if they do, my dear," Sir Robert told her with his little smile. "They cannot get inside Mordyn, and I do not think they will even try. But until we know more, I must take precautions. Come now, ladies, drink up your sherry. After such a frightening morning, I am sure you must need the restorative."

Miss Ward ran into the room, her eyes wide with terror. "Oh, dear sir, what will we do?" she moaned, coming to stand next to him and clutch his arm. "Oh dear, oh dear!"

"None of that now, Rebecca!" he said harshly, shaking off her hands as he did so. "I've no time for any more of your hysteria. I want you to see that rooms are prepared for our guests, and inform Mrs. Greene and Cook of their presence. Go now! Do as I tell you at once!"

Miss Ward straightened up and nodded. "Certainly, dear Sir Robert," she said. "You may be sure you can depend on me, as you always have. I shall take care of the matter personally. I rather think the blue chamber for Mrs. Brownell, and Phoebe, of course, must be next to her in the primrose room. Or perhaps it would be nicer if—"

"No one cares about the decor they are to have!" Sir Robert snapped, sounding harried. "Just take care of it—now!"

Miss Ward scurried from the room, but she paused

long enough to send Elinor a triumphant little smirk. Elinor ignored her.

"Where is Fiona, sir?" she said. "Perhaps I should go and keep her company."

"Well thought on, Elinor. You are such a comfort to me! Yes, do that, please, and tell Fiona of our guests and the situation. Keep her as calm as you can."

As Elinor left the room, he turned back to the visitors. "Now then, ladies, you must not worry. I am sure Horatio and Harry will be fine. There are all the servants and the farmers to help them, and Glyn is a solid house. I want you to try and be calm as well. Hysterics, while perfectly understandable, are only an added problem at a time like this. We must all be brave and do our duty."

Elinor was not even tempted to smile at his bracing lecture. She was much too worried. It was true *they* were safe inside the castle, but what of the others? The Brownells fighting off an invasion of Glyn? And what of the Wilkensons up at Trecarrag, and all their children? Surely the tinners would not hurt little children, would they? And then there were McCarthy and his lads in the stables, the farmer and his family, to say nothing of Gwyneth, all alone in her cottage!

Elinor stopped suddenly in her distress, and then she shook her head as she continued up the stairs to Fiona's room. No, she did not have to worry about Gwyneth. No one would hurt her.

But now Jonathan and Dick were outside as well, riding for Trecarrag. Suppose the tinners were attacking it even now? Dear heaven, suppose Jonathan was killed? Knowing him and his hot temper, she did not think he would obey his father and sound retreat if he ran into any fighting. Not he! She said a prayer for his safety, and one for young Dick Brownell's as well.

As she knocked on Fiona's door, she wondered again where Jason Grenville had gone. He, at least, was safe from the tinners' wrath. But they would not know who he was, she realized as she entered the room when Fiona opened the door. They might easily assume he was Jonathan, and shoot him too.

Elinor put Jason Grenville from her mind as she began to tell his sister what had happened. She was gratified that Fiona took the news calmly, although she did frown and shake her head. Still, as they waited for the luncheon gong to sound, she did not seem able to remain seated. Elinor wondered who in particular she was worried about as she paced to and fro. Her brother? Nigel Wilkenson, perhaps?

Luncheon was a subdued meal, leaving Miss Ward to chatter to her heart's content. Her face was quite pink as she set herself to entertain Mordyn's guests, often reassuring them that all would be well.

"For now that Sir Robert has all in hand, there is nothing at all to fear," she said brightly, completely forgetting those outside Mordyn's thick walls. "Although I am sure you blush to hear me say such a thing, sir. But you must not, for truly—"

"Elinor, you are not eating!" Sir Robert interrupted. "Now, I insist you do so. We cannot have you falling ill, my dear. Let me help you to the mushroom sauce for your chicken. Whitman, more wine for Miss Fielding!"

Thus ordered, Elinor tried to eat her luncheon. She saw Phoebe Brownell's eyes on her more than once as she did so. The girl looked speculative, and she wondered why.

"I have to leave you ladies after luncheon," Sir Robert announced as dessert was served. "I must go around the castle in inspection, make sure all is secure. But you will be quite safe if you stay inside. Do not even go to The Lady's Garden today."

"Perhaps you might allow us to go up on the battlements?" Phoebe asked shyly. "I know it possible to see a great distance from there, for Jonathan showed me once. And we would be in no danger, would we, sir?"

"No, I suppose not," Sir Robert said with a little frown. "Do not distract the men I have posted up there, however. They are our lookouts, and they have orders to warn me if the tinners are approaching."

"I shall not go to the battlements," Agnes Brownell

announced, shuddering a little. "It would be entirely too frightening."

"Certainly not to be thought of, ma'am. I quite agree with you," Rebecca Ward said, leaning over to pat her hand. "The young are so daring! I pray you will remain with me in one of the salons. We can talk, and in doing so, I can take your mind off other things. Indeed, it has been a long time since we have had a quiet chat, just the two of us, has it not? How delightful it will be! I quite look forward to it!"

"I would prefer to spend the time quietly in my room, resting and praying. Alone," Mrs. Brownell said with dignity. "You must excuse me, Rebecca."

Catching Sir Robert's stern eye, Miss Ward thought better of whatever she had been about to say, and subsided.

The younger women went to the battlements as soon as they left the dining room. Fiona led the way, running lightly up the flights ahead of Elinor and Phoebe. The bootboy and one of the footmen who were there keeping watch seemed surprised to see them until Elinor explained why they had come.

Phoebe went at once to the side of castle that faced Glyn, and Fiona and Elinor followed her. "There is no smoke. Thank heavens," she said, her voice relieved. "I did not like to worry Mama, but I have been so afraid the tinners might have torched the house."

"Surely they would not do such a heinous thing, Miss Brownell," Elinor protested. "For what would be the point of it? It would only make it more difficult for them when they are caught."

"I hope they hang the lot of them!" Phoebe muttered darkly. "And when they do, I'll go and watch them swing, I swear I will!"

Elinor felt Fiona start beside her, and she reached out to take her hand and squeeze it.

"Yes, it is understandable that you are worried, Miss Brownell," she said. "But all is quiet here. Shall we walk the perimeter? See if there is anything else we can spot? In what direction lies Trecarrag, Fiona?"

Fiona led them to the eastern walls and pointed. All

the countryside seemed calm. There was nothing to be seen or heard in any direction.

Elinor relaxed a little. She had never been up on the battlements before, and she was astounded at the view. She was able to see Downlong easily, and even Uplong and parts of the moor were visible. She stared down at Mordyn's stables and Home Farm next. It was from such a height that she felt a little dizzy, and she stepped back away from the wall that guarded the edge. She noted there were no horses in any of the paddocks, nor were the farmer and his hands working in the fields. No doubt they were on watch, too.

Elinor looked around then at all the other farms that she could see. They were, every one of them, very quiet. Not a single farmer was at work at what was ordinarily the busiest part of the year for them, nor was there a soul to be seen on the roads and lanes. It was eerie, as if everyone had gone away or disappeared.

They were still there an hour later when they saw some dust on the road that led to Glyn. Everyone leaned forward eagerly, and the boot boy left his post to run to the stairs. They could heard him clattering down them on his way to alert Sir Robert.

Eventually, two horsemen, followed by two liveried grooms, turned into the drive to the castle, and Phoebe Brownell exclaimed, "Why, it is Papa! And yes, that must be Harry with him! Yes, I'm sure of it, for he was wearing his blue coat this morning. Thank God they are safe! I must tell Mama at once!"

She hurried away without another word, but Fiona and Elinor remained to watch the gentlemen as they swept around the last bend and cantered up to the castle doors.

"I do believe both Mr. Brownell and Harry are smiling, Fiona," Elinor said in a wondering voice. "Come, let us go down and hear their news."

The two of them hurried after Phoebe, arriving in the medieval hall just as the bars were lifted off the doors, and the Brownells were admitted.

"Sorry to put you to all this fuss, my friend," Horratio Brownell said as he shook Sir Robert's hand. "It turned out to be a tempest in a teapot, but I did not feel I could take any chances with Agnes and Phoebe. And Phoebe insisted on coming to Mordyn so strongly! But where are my wife and daughter?"

"I've sent a footman to fetch them, so come, Horatio, let us adjourn to the drawing room. I would hear your story."

Elinor smiled at Harry Brownell as they all left the room, and he blushed, with a delighted smile of gratitude for her concern on his face. She saw he looked quite proud of himself, as well, and very anxious to tell the tale of their adventure.

After a tearful yet smiling Mrs. Brownell and her daughter had welcomed their men, and a beaming Rebecca Ward had offered her fulsome compliments, the two men took turns explaining what had happened.

" 'Tis my belief the tinners were only intent on robbery. Those shots that were fired at us were just a warning for us to keep away," Horatio Brownell said at last, nodding as he accepted a glass of Canary from the butler. "They did not try to attack Glyn itself, and we never saw them again."

"They knew we were waiting for them, and they did not dare!" Harry broke in to say.

"Whether they did or not, this must be dealt with!" his father said firmly. "They have gone too far this time!"

"I quite agree," Sir Robert said. "I sent Jonathan and Dick to Trecarrag first, and then on to Portreath. My son will arrange for the troops to come, and when they do, we'll root these dirty, thieving animals from their hiding places and deal with them severely!"

"Oh, how thankful I am that it was not worse!" Agnes Brownell said, her eyes never leaving her husband's face.

"I hope they hang every one of them," Phoebe declared. "And I said as much on the battlements."

"No doubt they shall, but there is no need to be so bloodthirsty, Phoebe," a cool, amused voice said from the doorway.

Followed by a beaming Dick, Jonathan strolled into the room. "All's well?" he asked. On being told the story briefly, he nodded.

"We went to Trecarrag first. They had no idea there was any trouble about, but when we left they were getting ready to protect the house if need be. Such pandemonium there was! All those screaming children! Frankly, after listening to them for a few minutes, I ceased to consider Trecarrag in any danger at all. The caterwauling of the younger Wilkensons would have discouraged even the most desperate men."

"We galloped to Portreath next," Dick Brownell hurried to add, over everyone's chuckles. His eyes were shining as he did so, and there was a beatic grin on his face. "I never made the ride in such a short time in my life before! Mr. Grenville spoke to the authorities there."

"The troops will be here by the end of the week, perhaps even sooner," Jonathan said. "And they will stay as long as it is necessary for them to round up all these tinners and take them to jail. We'll have no further trouble from the scum!"

As everyone else nodded and agreed, Elinor felt a sharp pang—a sudden coldness around her heart. That was the word Rebecca Ward had used this morning in the library to describe Elinor's mother and her family. She wished Jonathan had not used it too, and reminded her.

Now she could hear that same Rebecca Ward inviting all the Brownells to remain for tea—her high, breathless voice going on and on until Sir Robert excused her, supposedly so she could go and tell Cook and Mrs. Greene of the arrangement.

"We'll be delighted to stay, and our thanks," Horatio Brownell said with a twinkle in his eye as Miss Ward bustled away. "Harry and I are sharp-set, for we had no luncheon. Glyn was in chaos. However, we are expected back for dinner, and in truth, I do not care to be away for any length of time, nor will I feel at all comfortable again until the troops have come to protect us."

As the two elder gentlemen began to talk of the possibility of the tinners staging yet another attack before then, and how it could be parried, Elinor looked around. Harry Brownell and his brother were close beside her, and as Harry began again to tell of his daring and bravery during the attack—in a deprecating way, of course—Elinor's gaze went to the large windows that faced the sea.

Harry's voice faded from her consciousness when she saw Jonathan standing there with Phoebe. As she watched, the girl moved closer to him to put her hand on his arm. She even stroked it while she spoke at length, her face full of her concern. Fascinated, Elinor watched Jonathan pat that hand calmly, before he raised it to his lips and kissed it. As he replied a moment later, and smiled a little, Phoebe never took her dark eyes from his face. They were so close, they were almost touching. To a stranger, they would have seemed a married couple.

Heartsore, Elinor forced herself to look away. She noticed Mrs. Brownell had been watching them too, with a fond little smile on her face, and she wondered again exactly what Jonathan's plans were for the lovely Miss Brownell—and of course, for herself.

Much to Harry and his brother Dick's regret, Elinor quietly excused herself moments later. She did not think she could bear to remain and watch these old, aristocratic friends converse, watch Jonathan so easy and intimate with Phoebe Brownell. She was not one of them. She was an outsider, and a common one at that. She went to her private sitting room and sank down on a sofa there, disconsolate and confused.

She made herself take several deep breaths to steady herself, for she was determined not to weep. And she tried to make herself think logically. But as she did so, she was reminded of what Mr. Brownell had said, that Phoebe had been the one who had insisted so strongly on coming to Mordyn. Surely that was only the normal thing for her to do, under the circumstances, Elinor reminded herself. Mordyn's walls were high and thick. The tinners could not reach her or her mother here. Unless, of course, her primary motive had been to be close to Jonathan.

Perhaps Phoebe had noticed his jealousy of Harry on the sailing trip? Perhaps she had wondered, even as Elinor was doing now, what his intentions were? As for Elinor, she knew that if Jonathan were indeed her lover, his behavior just now with the pretty Miss Brownell could hardly be considered encouraging. Elinor's eyes were bleak as she recalled her earlier thoughts, that Jonathan might only be amusing himself with her, fully intending all along to marry the proper young lady he had known since childhood. For why shouldn't he make love to this guest at Mordyn even so? What man would not take advantage of something that had been offered so freely, and to an unknown stranger at that? If nothing else, it was satisfying, and it helped to pass the time he spent here.

He must have come to her room at first just intending to test the waters, to see if there were any possibility of a liaison between them. How delighted he must have been when she did not rebuff him, indeed, allowed him not only to take her virginity, but did so with such sighs and moans of delight.

Elinor writhed under her smart London gown, remembering her eager surrender, her involuntary cries. Ladies, she knew, did not behave that way. She wished she could die.

But I am not wanton! Elinor cried silently. I had never even kissed a man before, not that way. What I gave, I gave from love, not because I am common and abandoned. Or am I? Is it possible that all my prating about love is done only to try and excuse a base nature I never knew I had? One a true lady would scorn?

She rose to go to the window. Fiona and Phoebe were strolling the garden paths, and Elinor backed away from the window quickly, lest they see her and wave to her to come out. She could not bear to be in anyone's company right now, and certainly not in the virtuous Miss Brownell's, who, she was sure, would never have behaved so freely. No, no matter how deeply she loved—and longed—Phoebe would have waited for her Papa's approval before she even allowed her suitor more than a chaste salute on her cheek. That was the correct way a *lady* conducted herself.

Elinor knew her own behavior could call down nothing but censure on her head. And how quick others would be to point out that no one could *love* without knowing something more of a man than his kiss, the way his lean face and strongly muscled body felt under her hands, all his wonderful ways of loving. And the only argument she had to refute such condemnation was the simple statement that she knew she loved. How naive she was! How foolish!

She could not even blame Jonathan for what he had done, not really. He was a virile man, one who had spent much of his time in London. Elinor was well aware how easy it had been for him to set up a mistress there, whenever he felt the urge. Here in Cornwall, he had no such wealth of lovely, available feminine flesh to choose from.

But she had been here, she reminded herself, clenching her hands together and swallowing hard. Oh, yes. Miss Elinor Fielding, daughter of a London merchant and the granddaughter of a lowly tin mine manager, one with who knew what kind of—

No! Enough of that! Elinor told herself, lifting her chin and straightening her slumping shoulders. I know I am just as good a woman as Phoebe Brownell, no matter what vitriol Rebecca Ward spews at me, and no matter that I am not noble born. If I made a mistake, allowing Jonathan to make love to me, it was only that. A mistake. No one is perfect. Everyone makes mistakes.

Besides, Fiona loves me, and Sir Robert has welcomed me to his home as another daughter. I can tell from his smiles and concern that he cares for me.

But why has he never taken me to my father's boyhood home, then, as he promised? she asked herself. Her frown returned. What reason could he have for neglecting to do so? Because he did not want to be reminded of her humble beginnings?

Elinor put both hands to her temples and shook her

head. She did not know. She began to think she knew very little of anything anymore. But oh, how those words of Rebecca Ward had gone deep and hurt her so! She wondered if she would ever be able to forget them.

Teatime was an ordeal, but with so many guests, there was no need for Elinor to go to any lengths to be entertaining. She smiled at the appropriate times, and contributed to the conversations when directly queried, but she felt she had seldom spent a longer, more difficult hour.

It was only when she went to her room after the Brownells had taken their smiling farewell, full of their thanks, that Elinor realized that Jason Grenville had not been at tea, nor at luncheon either. In fact, she had not seen him since the Brownells' arrival that morning. She wondered briefly where he was, and if he were safe. But she was able to put him from her mind easily, for her own crushing problems were too demanding.

As she opened the long windows and carried a chair out to the balcony so she could sit and watch the ocean and the gulls, she wished she might talk to Gwyneth Grenville. She wanted to open her heart to her and tell her everything, so she might ask her advice. It would be such a relief to have a trusted confidante!

Elinor shook her head at her folly. She could never do that. How Gwyneth would stare at her if she did! Perhaps she might even draw away, ask her to leave the cottage, with all the disgust and revulsion she felt for Elinor's promiscuity clear in her voice. And Elinor knew she could not bear that, not from the woman who had become her closest friend. What she had done then must be her own secret. Hers, and her Cavalier's, of course.

Jason Grenville was in the drawing room with the others when Elinor came down to dinner later. For some reason, he made her uneasy tonight. It appeared he was staring at her, his gray eyes intent, as if to catch her every expression. Elinor made herself laugh at one of Jonathan's jokes, and she tried to appear most content with her lot and her life.

At the dinner table, Sir Robert asked Jason where he had spent the day. "I suddenly realized after luncheon that I had not seen you for some time," he remarked. "Can it be that you did not know of our latest troubles with the tinners?"

"Aye, I knew. I was here when Mrs. Brownell an' her daughter arrived. I went out riding shortly afterward."

"Out riding?" his father echoed, looking stunned. "But—but it might have been dangerous, with those tinners on the rampage! You were foolhardy, son."

"Not at all. The tinners pose no threat ter me. They might steal out o' want, but they wouldn't kill."

"Of course, you know them so well, don't you?" Jonathan asked, a sneer in his voice.

"Better than ye do," his twin replied, his eyes steady on his own image. "They're hungry men, is all, and their families is in dire need."

Before Jonathan could reply, Sir Robert interrupted to say, "Still, I am surprised you would just leave Mordyn at such a time. We are so few here. If we had been attacked, we would have needed every man."

"Since no one can get into Mordyn, where's the danger?" Jason asked as he cut his lamb. Taking a forkful of it, he pointed it at his father and went on, " 'Sides, Mordyn's none of m' concern. Not anymore, it ain't'."

"Then why do you linger here?" Jonathan asked in the uncomfortable silence that followed this blunt remark.

"That will be enough, Jonathan!" Sir Robert said harshly. "Jason is my son. He is welcome at Mordyn for as long as he cares to remain."

Jason nodded careless thanks. "Ter answer yer question, bro, I stay fer a very good reason. One I'm not at liberty ter divulge as yet. Ye'll know some day soon, I promise ye."

"I shall try to contain my impatience for that wondrous time," Jonathan murmured, picking up his burgundy and sipping it. His eyes went to Elinor's troubled face then, and he smiled at her. "Quite the thrilling day, was it not, Elinor? I'm sure you never expected such excitement, here in the dull countryside."

"It was excitement I could well have done without," she said. "I do so wish there was something that could be done for the tinners, though, and for their families."

"Do ye?" Jason Grenville asked. Somehow his tone of voice made it an insolent question, and Elinor concentrated on her dinner, and refused to look at him.

"As I have mentioned before, my dear, there is nothing that can be done," Sir Robert told her. "There is no work for the tinners here anymore. They must go down the line, perhaps even leave the country, if they want to continue to eat. I've heard there are vast tin mines opening in Africa, as well as Malaysia. If they thought beyond their next pint and their next bowl of porridge, they'd make arrangements to go there, and send money back to their families. But they are only animals, and as such, incapable of logical thought."

"Costs money ter travel," Jason remarked, signaling Whitman for more lamb.

"Are you suggesting we pay their way?" his twin asked, his brows raised. "You can't be serious!"

"Get 'em out o' yer hair, it would," Jason told him as he took some meat and vegetables from the platter the butler was presenting.

"What? Pay good money to lawless men to make themselves scarce? Never! 'Twoud be like paying blackmail, and that's no way to keep laborers in their place, son. It astounds me you would even suggest it," Sir Robert sputtered. After he had wiped his mouth on his napkin, he went on, "The troops will take care of them, in the only way they understand. Hanging, prison. They'll soon be gone."

"Perhaps we can suggest deportation," Jonathan suggested idly. "That way they might end up in a mine in some other part of the world. Why, it is almost altruistic, don't you think? Since they want to mine, that is.''

Elinor glanced up to see Fiona staring hard at Jonathan. Her face as she did so was strained and worried, and Elinor wondered at it. Was she frightened of the tinners still? But how could that be? She had not been in any danger today. What could be troubling her?

After dinner, Elinor excused herself from remaining with the family in the drawing room. She thought Sir Robert looked askance at her, and she noted the little frown between his brows, although he was quick to agree to it, and bid her a courteous good night.

Once in her room, Elinor summoned Betsy to help her undress. She had a headache, and she did not wonder at it. It had been a most unpleasant day, and the twins' sparring at dinner, Jonathans' cruel suggestions for the tinners' future, had not helped her mood.

She tried to settle down with a book, but she could not concentrate on the printed page. What was a novel, after all, compared to her own deep, confusing problems? Perhaps she should try to sleep?

But sleep eluded her tonight. She tossed and turned for what seemed like hours, until finally she threw back the covers and went to stand before the dying fire. It was chilly in the room now, and she picked up her green satin wrapper. One of the sleeves had become tangled, and she could not get her arm through it. Suddenly, as if that were the last straw, she burst into tears. As she wept, she knew very well it was not frustration with her robe that made her do so. No, it was all the horrid things Rebecca Ward had said to her today, all the agonizing thoughts she had tortured herself with ever since.

She sank down on a chair at fireside and put her face in her hands, trying desperately to contain her sobs.

''Here now, what's all this?'' she heard her lover ask, just before his hand touched her shoulder.

As she lowered her hands, her eyes flew open, but by then he had scooped her up in his arms to cuddle her close as he walked away from the dim, uncertain light of the dying fire.

"You'll catch cold," he scolded as he lowered her to the bed, and pulled the covers up over her. "Here, take this and blow your nose."

He handed her a large handkerchief, and Elinor did as he bade as he settled down on the bed beside her. She also wiped her streaming eyes, aware she must look a perfect fright.

"Now, tell me what is troubling you, love," he said more gently. He put his arms around her and pulled her close, and she sighed as she nestled against his hard chest. She could hear the reassuring beat of his heart, feel his warmth and strength, and in spite of herself, she felt a certain calm.

"I cannot," she whispered. "It is—it is too—"

"Too personal?" he prompted. "But nothing that concerns you, my dear, can be too personal or too awful or too painful for me to know. Come now, confess, there's a good girl."

"But I'm not a good girl!" Elinor wailed softly, her tears starting all over again. "If I were, I would never have let you make love to me, nor would I have come to care for you. I don't know you—why, I don't even know your name! Can you imagine what the polite world would say of my behavior? They'd stone me!"

"No, they would hardly stone you, my dear," he said, his voice a little unsteady. Elinor thought she detected some amusement in it, and she stiffened. But before she could accuse him of laughing at her, he added, "Even in backward Cornwall they are not so primitive. Oh, I must agree that we did not have a conventional wooing, you and I. Are you sorry for it?"

He kissed the top of her head and cuddled her closer as he went on, "I must admit I cannot be. It was all of it too perfect, too right for us. No, it *is* too right to regret the loss of a polite courtship, some little smiles and the teasing flirtations we seem to have managed to dispense with so easily. I knew right away, from the moment I first saw you, that I loved you. You cannot imagine my happiness when I discovered my love was returned. I felt—I felt so rich then, like the king himself. And you gave that to me, Elinor, out of your warm, loving nature."

His deep voice was intimate and reassuring, and Elinor found herself relaxing. But as she wiped her eyes again, she recalled some of her earlier thoughts.

"What you say is all very well," she replied so softly he had to bend his dark head closer to hear her. "You told me you had been watching me, listening to me, long before you first came to me. Perhaps you did come to love me that way. But—but I did not have even that excuse. I may have my suspicions, but I still don't know who you are. I have never seen your face, not here in my room. I know nothing of you, not really. And yet, I gave myself to you even so."

She twisted away from his comforting arms then, and turned her back on him. "It—it was not a fitting thing for me to do, and I am so ashamed."

Her voice was only a whisper, and when it died away, there was complete silence in the bedchamber. Elinor stared at the embers of the dying fire, her misery welling up in her all over again.

He did not touch her, although Elinor was longing for him to do so, longing for him to draw her back in his arms and somehow refute all her statements. Instead, he only said evenly, "Yes, I can understand how you might feel that way. But you must never be ashamed of what you did, Elinor. You are not like other women. You are sensual, the most sensual woman I have ever known. I could tell it from the very beginning. Your delight in the ocean, the storms and winds and mists. The way your eyes shine and your expression grows dreamy when a soft fabric like satin touches your skin. Your love of perfume and the good soap you use on that lovely skin. But even as sensuous as you are, I do not believe you could give yourself to a man you did not love. No, for you are also elegant and true. You must trust yourself, trust your instincts. They have not played you false. You love me, as I love you."

Elinor had listened hard, holding her breath as if afraid she might miss a single one of his word. How very much she hoped they were true!

"Come now, let me put you to bed, love," he said, reaching out at last to lower her to the pillows. As she stared up at him, he bent to kiss away the little frown that lingered between her brows, before he rose and arranged her covers so she would not feel a chill. "It's late, and you're tired, worn out from all the soul-searching you've been doing. Go to sleep now, and if you dream of anything, dream of happiness. Our happiness. This secrecy I practice will not last much longer."

Before Elinor could speak, he bent over her again, his hands on either side of her body. As he kissed her gently, the only part of him that touched her were his lips. It was the kind of kiss a father might give a beloved child, after he had heard her prayers and tucked her up in bed. "Sleep now, my love," he whispered, his mouth only inches from hers. "Sleep."

Elinor closed her eyes for a moment, and when she opened them again, he was gone. She wondered why he had not stayed and made love, but as a wide yawn escaped her, she had to smile. She was tired now. Sleep would come easily. And he had told her she was elegant and true, told her again that he loved her. She would be content with that, at least for now. Perhaps it would not be much longer before she could speak his name, and take his hand for all the world to see. She would dream of that day, she told herself, as she turned over on her side and closed her eyes again.

17

IT WAS A pearl-gray and misty calm morning that Elinor woke to hours later. Surprisingly, there was no rain, nor any wind, and she could not remember any weather like it since her arrival at Mordyn. As she stared down from her long windows in the direction of the ocean she could not see but knew was there, she could hear how lazy the swells were, the almost stately way they broke on the rocks before they retreated in equally august fashion. It was easy to picture them in her mind's eye. Far overhead, above the battlements, she heard a gull mew.

For some reason, even in the quiet peace of the morning, Elinor felt restless. Perhaps it was because she had been cooped up in the castle for most of yesterday, she thought as she went to ring for her maid. But there was no need for such caution any longer, and if it were too misty to ride, at least she could go for a walk. Perhaps she could persuade Fiona to join her, she thought as she selected a gown. She might even speak openly to Fiona, tell her what she had learned of the family, try to ease whatever problems were bedeviling her. For it was obvious Fiona was upset about something, and Elinor did not think it was only her part in Mischief's demise. No, there was something more, and she must try and find out what that might be. If only Fiona could talk, how much easier her task would be!

Fiona was agreeable to the walk when Elinor suggested it at breakfast. Rebecca Ward was there as well, and she tried very hard to discourage her charge from the excursion. First she talked about the lingering danger from the tinners, then the uncertain weather, and when these arguments had no effect but make Fiona look stubborn, she mentioned the girl's neglected piano practice, and how her music was suffering.

Throughout Miss Ward's long, rambling soliloquy, Elinor ate her breakfast quietly, and she was not surprised when Fiona threw down her napkin at last, rose to her feet, and drew her hand rapidly across her throat—her signal to her companion that she wished to hear no more. As she came to take Elinor's hand, almost pulling her from her seat in her eagerness to be gone, Elinor noticed the fierce glare Miss Ward threw in her direction, two angry red spots burning high on her cheeks. Elinor shrugged. She knew now how Rebecca Ward hated her. It could make little difference to what degree she was hated.

Outside, in The Lady's Garden, Elinor grabbed Fiona's red cape and said, "Now listen, Fiona! I do not intend to run after you, and so I warn you! Your legs are much longer than mine—you must shorten your pace."

She saw the little smile Fiona gave her as she nodded, and relieved, she relaxed as they left the garden together and started through the woods.

"Where shall we go?" she asked idly. "Would you like to visit the foals? Go to your Aunt Gwyneth's cottage?"

She saw Fiona did not seem interested in either destination, so she said, "Perhaps you might take me on a new walk, someplace I have never been before. It is the perfect morning for it—so misty and mysterious."

Fiona appeared to consider the suggestion for a moment before she nodded. Minutes later, she paused by a small side path Elinor had never noticed before. It led upward toward the cliffs, and she wondered Fiona would care to go that way. Eventually, however, the path twisted away from those cliffs, and the sounds of the breakers died away.

"We are certainly going somewhere I have never been before," Elinor remarked. The two were in single file now, for the path was narrow and overgrown.

"I feel hopelessly lost. I am not even sure in which direction Mordyn lies. Pray you stay close now, Fiona!"

Leading the way, Fiona did not bother to turn and smile, and for a moment, Elinor felt a chill. Gwyneth had told her Fiona was not dangerous—that she would not hurt a fly. Not ordinarily, anyway. But still . . . ? Had she put herself in danger by suggesting this strange walk, just the two of them?

The path opened up a bit, and she hurried forward as Fiona stopped and stared. Ahead of them was a small glade. There was a rustic wooden bench on one side of it, and its soft grass was carpeted with flowers. Elinor saw anemones and foxglove, clusters of violet leaves, for the flowers had gone by long ago, and wild thyme. A few blackberry bushes edged one side. There was even a rose bush, and in the center, a mossy old sundial.

"How pretty a place this is!" Elinor whispered. Instinctively, she felt there was something about the glade that would not welcome a normal tone of voice. "But where are we? Who made it?"

Fiona shook her head. Elinor saw that the sad look was back on her face and her mouth was drooping, and she wondered who or what she was thinking about.

"Shall we sit down over there and rest for a moment?" Elinor asked, taking her companion's hand and stroking it. She thought Fiona's nod a little reluctant.

For a while, the two sat quietly, side by side, each lost in her own thoughts. Elinor was beginning to feel uncomfortable, although she could not have told you why. But there was an atmosphere to this little glade, one that seemed a direct contradiction to its soft tranquility. At one time, someone had gone to a great deal of trouble to clear this secret spot, planted flowers and placed the sundial and bench, but she sensed that person had been gone a long time. Perhaps someone else had used it since? For some other reason than private contemplation?

She noticed that Fiona was wiping a tear from her eyes, turning her head away so she would not be seen, and Elinor was reminded of her original purpose for this walk.

"My dear, I have noticed your unhappiness for some time now," she said softly. "I do so wish you could tell me what is troubling you so I could help you. Has it anything to do with your eldest brother's death? Your father told me about that, and I am so very sorry!"

Watching Fiona's face all the time she spoke, Elinor saw how every expression disappeared from it, until it was empty and still, as blank as a child's clean slate.

"I see you do not care for me to speak of it. But tell me, are you upset because your brother Jason has come home?"

There was a long pause before Fiona nodded slightly and turned her head away.

"I see. Of course, I know you did not expect to see him ever again. His appearance here must have been a shock to you. And yet he does not seem that threatening a man now. Perhaps he has outgrown all those horrid traits he had as a boy—hurting small animals, doing whatever he had to so he could be first . . ."

Her voice died away as Fiona swung around on the seat to face her. There was a measuring expression in her gray eyes now—almost, Elinor thought wildly, a look of contempt there. But that look was gone so quickly, she could not be sure she had not imagined it. In its place came sorrow, and—could it be?—pity? But why would Fiona pity her? What had she said to bring about such a reaction?

"I just wanted you to know that I will stand your friend, Fiona," she made herself go on. "I'll watch Jason for you. You need not fear him . . ."

Fiona had risen, staring down at Elinor as she did so, and Elinor's voice died away. Fiona was shaking her head, her mouth twisted in wry exasperation.

"What is it?" Elinor asked. "Why do you look at me that way?"

Fiona shrugged and held out her hands, palms upward. Before Elinor could rise and take them in her own, Fiona whirled and ran for the path.

"Wait! Where are you going?" Elinor called as she

hurried after her. Cursing the ineptitude of hers that had driven the girl away, she hurried after her. But on her long legs, Fiona easily outdistanced her, and Elinor resigned herself to finishing her walk alone.

It was some time before she had made her way back to the main path, but in spite of the mist and her fears she might lose her way, Elinor felt easier the further she got from the little glade. It was as if something evil had happened there years ago—something so evil it lingered still, a dark miasma that would never be dispersed.

When she entered the castle, Elinor heard the sounds of a piano being played above her, and she went to her sitting room. Obviously, Fiona did not care for any more of her company this morning, she thought as she set out her pencils and sketchbook. But she had some drawings for Gywneth she wanted to finish, and now would be a good time to do them.

It began to rain right after luncheon, and Elinor spent the afternoon drawing and reading before her comfortable fireside.

A knock on the door stirred her from her absorption some time later, and her eyes widened as Jonathan Grenville stepped inside, a finger to his lips as he carefully closed the door behind him.

"What is it? What's the matter?" Elinor whispered, rising to smooth her gown.

She saw Jonathan's gray eyes were twinkling as he came to her, looking as devilish and handsome as ever he had. "Nothing is the matter," he said in a normal tone. "I wanted to see you, but I didn't want anyone to know I was here."

"Whyever not?" Elinor asked, confused and a little nervous.

"But my dear Miss Fielding, you are not thinking! Can you imagine what old 'Becca would say if she knew you were entertaining a single gentleman in the privacy of your sitting room? With the door closed?

"Tsk! Tsk! So bold and unprincipled! But then, I'm sure *I'm* not surprised," he said, in falsetto, an excellent imitation of Miss Ward's breathless voice. *"I've* had my suspicions of that girl from the beginning, and now I intend to tell my dear, *dear* Sir Robert about it as soon as I can run him to earth. And furthermore, I'll tell him what a bad influence his precious Miss Fielding is on Fiona, and . . ."

As Jonathan drew her down on the sofa, he reverted to his normal manner. "She does not like you, you know."

"Of course I know! She has made it very obvious," Elinor retorted.

"You must not let the silly pea brain upset you, my dear," he said, picking up her hand and pressing it. His other arm slid along the back of the sofa so he could pick up one of the curls that had come loose from her chignon, to toy with it.

Elinor's heart began to beat more quickly.

" 'Becca Ward is of no account. Even my father wearies of her constant boring prattle and silly ways. I'm sure I can convince him she must be sent away, and soon. Perhaps I should mention she is making you unhappy? My father would be very angry with her in that case. He's in a fair way of doting on you, my girl, or didn't you know that, too?"

"Miss Ward does a great deal of work about the castle," Elinor pointed out, determined to be fair as well as to ignore his last, mocking statement.

"Nothing Mrs. Greene and Whitman and the staff could not handle by themselves, and be delighted to do as well if it meant they would be free of her carping. But come, let us forget the boring, insignificant 'Becca, and speak of something much more interesting."

He paused before he picked up her hand and kissed it. "Us, for example," he said, holding it close to his lean cheek.

Elinor stared into his handsome gray eyes, saw the light in them, and realized she had neither a heavy book nor a slippery fish as defense today.

"I have been concerned for you lately, Elinor. You have not seemed as happy at Mordyn lately. Now why should that be?

"And someone as lovely as you are, must always be happy. It would be a crime if you were not. You are so perfect, so beautiful, so very, very desirable, my modern Pocket Venus. Yet yesterday you were almost distraught. I do not believe it was because of the tinners, either. Could it have been that you were concerned for *my* safety?"

Before she could frame a reply, he sighed and said, "But no. That was not the reason, much to my regret, for when I returned home from Portreath, you did not smile at me, or appear at all glad to see me. I had to make do with Phoebe's congratulations."

Reminded of his behavior with the pretty Miss Brownell, Elinor said, "I have heard several times that you and Miss Brownell are considered as good as promised. I am sure her concern for you was only normal."

His hand slid down to her waist, and he pulled her closer to him. "I shall not even ask where you heard such a falsehood. Its source does not matter. Ah, the country! There is so little to do here that people must make things up to gossip about to amuse themselves."

"But is there an understanding between you and Phoebe?" Elinor persisted. "If there is, you know you should not be here with me. I'll thank you to admit it, and take your hands off me as well!"

He dropped his arm, but only so he could cup her face between his two big hands. As he moved her head from side to side, he whispered, "Can it be that you are *jealous?* How encouraging a sign that would be!"

Elinor bit her lower lip, and his gaze wandered to her lips moments before he bent his head and kissed them.

To Elinor's surprise, he did not linger over that kiss, but let her go to rise and pace the floor. "You are a temptress, jade. You know that, don't you?" he said carelessly. "Here I came, all good intentions, determined to woo you as I ought, and with the greatest propriety, and I find myself kissing you! Perhaps I should take a seat on the other side of the room. It might be safer, for I am, after all, but a poor, mortal man, with all man's failings."

As he took a seat somewhat apart from her, and crossed one leg over the other, he went on, "As for dear Phoebe, you have no reason for jealousy. None at all. Any expectations of hers—and her dear mother's—are pure wishful thinking on their part. I have never given Phoebe any reason to suspect I held warmer feelings for her than I do for any other neighbor. We are not promised, nor shall we ever be. No. There was no chance of that even before I met you."

Elinor's heart was pounding in her breast. How cool he was! How sure of himself and his welcome! He seemed to treat her capitulation as a foregone conclusion. But of course, she reminded herself, blushing a little, after all that had passed between them, in the privacy of her bed, he would naturally do so. She wondered he did not remind her of it? Or was this some game he played still?

"Can you not bring yourself to speak to me, dearest?" he asked, putting one hand to his heart and rolling his eyes heavenward, for all the world like a bad actor. "Give me one word of encouragement, so I might know I have a chance with you?"

"You are being ridiculous, Jonathan," she made herself say, even as she wondered why he could not be natural with her, as natural as he was when they were together late at night. Had he forgotten how he had held her last night? Comforted her? Told her how much he loved her before he tucked her in bed and left her to sleep?

A terrible suspicion began to form in Elinor's mind then, and she rose in turn to walk to the window and stare out into the garden. Doing so enabled her to turn her back on him, and thus hide her horrified expression.

She heard him coming close to her, and she steeled herself as his arms stole around her waist and he pressed her back against him. He held her so close she could feel his arousal, and she shivered as he bent his head to kiss the nape of her neck. His chuckle was deep and lazy.

"Yes, as you can tell, it is only you I want," he whispered. "Say you will marry me! Say it now!"

Instead, she twisted away from him and went to put her desk between them. "I cannot," she told him, her gaze steady on his handsome, amused face. "Not yet. It—it is too soon, and I do not feel I know you very well."

His brows rose. "But you have been here several weeks now, and unfortunately, darling, you cannot get to know me any better until the ring is on your finger. Isn't that the way it is done in *your* circle of friends in London?"

Elinor lowered her eyes to fiddle with the strings of her sketchbook. Was he twitting her about her background? she wondered. Implying that perhaps a merchant's daughter was allowed more freedom than well-born ladies? There had been something in his tone of voice that sounded almost insolent.

"You must give me more time, Jonathan," she said at last. "You confuse me. First you are cold, and then you are hot. One moment you are possessive—jealous —and the next moment you ignore me. How can I say I will marry you? You have not even told me that you love me."

He came to put both hands on the desk and lean over it. "Dear me," he said, his voice openly mocking now. "Were you expecting me to go down on one knee like a lovesick swain? I do assure you that is not at all in my style. You may take it for granted that I love you, else I would not have asked for your hand. And do consider how very happy our union will make my father. You will be his daughter in truth, then. What a glorious way for you to repay all his kindness!

"Of course, I do not intend to remain at Mordyn much longer. As soon as we are wed, we shall travel to London. The Season is almost over, but there is still much of interest to do there, and no doubt you will need new clothes, be busy furnishing the house I intend to buy. In the best section of town, of course.

Your former girlhood home would not do for a man of my station."

Reminded of her situation, Elinor said, "You know I cannot marry until October, when my year of mourning is over. All this talk of matrimony is much too precipitate, sir."

She was surprised at the expression of impatience that crossed his face and was so quickly gone. "But who will know?" he asked. "We most certainly will not travel in the same circles you may have frequented before! I believe you have no living relatives? What can it matter when you wed? There is no one to call down censure on your head."

"Please, Jonathan, I must have some time to think about it," Elinor said quickly. "You are not kind to press me so!"

Again that little shadow of impatience crossed his face and darkened his eyes. He sighed. "Very well, since you insist on it," he said, bowing to her a little. "I shall leave you now, to ponder it. But know I shall ask you again, and again, and again, if need be. I am not a patient man. When I want something, I want it right away. I do advise you not to make me wait too long."

Elinor held her breath as she watched him stroll to the door. He turned there and bowed. "My bride. *Mine*," he said, and blew a kiss to her. A moment later, the door closed quietly behind him.

Confused, yet relieved to be alone again, Elinor sank down on the nearest chair. She did not know what to think. In fact, she was afraid of her thoughts, for the man who had just proposed to her so coolly could not be her lover after all. It was impossible! That man would never have treated her as Jonathan just had, nor would he have kissed her so lightly, spoken in that mocking way, as if he were playing a part. Nor would he have kept silent about their midnight trysts. Her lover had always spoken to her with warm words of love, but the man who had just left her . . .

But if her lover were not Jonathan, who could it be?

There was no one else, for the Cavalier was only a ghost!

Jason Grenville, she thought, her eyes widening. It had to be he. Elinor clasped her hand tightly in her lap. Was it possible that he was the one playing a part? Had he just pretended to be a boor, assumed that crude accent to do so? But why?

Staring down at a tiny china shepherdess on a table nearby, Elinor reminded herself he had not come to Mordyn until long after her lover had started visiting her at night. It would seem it could not be Jason Grenville after all.

She put her hands to her aching temples. She felt she was truly losing her mind. Perhaps she had made the whole thing up, dreamed it so vividly that it had become real to her? But why would she do such a thing? Perhaps she was not losing her mind after all. Perhaps she was already mad.

Elinor refused to go down to tea, but she knew she had to make an appearance at dinner. She spent the time watching and listening as much as she could, comparing Jonathan and his twin—their expressions, the nuances in their voices. And when the kindly Sir Robert asked her about her unusual quietness, she was quick to tell him she was suffering from a headache. She did not notice the fearful gaze Fiona gave her, nor Mr. Jason Grenville's ill-concealed sneer, for she was watching his twin's knowing little smile as he picked up his glass of wine and raised it in a toast to her.

Sent off to bed right after dinner, Elinor was delighted to be free of the lot of them. In spite of her good resolution, she paused for a moment outside her door to inspect the portrait of the Cavalier again. For some reason, he looked sad to her tonight, and his eyes did not twinkle as they always had before. Even, it seemed, he shook his head at her in regret, for what she did not know. Telling herself it was just a trick of the light, she hurried into her room and firmly closed the door behind her.

She spent a few minutes at the open windows that

led to the balcony, breathing deeply of the cool, damp air. But the evening was not conducive to lingering. Indeed, there was a bite to the air that reminded Elinor of her first days at Mordyn, in April.

Closing the windows, and pulling the draperies across them to cut the drafts, she settled down before the fire instead.

Both Jonathan and his twin had been just as they always were tonight. Jonathan had been full of light, drawling conversations one minute, and exuding curt boredom the next. Sir Robert had done his best, speaking impartially to all of them, but with Elinor's feigned headache, Fiona's silence, and Jason Grenville's few, terse remarks, he had had heavy going of it.

Now Elinor was reminded that that same Jason Grenville had stared at her again this evening—how uncomfortable it had made her. But she had noticed something else as well. He had done so only when his twin was preoccupied with other matters—cutting his meat, speaking to his sister, or turning to signal Whitman to bring him more wine.

For whenever Jonathan had been looking at her, Jason Grenville's eyes had been elsewhere. Elinor sat up straighter. Was there any significance in that? she wondered.

She felt she was grasping at straws. Still, she made herself review every moment she had ever spent in Jason Grenville's solitary company. Not that there many of those. Their one breakfast together, their meetings by the brook. And then, of course, there was the day he had come for her at the tinner's house, and put her up before him on his horse. He had spoken little at that time—indeed, he had always been a miser with words. But what had he said then? First, she remembered, he had ordered her to lean back against him, lest she fall. And then he had told her about his uncle's farmhouse, when she had asked why they could not go home to Mordyn. Why, he had even insulted her, by suggesting she "think—if she were capable of thinking, that is!"

Elinor stiffened. He was such a boor! But her eyes narrowed in thought. There had been something else, something else he had said after that, that teased her memory.

Think, Elinor! she ordered herself, leaning forward intently. She closed her eyes for a moment. It had been so dark that night, so wet. Even now she could remember how the cold rain had made its way under her cloak; how she had shivered. And he had said . . . he had said . . .

As clearly as if he were in the room with her, Elinor heard the words clearly now. "Trust me, Miss Fielding. I'll see all well." She was sure she remembered those words correctly, for they were the only kind ones he had ever spoken to her.

"All well, all well, all well," seemed to echo in her head. Her lover had used those words too. Not once, but many times, right here in this room. He would not let anything happen to her, he would see "all well." And again, everything would be all right, "all would be well."

Elinor jumped up so suddenly, she upset a small table nearby. She did not even notice. Her green eyes began to darken with her anger. It was true! It had to be true! And all this time she had fancied herself in love with a sadist—a murderer! A man who had pretended to be a crude boor for whatever perverted reason he might have had; one who had tricked her into thinking he cared for her . . . well! She would stand for no more of it!

She wanted to march right back down the stairs to the drawing room and confront him, but she could not do that. Sir Robert would think her mad. As for Jonathan, she shuddered at the very idea of his discovering she had had a lover before him, and that that lover had been his despised twin brother.

No, no matter how much it chafed her, she must wait till it was very late. If Jason Grenville did not come to her, why, then, she would go to him. She knew where his room was, for Rebecca Ward had gone on and on about the difficulty she had had in placing him in the castle. Not too close to Fiona, of course, nor to Mr. Jonathan—or, dear, how unfortunate that would be!—but not so far removed from the rest of the family as to give him the feeling he was being ostracized. Elinor knew Miss Ward's triumphant choice had been the green bedchamber that was almost directly under her, Elinor's own room, one flight down.

She summoned Betsy to help her undress. All the time she was being helped into her nightrobe, all the time her hair was being brushed and tied with a ribbon, Elinor thought of Jason Grenville, and planned the things she would say to him. Cruel things, cutting things. Things that would hurt him, as he had hurt her.

When Betsy brought her the red satin wrapper, Elinor wished she had chosen one more modest. Somehow the bright color seemed wanton to her now, and the slippery feeling of the fabric against her skin called to mind his remarks about her sensuality. Her color deepened as she dismissed the maid and told her she did not wish to be disturbed the following morning until she rang. As Betsy curtsied and left her, Elinor looked into her glass. Red, she decided, was the perfect color for a wanton after all. But oh, how she would make Jason Grenville pay for her downfall at his hands! How she looked forward to it!

It seemed an age before she saw the tapestry move, and he came around the end of it to glance at the bed. Elinor was sitting back in deep shadow on the other side of the room; he could not see her.

"I am not waiting for you in bed tonight, *Mr. Jason Grenville,*" she managed to get out over the tumultuous pounding of her heart.

He froze where he was for a moment, and he did not turn.

"It *is* you, is it not?" she persisted, rising and grasping the back of her chair for support.

She could feel the tension in the room, the currents that eddied between them as he turned toward her and moved to light a branch of candles on the dresser. As the candlelight flared up, and lit his dark, frowning features, she gasped. He looked as dangerous tonight as Jonathan had named him, and suddenly, she was frightened.

Still without speaking, he threw some logs on the embers that were all that remained of the fire, and he waited until those logs caught and began to blaze before he turned toward her again.

"Come closer to the fire, Elinor," he said calmly. "You must be cold. How did you discover my name?"

"You are very cold yourself, sir," Elinor retorted. "Never mind how I found out. It has been you all the time, why, even before you came to Mordyn openly, hasn't it?"

She waited then, staring into his dark, set face. When he nodded at last, his mouth a thin, uncompromising line, she lost control of herself. Gone was the cool lady she had intended to be earlier, freezing him with her scorn, humiliating him for his perfidy. Now the tigress had returned. She ran to him and began to pummel his chest with her fists.

"How could you?" she demanded, breathless with anger. "How could you do such an infamous thing to me?"

"Elinor, shh," he said, grasping her hands to hold them prisoner against the chest she had just been beating. Elinor struggled, but she could not get away, and when she tried to kick him, she realized her thin slippers could inflict no hurt.

"You are distraught, and I suppose you have every reason to be. Discovering my name was a shock to you, after the way I've been behaving. But I could not keep myself from coming to you. At first, I only meant to look at you, but soon that was not enough. You are a witch, my girl, and I am deep in your spell.

"Stop fighting me, Elinor! You'll hurt yourself, and I wouldn't want that. You see, I do happen to love you."

"*Love* me!" she panted, struggling anew. "What kind of love is that, to take advantage of a woman's naiveté, yes, even take her innocence, for your own ends? That is not love! But I guess I should not be surprised. Jonathan told me what kind of man you are.

Indeed, I have seen what kind from my own observations ever since you arrived here. You are nothing but a—a . . ."

Elinor sobbed, and shook her head. She could not say the word *murderer.* Not to him. She remembered again that Jonathan had warned her never to be alone with his twin. And where it had not mattered before, while he was kissing her, taking his pleasure, it was vastly different now. Perhaps she had angered him. Perhaps he would revert to his usual behavior, and attack her. And here she was, late at night, in a distant room at the top of the castle, with no one to hear even her loudest screams. The walls of Mordyn were so very thick. He had said he loved her, but who knew what such a man might do? He was not capable of love. It had been only lust that had brought him to her from the first.

"I hate you," she said suddenly. "How very much I hate you!"

He drew her closer in one arm, still holding her hands prisoner with his other big hand. Clamped tight against the long, lean length of him, Elinor felt faint. Faint, and a little nauseous, for even now her treacherous body was beginning to respond to him.

"No, you don't hate me," he said, in a firm, controlled voice. She realized that all the rough coarse accent was gone from that voice. Now he sounded as educated and elegant as ever his twin had. She wondered about it, but he was speaking again, and she forced herself to concentrate.

"As I told you before, you are a passionate woman. But even such passion as yours would not be enough to make you lie with a man you did not love. Be honest. Admit it."

Elinor sobbed in frustration. Of course she did not hate her lover. She only hated Jason Grenville for *being* that lover. To think she had given her heart to a sadistic man who had once murdered his own brother! It was the worst nightmare she could imagine.

"I cannot admit it. Not now, and not ever again,"

she managed to get out, in a voice so soft he had to bend his head to hear it.

His arm tightened around her waist, and the hand holding hers crushed them against her breasts. She could feel the warm flesh of his hand on those breasts, now exposed by her open robe and low-cut bedgown. "Let me go," she said brokenly. "Please, let me go."

For a moment, his grip tightened, and she was afraid until he released her. She backed away from him, carefully turning away to adjust the neckline of her robe and tighten the sash.

Finally, she forced herself to look at him, and as she did so, she lifted her chin. "There must be some explanation for what you have done," she said, proud of her even voice. "You have been playing a part here, not only with me but with your family, too. Why would you do that? What is your reason?"

"I have an excellent reason, but I cannot tell you of it. Not yet. I was serious when I said there was danger here in the castle."

Elinor went to hold her hands out to the blazing fire. As bright and glowing as it was, it did not seem able to warm her, melt that core of ice deep inside, that had returned, colder and harder than ever.

"Jonathan warned me of danger, too," she said over her shoulder. "But he called danger by *your* name."

She turned to look at him then, to gauge his reaction. To her surprise, he only shrugged. "I might have expected him to do so, I suppose. But even so, I must ask you to trust me. Things are not what they seem here."

Now it was her turn to shrug. "So you say. How can I believe you? I know of no danger. Fiona loves me, and so does Sir Robert. And today, Jonathan asked me to marry him."

She was watching him carefully, and she saw how his eyes narrowed, the way he clenched his fists at his side. His whole body was taut with fury. Why had she mentioned that? she wondered, quivering with nerves. Why hadn't she been more conciliatory, at least until he had left her and she had had a chance to tell Sir

Robert what he had done? For she knew his father would send him away in disgrace at once, and she would be free of him forever. Didn't she want to be free?

"No. You will never marry Jonathan Grenville," he said in a hard, cold voice that reminded her of his crude masquerade. Except, she realized, he was not masquerading now.

"I could not let that happen to you, Elinor, not even if I could somehow accept losing you. And I cannot lose you."

He turned to her dressing table, to pick up her comb and brush and rearrange her hairpins and perfume bottles. Elinor wondered why he did so, until she realized he was struggling to control himself. The sight of his big, masculine hands on her pretty belongings made her shiver.

"Very well," he said turning back to her. Elinor saw his eyes were bleak. "I had hoped it would not come to this, but I see there is no other way. You want to know Mordyn's secrets? You want to know why I disguised myself, why I kept my real identity hidden from you? Well, and so you shall, my girl. But I want you to think carefully before you agree. You will hear things you may not want to hear, see things that will change you and your perception of the people here. Eavesdroppers rarely hear any good of themselves, you know."

Elinor did not hesitate. "I agree," she said calmly.

He shrugged. "So be it. Tomorrow, after you have had breakfast here in your room and been dressed, dismiss your maid. Tell her you do not want to be disturbed, for any reason, until you ring. Give her whatever excuse you want—important letters to be written? Some thinking you must do alone? But you will know what would be best.

"Lock the door after she leaves. I shall come and fetch you at ten."

"How do you enter and leave my room?" she asked him, curious about that still. "I have searched, but there is no door to be found."

"It is there, cleverly hidden behind the tapestry. Mordyn is riddled with secret passageways and narrow stone stairs, as you shall see tomorrow. I discovered them by accident once when I was a boy, but I never told my twin, or Fiona, of them. I suppose I wanted them to be my secret. I am not sure even my father knows of them. I do not know why they were built, or by whom so very long ago, but it is possible to spy on everyone in the castle, and hear them as well, without them being aware of you."

He paused and came to stand before her, carefully not touching her. Elinor's heart began to race.

"Are you sure you want to do this, Elinor?" he asked, his gray eyes searching her face. "It might well be painful for you."

She nodded, not trusting her voice, with him so close to her. His face was bleak and intent; she wondered that he looked so sad.

"Very well. Do not investigate the passageways alone. It would not be safe. Wait until I come to guide you. Do you promise to do that?"

Elinor nodded again, closing her eyes for a moment to blot out his agonized expression. Even knowing what she did about him now, she wanted to take his face in her hands, kiss away all those harsh lines, lose herself in his arms.

And she was ashamed of herself.

18

ELINOR WAS READY the next morning long before the time Jason Grenville had named, for she had not slept well. After she had had her breakfast and been dressed, she dismissed Betsy, saying she wished to be completely undisturbed all morning. She waited until she was sure the maid had run down the stairs to the kitchen before she locked the door behind her, and pocketed the key.

When she saw the tapestry move on the last stroke of ten, she rose from the chair where she had been sitting and waiting. She took a deep breath as she did so, steeling herself for whatever unpleasantness lay ahead.

Jason was dressed simply in an open-necked shirt and breeches this morning, and his face was still set in harsh lines. Elinor remembered how she had once dreamed of seeing her lover in daylight—of taking his hand in hers in front of everyone—and her own eyes grew bleak. She could never do that now; she would never know that particular joy.

"You are ready?" he asked.

At her nod, he went on, "It is not necessary to speak in whispers when we are in the passageways. Mordyn's stone walls are thick, and no one will be able to hear us unless the peepholes are open. When they are, we must be very quiet. No matter how upsetting what you see and hear is to you, you must not make a sound. Do you understand? Do you think you can do that?"

Elinor bit her lip and nodded again, and he held

back the tapestry for her. "Very well then. Let us begin."

Elinor saw he had left an opening in the stone wall, and she stood back to allow him to precede her. Her heart was pounding now, and her breathing came short. In anticipation? she wondered. Or was it perhaps only dread?

After Jason had closed the stone door, and shut them into the cold, stuffy passage, Elinor was surprised at how much light there was. She had thought it would be dark. Jason led the way, till they came to the end of the passage and she could see a deep, narrow slit in the outside wall that admitted light. Fortunately, it was a sunny day.

Before her was a set of stone stairs leading down. They were steep and narrow, and she held tight to a chain that was fastened to the wall by heavy rings, lest she stumble. Why had these passages been built, and by whom? she wondered. Were they part of the original castle, or were they some unknown Grenville's later, secret addition? Perhaps the Cavalier had had them installed as an aid to his smuggling. But how strange it seemed to her to be creeping through them like a thief. Elinor shivered, hoping they would not meet any ghosts.

At the foot of the flight, Jason led her along another passageway. This one turned several corners, and there were others leading from it. Elinor was glad he was guiding her, for she knew by herself, she would soon become as hopelessly lost as she had been on the moor. Indeed, she did not have the vaguest idea where she was, nor how she could get back to her room.

Her guide paused then, and turned to stare down at her. His big shoulders almost touched both sides of the stone passage, although Elinor noted it was high enough so his head was in no danger of colliding with the vaulted roof.

"Be very quiet now," he said in his normal tone of voice. He waited for her nod of assent before he felt the wall before him and pressed two stones there. Elinor's eyes widened as the stones moved a little, and narrow slits about four inches long appeared. Holding her breath, and moving closer as quietly as she could, Elinor stood on tiptoe and looked through one of the slits into a room she had never seen before. It was nicely furnished in shades of rose, although it was cluttered and somehow fussy and prim. Why, this was almost what seeing a play in one of the London theaters must be like! she thought. As she watched in wonder she heard a sound, and the next moment, Rebecca Ward came into view. She was carrying a small striped box which she set down on the largest table and opened carefully. Her plain face was wreathed in a delighted smile as she did so, and she patted the cover of the box lovingly as she set it aside.

When she bustled out of sight again, Elinor turned to Jason, a question in her eyes. It was obvious they were looking into Miss Ward's bedchamber, and she wondered why he had brought her here. His eyes burned down into hers for a moment, before he nodded toward the peephole again.

Obediently, Elinor moved close again. Miss Ward had come back, carrying a tray containing a small black vial, a candle and napkin, and a knife and small spoon. She hummed as she put the tray down on the table, and she was still smiling.

Fascinated, Elinor watched as the woman took a mounded piece of chocolate from the box and turned it upside down on the napkin. Taking up the knife, she cut a precise small piece from the bottom of the confection, as carefully as any surgeon. Then she opened the dark vial and put several drops of its contents into the candy, before she lit the candle and held it close to the hole she had made. When the chocolate was softened, she placed the other piece of it back in place, and pressed the edges together.

"That's better. Much better!" she muttered moments later as she held it up to the light for inspection. "You really have to look hard to see it has been tampered with. I do believe I've got the knack of it now!"

Elinor watched as she repeated the operation with three other pieces of candy. One of them broke at the end of the process, and Rebecca Ward discarded it, shaking her head in exasperation as she did so.

Elinor was so intent on this strange behavior, and the woman's intensity, that she was startled when Jason Grenville touched her arm. Obediently, she stepped back, and he closed the peepholes.

"What on earth is she doing, and why did you show me that?" Elinor whispered after they had moved a safe distance away. Thick walls or not, a whisper seemed safer to her.

Jason stopped and turned to face her. "She is putting poison in that candy," he told her, speaking normally. "She has been doing it for the past two mornings, at just this time. It is the same poison Fiona used on her kitten. Miss Ward demanded my sister give it up to her, saying she was going to dispose of it. But as you could see, she never had any intention of doing that. Oh, no. She had quite another use for it in mind."

Elinor saw how intently he was watching her, and she took a deep breath. "You need say no more," she told him, her voice quivering. "Of course I knew Miss Ward disliked me, but how can it be she could hate me so badly she would try and kill me?"

"Because she is desperate to get rid of you. First, because you stole Fiona's affections, and her attention, and second, because she fears Sir Robert is falling in love with you. She has loved him for years, and she is afraid you are intent on marrying him."

"Marrying Sir Robert?" Elinor whispered in disbelief. "Is she mad?"

"Well, she is not sane, not if she is contemplating murder. Of course, she does not expect to be caught at it. For even if someone wonders about your sudden death from a gastric attack, and investigates the candy, the blame would most surely be put at Fiona's door, especially after her kitten's death. Rebecca Ward knows Fiona would be protected, no matter what; she places her in no danger. It is a fool-proof plan.

"She was going to give you the candy as a peace offering, after begging your pardon for all her harsh words, and after telling you how much she hoped the two of you might be friends. She's been practicing the speech. I've heard her."

Elinor grimaced, and he added, "You would never have seen those candies, you know. I intended to speak to her today, through the peephole. A slow, eerie whisper, to let her know someone was on to all her tricks. Knowing her penchant for hysteria, I am sure she would have taken such a warning as a direct message from God, and given up the plan. Of course, now I do not have to warn her, since you know of it."

He saw the distaste on Elinor's face, and her shock, and he turned away. "Come!" he ordered. "There is more. And you did say you wanted to learn all, did you not?"

Obediently, almost numbly, Elinor followed him, shivering with horror. What had she ever done that was so bad Miss Ward wanted to kill her? she wondered. It was ludicrous to think Sir Robert loved her that way, or that she would ever agree to marriage with him. Why, he was old enough to be her father, and she thought of him that way. Rebecca Ward had to be mad; a candidate for Bedlam.

Jason Grenville stopped again, and put his finger to his lips. After he opened the peepholes, Elinor moved forward reluctantly. She was nowhere near as eager to hear any more of Mordyn's secrets, but having come this far, she supposed she was committed. If she told Jason she wanted to return to her room, she was sure he would look at her with scorn. No, she must go on, show him she was made of stronger stuff.

The room she looked into now was familiar, and she had been there often, for it was Fiona's own private sitting room. Elinor could see the edge of the piano, the comfortable chairs grouped around a table, the window that looked down into The Lady's Garden.

Fiona was standing by that window, staring out. She did not move for a long time, but at last, she dropped the drapery she held and began to pace. Fifteen, sixteen times, Elinor watched her pass before the peephole. Fiona's pretty face wore a worried frown, and once she stopped to press her hands to her temples and shake her head.

To Elinor's surprise, they did not linger there. After Jason had shut the peepholes, he said, "She has been doing that for days, every time she is alone. I don't know why, but I wish I did."

"She looks so worried about something—or someone," Elinor said slowly. "I have wondered too, who or what it might be. In fact, Fiona has not been the same ever since the tinners' raid on Glyn. But she was in no danger then, nor is she now. And why would such a thing overset her? She is so safe inside Mordyn!"

Jason's expression eased somewhat. "Ah, now I understand. But you have it backward, you know. She is not worried *about* the tinners, she is worried *for* them. One, in particular. Come, we must go on."

Elinor longed to grab his sleeve and insist he explain to her, but he was moving rapidly now, and she picked up the hem of her skirt to follow. They came to the end of that passage, and descended yet another set of narrow stone stairs.

"Do these passageways and stairs go beneath Mordyn itself?" she asked, more than a little frightened now as they reached what she was sure must be the ground floor.

"Yes. There are various storerooms down there and even, a flight below that, what looks very much like a dungeon. No, you shall not have to see that, although it is empty, without a single skeleton languishing in its chains against the wall to frighten you. Further down, there is also a door to the outside. It looks like part of the cliff, impossible to see unless you know its whereabouts. That was how I got in and out of the castle before I came here."

Again, Elinor wanted to ask him why he had done such a thing, but he had turned to face the wall, raising one hand to ensure her silence.

The peephole she looked through revealed the library, and a serious Sir Robert, seated there at his desk. Sir Robert, her benefactor. Suddenly, Elinor felt shame at what she was doing. It was not right to spy on this dear, good man! Why had Jason brought her here?

She heard a door open and close, and Sir Robert looked up, his face grim as his son strolled forward and casually took a seat near the desk. On tiptoe again, Elinor could see them both clearly.

"She's told her maid she must not be disturbed by anyone this morning," Jonathan remarked in his usual drawl, and then he yawned. "I weary of such melodrama, such girlish reluctance! Weary of it as I do of this whole, ridiculous farce! Agh . . ."

He shoved his hands in his pockets and grimaced, his handsome face set in lines of sneering distaste.

"That is unfortunate, Jonathan," Sir Robert said, his voice cold. "But you know my mind. You will continue to pursue Elinor, and you will persist until you have won her promise to marry you."

"I cannot persuade you to choose another way, even now?" his son asked. "Marriage to one such as her is so distasteful!"

Elinor cringed at the revulsion she heard so plainly in his voice. This was the man who had told her how lovely she was—how desirable? The one who claimed he could not wait for her to become his bride? The one who had always been so insanely jealous if another man paid her even the slightest attention?

"Why do you say that?" his father asked, and Elinor made herself listen. "Elinor is lovely—nay, beautiful even—and—"

"She is common, vulgar, which quite outweighs her youth and pretty face, that voluptuous little body," Jonathan sneered, rising to go and pour himself a glass of wine. He did not offer to get his father one.

He was quite close to the peepholes now, and Elinor cringed away, unable to hide a tiny gasp at his proximity, those searing harsh words of distaste that were so different from the admiring way he had spoken to her yesterday. She felt Jason's warning touch on her arm. I must be still! she ordered herself, both fascinated and repulsed at the same time by what she was hearing.

"How ludicrous all this is!" Jonathan complained as he took his seat again. "To think I have been forced to give up an entire Season in town, and all for what? To play suitor to a merchant's daughter! I, Jonathan Grenville, heir to the baronetcy of Mordyn! I am sure to be laughed out of London when my friends hear of it!"

"How can you say that? Elinor is presentable, mannerly."

Behind the wall, Elinor smiled a little at the dear man. At least he liked her!

"Of course she is terribly overdressed, but you can soon correct that, as well as instruct her in the more genteel ways your wife should adapt. Poor little nobody! She does not understand our kind, but I am sure she can learn, with your guidance."

Elinor's smile faded.

"I might dress her as quietly as a churchmouse, confine that brassy hair of hers in a tight knot, but still it will be impossible to make a silk purse out of a sow's ear, and well you know it, sir. Someone will discover her origins, and how I shall be ridiculed then! They'll know I married her for her money—there could be no other reason for so disparate a match. It is humiliating!

"Come, father, let me end this distasteful affair. Send her back to that slum she came from, for my sake!"

"Elinor Fielding did not come from a slum. She came from a respectable tradesman's home. And I knew her father. Why he—"

"Please do not bother to tell me what a good friend of yours he was! Spare me the fairy tale you told her, sir, for I know better! You never kept in touch with Gerald Fielding after he left Cornwall all those years ago, and you would never have replied to his dying wife's plea to take care of his daughter if you had not learned how very, very wealthy Miss Elinor Fielding was going to be. Let us have honesty between us, if you please!''

''Sixty thousand pounds sterling, all safely invested in funds, real estate, and shipping. A tidy sum indeed, and one she has barely touched. Thank heavens I got her out of town before she could squander any more of it on showy finery,'' Sir Robert said, sounding pleased with himself. ''My man in London tells me the Compton Street house brought a goodly sum as well. All in all, a most respectable dowry.''

Elinor felt her stomach heave, and the bile rise in her throat, and she swallowed hard as he went on, ''But it might not have been necessary to align our family with any such lower class person as Miss Fielding if you had not managed to lose a fortune gambling and wenching!''

''Hardly a fortune, sir. It was only the matter of a few thousand pounds. You are so old-fashioned, so out of the way here, you do not realize that I have standards to uphold in London. It costs money to keep up. But my luck will change any day now, I know it will! And then we'll not need her grubby, ill-gotten money. Nor her.''

Sir Robert rose to lean on his desk. ''You are a fool, as well as an inveterate gambler!'' he snarled. ''Why, you've managed to lose more every time you've gone to Portreath this spring, and that town is hardly overrun with Captain Sharps! Nor is there any need for you to ''keep up'' an image there.''

''But one must find something entertaining to do in this quiet backwater,'' Jonathan complained gently. He sounded almost amused at his father's lecture. Perhaps he had heard it before?

''You will be silent!'' Sir Robert thundered. For a moment, the two stared at each other, and Elinor found she was holding her breath until Jonathan shrugged at last, and settled back in his chair.

''Listen to me! Your luck will never change, and I'll not throw good money after bad! No, instead you'll marry Elinor, if you wish to live in any comfort. I have promised you the interest, which is generous of me, after I had to save you from Newgate for bad debts.

"And I would remind you that I alone have the naming of my heir. The estate is not entailed. Take care! If you run into Dun territory again, I may have a change of heart, and choose your twin as my heir instead."

Elinor watched in horror as Jonathan rose and came to lean on the opposite side of the desk. She could not see his expression clearly from where she was hidden, but she could see that Sir Robert was the first to retreat, sitting down almost nervously and in great haste. But what had he meant? The estate was not entailed? That was not what Jonathan had told her!

"Come now, sir, you cannot be serious," Jonathan said in a silken voice that seemed even more threatening than the angriest bellow would have been. "What, name the uneducated boor my twin has become, master of Mordyn? And he the murderer of your beloved firstborn, too? Why, the very stones of the castle would weep at such blasphemy!"

"I have warned you. You know my mind," his father replied, clasping his trembling hands before him on the desk. "And I am still master here while I live, as I see I must remind you again."

"I live to obey you, sir," Jonathan said, his sneering voice contemptuous in spite of his courteous words. Elinor cringed.

"Since you insist, I shall continue my siege of Miss Fielding's defenses, however much it pains me to do so. To tell truth, I cannot imagine why she is being so damned coy! 'Oh, sir, I cannot even contemplate marriage until my year of mourning is over!' she simpered at me. And then again, fluttering her eyelashes, 'You really must give me more time to think of it!' Bah! It makes me ill just remembering her demure modesty!"

"Perhaps your charms are not as overwhelming as you have always thought," his father said wryly. "If so, I am glad of it. It might do you a world of good to have to extend yourself, winning her. And you might value her more, if you do."

"Should you care to wager on it?" Jonathan drawled. "That is one bet I am sure to win, for it has no chance of succeeding. No, I'll take her money, warm her bed, and use her body until I lose the urge to do so, and then I'll go my own way. And I'll send her back to Mordyn at the first sign of a child coming. She'll stay here from that time on. Why, eventually, the *ton* might even forget my defection from their ranks—forgive me—if I make sure she plays least in sight."

"Hardly much of a future for her, poor doll."

"She'll be Lady Grenville someday, and thus exalted. She must take the bitter with the sweet. And you'll have a grandchild to dote on, and Elinor can companion Fiona. Why, if you would only get rid of Rebecca Ward, you could be one big happy family. But you will be one without me. We have a deal, Father. Remember it.

"For you may be able to force me to marry her, but you cannot force me to provide devotion and endless attention. Still, I consider Elinor is getting the best of the bargain. I most certainly am not!"

His father shrugged. "I suppose I don't care what you do, as long as you do not run into debt again. I shall not rescue you next time—you have been warned! And I beg you to remember I shall have control of Elinor's money. You do remember that paper you signed?

"Elinor's a nice enough girl, pleasant and malleable. To my surprise I find I like her. I shall not mind her living at Mordyn."

"She is vulgar, in spite of her veneer of gentility, her superficial education. Why, she's only a little better than any peasant in one of our fields. Lord, what irony it is, when I think of all the commoners you have rejected before this, and with such scorn for their pretensions, too! First, Elinor's own father, when he and Aunt Gwyneth were all smiles and roses in May, or so I've heard tell from old 'Becca. That, of course, was long before my time, but I'm sure you remember it well. Sent him off with a flea in his ear, didn't you, for daring to aspire to the noble Miss Grenville's hand! And he such a *good* friend of yours, too!

"Did Aunt Gwynnie leave the castle and set herself up as savior to the herd to pay you back for banishing Gerald Fielding? I've often wondered.

"But I haven't had to wonder at how angry her defection must have made you, especially since she took the inheritance she had from that distant aunt with her. Indeed, took it right out of your control. How that must have pained you!"

Jonathan paused, but when his father had no comment, he went on, "And then there was Fiona's disastrous infatuation for the Coryton person when she was only fifteen. You nipped that in the bud as well, didn't you, sir? No, no, you must not become disturbed by the truth I tell. Why, your face is turning quite purple! I fear you will make yourself ill.

"Besides, I quite agree with your decision in both cases. Talk about unsuitable! But I do have to wonder why it is that the one Grenville who has never forgotten his station, and who has always had the most profound distaste for anything that smelled even faintly of the shop, should be the one who is forced to compromise his standards and make such a sacrifice. Ironic, is it not?"

"You must do it for Mordyn, of course," his father told him in a strangled voice.

"But Mordyn is not in a bad way, and you know it. No, 'tis only your own—ah, how shall I phrase it? Alas, no other word comes to mind but, er, greed."

"How dare you, sir!" his father demanded, jumping to his feet. "I am not greedy, I just have a concern for our estate and our name! One can never have enough wealth, and now the mine has closed, and I've lost that source of income . . ."

He paused and took a deep breath to steady himself. "You'll do as I tell you, damn your eyes! I'll have no more discussion with you! Set about the business sharply, and with your most polished address. I shall expect the lady's capitulation within a week's time. I want no more shilly-shallying!

"I do assure you, Jonathan, I am determined to gain her fortune."

"Very well, I'll marry the slut, but I think I must try other methods," Jonathan mused, rising to pace the room. "Ones more suitable for her station. I have restrained myself up to now, treated her with the same courtesy I would use seducing a duke's daughter. I thought it would thrill her. But force might be more effective, and pain can be a powerful goad."

What Sir Robert might have replied, Elinor never learned, for just then Whitman knocked and entered with a note for him, and the library was soon empty. Without a word, Jason Grenville closed the peepholes. Earlier, Elinor had thrust her fist against her mouth lest she cry out, but now she sagged speechless against the opposite wall of the passageway, feeling sick and faint and disgusted. The cold rough stone digging into her back hurt, and she was glad of it, for it gave her something to concentrate on, something that took her mind from the terrible things she had just heard.

"You are all right?" Jason asked in a cool, measured voice. To Elinor's ears, he did not sound any more interested in her well-being then than his twin had moments before, and her stomach lurched again.

"I told you you might not like what you would hear," he went on. "Come, let me help you back to your room. I imagine some fresh air would help."

Obediently, Elinor pushed herself away from the wall and tried to do as he had suggested. When he saw how white she was, how weak and shaky, he picked her up in his arms. Hating herself for her weakness, Elinor collapsed there, hiding her face in his shirt lest he hear her sobs.

By the time they reached her room again, that shirt was wet with her tears. He lowered her to the bed, and Elinor felt the room spinning. Quickly, she struggled to sit up and tried to rise, knowing she was about to be sick.

Jason must have known it as well, for he hurried to the dressing room, coming back moments later with a basin. He was just in time.

Elinor vomited her breakfast, loathing herself as she did so. It seemed so awful, with him standing there, holding her head. Oh, why doesn't he go away and leave me to my misery? she wondered, retching still even though there was nothing left in her stomach to lose.

Calmly, Jason put the basin down and took out his handkerchief to wipe her mouth and her brow, and remove all traces of the tears she had shed, before he lowered her to the pillow again.

"Rest now," he told her quietly. "Yes, it was a bad experience. I knew my father had asked Jonathan to come to the library this morning, and although I hoped they would say something about their plans to give themselves away, I had no idea they would discuss you in such painful depth again. But even though it has upset you, I have to be glad you heard it."

"Glad?" she asked, her voice faint. "Are you a monster?"

Jason stared down at her. She was lying with her eyes closed, one arm thrown over them, and as he watched, more tears escaped her lids and rolled down her white cheeks.

"Think!" he said harshly. "Would you have been any better off if you had never known? Better off if you had accepted Jonathan's proposal, perhaps? Think what a charming life he had in store for you! It will be all I can do not to throttle him at next meeting for his arrogance in daring to insult you that way!

"You must forget what he said. He is not worthy of you. You are too fine and good."

His words only made her cry harder, and he sat down on the bed and picked her up in his arms to hold her close. "Very well, if you must cry, go to it until all your tears are shed."

Elinor tried to push him away, but he was having none of that, and he was much too strong for her.

"Oh, no, Elinor, I shall not leave you. Not this way," he told her. "Besides, having laundered my shirt most thoroughly all the way up here, what can a few more tears matter?"

Elinor made a valiant attempt to control herself then, and soon her tears and sobs died away.

Jason spent the time cradling her head, caressing her back—and she found, in only a few moments, that she was nothing but grateful.

"Why does it overset you so much?" he asked. "You knew my twin was proud, my father as well. And certainly you have heard more than enough about your station in life from Rebecca Ward. I do not see how it could have come as any great surprise to you."

"It reminded me, rather painfully, of another time in London," she said faintly.

"You shall tell me all about it presently," he told her, releasing her and rising. "First, let me dispose of this basin, and fetch some water and a cloth from the dressing room so you might wash your face."

Elinor watched him as he left the room and, reminded that she was stretched out on the self-same bed where they had made love so late at night, she flushed and was quick to sit up and swing her legs over the side, adjusting her skirts as she did so.

He would not let her wash herself. Instead, he performed that service for her, and brought her a glass of water as well, to take the bad taste from her mouth.

At last she felt better, and he left her to go and open the long windows to the balcony. As the fresh, salty air blew into the room, she took several deep breaths.

"Why did you say it reminded you of another time?" he asked, coming to sit down on the bed beside her.

Elinor looked away, biting her lower lip. She had never intended to tell anyone what had happened to her in London, but his voice was so calm and concerned, she could not keep silent.

"It happened right after my mother died," she began, still not looking at him. "We had lived secluded in Compton Street, for my mother had a dread of the streets. Indeed, she never left the house after my father was killed by a runaway horse when I was fourteen. She had friends in the neighborhood, however, one in particular, a Mrs. Bertha Denby. Mrs. Denby was wonderful all through my mother's last days, taking care of all kinds of wearisome chores and details. I—I was very grateful to her, and to her son Austin, as well."

Elinor's voice died away. Jason wanted to touch her, to reach out and turn her toward him, but he did not do so. Her voice had been too full of agony as she spoke, of what he could tell was not only a painful, but a private matter.

She rose to pace the room, and as she turned toward him again, he saw how her green eyes had darkened with her memories.

"Mr. Denby was so good, then. He was a man in his late thirties, and he had often escorted me to church or to the libraries in the past. At that time, he took over the details of the funeral, and the burial. Even after everything was over, the Denby's continued attentive. Indeed, they were so often at my house, I had to beg them to moderate their calls. I—I only cared for Mr. Denby as a friend, and I knew people would begin to talk. I had had to listen to too much neighborhood gossip over the years, when ladies visited my mother, to imagine they would not.

"My maid—her name was Doll, and she was my best—indeed, my only—friend warned me. I knew she didn't care for the Denby's, but I heeded her, for there was something about them. They were almost too caressing and proprietary—almost smothering. Yet I tried to tell myself I was being ungrateful, after all their concern for me.

"Mr. Denby continued to call on me constantly, and it was not even two weeks after my mother's death that he proposed to me. I—I refused him as gently as I could."

Elinor stopped again, and clasped her hands before her, her eyes intent on some far distance only she could see.

"He—he would not take no for an answer, however," she went on at last. Jason leaned against the bedpost, never taking his eyes from her face.

"At last, I was forced to deny him the house, after

he—he attacked me one afternoon. Heaven knows what might have happened if Doll had not been there, and come to my aid when I screamed. He told me then that he would force me to marry him, for both he and his mother were determined to acquire the house and my fortune. They had been planning it for years. I am sure that in all their inquiring into my mother's affairs, and how things had been left, they had discovered the money my father had made. I—I was to blame for that, too, for when Mr. Denby offered to see my man of business for me, I had been only too happy to let him do so. I was such a trusting fool!"

"Everyone makes mistakes," Jason remarked in an even voice. "And you were still grieving. You could not know these people were not really the friends they pretended."

Elinor did not acknowledge his comment. "When Mr. Denby could not gain admittance to the house any longer, he tried another approach. I understand, from what Doll learned later, that he would take up a position on the doorstep, just before dawn. As soon as there was enough light, and some people abroad, he would make a furtive show of leaving, hurrying away still tying his cravat or buttoning his breeches, pretending he had spent the night with me and was now trying to hide all traces of our wrongdoing.

"People in the neighborhood began to gossip about it, and I was snubbed whenever I went out. Women turned their backs on me and sniffed, even hid their children's eyes, while their men snickered behind their hands and made rude remarks about me, not quite under their breaths. And—and when I went into one of the shops, I was told by the proprietor's wife that my trade was no longer welcome there. She called me a—a whore."

Jason saw how she swallowed, but when he rose to come to her, she held up a detaining hand.

"No, please, let me finish. There is worse," she said as he settled down again. "I was barred entrance at the church door the following Sunday, and as I went away, the vicar stood there thundering invective at me, and shaking his fist as he damned me. Some men lounging nearby picked up some stones and dung, and threw them at me. I ran as fast as I could, but I—I was filthy and bleeding when I reached the safety of my home. I was so afraid then! I knew I could stay there no longer, for they might well have burned the house down around me. They—they are very righteous on Compton Street, even if they are all commoners."

Jason had no comment to make to that bitter statement, and she continued, "Doll helped me. Indeed, I do not know what I would have done without her and her mother. They, at least, knew I had done no wrong. Doll fetched a hackney early the next morning, and escorted me to the solicitor's office so I could tell him I wanted the house sold as soon as possible. And she found us rooms in another part of town. It was then that I decided to accept Sir Robert's offer to make my home with his family. I could not stay in London any longer. I had no family, no friends, and I did not feel I could ever escape the stigma there, no matter how far I distanced myself from Compton Street. I was a young woman alone in the world, with only a maid beside me. A common maid, mind you, not an older lady companion to lend me consequence. I had to leave.

"I think that was why I was so upset this morning. It was painful enough to learn what they really thought of me—I do not deny that. But to learn as well that it had only been my money after all—that they, for all their noble name and beautiful manners, were just like the Denbys—well, that really did overset me. *Money.* It is always the money."

Jason came to take her hands, his gray eyes searching deep into her clear green ones as he did so. "All men are not like that, Elinor. I do not need or want your wealth. I would not care if you came to me without a pence, as long as you came. I love you, and I want to marry you."

Elinor pulled her hands from his and turned her back on him. "Please, no more," she said brokenly. "Please go away now."

19

To HER DISTRESS, he made no move to do so. "I cannot leave you, not like this," he told her calmly. "Come, Elinor, sit down beside me. I have things I must tell you, and there is little time."

She turned to stare at him. His voice was different suddenly, colder and more urgent.

"I had hoped to do so in another way, but that is not possible now, and so I must confess about a painful time in my life, even as you have just confessed to me. But before I do so, I have to know what Jonathan told you to turn you against me. I am still the same man who came to you at midnight all those times. The man who loves you. The same man you said you loved in return."

Speechless, Elinor only stood there until he led her to a sofa and pushed her gently down on it.

"Shall I have to guess then?" he asked, his gray eyes serious. "He told you I killed our older brother Rob, didn't he? Didn't he, Elinor?"

He took her chin in his big hand when she would have looked away, and forced her to meet his eyes. "It is all right," he told her. "He said as much right after it happened, which is why my father sent me away."

"Are you going to tell me he lied?" Elinor whispered. "But if that were the case, why didn't you defend yourself at the time?"

"First, because I was grieving for my brother, and I was hurt—hurt and confused. I was only a boy of ten. Besides, I was not sure that what Jonathan told my father might not have been truth after all. We *had* been wrestling at clifftop that day, Jonathan and I, and

I *had* brushed against Rob. I still remember doing so, and perhaps that inadvertent contact did cause him to lose his balance and fall. I didn't know then. I still don't. But I found I could not get on with my life until I at least tried to discover the truth, once and for all. It has bothered me all this time.''

Elinor saw how his face had darkened with his painful memories, and the harsh lines had returned to it, and in spite of everything, she felt a great pity for him. He had had to live with this for twenty long years! It made her own problem seem very small.

''I know I did not push Rob deliberately, but it is inconceivable that Jonathan would lie about such a thing,'' Jason continued. ''There had to be a grain of truth in what he said when he accused me of it.

''You see, even though Jonathan and I always fought as boys, and never really liked each other, I could not believe he hated me. And surely only hatred would drive him to such evil! But how could a young boy hate his twin? I may not have liked Jonathan, but I didn't hate him—why, it would be like hating myself! We had the same face, the same eyes, even the same voice. Sometimes, in these latter years, I have wondered if that might not have been the reason he disliked me so. Perhaps he couldn't stand having anyone just like him; felt cheated he was not unique. He always had to be first—in everything.''

Elinor felt chilled, for those were the same words Jonathan had used, describing his twin. She tried to forget them as Jason went on, ''That was the reason I pretended to be a crude, uneducated boor when I came here. I did not want Jonathan to think I might be a rival for your hand. It would not have been safe for you. He has always been unreasonably jealous—surely you have noticed that?''

Elinor nodded, remembering Jonathan's reaction to Harry Brownell.

''When I first arrived in the neighborhood, I stayed at my aunt's cottage,'' Jason went on. ''I was not sure of my welcome at Mordyn after all these years; not sure I wanted to return even for a visit. I intended to use the hidden passageways to spy on my family, see how they were. Of course then I saw you—fell in love with you—and I realized how even more important it had become to discover what really happened to Rob. For how could I ask you to share my life if I had somehow caused my brother's death?"

"I decided I would not tell you who I was, or speak to you of any future we might have, until there had been some kind of resolution. So I pretended to be a boor, assumed a coarse accent, and never touched you.

"In fact, that is why I told you I would not be coming to you at night for a while, right after I arrived here. Do you remember?"

He waited for her nod, before he added, "I had nothing important that I had to do then. I was just afraid that you might put two and two together and guess, if I were too close to you. I always know when you are near me, and not only from your perfume. You smell of sweet grass and honey."

Somewhat startled, Elinor asked, "But what of the night on the moors, when you put me up on your horse? We were close then."

"But the wind was in our faces, blowing away any scent of mine that might have recalled your lover."

"You did come to me that night, didn't you? It wasn't a dream?"

"No. I came. I had to make sure you were all right."

He turned away. "It was agony for me, only to be able to touch your hair, when all of me ached to take you in my arms, love you. I had been so worried about you all day, as I waited to hear word from Timmy . . ."

There was a long silence before he said in a completely different tone, "I have not pressed to find out more about Rob's death, no matter how much I want to claim you; take you away from Mordyn. First because of Fiona's problem; then, there are the tinners as well . . ."

He ran a hand over his dark hair in exasperation. "So many things to do! I had to know more of Fiona, and why she cannot speak. It seemed odd to me, that affliction of hers, after all these years. I can still remember her constant prattle as a little girl, her sunny laugh—the way she chased after me, calling me "Jase." I love my sister. I wanted to help her, if I could."

"Gwyneth thinks that perhaps she can speak," Elinor told him.

"Yes, she mentioned that to me as well. But if that is the case, it is imperative that I find out why she is pretending to be dumb—remove the cause of it, if I can.

"As for the tinners, I must help them too, since my father won't. They were my friends when I was a boy. I've already arranged for some of them to leave the area for other work. The day Glyn was attacked by a few hotheads, Coryton was in Portreath. No matter he was not the ringleader, for it's true my father hates him, not only for organizing the miners but for being Fiona's first love. He'll not be satisfied till Timmy swings. I must be sure to get him away!

"I was going to see about that this morning. Time is passing; the troops will be here any day. Yet I cannot leave you here alone, not when I know what my twin has in mind to do, to force you to accept him."

"I won't accept him. You need have no fear of that," Elinor told him, loathing in her voice.

"He is bigger and stronger than you are, and he has my father's sanction. I should not like another family murder laid at my door. If I were to return to find that he had raped you, I would kill him then and there, in the most painful way I knew how."

Elinor shuddered. "Please do not speak of it!" she said, looking away from the dark anger on his face, and remembering that Jonathan had said almost the same words when they had walked back to the castle after the sailing trip. Did they think alike, too, these Grenville twins? In that case, what was there to choose between them?

"We must speak of it," Jason said firmly, interrupting her depressing thoughts. "I have to leave, but

I have devised a plan to keep you safe, if you will agree to it.''

He waited until she nodded slightly, before he went on, ''I think the safest way would be for you to pretend you are ill. There is that basin in the dressing room to aid the deception. After I have left you, ring for your maid. Tell her you are sick, and ask her to send for Miss Grenville. I'll alert my aunt, ask her to join you here in the castle, supposedly to care for you. You must refuse to see Dr. Hepplewait, if my father suggests him—insist on Gwyneth. Once she is here, she can play watchdog, keeping not only my twin from you, but Rebecca Ward bearing dangerous gifts as well. I shall be as quick as I can, but I cannot promise I will be able to accomplish all that I must do in a day or two. Can you hold out until I return?''

''I'm sure I can,'' Elinor said, feeling vastly relieved that her ''illness'' would permit her to avoid the family. The thought of sitting down to a meal with them, listening to Sir Robert's feigned concern or having Jonathan touch her, made her feel as sick as she was going to have to pretend to be. And while she was confined to her rooms, she could make her plans to leave Mordyn. She knew Gwyneth would help her, and she did not feel she could stay here any longer, not now, not after all the things she had learned. Jason had been very logical, and his account of that fateful summer day so long ago had had a ring of truth. She wanted so badly to believe him, to believe he had not pushed his brother deliberately, but she did not think she could do that. Not now. Not anymore. She knew she had been too trusting in the past, first with the Denbys and then with Sir Robert and Jonathan. But she had been reminded today, and most painfully, too, that people were not always what they seemed. No, sometimes they could look at you with guileless eyes, and lie, and lie, and lie. How could she be sure Jason had not done that just now, for his own ends? She had only his word he did not need her money. She must leave here—to save herself.

The sadness on her face made Jason ask quickly, "What is it? What is troubling you?"

"No-nothing," she said, shaking her head. "I suppose it is only that I am still distraught at what I learned this morning."

She sensed he was about to take her in his arms, and she rose quickly and moved away. When she turned back to him from a safe distance, she saw he had risen as well. The bleak look on his handsome face tore at her heart, but she did not relent.

"Are you afraid of me still, Elinor?" he asked, his dark eyes searching hers. "Didn't you believe what I told you?"

"I don't know what to believe," she whispered. "I want to trust you, but I can't trust anyone blindly anymore. Too many things have happened. I've heard too many lies."

He stared at her before he nodded in defeat. "I see. Yes, I can understand your reluctance to align yourself with a possible murderer. So, it has become even more important for me to discover the truth. But know I love you. That is no lie. And know I always will. If there is any way that I can prove I did not push Rob deliberately, you may be sure I shall not rest until I have that proof, for it will be only then I can come to you openly.

"Wait until I am well away from the castle before you unlock your door and ring for your maid. That will give me time to alert Aunt Gwyneth before I must be gone."

He paused, and held out his hand to her. Elinor did not move closer, and he stared at her for what seemed an endless time. "Have a care for yourself," he said quietly, his hand dropping to his side again. "You are very precious to me."

Elinor could only nod a little. She saw how his mouth twisted for a moment before he turned abruptly and disappeared behind the tapestry.

When she knew he had gone, Elinor wandered out on the balcony, and stood there staring out to sea. The sky was darkening to the southwest, she noticed, desperately trying to think of mundane matters lest she cry again. Another storm was on the way. It would not matter. She would be closeted here in her rooms until Jason came back to the castle, unless she could figure out a way to leave Mordyn before that. But she would be safe here with Gwyneth, and survival was the important thing, she told herself stoutly.

Betsy was concerned when she came in answer to Elinor's ring almost an hour later. She agreed to fetch Miss Grenville at once, as she undid Elinor's gown and helped her back to bed.

Resting her hand on Elinor's forehead for a minute, she asked, "Be ye feverish, miss? Do you want another maid to sit with ye while I'm gone?"

Elinor thought quickly. Another maid would ensure her privacy, but she did not want one here. "No, I want you to stay with me," she said. "Send a footman to the cottage instead."

As the maid turned to do her bidding, she added, "And Betsy, don't tell anyone I am feeling ill, if you please. I—I would not worry them until I have consulted with Miss Grenville."

"But what about luncheon, miss? Sir Robert will think it a queer do if you don't go down."

"Inform Whitman I have asked to be excused. He can relay the message."

The maid curtsied and hurried away, and Elinor lay back on her pillows.

So, it begins, she thought. I wonder where it will all end?

She spent the time until Gwyneth should arrive, thinking over what she had learned that morning and trying to make plans for her future. It stretched before her, a vast, empty gray expanse of unhappiness, devoid of family and friends and love. She would have to go back to London. She knew of no other place, and at least Doll was there. Perhaps she should travel? Go see some of the places she had only known in books before? A long voyage might take her mind from her problems. But what at one time might have been entrancing, held no appeal for her now.

To think she had to spend her entire life without Jason! But what else could she do? She had no choice, for if she trusted him and married him, she might be putting herself in more danger than she would have known at Jonathan's careless hands. She remembered what Jonathan had said this morning. He would send her back to Mordyn forever, as soon as he got her with child.

She did not want to stay at Mordyn now, not a moment longer than she had to. Not anymore. What had once seemed the most marvelous place in the world, secure and welcoming, and full of love, had become a travesty. Commoner, commoner, echoed in her mind, and she tossed her head on the pillows.

"Here now, what's all this I've been hearing, Elinor? You're ill?" Gwyneth's deep voice asked from the doorway. Elinor's eyes flew open, and she quickly brushed a tear away.

"That will be all, Betsy," she told her hovering maid. "I—I would see Miss Grenville alone."

"Yes, run along and have a nice cup of tea," Gwyneth suggested. As the maid curtsied, she added, "I trust the fact your Mam has not summoned me again means your Grandda is feeling better now?"

"He's fine, ma'am," Betsy said, smiling a little. "Your tonic perked him right up again, it did."

Gwyneth nodded as she placed her bag on the table. She waited until the door closed behind the maid before she came and sat down on the bed, to take Elinor's hand in hers and pat it.

As soon as Gwyneth touched her, Elinor began to cry again, shaking her head at her weakness as she did so.

"Now, Elinor, where's your starch?" Gwyneth asked in a bracing voice. "Whatever has happened to turn you into such a watering pot?"

"Didn't Jason tell you?" Elinor asked, wiping her eyes on the handkerchief Gwyneth thrust into her hands.

"No, there wasn't time. He only said you would tell

me all—that it was important I be here with you until he returns. Quite a mystery! I am intrigued!"

Once again, Elinor was forced to review the things she had heard and seen that morning. As she spoke, Gwyneth looked affronted, indignant, angry, and even grimly amused in turn.

"My, my," she said, going to fetch a glass of water for Elinor's dry throat when she fell silent at last. "What a tale! Hard to believe, that it is. Oh, not about Rebecca Ward. She's plainly unbalanced, poor thing. But to think Robert would act as he has done, only for money, stuns me still. I knew him for a proud man, and one close with his money, but I never thought he would stoop so low as to plan to use an innocent girl to satisfy his greed.

"Jonathan's part in this is despicable as well. I never liked him as a boy—for reasons of my own—but I never suspected . . . Yes, all this must have been a terrible shock for you, my dear."

Elinor had not told her everything. She had decided she would keep the fact that she knew of Gwyneth's love for her father to herself. That was too private. There was no need to upset her friend as well.

"Let me see now," Gwyneth said, pulling a comfortable chair up beside the bed. "We must concoct some reasonable tale for Robert, some illness that is not so threatening as to require the doctor's intervention, yet still will mean bed rest. You vomited, I understand? Perhaps we can say you have a stomach infection. I've brought some harmless powders. They can't hurt you—they might even perk up your spirits a bit, which I can see are in dire need of it. We must also keep you secluded here, and I'll have to guard the door."

She snorted. "You may be sure I shall do so with a great deal of glee! To think you have been used so! It makes me so angry, I am determined to remain with you until Jason gets back.

"Now, where was I? Oh, yes, seclusion. No visitors, I think. Too upsetting for you, poor sickly lamb. I'll also have to alert Betsy that anything from the kitchen must be brought directly here; that Rebecca Ward is not to be allowed to get anywhere near your food and drink. Betsy will do as I say. She's a close one, too, not given to gossip with the other servants, and I know she doesn't like Miss Ward. None of them do."

She chuckled suddenly. "That woman will probably go down on her knees as soon as she learns the news, thanking the Lord for His intervention, and convinced that He wants you dead as much as she does. We'll take care of Miss Ward later, you and I, just see if we don't!"

"All this is very good of you, Gwyneth," Elinor told her, sitting up and preparing to rise. "I know you have many more important things to do, and it was not fair for Jason to ask you. But I must admit I am very glad you are here."

"I consider it a holiday," Gwyneth told her, her blue-gray eyes twinkling. "A few days of luxury will be a treat for me, and Philip Farlow is seeing to my animals for me."

As Elinor reached for her wrapper, Gwyneth said, "That is a beautiful color, my dear! What lovely material!"

"Bright red is common," Elinor remarked as she put it on. "No doubt that is why I was attracted to it."

Before she knew what Gwyneth was about, her friend reached out to grasp her shoulders and shake her, none too gently. "Stop that at once, do you hear me, my girl?" she demanded, her voice quite fierce. "You are not common! You are a lady! It is not the titles handed down over the generations, nor one's noble relatives, that makes any person a lady or a gentleman. Far from it. You are a lady worthy of anyone, and I'll thank you to remember it, lest you anger me further!"

"All right, I promise," Elinor said, somewhat startled by her friend's vehemence.

"For even if Jonathan cannot see beyond the peerage in his brazen arrogance, Jason is not so blind, now is he? He is noble too, moreover, with a great estate and much wealth."

Determined to be honest, Elinor asked, "Did you know that Jason and I have been lovers, ma'am?"

Her eyes darkened when she saw how shocked Gwyneth looked suddenly, and she twisted away from her hands and went to stand at the balcony doors with her back turned to her.

"No, I did not know that," Gwyneth said slowly. "I can see we have a lot to discuss. Just as well I'll be here for a while."

There was a knock on the sitting room door, and Elinor spun around to run back to bed.

"Don't you worry. I'll handle whoever it is," Gwyneth told her.

She did not shut the door to the bedchamber tightly, and Elinor could hear the subsequent conversation clearly.

"No, I cannot allow you to see Elinor, Robert. She is not feeling at all well, poor chick! It is some stomach ailment. She should be fine in just a few days. You are not to worry."

"But I do worry!" Sir Robert's voice came. He sounded so sincere, that Elinor began to doubt what she had heard in the library a while ago. At least she did until she was reminded that of course he would be concerned. Why, Sir Robert Grenville would lose over sixty thousand pounds sterling, all safely invested and paying interest every quarter, if she were to die before she contracted a Grenville marriage. No wonder he was upset!

"I'll send for Dr. Hepplewait at once!" he was saying now. "That's who we need here, not some unpracticed, uneducated—oh, I do beg your pardon, Gwynnie, but although it's good of you to come, I would prefer a medical opinion in Elinor's case. She is like my own daughter, and I would not feel I had—"

"Send for him if you like," Gwyneth interrupted cheerfully, "but Elinor has refused to see him. She wants me to care for her. Me, and none other."

"But—but . . ."

"There's no accounting for tastes, now is there, Robert?" his sister asked, chuckling a little. "Do run along. I'll tell Elinor you came, and relay your best wishes for her speedy recovery. Oh, and Robert, you might tell Jonathan and Fiona, and er, Miss Ward, that Elinor is to have no visitors, not a one. She will be better that much sooner if she is not bothered by company."

Elinor heard the door close then, and only a moment later, Gwyneth came back. "I do believe I'll send down for some luncheon, Elinor," she said as she rang the bell. "I'll order dry toast and tea for you, but never fear. I shall tell Betsy I'm feeling sharpset today, so there will be plenty for both of us. And I do believe I'll still be feeling hunger pangs at tea and dinner, too. Much safer if I take all my meals with you. Not that Robert would welcome me at his table!"

She laughed out loud as she indicated her faded old skirt and clean but unfashionable blouse. For the first time, Elinor was able to smile a little. Gwyneth might not look a lady, but she was the finest one Elinor had ever known.

After luncheon had been enjoyed, mainly by Gwyneth, and Betsy had removed the tray, Gwyneth questioned Elinor about her relationship with her nephew. It took a long time, but at last she knew all about his midnight visits, how they had made love and pledged themselves.

"And you did not know who he was? You never even saw his face?" Gwyneth asked at last, frowning, and looking as if she was having trouble comprehending this part of the story.

Elinor flushed. "It—it did not seem important at the time, and—and being with him seemed so right, almost fateful. Jason told me he could not reveal his name, that there was danger here, and I—well, I believed him." She shook her head, her mouth twisting. "I have believed a great many things lately that I would have been better not to."

"I knew Jason was in the castle," Gwyneth said slowly, her eyes distant. "He came to my cottage late one night, long before he appeared here openly as a visitor, and he asked me to keep his arrival secret. He would not even tell me why he had come back after all these years. He would only say it was a matter he had to settle for his own sanity. I understand now, about Rob's death and all.

"When you came and asked me if I believed in ghosts, told me someone had been in your room, touching you and kissing you, I knew it had to have been Jason. I could not break my promise to him and tell you so, however, but you may be sure I taxed him with his behavior the next day, for he did not come home at all that night. He said he could not help himself; that he loved you, and intended to marry you.

"I told him that what he had done, was still doing, was not at all fair to you. That he must wait until he could approach you openly. He never promised that he would, however, I am sorry to say.

"It was quite a while after that, that he announced he was going to stay at the castle. When I questioned him—and my! he did look black that afternoon!—he told me that he had seen something in the library that had forced his hand; that he could no longer delay. While he was packing, I could hear him mumbling and stamping around. As I remember, his twin's name was mentioned more than once. Generally preceded or followed by an oath."

She peered at Elinor, but Elinor did not notice. She was trying to remember when Jason had arrived. Was it before or after that night he had come to her room and looked at her, but made no move to touch her? Yes, of course! And that had been the same night of the day Jonathan had first kissed her in the library!

She told Gwyneth then what had happened since Jason's arrival at the castle. How frightened she had been of him, with his coarse accent, after Jonathan had told her of that fateful day at the cliff. How she avoided being alone with Jason ever after.

"I—I am ashamed to have to tell you that I was attracted to Jonathan, ma'am," she said. "I thought he was my lover for the longest time."

''I should be astounded if you hadn't been,'' Gwyneth said briskly. ''He was the only personable man in the vicinity. It is not as if you had a plethora of admirers to chose from. And he is so handsome, too, so charming when he puts his mind to it. Most understandable.''

Elinor told her of Jonathan's proposal, and how it had convinced her that Jason had been her lover all along. ''I was so angry with him! When he came here to my room last night, I flew at him, attacked him. It was then he told me he would show me Mordyn's secrets.''

She sighed. ''It is cowardly of me, no doubt, but a part of me wishes he had never done so.''

''Everyone hates to be disillusioned; in fact, most people go out of their way all their lives to try to avoid it. But I have to be glad you found out, Elinor. Jonathan would have made you a wretched husband.''

She hesitated for a moment before she asked a little diffidently, ''Do you still love Jason? Now, don't feel you have to answer me, if you would rather not! I am prying, and I admit it. My only excuse is that I am very fond of both of you.''

''Yes, I do,'' Elinor said. ''I cannot help myself. I think I will love him all my life. But when I remember he might well be a murderer, and a . . .''

''I do not believe for one moment that he is,'' her friend said firmly. ''If he said he cannot remember pushing Rob, then he did not do so. You told me he admitted brushing against his brother? If he could remember doing that, surely an outright shove would not escape his memory!''

''He might be lying,'' Elinor reminded her.

Gwyneth's mouth tightened. ''Yes, he might, but I cannot believe he would do so. Even as a child, Jason was never devious. Indeed, he was a happy, open little boy, full of fun and the sheer joy of living. He used to tag after Timmy Coryton as soon as he escaped his nurse's care; spend hours up on the moors with him, and some of the other miners' sons. And he was as kind to Rob as he was to Fiona. He had no reason to kill his elder brother, none at all."

"Perhaps you are right, ma'am," Elinor said politely, wondering why Gwyneth did not consider the inheritance of Mordyn, and the title, enough of a goad. "Still, I feel I must leave the castle, just as soon as I can contrive it. I'll have to ask your help to do so. Sir Robert will not let me go away, not just like that, when he has me, or so he thinks, so nearly in Jonathan's—and his own—grasp. There are those sixty thousand pounds . . ."

"You would go away now?" Gwyneth asked slowly, brows raised. "Now, before Jason returns? How can you even conceive of such a thing, you, who say you love him?"

Elinor rose and went to the windows to stare out over the ocean. Two fishing boats were beating their way back to the harbor ahead of the coming storm, and from the crowds of gulls that followed them, Elinor knew they had netted a large catch.

"I may love him, ma'am, but I can't trust him. Not anymore. I have learned too much about him, things, perhaps, of which you are unaware."

"Who told you these things? Jonathan? And you would take *his* word? Come, my dear!" Gwyneth said with scorn. "At the least you owe Jason a chance to prove his innocence. And for your sake, I pray he can prove it. A life spent mourning a lost love can be a sad one."

Gwyneth paused for a moment, and looked down at her work-worn hands. "I loved a man once," she said quietly. Elinor held her breath.

"He was your very own father. But Robert sent him away, and I was too much the coward to follow him. When you came to Mordyn, I could see Gerald in you—a certain expression about your eyes and mouth, your laugh. I have thought of you as the daughter I never had ever since. Of course, if you had been my child, you would not be such a dainty, lovely lady today, nor is it probable you would have fallen in love with your cousin Jason, so perhaps it's just as well."

She smiled at Elinor's startled face—her clear green eyes—and when she saw the pity there, she walked over and gave her a quick hug. "No, no, you must not feel sorry for me, dear child. I was young, and although it hurt at the time, I know now it was for the best. Gerald was driven by the need to make a fortune even in those early days. I know I could never have been happy spending my life helping him pursue such a silly goal. I wanted to work with the herbs even then, and I loved living in the country. Amazing, isn't it, how things work out?

"But you must not leave here, no matter how urgently you want to get away from Mordyn, not until Jason comes back. Don't you feel you owe him that much, even if it pains you to stay? Give him a chance to earn your trust, Elinor!"

As she had been speaking, Gwyneth had put her hands lightly on Elinor's shoulders to scan her face. Elinor could not look away, and at last she nodded, a little reluctantly.

"Good girl!" Gwyneth said briskly. "Now, I think we have had enough weighty discussions for a while. Come, I've some notes to write up, and I've brought you a sample of savory, and one of shepherd's purse, which you have yet to illustrate for me. Perhaps you could do so now, to pass the time?"

Elinor agreed. She did not feel like talking anymore either, and concentrating on reading was impossible. As for doing her needlepoint, that would give her too much time to think. Drawing, on the other hand, was absorbing.

After Betsy brought up her sketchbook and pencils, Elinor settled down across from Gwyneth at the large table. She was soon intent on her work, and so she did not notice how often her friend looked up from her notes, nor how her lined face softened when she did so. Elinor only knew she felt safe and comfortable because Gwyneth was there.

At teatime, Betsy brought a note from Jonathan, and a large bouquet of garden flowers. In the note, he told her how dismayed he was to learn of her illness, and how very much he was missing her already. He said he longed to see her again, as tempting and lovely as she was, so he might ask her a very important question—again.

He wrote smoothly, in an elegant, polished style, and although it was Elinor's first love letter, she handed it to Gwyneth with a grimace of distaste.

After Gwyneth had read it, she crushed it and strode to the fireplace to cast it away from her onto the burning logs. Brushing her hands together, she watched it turn to white ash before she said, "Hmmph!"

Even in her revulsion, Elinor could not help chuckling. That one homely sound had managed to convey not only disdain and disbelief, but a great deal of positively wicked satisfaction as well.

20

THREE MORNINGS LATER, the two were still secluded in Elinor's rooms. Time had begun to drag for both of them, even though Gwyneth had had books brought up from the library, a pack of cards, and a chess set as well.

Many times a day, Elinor found herself wondering when Jason would come back, and when Gwyneth finally left her locked in at night, and went to her own bedchamber next door, she could not sleep for worrying about him.

Betsy became their ear to the world. From her, they learned the news of the castle and the villages, how the troops had arrived at last, and how those troops were now busily combing the moors for the tinners. The maid was all smiles when she reported they had yet to find a single one. Later, Gwyneth told Elinor that some of Betsy's cousins were miners. Her relief and delight that they had all escaped down the line, was obvious and heartwarming. Elinor was glad for her, and the other village families, but still she could not be easy. Her own situation weighed too heavy for that.

Each morning brought another floral offering from Jonathan, and notes from a worried Sir Robert. Although, of course, there was nothing from Fiona, her father assured Elinor she was missing her friend, and longing to see her again. In this morning's note he begged Elinor to allow them to visit, saying that if she were not well enough for it today, he would have to send for Dr. Hepplewait.

"I cannot understand why you have formed such an aversion to the good doctor, my dear," he wrote. "He is a most capable man. Since Gwyneth does not appear able to restore you to good health, I must insist you see him. Mind now, I'll not take no for an answer! You are too precious to us!''

When Elinor showed her the note, Gwyneth frowned a little. ''Yes, I fear we have delayed up here as long as we can,'' she said slowly. ''I cannot imagine what is taking Jason so long, but surely he will be here soon!

''I think you must plan on making an appearance,'' Gwyneth added as she went to the balcony windows to peer out. ''It is going to be a nice day, after that awful storm we have been having. Shall we spend an hour or so in The Lady's Garden this afternoon?''

She saw the fright and reluctance on Elinor's face, and she added briskly, ''Come, come, my dear! Think of it as amateur theatricals! You must only play the part for a short time, just long enough to calm Robert's fears, and for Fiona to see you. Of course, you'll also have to see Jonathan, no doubt, but I'll be beside you the entire time. You need not fear him.''

She did not wait for Elinor to agree. Instead, she came closer to study her face. ''If only you did not look so well,'' she murmured. ''You're positively blooming! No sighted person would believe for a moment that you've been sick. Hmmm. Perhaps there is something we can do about that?''

Elinor's maid had been long in their confidence, for as Gwyneth said, anyone who claimed to have the appetite she had been showing, would have been not only fat, but fubsy. They did not tell Betsy why their subterfuge was necessary, but the maid was an eager conspirator even so, entering into the deception with a will. It was obvious to Elinor that whatever the loved and admired Miss Grenville promoted would win instant approval from her maid. Now, Betsy nodded as Gwyneth took her aside to speak to her for some moments, and there was a little smile on her face as she hurried away.

After luncheon, Elinor dressed in her most subdued gown. She was feeling very nervous and shaky, but she sat quietly as Betsy arranged her hair in a tight chignon, with none of the tendrils and curls that generally dangled from it and softened it.

Gwyneth nodded in satisfaction as Betsy opened a small jar containing some white powder.

"What is that?" Elinor asked suspiciously.

"Only a mixture of my own," Gwyneth told her cheerfully. "It is harmless, none of that white lead or mercury water that women have been ruining their health and complexions with for years. Now do sit still, Elinor, while Betsy applies your disguise. You did remember the black currant and saffron as well, didn't you, Betsy?"

The maid nodded as she indicated two small packets, and Gwyneth explained to Elinor how she had sent the maid to her cottage this morning to fetch these things.

Elinor kept her eyes closed while the powders were being applied. Betsy rubbed a mixture of saffron and currant under her eyes, before she liberally dusted Elinor's face with the white powder.

When Gwyneth bade her open her eyes at last, Elinor gasped. "Why, I look terrible!" she cried, turning her head this way and that. "I'm practically a hag!"

"Do you think we've overdone it?" Gwyneth asked from behind Elinor as she studied the results. "Yes, I agree it is a bit much. Remove some of the powder, Betsy, there's a good girl. If Elinor goes belowstairs looking like this, Robert will send for the doctor at once. Ah, a bit more I think. Good! Much better! After all, she's supposed to be recovering—even if it is very slowly. Just an occasional wan smile, Elinor, and if you can sigh every so often, it can only help the deception. Remember you are very tired. You won't have to talk much.

"Now, I think we're ready. Shall we go, dear?" she asked, coming to take Elinor's arm in support. Betsy followed with a rug, some books, and Gwyneth's black bag.

Elinor encountered only the concerned and sympathetic faces of the servants on their walk through Mordyn's halls. When she was seated in a long chair by the fountain in The Lady's Garden, she had to admit it was pleasant to be outdoors again. The sun shone down warmly, the flowers were lovely, and the birdsong and cascading waters eased her spirits. Still, she could not relax.

Fiona and Sir Robert were the first visitors. Fiona ran to Elinor with a delighted smile, but when she would have kissed her, Gwyneth took her niece by the arm and led her away. "I am not sure that what Elinor has had may not still be contagious," she said, smiling to soothe Fiona's hurt feelings. "Better not to take any chances, for there's no denying Elinor has been very ill."

"But she is improving, is she not?" Sir Robert asked, frowning as he studied Elinor's white face, the dark circles under her eyes.

"Oh, yes, I am feeling much better," Elinor made herself say slowly. "I'm sure in a day or so, I shall be my old self again, all thanks to Miss Grenville's excellent care."

"I still feel it would be wise for the doctor to see you. You are so pale!"

"No, no, sir, there is no need for that," Elinor told him.

"I'm sure you'll see a vast improvement shortly, Robert," Gwyneth added. "It took me a while to find the right powders and dosage—a stubborn case, Elinor's was. But she's on the mend now. Tell us, how are the troops progressing? We heard they had arrived, and we are so interested!"

Sir Robert's face darkened as he settled back in his chair, still holding Elinor's hand in his. "Not well. Not well at all. I cannot understand it! There is not a tinner to be found, although the moors have been most thoroughly scoured, including all those shacks they used. Why, even the fourgou was investigated.

"They're not lurking in the villages, either. I had all the cottages searched from top to bottom. It is as if the tinners were never here at all. But do not fear! Eventually, they must come out of whatever hiding place they have found for themselves. We'll have them then, every last man Jack of them!"

Fiona had wandered away to pick a few rose buds for Elinor, and he added, "Hunger will drive them out. Just you wait and see."

"No doubt you are right," Gwyneth told him as she

opened her bag to get her sewing. As she spread a gray cotton apron on her lap, her brother looked pained.

"I wish you would dress in a style more befitting one of your station, Gwynnie! And there is no need to do your own sewing. Nor is there any need to droop around looking like a peasant, for I know to the penny how much money Aunt Minnie left you. You are a wealthy woman!"

"If I do not care to squander it on my back, that is my choice, is it not?" his unrepentant sister asked as she threaded her needle. "Don't worry, Robert! I would never think of defiling your elegant dining salon in my common state. Elinor and I will continue to take our meals abovestairs."

"How you do take one up! I'm sure we would be delighted to see you at table, Gwynnie. That was not what I meant at all! Besides, we are all longing for Elinor to join us again. Surely she will be able to do so very soon. Jonathan has been disconsolate, my dear," he added, patting Elinor's hand. "*Most* disconsolate!"

Elinor withdrew her hand from his clasp as gently as she could, glad when Gwyneth spoke up before she had to think of a reply.

"I'm sure it will not be much longer. Of course, when Elinor is quite well, I shall return to my cottage. There are the villagers to see to, my herbs to gather, dry, and diffuse."

"I am so grateful that you took the time to care for me," Elinor said, smiling wanly. Gwyneth twinkled at her.

Fiona came back and handed Elinor her bouquet, and Elinor blew her a kiss in thanks. Smiling now, Fiona settled down on the grass nearby. Elinor saw she was very close to her kitten's grave. She wondered if Fiona had forgotten Mischief.

The two visitors were not allowed to remain for long. Gwyneth sent them away after only a few more minutes, claiming Elinor must not get overstimulated.

By the time Sir Robert had pressed her hand again, and uttered all his best wishes for a speedy recovery in his charming, concerned way, Elinor had the beginnings of a headache. She found it so difficult, this subterfuge, for always, in her mind, she could hear his cold, greedy words in the library that day. It was all she could do to give him a weak smile in response.

After they left, she and Gwyneth had the garden to themselves for quite a long time, and Elinor began to relax. Surely the worst was over now, she thought as she closed her eyes and lifted her face to the sun. Suddenly she heard Gwyneth snort in annoyance.

"What is the matter?" she asked, turning to see her friend staring up at the landing window. Almost fearfully, Elinor followed her gaze, and she gasped. The Lady was there again in her drifting white robes, wringing her hands and weeping silently. Her face was the mask of agony Elinor remembered from that other time.

To her surprise, Gwyneth rose and moved forward, waving her hands at the ghost. "Shoo!" she said loudly. "Get along with you now, *shoo!* We don't need any of *your* histrionics today, madam!"

Elinor grasped her skirt. "Do you think you should?" she asked fearfully, as Gwyneth continued to make shooing motions with both hands. "Perhaps it will anger her!"

"What of it?" Gwyneth asked. "The Lady's nothing but a ghost. She can't do anything, and she is tiresome. She always has been. I wish she would just lie in her grave peacefully, and let the rest of us get on about our business. I can tell she must have been a regular exhibitionist in life, and I suspect she is loathe to give that up. Shoo, there, I say! *Shoo!*"

Elinor looked up to the landing window again. To her surprise, The Lady had stopped crying. In fact, she looked almost bewildered, and only seconds later, her diaphanous image faded away.

"There!" Gwyneth said with a great deal of satisfaction. "She won't bother anybody for a while. I've found she always stays out of sight for quite some time after one of my scoldings. No doubt she's pouting and sulking, the ninny!"

"It certainly is a novel way to get rid of a ghost,"

Elinor said, chuckling in spite of her lingering fear, her fast-beating heart.

Gwyneth smiled at her as she folded her sewing. "I believe I'll just take a turn through the gardens, Elinor. I suspect Jonathan is out riding with the troops, since he has not made an appearance as yet. I do miss my exercise!"

"I too," Elinor told her. "But I'll be a good little invalid today."

As Gwyneth walked away, stooping every now and then to closer admire a flower, Elinor sighed. How she wished Jason would come back, and all this playacting could stop! And when he did, she reminded herself, she would be free to leave Mordyn. Deep in her heart, Elinor feared there was no way Jason would ever be able to prove he had not pushed his brother over the cliff. It had happened a very long time ago, and even if Jonathan had lied about what his twin had done, it was inconceivable he would admit to such a thing. She closed her eyes and sighed again.

"Such a sad, heartfelt sound!" a soft, mocking voice said from behind her. As Jonathan came to sit down beside her in the chair his father had vacated, Elinor looked around wildly, but Gwyneth was nowhere in sight. She drew a deep breath to steady herself before she forced herself to look into Jonathan's handsome, amused gray eyes.

"I wish I could say you are looking your beautiful self, Elinor, but I fear it would be the most terrible lie," he said as he took her hand in his and stroked it. "Poor poppet! You have had a time of it, haven't you?"

"Yes, it has been most unpleasant," Elinor murmured, wishing she might snatch her hand from his grasp, as her heart began to pound in her breast again.

"You have been missed," Jonathan said easily. "Fiona has sulked and had tantrums; my father has been positively distraught. It must be wonderful to be so dearly loved. I wish I were. By you," he added ruefully.

"Please, do not speak of that!" Elinor said quickly,

pulling her hand from his, and pretending she had to brush an insect away from her face.

As his brows rose in astonishment, she said in a weak voice, "I cannot discuss such things today. I—I am not feeling well enough."

"But of course, darling. Whatever you wish. We shall talk of other things. Isn't it a lovely day? Aren't the roses lush? When do you think my twin will reappear?"

"Ja—Mr. Grenville?"

"There is only the one, although he is more than enough. I found it passing strange that he left the castle at the same time you became ill. A weird coincidence, don't you agree?"

"I fail to see any coincidence," Elinor got out over her pounding heart. She bent to hide her face as she pretended to adjust the rug that covered her legs. To her dismay, Jonathan took that rug to arrange it around her himself. She could feel his hands on her legs, her hips and waist, how they lingered there, and she shuddered.

"Are you chilled?" he asked. "But it is such a warm day! Perhaps you made this trip to the garden too soon."

"No, indeed, I was weary of my bed. The air will be good for me," Elinor told him as she fiddled with the edge of the rug. "Do you, er, do you know where Mr. Jason Grenville has gone, and for what purpose, sir? I was not aware he had left the castle."

Jonathan shook his head, his eyes narrowing. "No. He did not say. He did not even leave a note for us. He has deplorable manners, doesn't he? But I'm sure we'll be able to send him on his way for good before much longer. I do not like such a boor near you. He is crude and offensive.

"I have been thinking a lot while you have been ill, Elinor," he said, changing the subject neatly. "In fact, I have been planning our bridals, in a week or so. Of course, you must regain your strength first, and I must get a special license. Perhaps we should have a quiet ceremony here in the garden, in deference to your mourning state. I have asked my father for my mother's ring. He was delighted to hear our news."

Elinor's stomach lurched as he smiled at her, a lazy smile that crinkled the corners of his eyes. He was a handsome man, and he looked so much like Jason—her lover—that it made her uncomfortable. Still, she realized she had not lied. She could tell them apart, for there was a difference, not so telling as subtle. Jonathan had a coldness, almost a blankness deep behind his eyes, that Jason, even when he had been pretending to be a coarse lout, had not.

Putting her thoughts aside, she said, "I have not told you that I would wed you. You take too much on yourself, sir, and you go too fast!"

"And you, jade, go too slowly," he said, bending closer. Afraid he might see the powder she wore, Elinor pressed back in her chair.

"I will not take no for an answer, you know," he murmured, the light she remembered back in his gray eyes. "I am sure I can, er, *persuade* you. One way or the other.

"Yes, a June wedding, and a honeymoon in London. As soon as we are married, Jason will take his leave. I'm sure of it."

"Why—why do you say that?"

He shrugged. "A suspicion I have."

He took her chin in his hand and held it as he whispered, "I suspect my twin is in love with you, in spite of his dark frowns. Of course you have not encouraged that love, have you? No, no, of course not! It would make me so very angry if you had done so. I am not at all pleasant, or, er, *kind* when I am angry."

"My word, I had no idea you were here, Jonathan!" Gwyneth exclaimed as she came around a bend in the path and hurried toward them. "Have you been here long? You must not tire Elinor, you know!"

Jonathan rose lazily to his feet and gave his aunt a sweeping, mocking bow. "Dear, *dear* Aunt Gwyneth! Now why do I have the feeling you are guarding Elinor?"

"Because I am," Gwyneth said coldly as she sat

down beside them. "I am Elinor's nurse, and I must see to her care. She has been very ill."

"I'm sure you are a formidable one," her nephew said lightly, although there wasn't a trace of a smile on his handsome, rugged face.

"As you say. Haven't you things to see to, Jonathan? We would not keep you, and Elinor should rest now."

Defeated, Jonathan bowed again, but he did not leave until he captured Elinor's hand and kissed it slowly.

"Yes, rest so you may get better soon, darling," he said. "I count the days."

Neither woman spoke as Jonathan strolled toward the gate that led to the stables and the Home Farm. As soon as he had disappeared, Elinor turned to her friend.

"He knows something, I know he does!" she whispered. "He talked so long about our wedding; mentioned Jason over and over. Gwyneth, I'm frightened!"

Gwyneth patted her hand. "I would not hide it from you. I think you have good reason to be," she said. "I wish Jason would come back! Jonathan's got something planned, and I don't trust him. I never did. Be sure you lock your door whenever I'm not with you."

Elinor nodded, and when Gwyneth suggested they retire to Elinor's rooms, she was quick to agree. She wanted to wash the touch of Jonathan's hands and lips from her skin as soon as she could.

Gwyneth insisted she keep the powders on her face till bedtime, however. Elinor was glad she had obeyed, for half an hour later, Rebecca Ward knocked on her door. Gwyneth had gone to her own room to change, but Elinor told Betsy to admit Miss Ward. She knew she was safe with her maid in the adjoining dressing room. Besides, she was not frightened of this ordinary, wispy woman, no matter what dark deeds she had planned.

As Miss Ward entered the bedroom, Elinor saw she was carrying the striped box she remembered, and she steeled herself.

"My dear Miss Fielding! What a pleasure it is to see you up and about!" Rebecca Ward exclaimed in her high, breathless voice. "I trust you are feeling better?"

"I am much improved," Elinor said through suddenly dry lips.

"Delightful! Sir Robert has been so uneasy! You were a naughty girl not to let him summon the doctor, although I am sure Miss Grenville did all she could.

"I—I have brought you some candy in celebration of your recovery. I realize things have not always gone smoothly between us, but while you were ill, my dear, *dear* Miss Fielding, I came to see how very wrong I have been. I am so sorry for it. I do hope you will accept my most heartfelt apologies, for I do so long to be your friend. Here. Do enjoy them *all* by yourself, dear. They are from Portreath's best confectioners."

She thrust the candy box into Elinor's hands, and stood waiting almost breathlessly for her to speak.

Without thinking consciously of what she was doing, Elinor let go of the box. It fell to the floor and spilled open, the chocolates it contained rolling out and breaking.

"Oh, my, oh, dear," Miss Ward said as she scrambled after them. "How very clumsy of you—er, I mean, me! I thought you had them secure, but they are quite ruined! What a shame! But do not worry. I'll send for some more this very day."

"I beg you will not, Miss Ward," Elinor told her, unsmiling. "I am not fond of chocolates. Some of the ingredients upset my stomach."

Miss Ward stared up at her from where she knelt on the floor, and two red spots appeared high on her cheekbones.

Gwyneth entered the room, her brows rising when she saw Elinor's visitor.

"Why, Rebecca, I did not know you had come calling," she said. "What have we here? Chocolates? Elinor cannot possibly eat candy. Her stomach is still delicate. But it appears there is no danger of that. How did they come to spill and break?"

"The box fell from Miss Fielding's hands," Rebecca Ward said stiffly as she rose to her feet, clutching the ruined candies, the box and papers to her breast.

Gwyneth stooped and retrieved one of the chocolates that had rolled under a chair and escaped Miss Ward's notice.

"Hmm," she said as she inspected it. "Havershams is not doing anywhere near as fine a job as I remember. Just look here, how clumsy it is made on the bottom."

Rebecca Ward practically grabbed the candy from her hands before she hurriedly excused herself and scurried away. Elinor and Gwyneth stood silently until all sounds of her feet clattering down the stairs had died away.

"Now I do feel ill," Elinor said as she went to shut the door.

"I do believe I shall call on dear Rebecca after dinner," Gwyneth said. "I must find out how her nerve tonic is working. And I remember that when she came and called on me to procure it, she mentioned a widowed female cousin of hers who lives in London. I think I will suggest she make plans to live with this relative—oh, in the nicest way possible, of course! I'm sure Robert will be happy to give her a pension."

"I doubt that will persuade her to leave Mordyn, ma'am," Elinor said. "She has been here too long, and there is her affection for Fiona, to say nothing of Sir Robert himself."

Gwyneth smiled as she reached into the pocket of her apron. She held up another chocolate as she said, "Something tells me that I will be able to change her mind, and without even threatening to go to my brother with what I have discovered. I do not believe in wagering, Elinor, but I think this chocolate that I am holding is what gamblers would call 'a sure card.' "

When she was alone that night, Elinor paced the floor of her room. Betsy had left her some time ago, after she had helped her undress and brushed her hair smooth, and Gywneth had gone yawning to her own room next door, pausing only to remind Elinor to lock the door after her.

It was very late now, but Elinor could not sleep. Even the good news that Miss Ward was already packing to leave the castle could not calm her. Perhaps it was all the upsetting confrontations she had had that day, she told herself as she paused before the fire, wondering if she should put on another log. She had heard the gallery clock strike midnight some time before, but still Jonathan's handsome face, his honeyed, lying words, came between her and sleep. And when his face faded from her mind's eye, Sir Robert's replaced it, all smiling, false concern. She shivered, and reached for another log.

She saw the tapestry move out of the corner of her eye, and she stood there hardly breathing until Jason came around the edge of it. He was not smiling. Instead, he only stood and stared at her for what seemed a very long time.

He looked sad and resigned to Elinor, and without thinking, she dropped the log back in the basket and ran to him.

"Jason! At last! It has been an age!" she said breathlessly as she reached up to take his face between her hands and pull it down to hers.

Still he did not smile at her, or touch her, and for a moment her heart stopped beating. It *was* Jason, wasn't it? It couldn't be *Jonathan*, could it? Dear God, what had she done?

As he enfolded her in his arms, and the lips that came down hard on hers were so dear and familiar, she sighed in relief. Yes, it was he. She could smell the distinctive scent of his skin, so warm and full of life, so—so *Jason*. She would know it anywhere.

He pulled her closer still, crushing her breasts against his broad chest. Elinor buried her hands in his hair, reveling in his nearness. His kiss was as consuming and urgent as if they had been separated for years, not days. His hands caressed her back, her waist, her hips—remembering her, claiming her.

When he lifted his head at last, Elinor felt heavy

and powerless with desire, and she clutched his shirt tight, lest she fall.

"You are all right?" he asked, his gray eyes searching her face.

"Now I am," she murmured. "It has been so hard!"

"Really?" he asked absentmindedly, his eyes intent on her soft, rosy mouth.

"Really," she breathed, admiring his own chiseled lips.

"Elinor?"

She did not answer him in words. She could not, her throat was so tight. Instead, she held up her face for his kiss again, and pressed even closer.

When he picked her up and carried her to the bed, he was still kissing her, kissing her as if he could never get enough of her.

What am I doing? Elinor wondered as she helped him remove her nightrobe in a kind of frenzy. I still do not know if he is a sadist and a murderer! I must be mad!

She realized she was mad. Mad for him. His touch left fire she could not live without. His mouth was a snare she did not want to escape. His arms were too strong, too wonderful to deny. And when he lay down beside her, all the long, naked length of him—those smooth muscles of his hard chest, his flat stomach and powerful thighs—he made her feel even more abandoned. Her hands and mouth were as urgent as his. Neither spoke. It was not a time for words.

Later, as she lay quiet beside him, still held tight in one of his arms, reason returned. She must leave here, she must! she told herself fiercely. If she did not do so, it would not matter what horrible manner of man he turned out to be. She was completely in his spell; helpless when passion overcame her; as much a slave to him as if she were in fetters. That would not do at all. To save herself, she must go someplace he could never find her, and she must do it soon, while she still had a tiny tattered remnant of will and pride left to her.

She moved a little, and he let her go. Without looking at him, or speaking, she rose and put on her wrapper before she went to stand before the fire with her back turned to him.

"So, nothing has changed, has it?" the quiet voice that came from behind her asked.

She shook her head. "I don't know what made me run to you like that," she murmured.

"I do," he said evenly.

She turned to see him buttoning his shirt and tucking it into his breeches, and she had to swallow, hard.

"Tell me what has been happening here since I left," he said, running a hand through the hair she had disarranged in her passion as he came to take a seat by the fire.

As she told him all the news, Elinor took the seat across from him. He frowned when he learned of Jonathan's visit to the garden that afternoon, and what he had said, and his scowl was even blacker when she mentioned Miss Ward and her gift of chocolates.

"You say she is going away soon?" he asked. "That is good. I don't want her anywhere near Fiona; she's mad as a March hare. As for my twin, the time has come to take the initiative. The tinners are safe away. Timmy was the last of them to go. He left Falmouth on the afternoon tide on a ship bound for Canada. He was the reason it has taken me so long. I had to be sure he got safe away, and he would not go until all the others were safe."

He paused for a moment before he said, "You must come down to luncheon tomorrow. I will be there as well, as if I had just come back. I'll sleep at my aunt's cottage tonight. I arrived only a short while ago, but I could not wait till morning to see if you were all right."

Elinor looked away from him to stare into the fire, and he studied her calm, pure profile. What a contrast of moods she was! he thought. A hot passionate vixen one moment, demanding and seductive, and all warm, satiny curves, and the next, a cool distant lady, poised and controlled, who held her robe closed tight with a hand at her breast. He realized he adored her in any mood, but she was especially breathtaking when she was naked in his arms. In spite of their lovemaking only moments ago, he wanted to go to her, pull her to her feet, and rip that robe away. Right now.

"I think I will ask Gwyneth to come to luncheon with me, if you don't mind," Elinor was saying, and he forced himself to concentrate, forget the ache in his loins.

"No, of course not. Aunt Gwynnie has a right to be there, and it might be she can help."

"What are you going to do? Going to say?" Elinor asked. "You don't really believe Jonathan will admit he lied, do you?"

"No, he won't do that. But perhaps if I can force him to relive that day, he will make a slip. It is all I can think of to do."

He saw Elinor shake her head in defeat, and he added, "I know. It is a slender reed at best, not the kind of sturdy lifeline I would like. But it is all I have, and I must make the best of it. I'll try to get him to lose his temper. He always did have a fearsome temper, and if he loses control, it might be easier to get at the truth.

"Don't be surprised or frightened by anything I might say or do tomorrow, Elinor. Remember, I am fighting for our life together."

He waited for her nod before he came and put a hand on each arm of her chair, and bent over her. He noticed the stubborn set of her jaw, and saw the refusal deep in her clear green eyes, and he drew back, not kissing her as he had intended to do.

"Go to bed now and sleep," he said in a quiet voice as he straightened up and moved away. "Thank you for tonight. It makes me even more determined not to lose you—ever."

21

THE MIST DRIFTED in on the change of the tide, and by morning it was impossible to see past arm's length. Elinor had risen early after a restless night, and as she stared out at the whiteness that curled around the windows as if it were trying to seek entry there, she wondered if Jason would even be able to find his way from Gwyneth's cottage to the castle.

She felt nervy and on edge this morning, her heart beating erratically as she considered what the day might bring. She was not looking forward to it at all, and she was afraid for Jason. Afraid he would be hurt and disappointed, for she saw no way he could ever get his twin to admit to lying about their elder brother's death—if, indeed, Jonathan had lied at all. She might not like the man, and she most assuredly had no intention of marrying him, but she found it impossible to believe that anyone would have been so evil as to have blamed his twin for such a deed. When she remembered he had only been a child of ten at the time, it was even more preposterous.

So now, she had no recourse but to begin planning to leave here in earnest. She grimaced as she remembered that Miss Ward would also be leaving Mordyn. She must not travel with the woman. Indeed, to avoid her she would even consider the long overland journey.

She would have to ask for Gwyneth's help again, but she could not ask for it yet. No, first she must allow Jason to try and clear his name. She owed that much to him. Her love—her love.

She closed her eyes and willed the threatening tears

begone. There was no time for tears now. Besides, she would have all the rest of her life to weep in regret.

Gwyneth seemed to sense her preoccupation when she joined her for breakfast later. She only nodded when Elinor told her of Jason's return; how he wished both of them to come down for luncheon.

It was a long morning, and as the two walked down the stairs after the luncheon gong sounded, Elinor wondered at her companion's grim, determined face. She saw Gwyneth had put on a clean blouse in honor of the occasion, although she still wore one of her faded skirts and her stout shoes.

As they reached the ground floor and a footman hastened to open the door of the dining salon for them, Gwyneth grasped Elinor's arm for a moment. "Courage, my girl," she whispered. "Courage!"

Elinor could not even smile.

Everyone was there before them, a smiling Sir Robert, a serious Jason, a faintly amused Jonathan, and a silent Fiona. Only Miss Ward was missing. Elinor wondered briefly if she was packing.

"How delightful it is to see you with us again, Elinor," Sir Robert said as he came toward them. "And Gwynnie! It is a pleasure to welcome you! I do wish you would reconsider coming back to the castle to live, dear sister. You have been missed, and now that Rebecca is going away, Fiona would be glad of your company."

"Now Robert, don't start up on that again," Gwyneth told him tartly. "I'll not give up my cottage, and my freedom, as I have told you many a time. Fiona can run down and visit me any time she likes. Come! Where would you like us to sit? I'm hungry."

"You must sit opposite me, at the foot of the table, Gwynnie," Sir Robert said as he led her to her chair. "I have placed Elinor beside Jonathan, which I am sure will please him very much. Jason and Fiona will be across from them. How cozy this is today, just the six of us family!" As he took his seat, he beamed impartially.

"You look vastly improved today, Elinor," Jonathan said as he held her chair for her. ''Almost a miraculous recovery, wouldn't you say?''

''Perhaps she had a good night's sleep,'' Jason remarked as the footmen began to serve the soup.

''I told you I would be better soon,'' Elinor said, glad the length of the massive table placed her some distance from Jonathan. Snippets of the things he had said about her to his father in the library echoed in her mind, and she forced herself to forget them, lest she be unable to eat her luncheon.

''When did you arrive back at Mordyn, Jason?'' Gwyneth asked. ''If you came this morning, you must have tracker instincts. I've rarely seen the mist so thick.''

''It's not as bad as you think,'' her nephew said, stirring his hot soup.

''But where have you been these past days?'' Sir Robert asked. ''You have yet to tell us.''

''In various places in Cornwall. I was making sure all the tinners got away safe.''

''What?'' Sir Robert demanded, so startled he dropped his spoon in his soup. ''You were helping them get away? But—but . . .''

''You mean you actually spent time and money on those crude, thieving animals?'' Jonathan asked with a disbelieving sneer. ''They should have been hung for their crimes!''

''Ah, but they are in no danger of that. Not now. I never thought them guilty of anything more than want. Want that was not their fault. I know them. Ordinarily, they would never steal, but they were starving men, and they had starving families.''

''How—how altruistic of you! How positively saintly,'' Jonathan remarked, wiping his mouth on his napkin and signaling Whitman for wine.

Elinor tried to eat her soup. She wondered how long it would be before Sir Robert and Jonathan noticed Jason's coarse accent had disappeared. Now he sounded as cultured as his twin, and just as well educated.

Sir Robert was still frowning, his face red. ''I most

strongly disapprove of your actions, Jason. Indeed, I have to say I am ashamed of you! To think the troops were called to a wild goose chase, and all because of the intervention of one of my sons! I do not know what to say to you, sir!''

''Perhaps it would be wise not to say anything at all,'' Jason replied as he took a roll. ''We are not like to agree on the matter. Indeed, we have been at odds over it ever since my arrival. I am not a child, father. I am a man of thirty, and no longer under your aegis—or your authority.''

''No doubt you'll be making plans to leave here soon?'' Jonathan asked, as his father subsided, sputtering. ''I mean now that your 'business' here has been concluded? I wonder we never guessed the nature of that 'business.' But you have always had a common streak about you. If you did not look exactly like me, I'd swear you were a changling.''

''It pains me to have to acknowledge you, too, twin,'' Jason remarked evenly.

''Do stop your bickering,'' Gwyneth said, smiling at Fiona, who was beginning to look a little apprehensive. ''I believe I smell pigeon pie, and I see there are prawns as well. Let us enjoy our luncheon! Yes, indeed, Whitman! I'll have a slice, and some of the brussels sprouts, too. If there is one thing I envy you, Robert, it is your cook.''

Sir Robert did not answer, for he was frowning still. Elinor thought to ask Fiona a question about the foals then, and the awkward moment passed.

It was during the dessert course of saffron cake that Jonathan suddenly frowned. Jason had been talking to Fiona, and Jonathan interrupted to say, ''My word! To what do we owe this miracle, bro?''

Jason looked up to stare at him.

''You seem to have lost your crude accent overnight! Now why is that? Truly unusual!''

''The accent was assumed for a reason,'' Jason replied, sipping his coffee. ''There is no need to employ it any longer. I took my degree at the University of Edinburgh, my Uncle Lawrence's old school.''

"Mystery upon mystery," Jonathan murmured, sneering as he pushed his plate away. "There is another mystery I would have explained. Tell me, if you would be so good, bro, why you skulked about the castle, spying on us all, long before you came openly to Mordyn, begging hospitality."

When Jason only stared at him, frowning, he went on smoothly, "I know you were here. My sweet Elinor let it slip, the day I first told her what happened to our brother Rob. I know it was not *I* who saved her from the crumbling cliff steps that day, long before your open arrival."

Elinor stared at him aghast, before she looked across the table at Jason. Of course! It *had* been Jason that day; that was why Jonathan had always seemed to have forgotten the incident so completely. Why, he had never even known of it until she had mentioned it so innocently. Dear God! What else did he know?

Jonathan was leaning forward in his chair now, glaring at his twin with narrowed eyes. Elinor could feel herself trembling.

"What's this you say, Jonathan?" Sir Robert asked, sounding confused. "Were you here spying, Jason? But for what reason? It is incomprehensible to me that you would do such a thing!"

"Sir, would you clear the room, please?" Jason asked. "I will be happy to explain, and there are other matters we should talk about as a family, but it must be done privately."

Sir Robert stared at his difficult, disappointing son before he nodded and waved to the servants. Whitman bowed and ushered the two footmen from the salon, carefully closing the doors behind them all.

"To answer your question, twin, yes, I was here," Jason began. "I stayed at Aunt Gwyneth's cottage. I was not sure of my welcome at Mordyn, nor was I at all sure I wanted a reunion, even though I had come back here with the purpose of trying to find out the truth of Rob's death. The day Elinor climbed the steps from the beach, I was there at clifftop, trying to reconstruct that day twenty years ago in my mind. When

I saw she was in danger of falling to her death, I saved her, pretending to be you. I still had not decided whether it would be better to go quietly away—forget you all, and concentrate on my new life in Northumberland.''

''To think you were sneaking around, watching us,'' Jonathan mused. ''Hardly the act of a gentleman, now was it, old boy? If you had a shred of honor left, you would have approached us openly, to ask.''

''I am asking now,'' his twin said. He reached out to pat Fiona's hand before he continued, ''I know it is a painful subject, but it is important to me.''

Elinor saw Fiona's face paling, and as she braced herself for the unpleasantness to come, she wondered if her own face had paled as well.

''I wonder why you think it necessary?'' Jonathan drawled, at his most world-weary as he sprawled in his chair. ''It all happened such a long time ago, and what you did that day cannot be changed by any amount of discussion. Why should we go over it again? It will only upset our father, and Fiona.''

''We must go over it. I am not at all sure, you see, that I *was* responsible for Rob's death, and I would have the truth.''

Jonathan sighed. ''With your permission, sir?'' he asked his father. A silent Sir Robert nodded.

''Very well. Since you insist. I remember it as if it were yesterday. I shall never forget it,'' Jonathan said, staring coldly across the table at his twin. ''We were wrestling at clifftop, and Rob was at the top of the steps, pressed against the railing. I saw you push him. Do you hear me? I *saw* you do it!''

''I have no recollection of it,'' Jason said evenly. ''I only remember brushing against him slightly, and that contact would hardly be enough for him to lose his balance and fall over. The railing was too high for a boy, for that. Could it be that your memory is at fault? Even that you lied about it, for some dark purpose of your own?''

Jonathan rose slowly to his feet, looking menacing. ''You accuse me of *lying*, sir? I, at least, am a gentleman. I told no lies then. I tell none now. How unfortunate that you must take my word for it, since Fiona cannot speak to tell us what she saw that day.

"Now, I suggest we drop this subject." He took his seat again, turning to face Elinor and pick up her hand. As he raised it for everyone to see, he said, "My sweet Elinor will think she is marrying into a terrible family!"

Elinor looked around. Sir Robert was nodding and trying to smile, Gwyneth was staring at Jonathan, and Fiona sat gazing intently at her empty dessert plate. When Elinor looked at Jason, she saw he did not look at all resigned or disappointed, and she wondered at it.

"It is for Elinor's sake we must continue to discuss it. I do not want her thinking her husband is a murderer," Jason said calmly. "Release her hand. She is not to be your bride; she will be mine."

"WHAT?" Jonathan exploded, dropping Elinor's hand as he jumped to his feet.

"You heard me," Jason said in measured tones as he rose slowly to face his furious twin, only the width of the table separating them. "Elinor is going to marry me. We love each other. We have for some time."

Quick as a snake, Jonathan reached out to pull Elinor to her feet; drag her close to him. She shuddered as his arm went around her waist to hold her prisoner. "Damn you!" he swore. "You sneaky bastard!"

"Not sneaky, cautious. I kept it a secret because I knew what would happen if I did not. You would want Elinor then, whether or not you loved her. You were that way from the time we were children. I learned early to pretend I did not care about my most treasured toys, for if I had not, you would either have stolen them or broken them. You have always been insanely jealous, wanting for your own what others held dear. A bad failing that, twin.

"But the story can now be told. I came here, met Elinor, and fell in love with her. She assures me she loves me too."

"You'll never have her! I'll strangle her first!" Jonathan panted, his grip tightening cruelly on Elinor's waist.

As she cried out, Jason rose to his feet and started around the table. "Let her go at once!" he ordered. "You are hurting her, and I'll not stand for it!"

"Jonathan," Sir Robert pleaded, looking white and strained. "You are not thinking, my son—you are distraught! You would never do such a thing, never! Let Elinor go, I beg you! Jason, sit down, sir!"

As he spoke, the door to the dining salon opened and Rebecca Ward slipped inside, closing it quietly behind her. No one in the room even noticed her, so intent were they on the drama unfolding before them.

Miss Ward was dressed in a drab traveling costume with a matching bonnet, and she looked as ordinary and forgettable as ever she had. In her tightly gloved hands, she clutched a large black purse.

Completely ignoring the tension in the room, she said, "You will face me for your judgment day, Elinor Fielding."

Startled, Jonathan spun around, Elinor still in his grasp.

Miss Ward pointed a finger at his captive. "Jezebel. Witch. Whore," she crooned in a quiet voice that was all the more menacing after Jonathan's impassioned threat. Her voice sent shivers racing along Elinor's nerves.

"All of this is your fault, bitch," Rebecca Ward went on, slowly and carefully. "If you had not come here, none of it would have happened. I would not have been forced to leave my beloved Sir Robert; been driven from my dear Mordyn home; been required to abandon Fiona. But you saw to it that I was to be banished, didn't you, you *common slut?* You wanted Sir Robert and Mordyn for yourself. Well, I may not be able to have them, but neither will you. No, instead you must pay for what you have done.

"Don't anybody move! I see you trying to edge toward me, Mr. Jason. Stand still!"

In the astonished silence that followed, she reached into her bag and withdrew a pistol. Elinor gasped in horror.

At the sight of it, everyone in the salon froze in place like wax figures in an exhibition. It was deathly quiet. Into that quiet, Fiona uttered an agonized squawk. Jason Grenville's head whipped around, and his eyes narrowed as he saw his sister's mouth opening and closing—heard the animal sounds that came from it. Not words—just painful sounds, wrenched from somewhere deep inside her.

Miss Ward paid no attention to her erstwhile charge, she was so busy raising the pistol in both hands and taking aim at Elinor.

Jonathan seemed to realize suddenly that he was much too close to Rebecca Ward's intended victim, and he released Elinor and pushed her in front of him.

As he did so, Miss Ward closed her eyes and fired. The sound of the shot echoed through the room, as first Elinor and then Jonathan fell to the floor.

"Oh, no, no!" Gwyneth wailed, pushing back her chair to go to them.

Jason reached Elinor before his aunt could, and as he dropped down on one knee beside her, the servants rushed into the room.

"Take that gun away; restrain Miss Ward!" Sir Robert ordered. "She is mad—mad!"

Rebecca Ward made no attempt to resist. Indeed, all the time the gun was being confiscated, and two tall footmen grasped her arms tightly, she wore a happy, satisfied smile.

The echoes of the shot were still reverberating in Elinor's stunned ears as she struggled to stand. When her would-be murderess saw that she had not succeeded—that Elinor still lived—she went berserk, and the two footmen had their hands full restraining her.

"Thank God," Jason murmured over the din she made as he gathered Elinor in his arms. "You are all right, love?"

"My son! My son!" Sir Robert exclaimed, and everyone looked at the prone figure on the floor, and gasped. Jonathan Grenville lay on his face, very still, and as they watched, a trickle of blood crept from beneath his body to stain the gleaming parquet floor.

Gwyneth went to kneel beside him and put her fingers on his pulse. She shook her head sadly, and as she did so, Sir Robert collapsed sobbing, his face down on the table before him.

Rising, Gwyneth ordered the servants to remove the still raving Rebecca Ward to a safe place, and keep her under guard until the authorities could be notified.

Elinor was still shaking, and trying not to sob. As if through a shimmering veil, she saw Gwyneth go to Fiona and put her arm around her and whisper. As she did so, she turned her niece away so she would not have to look at her dead brother, and that widening pool of blood.

She felt Jason's arms tighten around her, felt his breath in her hair as he whispered, "Come now, Elinor! I know this has been a terrible shock to you, all of it, but you must not break down now. I depend on you."

Valiantly, Elinor tried to nod. Jason took her back to the table and held up her wine glass so she could sip from it. She was grateful he had done so when the world stopped spinning moments later, and she felt warm all over at the loving concern in his intent gray eyes.

"Jason, I am going to take Fiona away," Gwyneth told him. "Do not let anyone touch the body until the authorities have come. Perhaps you could get your father to leave the room; Elinor, too?"

He nodded as she led a weeping Fiona away, a Fiona now as silent as she had ever been.

Elinor sank down in her chair as Jason went to his father to grasp his shoulders tightly.

"Come away, sir," he said gently. "Let us adjourn to the library. I think we could both use a brandy."

Sir Robert wiped his eyes on his napkin before he allowed his only remaining son to help him from the room. As quickly as she could, Elinor rose to support him on the other side.

When they reached the door, the servants were still clustered there, whispering to each other and gawking. Jason stopped to have a quick word with the butler.

"Send a groom to the nearest magistrate, Whitman, and guard this door. No one is to enter the salon until he has inspected it, and heard what happened. Is that clear?"

"Aye, Mr. Jason," the old butler said, his voice

quavering. One of the maids began to weep in that gusty way that precedes hysteria, and as Whitman spoke sharply to her, it seemed to steady him. The hall emptied almost at once.

In the library, Sir Robert collapsed in the chair behind his desk. He opened one of the drawers before him, and stared down into it in horror.

"My son!" he murmured brokenly. "My poor, handsome boy, shot with my own pistol! I always kept it in this drawer, loaded, and somehow Rebecca must have known of it.

"But why did it have to happen? Why did I have to lose Jonathan as well as Rob? What have I ever done to deserve such a cruel fate?"

Jason brought him a large snifter of brandy, and insisted he drink it as Elinor took a seat somewhat apart. She was not one of the family—she must not intrude on Sir Robert's sorrow.

Much later, after Jason had tried to comfort his father, he came to Elinor's side. Sir Robert was lost in some sad revery now, and did not appear to notice them. Jason lowered his voice even so.

"I saw Jonathan push you toward Rebecca Ward myself, Elinor," he said, taking her shoulders in his hands and pressing them. "I do not know how you managed to escape her bullet, but I am everlastingly grateful that you did."

"Yes, he pushed me," she whispered. "As he did so, I slipped on the polished floor and fell. The bullet must have gone over my head and struck him instead."

She gripped her upper arms for a moment and hugged herself as she relived the horror of that moment. "He meant for me to die," she said slowly. "He was using me as a shield to save himself."

"I know. Gwyneth does, too, and when my father has had a chance to think it over calmly, he will remember it as well. For that coward's act alone, I am glad Jonathan is dead, even though it means I will never know the truth about Rob now."

He sounded bleak in his disappointment, and Elinor

reached out to take his hand and hold it against her cheek. "It does not matter, my darling," she said, and knew she spoke the truth. "When I thought I was going to die—that there was no way to escape it—I realized that my biggest regret was that I was going to have to lose *you*. And I knew then how very much I loved you. Too much to give you up. It does not matter—no, not at all—if we never discover what really happened that fateful day."

The dark frown Jason had been wearing had disappeared as she spoke, and now his gray eyes filled with light and wonder. Unable to speak, he shook his head a little, and lifted her hand to kiss it in tribute.

A week later, a sorrowing kind of peace had descended on Mordyn's halls again. The authorities, headed by a discreet Horatio Brownell, who was the local magistrate, had concluded their investigation and withdrawn. No mention had been made of Jonathan's last cowardly act. Instead, it was implied that Miss Ward, unused to pistols as she had been, had simply missed her target.

Jonathan had been buried in the family graveyard beside his brother Rob, and the black crepe on the castle's front doors was all that outwardly remained of the tragedy.

Rebecca Ward had been buried as well, although not on the grounds of her beloved Mordyn. After the servants had taken her away from the dining salon, they had locked her in a small, windowless storeroom in the depths of the castle to await the attention of the magistrate. Unfortunately, no one had thought to tie her hands, or remove her large bag, and when they went to fetch her later, they discovered she had stabbed herself to death with a pair of scissors she carried.

As had Jonathan's, her death came at the ebbing of the tide, and the older servants nodded amongst themselves and whispered, "Aye, for that is when death always comes."

Elinor could only be relieved for Rebecca Ward, for she would not have wished an asylum for the criminally insane on any human being, not even the one who had tried to kill her. The storeroom was washed clean of the blood, and padlocked, but she had heard from Betsy that some of the maids were already prating of a new ghost in Mordyn's halls. Elinor shuddered.

Gwyneth was still at the castle, lending her strong support to her grieving brother and a distraught, silent Fiona. Jason, as well, had taken as many of the burdens from his father's shoulders as he could. Only Elinor did not seem to have any role to play here. Jason had not used the secret passageways again to come to her at night, nor had he been able to see her alone during the day. They had had only a few, short and prosaic conversations. Elinor found she spent a great deal of her time alone, thinking about everything that had happened, and wondering about the future. As she did so, she discovered she was glad to have this time to herself—glad to be able to recover her equilibrium and try to forget that if she had never come to Mordyn, none of it would have happened at all.

Rebecca Ward had been right about that, but I could not know it—I must not blame myself, she told herself stoutly, even as she wondered if she would be able to take her own good advice. How she wished she and Jason could leave Mordyn now; put all this pain and darkness behind them forever! But she had no idea what Jason planned to do, and so far it had never seemed to be the right time to inquire.

When she returned from a solitary walk early one morning, Whitman said that Mr. Jason had requested that she join the others in the library as soon as she came in. Elinor nodded, wondering what such a summons meant.

As she entered the library and curtsied, she noted Jason's look of purpose, Gwyneth's serious face, and Fiona's now customary shrinking demeanor. Sir Robert was there too, seated behind his desk again. Elinor was glad his color was better now, and except for his usual gravity, he seemed to have himself well in hand.

"Before you begin to discuss whatever you have

summoned us here for, son, I would like to make an announcement,'' he said.

''Yes, an announcement. I am going to name Jason my heir, and I will notify my solicitor of my intent by post today. In due course, I hope Jason will marry Elinor, as he planned. The union has not only my sanction, but my blessing.'' He turned to Elinor then and attempted a smile.

''Elinor, my dear, you will become my daughter in truth, and I am delighted. Mordyn could use some happiness. With both of you in residence, I am sure it will have it.''

Elinor looked quickly to Jason, to discover he was looking back at her, his face serious and his eyes intent on her face. She wondered if he were thinking what she was—that even in his grief, his father had managed to conceive a whole new plan to get control of her fortune. Dear Lord, she thought, how she hated this new knowledge of human failings she had acquired, most particularly Sir Robert's. Surely it was making her cynical!

After what seemed a long silence, Jason said, ''Of course I am honored to be named, sir, but I must tell you I have no intention of ever living at Mordyn again. There are too many unhappy memories here, not only for me, but for Elinor as well. After we wed, I will take her to my estate in Northumberland. I want us to have a fresh start, make our own memories. Happy ones, this time.''

Elinor's heart resumed its normal beat as Sir Robert said, ''What? Leave Mordyn? But Jason, my son, you are not thinking! This will be your inheritance; you will be Lord Grenville someday! I suppose I've no objection to your retaining Great Oaks, although I will admit I had hoped you would sell it and put the money into Mordyn. It is your birthplace, after all, and must be primary with you. You can oversee your uncle's estate from here with a good agent in charge, if you insist on retaining it. Perhaps you could even visit it once a year or so. But your place is here!''

Jason shook his head. ''No. Uncle Lawrence does not deserve that. Great Oaks was his life, which he left in trust to me. I loved my uncle, and I would honor his memory. I intend my sons to be the Grenvilles of Great Oaks."

There was a pregnant pause before he added gently, "You are not like to change my mind, sir, for I am determined on this course. I have gone my own way for too many years to be swayed by any argument you might expound."

Sir Robert opened his mouth, and shut it thoughtfully again. Unspoken, but implied, was the knowledge that, having cast him off twenty years before, he had no jurisdiction over Jason now, nor did Jason owe him allegiance.

Gwyneth cleared her throat. "I think you have the right idea entirely, Jason!" she said. "Yes, get away from here, both of you. Be happy! We shall do very well, if you but visit once in awhile."

Sir Robert was strangely silent, as she went on, "Now, what is this matter you have brought us here to discuss?"

Jason rose and went to stand by the mantel. To Elinor he looked very much in control of the situation, and easy, in spite of his somber face. She wondered again what he had planned.

"If you remember, the day Jonathan was shot, and when she was so frightened, Fiona uttered some sounds," he began, looking at all of them in turn. "They were not words, but those sounds made me sure she could learn to speak again, if she put her mind to it."

"Fiona, am I right?" he asked, turning to his sister now. "Come! There is no need to pretend you are such a timid rabbit anymore," he added, smiling kindly at his sister's shocked face, her shaking hands. "If my surmises—and Aunt Gwynie's—are correct, you have hidden behind a supposed muteness all these twenty years. Why?"

Fiona shook her head, looking stubborn, and when Sir Robert would have spoken up to defend her—told his son to stop bullying her—Jason raised a warning hand for his silence.

"Then I shall guess, but you will have to tell me if

I am right," he went on. "It was all because you were afraid of Jonathan, wasn't it?"

Fiona sat immobile, and Jason went to kneel and take her hands in his. "This is important to me, Fiona, very important! And it is important to your good friend. Won't you help us? Tell the truth? If you do not, Elinor will be marrying a man who has been named a murderer."

There was a long silence in which the ticking of the mantel clock sounded very loud. Elinor found she was holding her breath.

"Fiona, listen to me!" Jason ordered, staring down in his sister's eyes. "Jonathan is dead, do you hear me? *Dead!* He cannot hurt you now, or ever again. Come, tell me! Were you afraid of him?"

After what seemed an age, Fiona bobbed her head once.

"But *why* were you afraid of him? I have thought about this endlessly, and the only conclusion I can reach is that you must have seen something that day at the cliffs when Rob fell from them. Something that was vastly different from the story Jonathan told our father. Am I right?"

Still Elinor stared at Fiona, gripping the palms of her hands so tightly, her nails bit into the soft skin. Again Fiona nodded, stealing a glance at her father's shocked, disbelieving face as she did so.

"Did you see me push Rob over the railing?" Jason persisted.

Fiona shook her head this time, and in her relief, Elinor smiled joyfully at Jason. He did not notice, for he was leaning toward his sister now, as if to pull the truth from her by the force of his will.

"Why, it is just as I thought," Gwyneth mused, almost to herself. "I wish she could tell us what really did happen!"

To everyone's surprise, Fiona got up and went to her father's desk. She picked up a pencil and paper there, and began to write.

"You can write?" Sir Robert asked in wonder, as he stared at her nimble hand, flying over the paper.

"All these years you have been able to write? But . . . but . . ."

"No questions about that now, sir," Jason said quickly. "Go ahead, Fiona. Write down what you saw."

"I saw the whole thing," Fiona scribbled as everyone crowded around to read. "You and Jonathan were wrestling, and you did brush against Rob. But when Rob cried out, you drew back. It was then that Jonathan thrust his foot under Rob's legs and tripped him. Rob lost his balance and fell."

"No! That cannot be!" Sir Robert exclaimed. "It would mean that Jonathan lied to me! Why, to put the blame on his twin when he himself had done such a dastardly thing—no! Not Jonathan, my son!"

Gwyneth put her hand on his shoulder. "Jonathan was never what he seemed, brother. But please, let Jason go on!"

Sir Robert settled back in his chair, nodding weakly. Elinor saw the tears in his eyes, and she was sorry for him, but Jason's next question to Fiona made her forget him in a minute.

"You must have known Jonathan had seen you watching, isn't that true?'

When Fiona would have written something, Jason went on, "Of course! You decided then it would be safer to pretend you could not tell anyone what you had seen, so he would not kill you, as he had killed Rob. Am I right?"

When Fiona nodded, he went on, "I imagine my banishment from Mordyn only reinforced your resolve?"

"Yes," Fiona wrote quickly. "That was why I pretended I could not learn to write, even while I taught myself in secret. If I had had that skill, I could have told our father what Jonathan had done, and I might have been killed, or sent away, too. I was so frightened!"

"But why did you kill Mischief?" Elinor asked in the stunned silence that followed.

"I had to kill him after he scratched Jonathan," Fiona wrote, looking sad again. "I saw how angry Jonathan was. I didn't want Mischief to die slowly—

suffer—like all those other animals he used to torture in the glade."

"Yes, I remember that place. Your mother had it made for her own private retreat," Gwyneth said, her brow furrowed in thought. "Once, when I was searching for plants in the wood, I caught Jonathan there with a wingless bird. I gave him a tongue-lashing and a caning he never forgot, for he avoided me ever after."

Elinor was reminded of her uneasy feelings in the glade Fiona had taken her to—how eerie it had been, so full of dark lingering—and she shivered. Yes, it all made so much sense now! Of course Fiona would put her kitten to death as kindly as she could, to save him from Jonathan's cruel hands.

Suddenly she remembered that Jonathan had told her it was Jason who had tortured animals as a boy. He had lied about that, as he had lied about everything. In fact, now she thought about it, he had told her his own story, only naming his brother as villain. How evil he had been!

"Well," Sir Robert said, sounding stunned. "I am sure we are all glad you can communicate, Fiona, but I do wish you had told me all this years ago. Why, when I consider I sent Jason away, not knowing, and paid all those debts . . ."

"She could not tell you. What are you thinking of, Robert?" Gwyneth interrupted. "Fiona was a small child, only six years old, and she was frightened out of her wits. And once having begun the charade, she had no choice but to continue it."

"Fiona, when you were older, did you ever consider going to our father? Confessing?" Jason asked. He was smiling at his sister, to reassure her, and his voice was kind.

Fiona frowned. "Yes, I did," she wrote. "But every so often, Jonathan would say something to me—just a hint, you know—or look at me a certain way, and I did not dare! As time passed, it was easier. You had gone away, and I was able to forget."

She looked around, and seemed to see some condemnation on everyone's faces, and she went to stand close to her aunt, as if for protection. The lost, simple-minded-child look was back on her face. As her father frowned, she stared fearfully at him.

Gwyneth turned and caught her at it. ''Now, that will be quite enough of that, Fiona!'' she said briskly, shaking her to emphasize the point. ''You are not a little girl, nor are you the least bit backward. I've known it forever! You will stop pretending to be one, and begin to act your age. And we'll have no more of your spoiled tantrums when you can't get your own way, as well. You are twenty-six years old—a woman grown—and it's more than time you began to behave like one. I'll teach you how.''

Fiona looked amazed, her mouth falling open in shock, as Gwyneth added, ''There are many advantages to being a woman. You have only to ask Elinor. She'll be glad to tell you of them, if you won't take *my* word for it!''

The luncheon gong sounded outside the door, and everyone jumped. As Sir Robert rose, he bowed deeply to his son.

''Jason, I thank you for what you have discovered this morning, as painful as it has been for me,'' he said slowly. ''I'm sure Fiona will thank you, too, as soon as she's able. But tell me, do you really think she will speak normally?''

''I do,'' Gwyneth interrupted. ''Fiona's very intelligent, and we'll begin working on her problem this very afternoon, won't we, my dear?''

Fiona made a valiant attempt to say something, and when at last a little sound escaped her lips, everyone smiled and applauded.

Her answering smile was radiant.

22

THE CONVERSATION at luncheon was all of Fiona—her future as Mordyn's hostess, and the life she could begin to lead at last. By unspoken consent, no one mentioned Jonathan's part in her dumbness. Elinor saw that the servants were to be kept unapprised of the real story.

"Let them—let everyone!—think it was shock that caused her to lose her speech, and shock that restored it," Gwyneth said when they were alone at the table after luncheon was over.

"Ahhh . . . ehh . . . ssss," Fiona managed to get out.

Sir Robert smiled at her, but Elinor could see he was still struggling with his feelings; all the horrible things he had just learned. Poor man! she thought as she sipped her coffee. He is only greedy. I have never thought him evil, nor do I now. But to have lived all these years believing his exiled son was a murderer, only to discover he had sent the good son away, and sheltered and abetted the bad one, must be dreadful for him. No wonder he looked so white and strained. Still, she was delighted that earlier in the library, Jason had said they were to leave the castle. Mordyn was no more a haven of love and safety to her, nor could it ever be again, after what had happened here. No, not even with Jason beside her.

As they all rose, Jason came to her and detained her as the the others left the room.

"Have you noticed, Elinor? It is one of those perfect summer days that everyone in Cornwall extols," he whispered. "Shall we share the rest of it together? Alone?"

Elinor smiled up at him and nodded, unable to reply for the happiness she felt bubbling up deep inside her.

"Good! I'll just have a word with Whitman, and change into something more casual. And you, my dear, must change as well. Shall we meet in The Lady's Garden in half an hour?"

"Where are we going?" Elinor asked as they walked to the door.

"That is my secret. Someplace near, yet far away. Someplace you have never been. Bring a hat. It will be sunny."

"Must I wear gloves as well? Perhaps even a stole?"

"You wouldn't wear any of them for long," he told her as he opened the door and bowed her out. His gray eyes were full of deviltry, and Elinor blushed.

When she came out to The Lady's Garden later, she had on her lightest black muslin, and a broad-brimmed straw hat trimmed with white flowers and ribbons. She had neglected the gloves, her reticule and stole. Wherever Jason was taking her, she was sure it was not going to be calling.

He was waiting for her by the fountain, clad in an open-necked shirt and buff breeches. There was a large wicker basket at his feet.

Elinor waited breathlessly, but he did not take her in his arms and kiss her, as she had expected and hoped. Instead, he bowed and held out his arm.

"Shall we?" he asked as courteously as if they were in a crowded London drawing room, with everyone watching them.

They went around the castle to the cliff walk. It *was* a beautiful day, Elinor thought as she stared past the breakers to the ocean beyond. Blue and turquoise and green and white, with a golden sun casting its benevolent smile over all. The gulls were quiet today, and there was only enough breeze to ruffle the edges of her skirts.

Still, she wondered Jason had not kissed her. She was longing for him to do so—longing to put her arms around his neck and whisper her love for him in his ear, to run her hands through his hair . . . across those broad, powerful shoulders . . . down to his narrow waist . . .

"Do you know, sometimes your eyes turn smoky?" he remarked as they started down the cliff walk. "Do I dare to ask what you are thinking?"

"Much better not," Elinor said, looking down so he would not see what she was sure was naked longing for him written plain on her face.

Further along the path, she stopped to look back at the castle they were fast leaving behind. Her eyes went up, way up those thick gray stone walls to its battlements, where the Grenville banner flew. She admired the castle's rugged doggedness as it clung to its precipice—strong, invincible. Yes, Mordyn *was* invincible, she thought. Not the humans inside it, only Mordyn itself. How many years had it stood here, immune to war and weather, treachery and time? All the Grenvilles who had once inhabited it had come and gone in the fullness of their years. Only Mordyn itself remained.

"You won't be sorry to leave here, will you?" Jason asked, searching her face. "I meant to discuss it with you, but my father surprised me this morning, and I was forced to cut short all his plans for us to live in the castle."

"No, I'm not sorry, not a bit," Elinor told him. "When I first came here, I thought of Mordyn as a sanctuary—a place that would be full of friends and family and all the encompassing love I had always dreamed about and never had. I felt safe here, protected."

She shook her head. "But it was a false security. If there is anything at all I regret, it is that those dreams I had—of friends, a whole circle of them, and a real family at last—did not come true."

"You will make friends in Northumberland, Elinor. There are some wonderful people there," Jason said. "And you and I will have our own family. Of course, it will take us a while, but I, for one, am looking forward to its creation. More eagerly than I can say."

They began to walk again, and as they turned a bend and Mordyn was lost from sight, he took her hand and squeezed it.

"What is in that basket you are carrying?" Elinor asked, to change the subject. She was feeling a little breathless. She thought she had never seen anyone as handsome as Jason was this afternoon—so tall and broad-shouldered and strong, his rugged face alight with happiness and his chiseled lips curved in a warm smile. The dour, crude Mr. Grenville had disappeared—forever, she hoped.

"Supplies, of course," he said, grinning down at her. "You can't go off for the afternoon without supplies."

They had reached the cliff steps by then, and by mutual, unspoken consent, they both stopped and went to sit on the wall that closed them off.

"What do you think will happen here at Mordyn after we're gone?" Elinor asked.

Jason shrugged. "I suppose life will go on much as it always has. When Fiona learns to speak, gains some confidence, she may well marry. I noticed Nigel Wilkenson seemed smitten with her, even when she was dumb."

"Yes, I thought he was, too. But what about her love for Tim Coryton? I wondered that he could go away and leave her."

"Theirs was a childhood romance, one that Tim knew had no chance of coming to fruition. He accepted that long ago. Fiona still clings to the dream. But she is immature. She will love again—as a woman this time, not a young girl deep in her first calf-love. But even though she will forget Tim, he is older. It might take him longer to forget her—if he ever does."

Elinor remembered Coryton's face at the miner's shack that day he had found her on the moor. She had asked him then if he had a family, and he had told her that he had been cured of the thought of marrying "long ago." She shook her head, pitying him, even as she wished him well in his new life, far from Cornwall.

"Then, of course, there is my father. He is not an old man, for he married at twenty," Jason said, recalling her to the present. "He might well decide to marry again, even have another family. If he does, I hope it brings him more joy than ours did."

"Don't think of it—forget it!" Elinor ordered, grasping his arm in her earnestness. "We've all the future ahead of us, my dear. What's past, is past."

He smiled at her before he turned to face the sea again, his eyes narrowing as he searched the horizon. The breeze ruffled his dark hair, blew his linen shirt against his chest, and Elinor looked away to compose herself.

Staring down at the beach below, she murmured, "I am so glad that Fiona told the truth about that day so long ago. Now we can start our life together without any dark shadows lingering over us."

"Yes, it was a great relief to me," Jason replied, frowning a little now. As Elinor reached up to smooth that frown away, he turned to her and grasped her shoulders. "But what was more important was that you admitted your love for me, long before you knew the truth," he said. "You trusted me, Elinor. I will never forget it, nor will I ever betray your trust."

She held up her face for his kiss, but he only shook his head. "Not yet," he said, smiling again and teasing her. "We have quite a way to go, and I do not want to get, er, so preoccupied, I forget our original destination. Come!"

"Let's hurry!" Elinor said, laughing back over her shoulder at his delighted face as she began to run. He looked young suddenly—so carefree!

She was breathless when they reached the end of the cliff walk.

"Where do we go from here? Down to the beach?" she asked.

Instead, Jason pointed to an overgrown path that led away from the shore. "No, this way," he said. "Let me go ahead and hold the brambles back for you. It's overgrown. No one comes this way anymore."

As Elinor followed him, he said over his shoulder, "This is a path that leads to the cove below Aunt Gwyneth's farmhouse. She often swims here—I did myself as a boy—but we will have it all to ourselves this afternoon, now she's closeted with Fiona teaching her her vowels. It's a pretty spot. You'll see."

As they came out of the woods onto the shore of the cove, Elinor saw he was right. There was a small sandy beach there, and little waves lapped the shore. She also noticed the beach could not be seen from the ocean, for there was only a narrow cut between the two shores, too small for anything but a small rowing boat. Once past that cut, the cove opened up, deepened.

Over to one side, a small brook left the woods to cascade over some rocks to a pool below before it ran away into the sea. The whole place was peaceful and quiet and remote.

But Elinor felt none of those things. She turned to Jason and he swept her into his arms, his mouth coming down on hers with a matching hunger. His hands caressed her shoulders and her back, and she clutched his arms, losing herself in his embrace.

When he lifted his head, Elinor sighed, regretting the end of their kiss. Gently, Jason lowered her to the sand, to drop to his knees behind her. He began to undo the buttons of her gown, and as he opened it, his lips caressed every inch of the satiny flesh he uncovered, all the way to the low back of her chemise. Elinor shivered.

"Do you think we should?" she whispered, staring around a little fearfully. Somewhere in the woods a cuckoo gave its breaking cry.

"This is Mordyn property. No one comes here except Gwyneth, and she's not likely to today," he told her, his voice husky as he slipped the straps of her chemise from her shoulders. "Do you remember the time I told you I wanted to see you—all of you—in the sunlight? Wanted you to see me? Today we can."

Elinor bent her head as he kissed the nape of her neck, his tongue tasting her before it circled around to her ear.

"Ah, Jason, I have missed you! Wanted you so!" she cried.

"And I, you. But I could not come to you inside the castle walls after Jonathan's death. Somehow, it did not seem right. That was not our place anymore. I had to wait until we could be alone, outside. Today we can begin our life together, openly and freely, as I have longed to do since the beginning."

She twisted in his arms then, and ran her fingers down his chest. "Take your shirt off," she said. "Let me see you."

Together they undressed, exploring each other as they did so. Elinor never took her eyes from him. She was so afraid she would miss some expression on his face—some light in his gray eyes—and she was as anxious to see all of him as he was to see her. It was all so much more intense now that sight reinforced touch.

She heard his gasp when she stood up to drop her gown and chemise to the sand, and she stood proudly for him for a moment before she dropped to the beach again.

"How beautiful you are, my darling Elinor," he murmured as he pulled her close again. The sun beat down on them, making them warm all over, but it was no match for the fire that was burning inside.

Jason left her for a moment to open the basket he had brought and take out a soft rug. Observing the long sculptured curve of his spine, his tight small buttocks and powerful thighs—knowing how they all felt under her hands—Elinor had to swallow. He is beautiful too, and I must tell him so, she reminded herself as he came back and lifted her to the rug. But somehow she forgot, for his urgent hands and passionate mouth were on her again, and reason and purpose left her.

They shared a lovemaking unlike any they had known before, and Elinor wondered why that should be so. Surely she had felt this same way each time with him—breathless with passion, consumed by it. But today it was different. As he came to her, and she welcomed him, she realized that what he had said was true. Today—right now—they were pledging themselves, beginning their life together.

As Jason moved more urgently, and Elinor was caught up in sensation, she forgot everything. When her world dissolved, she cried out, raking his long back with her nails. And where they had been two people, a man and a woman, before, now they had been made one by love, not only for today, but for all their tomorrows.

And not for a moment had either of them closed their eyes.

Elinor knew she would never forget her perfect Cornish summer day, even if it were the only one she was ever to have. The two of them dozed in each other's arms for a while before Jason coaxed her into the water. Elinor could not swim, and she was frightened once she got beyond her depth, but Jason held her in his arms, and the cool brine of the water felt so good, she began to enjoy the experience.

Out in deeper water, he even put her on his back, her arms tight around him, to swim.

He teased her then, saying if he weren't so bewitched, he would extract all kinds of promises from her now he had her at his mercy. Some of his suggestions for her future behavior made her sputter and laugh, and some made her press even closer to him, her heart racing.

After their swim, he took her to the little pool under the cascading brook, so they could wash the salt from their skin and hair—together. This time they made love in the soft grass that lined the banks of the pool.

Later they ate the picnic tea that Mordyn's cook had packed for them—her usual lavish spread. The sun and salt air, and the exercise, had made Elinor ravenous, so ravenous she insisted they draw straws for the last piece of cake.

"I wonder if I have been wise," Jason mused as she

crowed in delight when she won. "It appears you have more than a healthy appetite, madam. Shall you eat me out of house and home? What other faults do you have, that I have yet to discover?"

Elinor licked her fingers clean of icing before she replied. She was naked, although at his insistence she wore her fashionable broad-brimmed hat. To Jason, she looked like a fey water sprite, all cream and pink and gold, who had somehow wandered into one of London's smart hat shops.

He was about to reach for her, when she said, "Well, as you yourself pointed out once, I am much too short for the likes of you."

Pointing an accusing finger at him, and feeling giddy, she went on, "And you do remember I've a temper on me? You said so yourself, to say nothing of the fact that you mentioned you'd seen better! I was never so insulted, and I'll make you pay for it, if it takes me years!"

"I lied!" Jason exclaimed as she threw a large piece of kelp at him. "You know I did!"

She refused to accept his most fervent apologies, or his fulsome compliments on her hair, her mouth, her breasts, her—

Elinor put her hand over his mouth.

"All right. I believe you," she said breathlessly, just before he bent to take her in his arms and kiss her again.

They came back to Mordyn at dusk. The evening star was shining over the sea, and a sliver of quarter moon sailed in the sky. Elinor saw the tide was coming in, and the last of the fishing boats had long since made harbor with their catch. There wasn't a sail anywhere, all the way to the horizon. It was as if they were the only two people in the world, lovers strolling the cliff walk with their arms around each other.

She prayed they would not meet anyone as they entered the castle through the side door. She did not want to see any smiles, or knowing glances. But as if today were truly magical, no one was in the halls as they passed through them.

Jason left the basket at the foot of the stairs, for he insisted on escorting her to her room. "Just so I can say that once, I came to your door properly, like any other man," he told her, bending to kiss the top of her shining head.

The candles had not been lit as yet, and to Elinor it was as if they moved through an enchanted mist in the soft dusk.

As they climbed the stairs, she suddenly remembered something.

"Jason, did you ever come to my room late at night sometimes, and only stand there, watching me sleep, or just touch my braid?" she asked.

His brows rose. "Oh, no," he said. "I could never have stopped at that."

Elinor thought for a moment. "Well, did you help me find my way when I was lost in the woods one misty morning? Whisper to me there?"

"No, I didn't. Did someone do that?" he asked.

She nodded, biting her lower lip. "I wonder—" she mused.

"It must have been Jonathan, playing some sort of trick on you," Jason said.

Elinor nodded in agreement, but she was not at all sure it was so.

They had reached the gallery now, and Jason paused before the portrait of the Cavalier. "I've always been drawn to that painting," he said. "Perhaps it is because I bear one of the gentleman's names. To me he has always seemed so alive, and have you noticed? His eyes follow you, no matter where you are in the gallery."

As Elinor agreed, she stared up at the handsome Cavalier. She had proof now he walked. When would he ever rest? she wondered.

As they stood there together, in the quietness of the gallery, Elinor held close in Jason's arm, she felt a hand on her shoulder. Not Jason's hand, but the one that had touched her here once before. Beside her, she felt Jason stiffen, and she knew he was feeling a hand as well.

"Don't be afraid, Elinor," Jason told her in a soft, calm voice. "It's all right."

"I'm not afraid," she whispered, still staring upward, mesmerized as she had always been.

As before, the portrait of the Cavalier seemed to dim as she watched, even to waver in its frame, and the air around them grew chill.

"I have her safe now, sir," Jason said in his normal voice. "And I will keep her safe always. She is *my* love. Not yours."

It was deathly still then. After a long moment, Elinor felt the pressure of that ghostly hand withdrawn. As she watched, her eyes wide, the portrait took on its normal, colorful tints again, and the chill surrounding them dissipated.

Jason smiled down at her and turned her to him to kiss her gently.

As he walked her to her door, Elinor looked over her shoulder. She saw the Cavalier was watching them both. She wondered he could still smile, when his eyes looked so sad.

Jason opened the door to her rooms for her, but he would not let her go until he had kissed her again, all his love and all his homage in that one last, fervent embrace.

Behind them, high on the wall, the Cavalier watched.

And he smiled.

ABOUT THE AUTHOR

Barbara Hazard is the award-winning author of twenty-five regency romances. *Midnight Magic* is her third historical romance. It was preceded by *Call Back the Dream,* and its sequel *The Heart Remembers.* Both are available in NAL/Onyx editions. There are almost three million of her books in print, both here and abroad.